"YOU'RE T[...]
TO BE REAL, BLAINE."

Garrath's whisper was gruff, but his fingers were gentle as they brushed back the curtain of her hair. Then his lips touched hers.

Blaine was instantly on fire. She moaned as an exquisite ache blossomed inside her, as their heartbeats synchronized into one strong pulse. For heady moments she forgot everything—the oil rig, the metal deck, the brewing storm. Then lightning flashed in the night sky.

Garrath's voice was abruptly businesslike. "Get inside, okay? I'd better check the rig."

"Of course," Blaine answered numbly. He was leaving her now—to check his precious rig!

What a fool she was! She should have remembered that Garrath was an oil man first and foremost, that caring for him would result in misery. Should have remembered before she lost her heart to him . . . .

AND NOW.

SUPERROMANCES

Worldwide Library is proud to present a
sensational new series of modern love stories —
SUPERROMANCES

Written by masters of the genre, these longer,
sensuous and dramatic novels are truly in keeping
with today's changing life-styles. Full of intriguing
conflicts, the heartaches and delights of true love,
SUPERROMANCES are absorbing stories —
satisfying and sophisticated reading that lovers
of romance fiction have long been waiting for.

SUPERROMANCES
Contemporary love stories for the woman of today!

THE FOREVER SPELL
ROBYN ANZELON

A SUPERROMANCE FROM
W RLDWIDE

TORONTO · NEW YORK · LOS ANGELES · LONDON

In memory of the real Walter Cobb,
who knew nothing about computers,
but a lot about love.

———————◆———◆———————

Published January 1983

First printing November 1982

ISBN 0-373-70049-0

Printed in Canada

CHAPTER ONE

AFTER AN HOUR AND A QUARTER in the pulsing helicopter Blaine Christensen no longer wondered where the grayish blue of the late afternoon sky ended and the blue black of the North Sea began. She even stopped leaning forward anxiously to search the endless stretch of mist ahead for a first glimpse of her destination. She was just too numb to care.

Her hands and feet ached with the cold. Her ears rang with the whine of the helicopter's jet engine and the thundering beat of its huge blade. And her mind as well as certain other parts of her anatomy were dulled senseless by the long sleepless hours she had been traveling—and worrying. But even her fears and apprehension didn't seem to matter much anymore. Nothing did.

Then the pilot beside her shouted above the roar, jabbing a finger toward the bubble-shaped window before him. "There it is! There's Sithein One!"

Numbness instantly gone, Blaine strained forward. At first she saw nothing, then a gust of wind buffeted the helicopter, the round nose dipped a bit, and she saw an orange flame. No bigger than candlesize, it burned in the murky emptiness.

She knew what it was: a safety flare high atop the derrick, burning off the natural gas coming up with the oil, on one of the newest and largest offshore oil-drilling platforms in the world. Sithein One. Or "Sheean One," as the pilot pronounced it in his rolling Scottish lilt.

Blaine shuddered and closed long dark lashes over her spring-green eyes. To anyone else that tiny flame would be a welcoming beacon in the vast ocean wilderness offering safety, assurance and journey's end. To her it meant a resurgence of memories, the painful stabbing memories she had been trying to escape for nearly two years.

What am I doing here? Why am I putting myself through this, she asked herself for perhaps the thousandth time since she had left home. But the questions were unnecessary. She had known the answer from the moment she'd agreed to come. She was there because of two men: one the man she loved, the other a total stranger, nothing but a name. Garrath St. Clair.

Blaine squirmed restlessly. Helicopters were definitely not designed for comfort, she decided. The seat was hard, unbearably hard, and the restraints of both the safety belt across her lap and the yellow life jacket chafing her neck allowed little leeway for shifting into a more comfortable position. But it wasn't really the physical restraints that caused her restlessness, Blaine acknowledged. It was the effect of that name: Garrath St. Clair.

An intriguing combination with the first name so harsh, the last so delicate. How many times during this dreadful trip had she found herself wondering which suited the owner better? Too many, for each time the name crossed her mind a shiver tiptoed up her spine, just as it had the very first time she'd heard it. From Richard.

"Blaine, I want you to go to Scotland for me," Richard had said just yesterday evening as they were driving home from Computec, his computer systems company. He had started the business in his garage and had guided it into a multimillion-dollar enterprise headquartered in a suite of San Francisco offices.

"Scotland? Why?" Visions of flaming-haired clansmen swinging claymores and squeezing mournful tunes from bagpipes floated through her mind.

"The monitoring system we installed for St. Clair Corporation is malfunctioning. It's already shut down the drilling three times without apparent cause. The technician there hasn't been able to find the problem. I got a call this afternoon from St. Clair himself, raging about wasted time, money and manpower and demanding that I get someone out to the rig immediately who can fix it."

"Rig?" Blaine had barely been able to force the word past her lips. "Richard, you don't mean an oil rig? You know I can't. . . ."

Richard, usually so casual behind the wheel of his silver Cadillac, was paying strict attention to the road. "I wouldn't ask you if it wasn't crucial. St. Clair's holds a pile of exploration leases in the North Sea. It's one of the fastest growing companies in Britain. They're trying our system with the option of including it on all their future rigs if it's successful—which it isn't at the moment. I really need your help."

You can't ask that, Blaine nearly cried, staring at Richard's familiar profile. *You're breaking your promise. It isn't fair.*

Her cries were never voiced. Richard Perry was not

just her employer or even just a friend. He was the man she loved even though, for some unexplainable reason, she still hadn't said yes to one of his casually offered marriage proposals. It was Richard who had helped her through the worst time of her life, letting her lean on him when every other bit of stability in her world had been cruelly snatched away. If he asked for her help now, fairly or not, she would give it. She had to.

". . . and we've just got to get that system going." Richard was still pleading his case, not knowing he had already won. "Garrath St. Clair doesn't tolerate failure."

She had shivered then at the name, with awe, curiosity and something else. Awe because this stranger was important enough to make Richard ignore her feelings and the promise he had made. Curiosity because she sensed in the way Richard said it, the power of the man himself. And something else. . . some tingling rush of emotion she didn't understand. And didn't want to understand.

The strange feeling had continued to plague her, keeping the name uncomfortably in her thoughts throughout her rushed preparations for the trip, throughout the long transatlantic flight, throughout the final connecting flight out of London. But shortly after her arrival at the Aberdeen airport it had ceased to bother her, being superseded by a much less confusing emotion—anger.

At first she'd been angry with herself. After all, she was the one who had somehow misplaced the tortoiseshell clasp that secured her thick sandy-blond hair at the back of her head. For comfort she'd removed the clasp during the flight, freeing her hair to tumble over her shoulders and down to the middle of her back. And she had put the clasp...somewhere.

So she could blame only herself for leaving the plane looking more like a sixteen-year-old girl on her first date than a mature twenty-five-year-old woman on a business trip. That didn't make it any less embarrassing.

The cold salt bite of the wind made her tremble as she walked, head held high, toward the terminal building. She had thought herself acclimatized to the chill of ocean breezes; San Francisco certainly had its share. But this North Sea wind blew with an icy savagery that never came off the Pacific. And it was only September. What would it feel like in the depths of winter? She wanted to bolt for the protection of the building but didn't dare. There were too many faces at the wide windows, and one of them might be looking for her.

Only none of them were. Once inside the terminal door Blaine stopped, pushing the wind-whipped strands of hair out of her eyes and searching for a face to match the name that had been haunting her. There wasn't one. There were plenty of people hurrying by, but none of them seemed interested in her.

Was he late? she wondered. Or did he expect her to find her own way to the St. Clair office?

Late, she decided promptly. It fitted the image she had formed of him—arrogant, self-centered, completely uninterested in the feelings of anyone else. He would typically make others wait, not caring if they were inconvenienced, rather than waste a minute of his precious time. But if that were the case, what should she do? Where should she go?

All at once Blaine felt lost. Everyone else seemed to know exactly where they were going and to be in very much of a rush to get there, while she was disoriented and exhausted. She had been traveling for over fourteen hours, all spent trying to steel herself to face the man who impressed unimpressible Richard. With the eight-hour time difference that made it late afternoon in Aberdeen, she felt as if she had been awake for nearly two full days and fretting the whole time. To have finally arrived, all geared up for the meeting, and find no one waiting was just too much. It would serve the rude Mr. St. Clair right if she booked herself back home on the next flight. Obviously he didn't care enough about his precious system to meet her, despite all his fuss and rush and demands.

She was so busy fuming that it took her a few moments to realize that the name being called in loudspeaker monotones was her own. "B. A. Christensen, to the information center, please. B. A. Christensen...."

Blaine followed the signs pointing the way, regirding herself for the meeting to come. But when she reached the information desk she discovered she hadn't prepared herself for the right encounter. Nothing could have prepared her for this particular meeting.

A young man lounged carelessly against the counter. His long legs were clad in blue denim jeans tucked into well-worn brown leather boots. His upper body was doubled in size by a thickly pile-lined cowhide jacket. And his face was obscured by the wide brim of a beige cowboy hat.

A cowboy hat! Blaine had expected tartan kilts and

tams. But it was the casual stance of the man—lanky arms and legs jutting every which way, the slight tilt of the head beneath the hat as he scanned the moving crowd—that stunned her and brought her to a shocked standstill in the middle of the room.

He looked like Len, so very much like him that it felt as if some giant hand was squeezing all the breath and life out of her. She knew it wasn't Len—knew it was never again going to be Len she glimpsed in a crowd—but the similarity was there. And it hurt.

His dress shouldn't have surprised her. Oil work was multinational. Oil men traveled from job to job, place to place, at the whim of wages, bosses and the substance itself. Those were facts she had learned growing up with both a father and a brother, Len, who, as her mother contemptuously put it, had oil in their veins.

But, absorbed in her qualms about facing the rig and Garrath St. Clair, she hadn't considered that Aberdeen, known since the discovery of the great North Sea fields as the Houston-of-the-North, would be filled with as many cowboys as clansmen.

Blaine knew she should move. The young man was searching the crowd, obviously waiting for someone. Any moment he would notice her standing there, eyes blurry with tears, and...and then it struck her. He was waiting for her!

This was not Garrath St. Clair; she knew immediately without any reason for being so certain. And now she realized that expecting him to meet her plane had been foolish anyway. Heads of important companies did not wait around airports to meet employees. They sent assistants—like this one.

Suddenly Blaine didn't want to be found. She

shouldn't have let Richard talk her into coming. She should have held him to the promise he'd made when she agreed to work with him—that she would never have to be closer to an oil rig than the scaled drawings she used for computations.

It didn't matter that Garrath St. Clair would be justifiably outraged or that Richard would never forgive her. She simply couldn't face the oil rig, the reminders like this one, the memories. She wanted to go home.

It was too late; the cowboy had seen her. He pushed himself upright and strode across the floor to where she stood. He stretched at least eight inches above her five foot four and though the hand he put on her arm was gentle, it felt very much like handcuffs closing.

"Can I help you, ma'am?" The drawl matched the hat. She was trapped by a boyishly freckled face, the reddish brown of the freckles duplicating the color of a thin mustache and the curly hair showing beneath the wide brim of his hat. A "V" between his brows confessed his concern, but even concern couldn't keep a grin from his mouth. Blaine liked her captor's smile.

"I'm Blaine Christensen," she admitted.

"Yes, ma'am?" he said, clearly not understanding.

Had she guessed wrong? Wasn't he waiting for her?

"B. A. Christensen." She waved a finger in the air. "Aren't you the one who had me paged? Aren't you from St. Clair's?"

"But you can't be the one I'm after!" he exclaimed. "You're a...." He gulped down the rest of the words, blushed apple-red, then whipped off the hat.

"Excuse me, ma'am, but I was expecting a—that is—I was told to pick up a. . . ."

Blaine understood. One of Richard's little surprises. He wasn't above using her initials and the old once-she's-there-what-can-they-say ploy—and not telling her about it—if for some reason he thought her gender might present a problem. And in this instance there was only one person whose opinion counted.

"You were sent to meet a man?" she asked.

The cowboy nodded, somehow managing to shake his head in disbelief at the same time. "And you're from Computec?"

"I am," she said, trying to sound amused at the situation. "And you're. . . ?"

"Sorry, ma'am. I'm Andy Walker. They call me Tex on the rig."

What else, Blaine thought, smiling, and a dimple appeared in her left cheek. "Glad to meet you, Andy. Where do we go from here?"

He slapped the hat nervously back and forth across his leg. "Well, I was supposed to take you directly to Mr. St. Clair, but maybe I ought to call first and let him know that—"

"Stop right there," Blaine interrupted. It wasn't hard to guess what Andy had been about to say. Richard had obviously gauged his client correctly. The boss wasn't going to be pleased at the unexpected packaging of his technician.

Anger surged through her. It was bad enough that Garrath St. Clair had dragged her halfway around the world to a place she had no desire to go. She shouldn't have to endure an outmoded insulting attitude, too.

"Look, Andy," she said curtly. "I'm the best person Computec could send to fix the monitoring system. I'm also a woman. In my opinion neither one of those facts negates the other. If Mr. St. Clair wants his system repaired as badly as I think he does, he's just going to have to survive having a woman do it for him. It's about time someone told him we're not living in Victorian times any longer, a bit of information I will gladly impart if you will just follow whatever directions you were given. Okay?"

"I don't think you understand—" Andy began, but Blaine cut him off.

"I don't think *you* understand. I want to meet Mr. St. Clair. Now!" And then she softened the order with a smile. After all, it wasn't Andy's fault he worked for a tyrant straight out of the Dark Ages. "Please," she added.

"If that's the way you want it, ma'am." He grinned and plopped the hat back on his head. "Let's gather your bags and face the storm."

"Storm? The pilot on the plane said no storms were expected tonight."

"True enough, I suppose, though the weather does change mighty quickly in these parts. But it wasn't the weather I was thinkin' of." He chuckled and without another word steered her toward the baggage area.

Blaine made a face worthy of her teenage appearance. Andy might think her meeting with his boss was going to be stormy, but she was feeling more confident now than she had since she left home. Mr. St. Clair might be rich and powerful, but it seemed he was also a chauvinist, one of the lowest of the low in her books. She had dealt with chauvinists before; she could handle one more. In fact, she was almost looking forward to it.

But her euphoria lasted only as long as it took to gather her bags. Andy led her, not to the car she was expecting, but to a glass and metal insect crouching uneasily outside the terminal.

He misinterpreted her horrified gasp.

"Beautiful, isn't it?" He gazed at the wretched thing with obvious pride. "Handles like a well-trained mare. But she can take the rough stuff, no sweat."

"A helicopter," she moaned.

"Well, of course. We only make roughnecks swim out to the rig," he teased.

"To the rig," Blaine echoed dully, her stomach doing intricate and uncomfortable maneuvers. Oh, she knew helicopters were the main mode of transportation out to offshore oil platforms, just as she knew roughneck was the term applied to the newest, and therefore lowest-ranking members of the rig crews. She just hadn't realized she would have to face her first helicopter ride, and the rig, so soon after her arrival. And in the totally inappropriate clothes she was wearing.

Her suitcase was filled with sensible warm clothing—slacks, jeans, fur-lined gloves, thick sweaters, rubber-soled shoes. But when it had come time for her trip, and just incidentally her first meeting with the intimidating Mr. St. Clair, she had found herself discarding the comfortably functional wool pantsuit and heavy melton jacket she had laid out to wear. Instead she chose a silk shirt in a deep turquoise that

flattered her fair skin and blond hair, a pleated skirt
that showed off her small waist and slim legs and the
high heels that usually gave her confidence as well as
height. But not in this case.

She prayed her face didn't look as hot as it felt.
She suspected Andy already knew she had expected
to be taken to an office building, not an oil rig, that
he'd been trying to warn her when she'd imperiously
cut him off. She didn't want him to also guess how
afraid of the strange little vehicle she was.

Taking a deep breath, she lifted her chin and
marched toward the helicopter. But no one could
possibly maintain a nonchalant facade when clam-
bering over a helicopter's huge black floats and up
into the seat beside the pilot. Especially not in wob-
bling heels and a skirt the wind was making indecent.
She did the best she could and didn't meet Andy's
eyes as he leaned in after her to place a life jacket
over her head and buckle her seat belt.

The trip wasn't as horrible as she had anticipated.
She clenched her teeth when the pilot, isolated by
mirrored sunglasses and black earphones, punched
various buttons, starting the soft scream of the jet
engine. She dug her fingernails into her palms as the
scream built into a banshee's wail and the huge overhead blade began to rotate, beating the air with a
steady pulse soon echoed by the pounding of her
heart. She gasped as they lifted gently off the ground,
rose quickly above the terminal building and then
hurtled out over the sea.

Once airborne, though, Blaine wasn't afraid. The
helicopter, gliding swiftly over the dark blue silk of
the ocean, became a little world of its own. An uncomfortable world, to be sure—noisy, cold, existing

in a bluish void where the scenery never changed. But that very sameness was lulling, draining away her fear, her anger and her misgivings.

Until the pilot shouted "There's Sithein One." And Blaine glanced once at the orange flare atop the platform, then squeezed her eyes tightly shut.

Damn him, she thought. *Damn Garrath St. Clair!*

CHAPTER TWO

SHE DIDN'T OPEN HER EYES until a light thump told her they had landed. Then she knew she had to—had to force open her eyes, force herself to take the hand Andy was holding out to help her down from the helicopter, force herself to take that first step onto the platform. After that she would be all right. She would meet Mr. St. Clair as one executive to another, be briefed on the problems with the system and then work on solving them. Once she was working with the instruments and programs she had helped design she could forget where she was. Work would keep the memories at bay here just as it did at home. All she had to do was take that first step.

It wasn't so bad. She didn't have to really look at the rig. Couldn't, in fact, with the helicopter's blade still chopping noisily over her head and Andy pulling her past the curious stares of several men hurrying toward the waiting craft. All she had to do was watch her feet as Andy guided her down three steps and around the corner of a building.

There the noises changed. The whine of the helicopter rose and then lessened as it lifted again into the air. Immediately its sound was replaced by a cacophony of others: booming, clanging, the crash of heavy metal on metal, rumbling, screeching, scraping. A symphony of strange noises punctuated by an occasional shout.

They were on one corner of the rig, high up, facing the derrick. Now there was no avoiding it. A giant metal Christmas tree, it stretched two hundred feet above them, lights dotting its triangular form. At the top, burning and hissing like a gigantic pilot light, was the flare, no longer candlesize. Nearby two huge cranes arrogantly thrust out their latticed arms. And all around, eerily outlined by cold white lights, lay a jumble of box-shaped buildings, machinery, monstrous tanks and metal stairways. The whole thing looked like pieces of a child's building set that had been haphazardly tossed into the sea and somehow fused into an island.

"It's incredible," she breathed, her lips parted, her fears and memories lost for the moment in amazement.

"It does take some getting used to," Andy agreed, grinning. But the "V" was back between his brows and Blaine realized he was waiting for her impatiently.

She could guess the reason. His boss was expecting them and Andy was anxious to get the meeting—and the storm—over with.

Until that moment Blaine hadn't noticed the cold. Now she did, intensely. The chill of the helicopter had been pleasant compared to this slashing sea-wet wind. It flew in her face, stinging her lips with iced salt and snapping her hair out behind her like a silken sail. It parted the flaps of her coat and rushed under her skirt, making her legs tremble unsteadily and confirming the unsuitability of her outfit.

Andy led her to a steep metal stairway. "Watch your step," he warned. "It's a long way down."

"You have a way with understatement," she replied lightly, trying to mask her apprehension.

It was a walk on a steel tightrope in high heels. Her first glance down reinforced the image. The perforated metal slats that caught at her heels also gave a dizzying view of glistening black ocean below, not the most comforting of nets. One look and she kept her eyes carefully averted, clutched the icy guardrail and hoped for the best.

She almost made it. There were just a few of the treacherous slats left to go when a figure appeared at the bottom of the stairs—a man whose broad shoulders nearly filled the stairwell. A light glared behind him, throwing his face into shadow, but Blaine knew his eyes were on her. She could feel them moving over her, from her startled face to the long expanse of legs visible from his angle below. His look boldly and leisurely traveled the length of her body, and suddenly she wasn't cold. Not at all. And she never wanted to move again.

His voice broke the spell. "I hope you're enjoying the view as much as I am," the figure said, derision spiking each word.

All the warmth she'd been feeling rose to color her cheeks with humiliation. She knew that a leer accompanied the coarse comment and that she deserved both. She had been standing there as if she were enjoying his gaze, as if she were inviting it.

Her only thought was to get away from that stare as quickly as possible, even if doing so meant moving past the man. She took a hurried step and gasped as her heel caught in the slat. Her ankle twisted agonizingly and she fell forward, right into the man's arms.

He took her weight effortlessly, his arms going around her waist beneath her open coat. Her arms had automatically flown around his neck, and they were face to face as he held her firmly against the taut muscular length of his body, her feet inches from the floor.

Now she could see the eyes that had warmed her with their glance. Deep rich brown with flecks of fiery gold, they burned into hers. Then she took in the rest of the man's face, and caught her breath.

One of her most treasured possessions was a book her brother had given her one Christmas, a collection of beautifully illustrated fairy tales. She had been thirteen then, in the process of abandoning dolls and storybooks for records and fashion magazines. But Len had understood the struggle of growing up and had given her a bit of childhood to hold onto. She loved it for that reason but also for another. There was one illustration—she couldn't even remember now to which story it belonged—of a prince kissing a beautiful princess. The prince was dark and fierce, ruggedly handsome with thick black hair and oddly gentle deep-set brown eyes. Arrogance, bravery and determination were written in the prominent cheek and jaw lines of his face, and there was something in- triguing, even puzzling, in the shape of his mouth. Later, years later, she had recognized what that something was. The illustrator had given the prince a very sensual, very demanding mouth.

And now that face, and that mouth, were inches from her own.

She pulled her arms from his neck and pushed against his rock-hard chest. "Put me down," she breathed.

He loosened his grip, but his hands moved to circle her waist and stayed there, supporting her.

She wriggled. "Let go of me!"

Aided by the slipperiness of her silk shirt, she slid through his hands—slowly because he didn't release her. And his hands moved provocatively up her body as she did.

Blaine couldn't force her eyes from his as a tingling current followed his touch on her ribs, her breasts, under her arms. Shock waves stabbed through her, a mingling of warmth and longing where there should have been outrage. It was an eternity before he relaxed his hold and let her feet touch the ground.

Blaine gasped then, as pain blotted out everything else. Instantly his arms were around her again. She felt his muscles ripple and his weight shift, and then she was cradled in his powerful arms.

Her head dropped to his shoulder as she bit her lower lip, fighting back the tears that welled in her eyes at the throbbing of her ankle. But it was his shouting over her head that made the pain subside— into anger.

"What the bloody hell is going on here, Tex?" He thrust her recumbent form in the direction of the stairs. "What's this girl doing out here and where's the man from Computec?"

His voice was as rich as the velvety brown of his eyes, the soft burr of his accent at odds with the harshness of his words, words that sparked Blaine's temper. She didn't enjoy being handled like a sack of unwanted merchandise or being called "girl" in a manner clearly not complimentary.

"You have your grimy hands all over the 'man' from Computec," she snapped. "And I must congratulate you on how quick you are to take advantage of an unexpected situation."

He stared down at her, his lips—those tantalizing

lips—compressing into a hard line. "You can't be."

"Can't be what? A man? No, but I am the Computec technician. Now, if that's all straightened out, would you please put me down? As gently as you know how."

He eased her back to the floor, supporting her weight until she had grasped the railing and balanced on her uninjured foot. It was done silently and considerately, and Blaine was going to offer a grudging thank-you when she saw that his frowning gaze was no longer on her face but had moved lower. She looked down at her blouse.

Two greasy smudges ran up the blue silk, following the all too intimate path his hands had traveled. Blushing hotly, she yanked her coat closed, then twisted to call up to Andy. "Can you help me? I think I've hurt my ankle."

Andy was gaping at the two of them, but at her question he hurried down to her. Leaning against him she managed a few slow hobbling steps, letting him guide her out onto the main deck. But there were too many things to step over or around, and she was just about to swallow her pride and ask Andy if he could carry her when she was lifted off her feet. Not by Andy.

"Put me down!" she shrieked, dismayed by the finger of flame that touched her skin where the arms of the dark-haired man rested beneath her knees and back. "I can do without more of your mauling."

"And my men can do without the distraction you're providing," he snapped back. "Inattention causes accidents in this business."

She'd been too busy trying to walk to notice her surroundings or the faces turned in her direction. But they were there. Each figure wore a hard hat, yellow, white or silver; coveralls that had once been white; heavy black work boots; and a broad knowing grin. Blaine stopped struggling.

Her rescuer strode across the deck as if he were unencumbered. Andy rushed ahead, opening the door of a gray building. When it closed behind them the noise was cut to a low vibration and the comparative silence burned in Blaine's ears. She was carried down the corridor past an empty television room and a crowded galley and into a miniature medical office.

"Get Doc up here, Tex," the man ordered sternly as he deposited her on the examining table. He didn't look to see if his order was being obeyed, and Blaine could tell he was supremely confident it would be—this time and any other time he gave one.

Andy disappeared, and she was faced with a broad scowl and arms folded across an even broader chest.

"All right. I want to know what's going on here."

She heard his accent more clearly now, a slight lengthening of the "Os" and a rolling of the "Rs." Scottish, and he certainly had the flaming Celtic temper to match.

Blaine didn't know which part of her own mixed bloodline she owed her temper to, only that it was aroused. "I don't have to explain anything to you or to anybody except Mr. St. Clair. He's expecting me."

"I doubt he's expecting *you*, *Miss* Christensen. And you obviously have no business being on a rig. The greenest roughneck knows enough to dress properly. Did you think this was a cruise ship doing a bit of drilling on the side? I suppose your suitcase is full of bikinis for sunbathing and white shorts for shuffleboard.''

She wanted to slap his taunting handsome face, but she couldn't. He was justified in his disgust. She was dressed wrong—dangerously wrong, as her fall had proved. If he hadn't caught her. . . .

But at that thought her skin tingled with the remembrance of his touch, his brazen sense-stirring touch. Her cheeks burned again, and all she wanted to do was get away from this man who so confused her, plaguing her with feelings and emotions she didn't understand.

"The contents of my suitcase are no concern of yours. Just send for Mr. St. Clair, please, and then you can get back to your grubby work. I don't think the doctor will appreciate you getting his office all dirty.''

"You're nearly as greasy as I am if I recall correctly," he said slowly, while his eyes glided down the front of her coat. He smiled wickedly and raised one black eyebrow as if he were seeing her smudged blouse beneath the coat—and even beneath the blouse.

Blaine's ragged control broke. "You vile. . . crude. . . horrid. . ." she stammered, unable to think of an appropriately foul finish. "I'll see to it that you're thrown off this—"

"What's the problem, Mr. St. Clair?" A Ben Franklinish little man was hustling through the doorway, followed by a gawking Andy. Blaine hardly saw them. Her green eyes were fixed on the man she had just called vile, crude and horrid—the owner of Sithein One.

"My men," he'd called the workers out on the

deck. She should have known; would have known immediately that he meant exactly what he said if she hadn't been blinded by the strange sensations his touch had caused. This was Garrath St. Clair.

He fitted the name—both names, the hard and the soft. The angles of his face were strong and fierce, and there was power as well as sensuality in his mouth. Yet his eyes were gentle, fawnlike, even when he was angry. And his touch had been gentle, too, softly caressing. Too softly caressing. The contrast in the names had fascinated her. The contrast in the flesh was almost hypnotic.

Her reaction infuriated her. She was acting like a schoolgirl—star-struck, moony-eyed, unable to think logically, a way she had never acted even when she was a schoolgirl. And she couldn't understand why. Actually, she despised him. His orders had turned her world upside down and had brought her to an oil rig, where she'd been injured, insulted and humiliated. How could she feel otherwise?

He wasn't taking advantage of this situation, though, Blaine had to admit. Instead of gloating over her embarrassment he seemed to be giving her time to recover by purposefully not looking at her.

"This young lady slipped on the stairs, Doc. Twisted an ankle. See if you can make her comfortable for tonight. She's going back to the Bank tomorrow."

Blaine was about to ask what the "Bank" was and refuse to go there on principle when Garrath turned to Andy.

"Right now I want to talk to you, Tex. I knew you were as reckless as a child, but I didn't know you were equally as brainless. Surely one look at that—"

he jerked his head toward Blaine "—should have told you something. How could you bring her out here without at least consulting me?"

"I insisted," Blaine cut in. "And I think he did try to warn me that I wasn't dressed properly. But I was...well, I didn't listen. So it's not his fault, it's mine. Andy was very nice."

Garrath stretched a glare from her to Andy. "Oh, I'm sure he was. Tex has a way with the ladies, don't you, Tex?"

Andy's mustache twitched. "Look, Mr. St. Clair, that's not fair. I know you don't think I'm right for Janet, but—"

"Forget it! Just be in my office in half an hour. That should be time enough for you to change and clear out your room. Since you're responsible for this mess, I'm sure you won't mind volunteering to find other accommodations for the *one* night." He punctuated the order with a black scowl that dared both Blaine and Andy to argue before he stomped out of the room.

" 'Storm' is right," Blaine whispered to Andy, and the two of them grinned at each other like naughty children.

The doctor, ignoring the turmoil around him, had removed her broken shoe and completed his poking and prodding. His smile held a grandfatherly concern as he asked her a few questions about how she felt.

Confused, angry, frightened, jumpy, crazy, she thought. "Fine," she said.

"Well, I doubt the ankle is broken. Just a sprain, probably a mild one, though I know it doesn't feel mild right now. If you go into the other room and remove those stockings, I'll bandage it. You can rest on the bed in there while Andy gets your room ready."

Blaine didn't mind the doctor's orders at all. They bore no resemblance to the dictatorial commands of his boss. Getting the panty hose off over her already swollen ankle wasn't easy, but once she'd done so and settled herself on the bed, she wondered if she would ever get up again. Lying down felt so good.

Andy returned just as the doctor handed Blaine an ice pack, saying, "Use this and keep it elevated tonight and it will be nearly as good as new tomorrow. Call me if you feel you need something for pain later, but I think you'll be fine."

"Thank you, and I'm sorry I disturbed you," she apologized.

"And I'm sorry I don't get disturbed by patients as pretty as you more often," he said, patting her arm before he left.

Andy had changed into coveralls, had replaced the cowboy boots with work boots and carried a hard hat. The long line of the coveralls added to his lanky height, but height couldn't compensate for his boyish face. Andy looked too young to be going off to work anywhere, much less on an oil rig.

"What do you do out here?" Blaine asked him, expecting roughnecking to be his answer.

"I'm night drilling foreman," he replied, a blush creeping up beneath his freckles.

Blaine was surprised. The drilling foreman was in charge of the actual work on the platform and answerable only to the headman—the toolpusher—and the owner, in this case, Garrath St. Clair. He was in charge of a drilling crew and of keeping the drilling on schedule. It was a position of enormous responsibility, requiring experience and self-confidence, and Andy appeared too young and unsure of himself to have either. She began to suspect there was more to Andy Walker than simply a freckle-faced boy.

"Then how did you end up waiting for the 'man' from Computec?"

"The boss likes to give me all the . . . special jobs."

"Well, I'm sorry I made it so difficult for you," Blaine apologized. "I know I was headstrong and overbearing, two of my less than endearing traits that commonly get me into trouble. But I didn't mean to cause problems for you."

Andy stared down at his boots. "Aw, don't worry yourself none, ma'am. The boss and I have a basic difference of opinion that has nothing to do with you. If he hadn't barked at me over this, it would have been over something else. It's his way of saying hello when I come back aboard. You know."

Blaine wasn't sure she did. But it had something to do with the mysterious Janet, of that she was certain.

"If he's so disagreeable and unfair, why do you work here? Surely there are other companies with openings."

"Plenty, but none like St. Clair's. The boss really cares about his men. We get the best grub, the best accommodations, the best facilities possible. He's even got a profit-sharing plan. But more importantly he really cares about safety. This rig has more safety systems, both environmental and personnel, including your computers, than any other rig I've ever been on. Most places, the safety rules are known and basically ignored. Here you don't ignore the rules more than once. The first time you do, you find yourself back on the Bank. . . ."

"The Bank?"

"Ashore. And looking for a new job. Where I'm going to be if I don't get back to the boss soon. Are you ready to head upstairs to your quarters? I can't promise luxury, but it's got the necessities."

"Let's give it a try," Blaine nodded.

It wasn't too difficult, mostly because Blaine's mind was occupied elsewhere. With Garrath St. Clair.

She was surprised to find that she and her new boss had something in common after all. Safety was the reason she had gone to work with Richard, why she was willing to take a job that dealt with the industry she hated. The system they had developed was a great aid in protecting workers. If the rig Len and her father had been on had used such a system, they might not have died. That the system could also speed up production, cut costs and allow drilling under formerly prohibitive conditions didn't matter to Blaine. Those were fortunate by-products. Safety was what counted.

But the system wasn't working here. That was the one fact Blaine hadn't actually thought about till now. It was true that Richard could have—and should have—sent someone else; they had a large, well-trained staff of troubleshooters for cases like this. But he had asked her to go and she hadn't been able to refuse him. From that moment whether she'd realized it or not, the safety of all the workers on this rig had become her responsibility.

She hadn't wanted to come; she didn't want to stay. But if she let Garrath St. Clair's chauvinism and his rude manner send her away, and there was an accident between then and the time a new technician got out here, she would be responsible—in her own eyes at least.

"Welcome," Andy said, pushing open one of the doors off a corridor that was the duplicate of the one below.

The cabin was small, about the size of a college dormitory room, but with several touches that raised it above that class. There was a private bath, for one thing. And the dresser with Blaine's suitcase sitting before it, the built-in desk and the bookshelves were all of dark-grained walnut. A large sheepskin rug softened the hardwood floor between two oversized and very inviting single beds. Blaine ignored their beckoning.

"Andy, I need to ask you one more favor."

"Sure thing," he agreed, tilting his head questioningly.

"Wait for me to change my clothes and do something with this unruly mop of hair, and then take me to the Computec unit."

"But Mr. St. Clair said you were going home."

"Tomorrow. He didn't say anything about what I should do tonight. I want to look at the system."

Andy jiggled his hard hat against his leg, staring at Blaine as if he was trying to guess whether or not she could be talked out of her plan.

"I don't think the boss would approve."

"I'm sure he wouldn't," Blaine said, "So let's just not mention it to him until it's done. I intend to fix that system before I leave."

Andy grinned. "I can see that you do, ma'am. I can see that you do."

CHAPTER THREE

FOUR HOURS LATER Blaine put her head down on her arms, which were folded on top of the computer terminal. She was ninety-five percent certain she had found the cause of the monitoring system's malfunction—a faulty circuit. Locating the specific circuit, replacing it and conducting some lengthy tests would contribute the other five percent certainty. But she almost didn't want that last bit of proof, not when there was no logical explanation of how a circuit could have failed in just the way this one obviously had.

She couldn't think about it anymore tonight, however. Or was it morning? She was totally disoriented by the combination of the long flight, the time change and the hours she'd just spent in the windowless yellow Computec trailer. The trailer held the system's equipment—numerous television monitors focused on points around the rig, information converters, printers, several computers and the emergency generator that protected against power failures.

Morning or night, it didn't matter; she *had* to have some sleep. She wasn't thinking straight any longer, she couldn't be. Not when for the past half hour her thoughts about the "how" of the malfunction had kept returning to one utterly illogical impossible idea.

She thought of testing her notion on the man in the

trailer with her, and lifted her head long enough to glance at him. Walter Cobb was barely five feet tall, with owlish eyes that blinked slowly behind round wire-framed glasses when he was thinking. He was also the best technician at Computec, a fact Blaine was justifiably proud of since she'd fought Richard over hiring him in the first place. Richard had objected to Walter's age—fifty-seven at that time—and his lack of experience in the field, saying Computec couldn't afford to subsidize old men looking for new careers. But Blaine had pointed to Walter's excellent training credentials and had insisted he was a natural, and her instincts had been proved right. Walter was dedicated to his work and devoted to Blaine and Computec.

Which was precisely why she rejected the idea of confiding her suspicions to him now. She wouldn't yet, not until she was sure. Because if her hunch was correct, some nasty implications were going to arise, some of which would reflect badly on the technician. Walter would be the first person to think of those implications and take the blame on himself.

Watching her old friend brought home to Blaine once again how important this job must be to Richard. She'd been very surprised to find Walter on Sithein One. His expertise was usually reserved for overseeing the complex installation of Computec units, not manning their day-to-day operations. But for Garrath St. Clair, Richard had sent the best. And when the best technician hadn't been good enough, he'd sent Blaine herself.

If he knew what she was thinking now he would probably regret that decision, Blaine thought, shaking her head. Her idea was crazy; just how crazy would be obvious after she had a bit of sleep to clear her head. The only question she should be asking herself at the moment was whether or not it was worth making her awkward way through the dreadful cold to Andy's room to sleep in a bed.

Her head drooped forward again, answering the question for her. Although the terminal wasn't comfortable and she could already feel a crick developing in her back, falling asleep there didn't require any effort. All she had to do was close her eyes.

A blast of grinding noise and frigid air ruined her intentions. Groggily Blaine lifted her head and looked toward the door that had opened.

"Oh, no," she moaned.

He was standing there, hands jammed on narrow hips, a chief of the clan enraged by the flaunting of his edicts. His sparking eyes quickly found her in the small room, and she could almost hear his battle cry.

Just let it be mercifully quick, she thought, knowing she wasn't strong enough to defend herself this time. She let her heavy head sink back to her arms.

The attack came quietly. He didn't say a word. He just pulled back her chair and scooped her up into his arms. At his barked order Walter placed her coat over her, and Garrath carried her out into the cold.

Was snatching up women and rushing off with them like some wild caveman the only way he knew how to deal with the female of the species, Blaine wondered, but without the rancor she had felt earlier at his high-handedness. Right now she was just too sleepy to object. Besides, she was infinitely more comfortable than she had been at her computer terminal. His firmly muscled arms and massive chest made the perfect cradle, warm and secure. The soft niche at the meeting of his neck and shoulder was a made-to-order cushion for her head. The strong steady beat of his heart soothed like a tranquilizing lullaby. If he would let her sleep like this for even a few minutes, she would forgive him the rest.

For a single moment her mind tried to offer resistance. *Sleep! In this big bully's arms! Where's your pride, woman?* But it was only token resistance and had no more effect than the pounding noises of the rig. Her eyes closed and her mind drifted away.

Blaine barely stirred when the strong arms were exchanged for a bed, and a blanket was tucked gently around her. A voice was speaking, but she hardly heard it.

"Bloody little fool," it might have said. "Don't you ever listen to anyone?"

But the voice wasn't angry or disturbing. And it was accompanied by the pleasurable touch of hands removing her shoes, lifting her head to unfasten the silver clip holding her hair at her neck and fluffing the long strands over her shoulders. When the voice came again it was deeply soft, like a caress.

"Sleep, silly princess." It almost seemed as if there was a brief pressure on her lips, like the kiss of a prince. Only kisses usually woke up sleeping princesses, Blaine thought. This kiss was easing her directly into her dreams....

IT WASN'T THE RIGHT DREAM, Blaine wanted to cry out. A prince didn't lead his princess into a nightmare, a horrible terrifying nightmare. This couldn't be right.

But it was familiar, all too familiar. And even when some part of her consciousness recognized it as

the same old dream, she still couldn't force herself
awake, couldn't escape its cold cruel clutches.

She was on an oil rig, and never before had the rig
been so vividly alive with sounds and movements and
leering faces. She was running across the main platform, into the buildings, up and down the treacherous stairs. And all the while she was calling
frantically, "Len! Dad! Where are you? Len? Dad?"

Then the whole world exploded. She heard the
screams of panicked men, saw the hellish glow of fire
out of control, felt the searing heat of oil-fed flames
that were reaching out—for her. She screamed.

As always, the scream freed her from the nightmare. But not from the aftereffects.

She was sitting up in bed, her face already wet with
tears, her head aching with thoughts of the pain and
fear and hopelessness of men—of Len and her father—caught in the hell of a blowout. Soon the trembling would start, as wave after wave of horror
washed over her. And it would continue until she was
too drained and exhausted to hurt anymore.

Blaine pulled her knees up to her chest, hugging
them, huddling into a ball like a frightened child just
as the door flew open with a resounding bang.

Etched in the light from the corridor was the same
bold figure that had stared up at her earlier from the
bottom of the staircase.

At my worst, she thought; *he's seeing me at my
worst again.* She wanted to order him out of her
room. What right had he to come bursting in this
way? She had been so determined not to show the
slightest weakness to this powerful domineering man,
and now he would see her totally undone, uncontrol-
lably shaking, with silent tears coursing down her

cheeks. And she didn't have the strength to do a thing about it.

"Are you all right?" he demanded. But he stayed in the doorway as if wanting permission to cross the threshold.

Blaine knew then that all she had to do was say, "Yes, I'm fine. It was just a silly dream," and he would leave. Leave her alone with the memories.

"No, I. . . ." Her teeth clattered over the words.

In two strides he was across the small room, the door slamming behind him. His hands found her in the dark. He didn't say a word, simply grasped her shoulders and pulled her huddled and unresisting form against him, lifting her onto his lap so that he could fold both arms around her. Ever so slightly he began to rock forward and back, forward and back.

Blaine pressed her face into his shoulder and sobbed, great gasping sobs that shook her whole body. Through it all he held her firmly against his warmth and rocked.

It didn't last long. After a few minutes the sobs ended in four silly hiccups, and Blaine realized the nightmare was gone. Completely.

Never before had the fear left her so quickly; never before had she given in to racking sobs. Now she felt drained, as she always did, but in a somehow different way. As if instead of being just too exhausted to suffer any longer, she was drained of the fear itself. As if it had been drawn out of her by the strong arms that held her and was gone. Forever.

Not that she believed it. She'd lived with the nightmare too long now to believe it would ever go away permanently. But this feeling of freedom, no matter how temporary, was wonderful.

A huge sigh of relief came from deep within her. Her arms fell away from her knees and she stretched out her cramped legs.

"You feel like a kitten stretching on my lap," the man holding her said.

His voice, warm with a smile, startled her into an awareness of her position. Immediately she tried to sit up, tried to move off his lap, but his arms held her tightly.

"Don't fidget, kitten. You didn't seem to mind where you were a few moments ago and I was certainly enjoying myself. What happened?"

"Oh, but I . . . I just didn't realize. I'm so sorry."

"I'm not. Sorry, I mean. But then you did accuse me of taking advantage of pleasant situations."

Afraid that even in the dark he might see the burning of her cheeks Blaine turned her face into the only place she could hide, the softness of his shoulder.

"I had a nightmare. I just wasn't quite awake when you came in. You know how that is."

"I know you screamed and that you were terrified of something. I'd like to know what it was."

Wondering why she was doing so, she told him.

She had told only one other person about the dreams—Richard—and then only after he demanded an explanation for the gray circles under her eyes, the lost weight, the hands that constantly shook. But the story poured out easily to Garrath. It was dark, his arms were sheltering and he had saved her from hours of despair. She was grateful: he deserved the truth.

When she finished he was silent for a moment. One of his hands moved to the back of her neck, beneath the fall of blond hair, and rubbed gently. From that one touch a glow spread slowly throughout the rest of Blaine's body, and she decided she wouldn't mind staying as she was forever.

"Why on earth are you working on rigs then?" he asked at last.

"I don't. At least I never have before. I work in design and I helped design this system. So Richard thought I could solve your problem quicker than anyone else."

"Why didn't you tell him about your family, your nightmares, your fears?"

"He knew," she whispered, and the two words hurt.

Of course Richard knew. He knew everything about her. How could he not know when his was the shoulder she had been crying on, and leaning on, since she was a teenager?

It was hard to recall a time when Richard Perry hadn't been in her life. He and Len, close friends and both ten years older than she, had typically ignored her and resented her trailing after them when they were young and she was little more than a baby. But the years had passed, and when Len left home to join his father working in the oil fields, it was Blaine Richard came to see. As a stand-in for Len, he explained, and that was just what the lonely fourteen-year-old Blaine needed.

Richard also sparked her interest in computers. He went to work for a computer company already known for its innovations in a very innovative field, and he loved having an audience for his theories, his experiences and his knowledge. When, later, her interest turned into a career choice, his encouragement bolstered her against the ridicule of her family for her "unfeminine" pursuits.

But when her training was completed, she refused

Richard's "brotherly advice" that she take a job in his company. His company dealt mainly with the oil industry, and Blaine wanted no part of the world that had separated her from her father and brother. She chose a firm specializing in computer-game designs, over Richard's loud protests that she was playing instead of working.

Then the blowout at a drilling site in the Gulf of Mexico killed Len and her father—and her mother, too, for she seemed to will herself to die from the moment they heard the news. It took her just three months.

Blaine was suddenly alone. There had never been ties with other relatives. There was no one for her to turn to except Richard.

And turn she did, completely. She let Richard make all those first difficult decisions and arrangements while she concentrated on surviving the shattering of her world—and the recurring nightmares. By the time she recovered from the worst of the shock and pain Richard was handling everything so well that there was no need for her to do or decide anything. She followed his advice—sold her family's home and moved into an elegant Sausalito apartment in the building where he lived. He handled her finances, so it was months before she began to suspect that the apartment was much more expensive than he had led her to believe, and that he must be making up the difference.

"I want to," he said when she challenged him about it. "Please let me help you. Just for a while. The way Len would if he were here."

She did. And then he asked her to quit her job and come to work with him. Not in his old company; he was leaving there to start a company of his own to work on an idea for a computerized monitoring system, a totally new concept. He was having difficulties with the design but was convinced the problems could be solved.

"A system like this one might have saved your father and Len," he argued. "It will save other lives. But I can't do it alone, Blaine."

The one argument she couldn't resist. She agreed, after exacting a promise from him that she would be involved in design only, that she would never have to face the root of her nightmares.

It was a promise he'd kept through the months they spent designing, testing, redesigning. Through that first crucial installation and its success, starting a trickle of orders that grew into a flood as wells were drilled deeper and in more treacherous territory. He kept his promise through the move to new offices, the purchase of two jet helicopters and the growth of their own construction company. He kept his promise through everything—until Garrath St. Clair.

Yes, Richard had known about her nightmares and all the rest. But he had ignored that knowledge to please Garrath. Blaine told herself that Richard didn't know how really terrifying her dreams were or even that she continued to have them. But even so, his broken promise hurt. Deeply.

"He knew and he sent you out here anyway," Garrath said, his voice a growl. "Why, that unfeeling son of a—"

Blaine put a hand to his lips. He finished the epithet against her fingertips and the movement was soft, sensual, very much like a kiss.

She snatched her hand away as if it had been scalded, but that didn't stop the tingling that shot through her body. It was a feathery fiery sensation that made her long to press her fingers once again to those tender lips, to put her arms around his taut neck, to press her body against the hard leanness of his.

No! The unvoiced cry ricocheted madly within her and she struggled out of Garrath's arms. This time, absorbed by his own thoughts, he let her go.

"Well, at least you won't be arguing with me about leaving tomorrow—or is it today," he mused.

She'd been totally absorbed in getting as far from Garrath as possible on the narrow confines of the bed, but the words "arguing" and "leaving" cut through her daze. "What do you mean?"

"Just that this afternoon, when I said I was sending you back, I thought the only way I might get you off my rig would be to put you off bodily. And when I found you in the lab tonight I was certain I'd read you right. But this—"

"You did read me right, Mr. St. Clair," Blaine cut in, bristling.

He chuckled, unconcerned by her outburst. "Don't you think we can be a little more personal than that, Miss Christensen? After all we've been through together? Make it Garrath."

Blaine flushed at the memory evoked by his knowing laugh and his suggestive words—a memory of the electrifying warmth of his hands running roughly over her, the hard strength latent in his body pressing against hers and her dismayingly ardent response. She remembered, just as he'd meant her to. He was trying to embarrass her into acquiescence.

She pressed her lips tightly together. It wasn't going to work. She was embarrassed, all right, but she

was also angry. He was taking unfair advantage of
her sex, and using her emotions against her, believing
she would crumple under a little pressure just because
she was a woman. Well, he was in for a surprise.

"I'm not leaving, Mr. St. Clair, not until I've fixed
the system," she declared.

There was no chuckle this time. He stood up slowly
and deliberately, and Blaine felt his tall form leaning
threateningly over her. "You'll leave if I tell you
to."

She refused to flinch. "Computec's contract with
you says we will send out repair technicians when
needed. It doesn't give you a choice of personnel."

"On my rigs I always have a choice. And I'm always obeyed," he said, his voice harsh and low, a
warning snarl. "You'd best not forget that."

"But I've already found part of the problem."
Blaine tried a different tactic, wishing it didn't sound
so much like pleading. "And there's something...
unusual that I need time to investigate."

"Your replacement can do that. When the helicopter comes in the morning you'll be going back to
the Bank on it, sweetly and quietly or kicking and
screaming. It's up to you."

His footsteps thumped toward the door, each one
an obvious dismissal. But Blaine refused to be dismissed.

"It'll have to be kicking and screaming then," she
called out. "That's the only way you'll get me off
this rig before my job is finished."

Light from the corridor spilled cruelly over her as
he yanked open the door. She felt herself fixed by the
same bold stare and taunting smile that had so un-
nerved her at their first meeting, and a strange mix-

ture of warmth and chills swirled through her veins, leaving her weak.

"Fine with me," he said slowly, so that each word was heavy with implication. "It sounds...enjoyable."

"Why, you rotten, egotistical..." Blaine sputtered.

Garrath's laugh surged across the room. "Why, my dear Miss Christensen! Didn't anyone ever tell you nice girls don't say things like that?"

With an outraged gasp, Blaine heaved her pillow at him, but the missile fell short of its target. In an instant it came flying back at her, plopping into her lap with infuriating accuracy.

"Get some sleep, kitten. I'll see you in the morning. Early," he said, pulling the door closed behind him. But even that galling remark wasn't the end of it. Just before the latch clicked shut, he added, "Sweet dreams."

Blaine sank back in the bed, punching her pillow. *Sweet dreams, indeed,* she thought. *Kitten!* How dare he order her to sleep as if she were a disobedient child. Well, she wouldn't sleep and she wouldn't leave in the morning, at least not without a fight. If it was a battle he wanted, she was more than willing to give it to him. But she wasn't going to abandon her responsibilities by meekly obeying irrational, unfair and unprofessional orders. And she certainly wasn't going to sleep. Not a wink, she told herself.

It was her last waking thought before morning.

CHAPTER FOUR

BLAINE STIRRED JUST ENOUGH to grope along the shelf above the bed, groggily searching for her small travel clock. When her fingers closed over its squat body, she drew its face close to her own, blinking her sleep-fogged eyes until the luminous green hands came into focus. They pointed to 6:30.

Early, she thought, smiling and wriggling back down in bed. Still early. But the word stuck in her mind, echoing there until it struck a chord that brought her suddenly upright and wide awake.

Early! As in "I'll see you in the morning. Early." As in Garrath St. Clair's parting statement, which had not been an invitation to breakfast.

Frantically she kicked at the blanket tangled around her legs. A twinge of pain reminded her of her injured ankle but didn't halt her efforts to free herself. From what she knew of Garrath, his "early" would be *early*, especially in this case. If she didn't want him to find her sitting in her room docilely awaiting deportation—and she certainly didn't—she had to move.

She stood up cautiously, testing her ankle against her weight. It was tender but much improved over the night before. By favoring it slightly she was able to hurry to the bathroom without any significant problems.

Though she'd crawl all the way if she had to, she thought. She intended to defy Garrath for as long as she could, and that meant getting out of this room and to work. A little sprain wasn't going to stop her. Nothing was.

Her defiant resolution slipped a bit when she flipped on the bathroom light and faced her reflection in the mirror. The vision was familiar—ashen complexion, smoky shadows beneath eyes drained of sparkle and color, the tight thin line replacing her usually soft full-lipped mouth, and the limp tangled mess of her hair. She had seen it all after every bout with the nightmare.

And each time her feelings had matched her appearance. A dreadful crushing loneliness always lay beneath that perfect picture of despair. Loneliness and self-pity and a wish that she could huddle under the covers all day, licking her psychological wounds. It had been that way every time—until now.

"Sorry to disappoint you," she said to the wan face in the mirror. "I just don't have time to feel miserable this morning."

She shed her sleep-rumpled clothing like an outgrown skin, then turned on the shower. Smiling, she brushed the tangles out of her tousled hair and twisted it into a knot on top of her head. She unwound the bandage on her ankle, then stepped beneath the cascade of water, all the while savoring the thought of the look on Garrath's devastatingly handsome face if she could present him with a working system when he arrived to throw her off his rig. That would show him! And he certainly deserved showing. He'd been unbearably rude, thoroughly arrogant and totally disagreeable in every way from the moment she'd met him.

Well, maybe not in *every* way, she relented, the tingling warmth of the shower spray forcing the admission from her. There had been a few moments last night when he had been. . .different. The Garrath St. Clair that had held her, rocked her and eased her through the horror bore little resemblance to the man who barked orders and expected everyone else to jump.

So which was the real one? Was he even more complex than his name implied? Had she misjudged him as badly as he had misjudged her?

With an exasperated sigh Blaine switched off the water and stepped out of the glass enclosure. She rubbed a towel briskly over her body as if the friction of the terry cloth could rub away the memory of the soothing security of Garrath's arms.

She wasn't wrong, she told herself sternly. She was just reading too much into his casual attentions. He had played nursemaid simply to keep his sleeping crew from being disturbed. Certainly his gentleness had disappeared quickly enough the moment she had disagreed with him. And in every other instance he had acted horribly.

But this time, too, a memory rose to contradict her. Blaine froze with the towel pressed tightly against her chest as a picture formed—of herself cradled in Garrath's strong sheltering arms yet another time.

Her forehead wrinkled as she tried to see the picture more clearly. She had been half asleep at the time, so the episode was vague and hazy, like a badly shot movie sequence. She did remember his appearance in the Computec trailer and being swept up into his arms and carried to her room. But once there, had he removed her shoes and covered her with a blan-

ket? Had his fingers trailed sensuously through her
freed hair? Had he called her "princess" and...
kissed her?

The towel slid from Blaine's hands. Staring wide-
eyed into the misty mirror she saw was a very different reflection from the one she'd seen minutes
before. This face was flushed with rosy color, its eyes
shone a deep emerald green and its lips were soft,
moist and slightly parted in surprise. She raised a
fingertip to lightly touch her mouth. Had Garrath St.
Clair kissed her?

Blaine snatched her finger from her lips. *Fool,* she
chided herself, shaking as she bent to retrieve her
towel. Garrath might have offered the comfort she so
badly needed after her nightmare because it suited his
purposes to do so, but he had not been playing Prince
Charming to her Sleeping Beauty earlier. His sole interest in her was to get her off his rig with the
minimum amount of fuss. All because she was a
woman and he didn't believe a woman could do the
job. And if she didn't quit wasting time imagining
impossible things, he was going to be proved right.

She quickly pulled on a pair of jeans and a sea-
green velour top and brushed her hair into a severe
and very businesslike French twist. Feeling ready but
not *ready*, she crossed her fingers in the hope that
she could avoid Garrath long enough to find her way
to the trailer and looked around for her melton
jacket.

She didn't find it. Thunderous pounding burst
suddenly against the door and all thoughts of her
jacket flew from her mind.

"So much for crossed fingers," she muttered,
knowing there was only one person who would beat

on her door with such aggression. She held her breath, wondering if there was a chance he would leave if she didn't answer. A second, louder round of thumping assured her he would not. He would break the door down first, and the flimsy lock on it would be no deterrent.

The lock! Blaine stared at the small gold latch, but instead she was seeing Garrath standing in her open doorway the night before while she cowered miserably in bed. She hadn't been able to move, much less cross the room to let him in. . . .

She yanked open the door, demanding, "How did you get into my room last night?"

If her verbal attack surprised him, Garrath didn't let it show. There was only relaxed amusement in the glint of his eyes, and he didn't answer until his glance traveled slowly over the length of her.

"Does it matter?" he asked at last, each word barbed with innuendo. At the same time he leaned a bit to one side to let Blaine see the figures in the hallway beyond him. Figures that were studiously ignoring the scene at her door while moving slowly down the hall. Very, very slowly.

Blaine didn't need an instant replay to know how the exchange had sounded. She spun away from the doorway, retreating into her room. Garrath was right behind her as the door clicked shut.

"Do you enjoy making other people feel ridiculous?" she asked, not looking at him.

"I might if they all were as beautiful as you are when they got mad," he replied. "But I can't take all the credit. After all, you're the one who answered the door in such a provocative fashion."

"Oh, you. . .!" Blaine whirled around and her

hand flew up automatically, aiming a slap at the in-furiating smile she'd known she would find.

She never made contact. Almost as if he'd expected the attempt, his hand caught her wrist easily in midair. His fingers closed and she was pulled against him.

"No," he said. One word, spoken softly and with-out apparent anger, but it lashed with the force of a whip snapped warningly over her head. Blaine stared up at him, at the set line of his jaw and the mouth no longer taunting or amused but simply determined, and the fight drained out of her. She wouldn't at-tempt to strike Garrath St. Clair, not now, or ever again.

When her lack of further resistance was obvious he released her. "To answer the question that started all this," he said as if nothing had happened, "I have a master key. So if you were contemplating trying to run and hide...." He paused and ran a finger along the collar of her top, lightly brushing the nape of her neck. Blaine's hands closed into fists until her nails dug into her palms as lightning zigzagged down her spine.

"You might as well forget it," he went on. "There are no doors to keep me out on Sithein One."

"How nice for your crew!" she snapped, more up-set by her reaction to his touch than by his renewed teasing. She took a step backward. "I wasn't going to hide, though. I was going to work."

She prepared herself for his outrage, his fury, his condemnation. She wasn't ready for the slow arching of one black eyebrow.

"And why am I not surprised by that information, I wonder?" he asked wryly.

Blaine bit the inside of her lip to keep from rising to his bait. When she didn't respond, his brow quirked even higher.

"Well, never mind. We'll leave it that I'm not. In fact, I'm so unsurprised that I brought you these." He held out a pair of glaringly white coveralls and a yellow hard hat. "The coveralls are optional but recommended. They might save your very becoming outfit from stains."

Blaine saw an echo of the compliment in his bold brown eyes, and the clothes that had always seemed comfortable and functional before all at once felt too tight, too clingy and too accentuating. It was all she could do to not raise her hands in a classically shielding gesture. But Garrath's attention shifted back to the items he held.

"The hard hat, though, is not optional. It will be on your head any time you go outside the building, regardless of how short a trip you're planning, how unchic it looks or whether it messes up your hairdo. Have I made that clear enough?"

"Quite clear enough," Blaine answered coldly, snatching the hat from his hand. "I'm not a child, you know."

His smile claimed that he knew nothing of the kind. Furious, Blaine plopped the hard hat onto her head. But the picture of professionalism she intended to present was ruined when the hat slipped forward over her eyes, its hard brim hitting the bridge of her nose painfully.

The sharp sting of the blow stunned her for an instant, and she stood very still, fighting back the tears that sprang into her eyes. She would not give Garrath any more reasons to consider her an incompetent child. She would not cry.

But before she could gain control, his hands were lifting the hat from her head. "Are you all right?" he asked gently.

"Fine," she forced out between stiff lips. "I don't think much of your haberdasher though."

Garrath stared at her for a moment, and then laughed, a deep vigorous laugh.

Like wine, Blaine thought, and a dimpled smile sprang to her lips. His laugh was like good wine, rich, full-bodied and warming. Warming deep down inside, drowning out all the tension, all the anger. One taste made her long for more.

"My apologies, madame," he said, sketching a mock bow. "This unfortunate situation will be remedied forthwith." He turned the hat over and tugged at the network of straps inside. Blaine watched the deftness and strength of his fingers as he worked and couldn't help remembering the light touch of them brushing her neck. She was so deep in the remembered feel of his hands that she was caught off guard when he raised the hat above her head.

"Now, let's try again," he said.

The tension returned, doubled. "No, I can . . ." she stammered, reaching out to take it from him.

"Stand still, woman," he ordered lightly.

She did. To do anything else would make her look ridiculous. She was overreacting again. He wasn't going to attack her, after all; there was no reason for her to feel like bolting to the other side of the room, not even if he was standing unnecessarily close. Not even if she didn't dare fidget the slightest bit and so was forced to stare at the broad expanse of his chest, the taut muscles softly hugged by his cashmere sweater—no grimy coveralls today—and the golden skin of his long lean throat. Not even if he was taking forever.

At last the hat came down on her head, snugly this time. Its weight was considerable, and the protective brim jutting over her forehead was like blinders above her eyes. But she didn't mind that, not while it shielded her burning cheeks from Garrath's sight.

The protection didn't last long. Before she could thank him and move away he placed a finger beneath her chin and pressed upward, tilting her face toward him.

"That's better," he said. His finger moved from her chin up her jawline and over her cheek to touch the tender bridge of her nose. "There's a red mark. Are you sure you're okay?"

Blaine's breath was caught somewhere deep in her throat, so her yes came out small and uncertain. But it satisfied Garrath. He dropped his hand, and freed from his spell she was at last able to take a step away.

Distance wasn't enough to end her turmoil. He proved that by holding up the coveralls, a wickedly teasing smile playing on his lips. "Do you think you'll need help getting these on, too? I estimated your size—from memory." He made a motion with his hands that left no doubt that their first intimate contact had been the basis for his guess. "And I'd be happy to—"

"No!" Blaine blurted, unable to stop the panicky refusal, but mentally kicking herself at the same time. She couldn't understand what was happening to her. Never before had she had trouble maintaining a cool unflappable facade in her business dealings. Why was it so impossible now?

Grinning, Garrath tossed the coveralls onto the bed. "All right then, I'll take you down to breakfast, and after that you can get to work."

"Work?" Blaine's eyes opened wide, their green deepening to emerald as the implication of his bringing her the outfit hit home, an implication she'd been too rattled to notice before. Her expression changed to one of suspicion. "What about the helicopter? And your orders?"

Garrath shrugged. "I spoke with Richard Perry late last night. He explained your familiarity with the system and your position in the company. Although I had some difficulty accepting his assurances that the teenage fashion model that threw herself down the stairs at me—"

"Threw!" Blaine exclaimed. "I most certainly did not throw—"

"—last night was a fully qualified computer engineer, I'm willing to give you a try." He hadn't even paused.

"How very generous of you," she grumbled. But even as the words came out, laced with all the sarcasm she'd intended, even as she rebelled at his being *willing* to give her a *try*, she was mentally jumping up and down like a four-year-old. He had changed his opinion of her, no matter how grudgingly he was admitting it. He was giving her a chance instead of dismissing her out of hand. Why that should matter so much she didn't know, but it did. And while she knew it was ridiculous to feel grateful for being allowed to do the job she had been sent to do, logic couldn't suppress the warm burst of happiness inside her.

But Garrath could, and did, with his next comment.

"Very generous, I thought. Of course it helps that you look a little less in need of a nanny this morning."

"A nanny!"

His eyes roved again, his smile broadening as his gaze swept over her, ending at her furiously reddened lips. He nodded.

"I think a chaperon should be sufficient now. So if you're just about ready, I'd like to get going. I've got a meeting in a few minutes. I'll drop you at the galley on the way."

Like a sack of old potatoes, Blaine raged inwardly. And outwardly. "I don't require a nanny or a chaperon, Mr. St. Clair," she said frostily. "And since I'm sure you don't escort all your employees to breakfast, I'll find my own way when I'm ready, if you don't mind."

Garrath was ominously silent for a full minute and a muscle twitched at the edge of his no longer smiling mouth. But when he spoke his voice was coolly unemotional. "I don't mind," he said. "I'll check on your progress a little later then."

"I'm sure you will," Blaine retorted.

His brown eyes sparked dangerously in response, a flash of lightning closely followed by the thunder of his slamming out of the room, leaving Blaine alone.

"Good," she muttered. "Good." Though she didn't feel good at all. She would be fine once she was working, however—as always. With that objective in mind she pulled on the coveralls and headed for the galley.

Surprisingly she found she was starving. She'd

been too preoccupied before to notice the gnawing
feeling in her midsection, but now it was painfully
obvious. Her last meal had been a very long time ago
and had probably been breakfast, too. But she
doubted her empty stomach would object to a repeat
as long as there was food, and plenty of it.

She found her way with no trouble, guided by tantalizing cooking odors. But just outside the galley she
hesitated. A long line of hooks held a multicolored
mosaic of hard hats, evidence of a crowded room
beyond. Suddenly her stomach was filled with but-
terflies, and she wished she hadn't been so quick to
reject Garrath's offer of an escort. Even his company
was preferable to facing alone a roomful of stran-
gers, men whose attitudes toward a woman on board
most likely resembled that of their boss.

But hunger overcame hesitation and hooking her
hat next to the others, then taking a deep breath and
tilting her chin determinedly, she marched through
the door.

She found herself at the end of a line of men moving past cafeteria-style counters loaded with pans and
platters of food. Plates were being efficiently loaded
by white-aproned attendants, and her appetite took
over, countering her uneasiness. All her thoughts
concentrated on the delicious-looking food. She
didn't try to decide between the various dishes but
held out her tray for almost everything, ending up
with three butter-dripping blueberry muffins, twin
mountains of fluffy scrambled eggs and buttermilk
pancakes, crisp bacon as well as juicy sausage and a
sectioned and sugared grapefruit.

The only time her attention was diverted from the
food was when she reached the coffee cart. She

looked up in response to the question "Black or white?" and into the face of a pert pretty young woman.

"Black," she managed to reply, but her mind was far from coffee, puzzling over the discovery that she wasn't the only female aboard. She'd assumed the rig population was all-male, but here was evidence distinctly to the contrary.

So why had Garrath been so anxious to get her off Sithein One? Was it just women in professional positions that bothered him? Or was it, for some unimaginable reason, her specifically that he objected to?

A steaming mug of coffee was placed on her tray. "You're new here," the girl stated with a friendly smile.

Blaine nodded.

"Well now, you'll be lovin' it; never mind the strangeness at first. Everyone's so nice. Especially Mr. St. Clair."

Especially Garrath? Of course, Blaine thought irritably, aware of the girl's well-rounded figure unabashedly hugged by the white uniform, the knowing sparkle in her eyes, the saucy toss of her head. Of course Garrath would be nice to such an eager and compliant female.

A shuffling behind her told her she was holding up the line. With a quick "thank-you," she moved on, the lilting tune of the girl's bubbly "Cheerio, miss," accompanying her to the door of the dining room.

The same care in design that had lifted Andy's room a notch above dormitory quality was present in the dining room. Blaine had expected cafeteria metal and plastic glaring coldly beneath harsh fluorescent lights. Instead there were long tables and captain's

chairs of polished oak, parquet flooring and soft dif-
fused overhead lighting. It wasn't four-star elegance,
but it was attractive. As Andy had told her, St. Clair
Corporation provided the best for its crew.

Not that the crew seemed all that aware of their
surroundings—or anything else. The crowded room
was unexpectedly quiet, with conversation minimal.
Most of the men were giving total attention to their
plates, while the few looking elsewhere were doing so
with blank unfocused stares.

The glassy expressions touched her memory and
Blaine realized what she was seeing. "Oil rig trance,"
Len had described it to her after his first tour on a
rig. It was an appropriate name for the daze that
often came over men just after a grueling twelve-hour
shift. Only two things mattered—getting some food
and getting to bed. Very little else roused them from
their lethargy.

Blaine smiled as she quickly scanned the room. She
was hoping to find Andy or Doc, or at least an empty
spot where she wouldn't feel she was intruding. Her
search was cut short, though, by a raspy thickly
burred voice. From somewhere amidst a knot of men
in a corner of the room it grated through the quiet,
reminding her that there was a third thing that interested rig crews—gossip.

"First we get fancy American machines, now we
get a fancy American woman to fix the daft machines. 'Tisn't right."

Blaine froze in the doorway, in no doubt as to who
was being so unfavorably discussed.

"Those machines have done nothin' but cause
trooble from the beginning, shuttin' down drilling
for no good reason, wastin' time. And that woman—

did ye see her when she arrived, all indecently dressed. Why, a body could see everythin'...."

"Oh, go on, Rory," another voice cut in. "You weren't even on shift when the lassie arrived. So how do you know what she was or wasn't wearing?"

"'Tis hearing things, I've been," came the gruff reply.

"And you see things, too, and not always things that are there."

Light laughter followed the rejoinder, but Rory ignored it. "I still say American machines and American women have no place on a Scottish rig. Scottish oil should be for Scotland."

"Here we go again," came one grumbled response, and others followed. Whether in agreement or not, Blaine couldn't tell and didn't care. She was too busy wishing she could vanish into the polished woodwork. She didn't dare move for fear of attracting attention, yet she couldn't just stand where she was forever for the very same reason.

Her disgruntled critic spoke again, and it was all she could do to keep from dropping her laden tray as the shock of his words hit her.

"There's goin' to be trooble on this rig," the voice rasped. "Big trooble, if St. Clair willna be rid of those machines and that woman. Mark my words, lads. There's goin' to be trooble."

CHAPTER FIVE

OTHER QUIETER VOICES TOOK OVER after Rory's dramatic pronouncement, but Blaine had already lost her taste for breakfast. Thinking only of finding somewhere to be alone, she swung around quickly. Her elbow bumped into a mug of coffee—very hot coffee, she discovered, as the steaming brew sloshed over the rim of the jostled cup and onto her arm, where its heat soaked through her coveralls and sweater. She jumped and the dishes on her tray rattled noisily.

"Steady on there," came a voice, and a hand reached out to balance her tray.

"I'm so sorry," she apologized hastily, and looked up into a smile straight out of a toothpaste commercial. "I was...I just wasn't thinking."

"How nice for me that you weren't." The clipped British formality of the words didn't disturb the smile. "This way I don't have to contrive some ridiculous excuse to introduce myself. I'm Miles Ramsey. And you must be our new computer technician."

Looking past the man's too-wide too-brilliant smile, Blaine saw that the rest of his appearance was made to match. Everything about Miles Ramsey was just a shade overdone.

She wasn't sure of his age. Anything from thirty to fifty was possible, though she guessed it was closer to the fifty end of the span simply because he seemed to be making such an effort to look young. His smile flashed in a face too deeply tanned to be a result of working under the often stormy skies of the North Sea. He was of average height and stocky in build, but snug-fitting coveralls showed off muscles as carefully nurtured as was the stylish wave of suspiciously blond hair that dipped over his high forehead. And the glint in his blue gray eyes was full of such typical predatory male appraisal and appreciation that it had to have been practiced in a mirror—for hours.

"Yes, I'm Blaine Christensen," she replied cautiously.

"Marvelous. I was hoping to get a chance to talk to you about your monitoring system, but I'd heard you weren't staying long. Does that mean you've already completed the repairs?"

"Not quite," she answered, wondering if he knew more about her stay than he was saying. "I have an idea of the problem, but it's going to require a lot of testing to be sure. I expect to stay until that's finished." I hope, she added silently.

"Well, I'm glad to hear that." He paused, and his smile blinked brighter. "And not just because I want to see the system fixed."

Blaine couldn't help smiling back. His line was as contrived as his appearance, but she sensed with relief that it was a definite case of a lot of big talk and very little action. Right now her battered ego welcomed the balm of some light harmless flattery and eyes that held something besides scorn.

"I was just getting a refill," Miles continued, lifting his now half-empty cup. "Can I persuade you to join me for a little shop talk over your breakfast? I'm the toolpusher on Sithein One, so I have a professional interest."

Blaine agreed quickly, surprised and pleased at the twist of events. The attitude of the toolpusher was very important to the success of the Computec system. He was the rig boss, second in command only to the owner. His job was to bring up the oil as rapidly and efficiently as possible. To do that meant making decisions about when, where, which direction and how fast to drill based on available data. It also meant deciding when drilling should be suspended to prevent accidents or even a blowout. Thus his decisions meant life or death for every person on the rig.

Which was why the Computec system had been designed to make many of those decisions automatically. The computers could analyze the incoming data and institute changes, even shutting down drilling, much quicker than a human being could. Because the emphasis was different—the toolpusher's job was bringing up the oil safely, while the monitoring system's was maintaining safety while bringing up the oil—there were bound to be some conflicts over those decisions. Therefore the toolpusher's acceptance of the system was crucial.

So it was doubly nice to find Sithein One's toolpusher not only interested in the computers, but, unlike his boss, not at all outraged by her gender. On the contrary, she decided, as Miles put a guiding hand beneath her elbow.

Her pleasure rapidly evaporated, though, when he steered her across the dining room to the very corner from which Rory's irate speech had come. She realized Miles had probably been away getting his coffee refill at the time of the angry outburst, so was unaware of what had occurred. It was too late at this point to try and explain or come up with a graceful retreat.

So she pasted a smile on her face and glanced tentatively at the men sitting on either side of the chair Miles pulled out for her, praying that she'd misjudged and Rory was somewhere farther—much farther—down the table. She received a few curious stares, a quick nod or two, and one outright leer in return. But none of the nearby faces contained the malevolence she'd heard in Rory's tirade. With a sigh of relief she sank down into the proffered chair.

Her sigh came a moment too soon. She had just scooped up a section of grapefruit and was raising it to her mouth when she looked in the one direction she hadn't before. Directly across the table—at Rory.

That venomous glare couldn't belong to anyone else. He resembled a badly dispositioned gremlin, with tufts of rusty brown hair poking out from a round skull, huge flaring ears, a pouting lower lip swallowing the upper one and bright hard beads for eyes. If gremlins could fashion curses, Blaine knew she was being cursed.

Miles verified the man's identity as he introduced her to their table mates, saving the unfriendly face for last.

"Rory MacPherson, our most revered crew member,'' he said sincerely. ''Rory has been working on rigs for. . .how many years is it, Rory?''

The lower lip twitched slightly, the rest of his expression not altering. ''Comin' twenty-five years, since early days. Days when drillin' was a lad's job and takin' care of bairns was a lassie's.''

''Isn't it nice the way things have changed,'' Miles interjected with a tolerant smile for the old man. ''I'd certainly rather look at Miss Christensen's pretty face than your ugly mug.''

''Oh, I dinna mind lookin' at the lassie's face. Sure an' if I were a wee bit younger I wouldn't object to lookin' at the rest of her either. But not on the job.'' The crook of his lips was a nasty sneer.

There was a ''Now, Rory. . .'' from Miles and a snicker or two from down the table but mostly silence as the others watched and waited for Blaine's reaction.

She could guess what they expected—from a female. Blushes, tears, hysterics, an outraged dash from the room. And nothing would more quickly earn their scorn, for in the close confines of the rig communities a sense of humor was a necessity.

Fortunately the lessons painfully learned as a baby sister had taught Blaine early in life the best way to deal with bullying. By giving back a large dose of the bully's own medicine.

She smiled broadly, knowing her dimple would add dramatically to the effect. ''Well, Mr. MacPherson,'' she said, her voice a soft sensual purr. ''If you were a *lot* younger, I might not mind your looking either.''

Laughter boomed around the table and her opponent's scowl deepened. ''In my day women knew their places, and the decisions on a rig were made by men, not machines. And definitely not by women,'' he growled.

"Yes, I know—'' Blaine fluttered her long eye-lashes innocently ''—but don't worry, sir. We're working hard to change all that.''

Rory's reply was something between a snarl and a snort. With a glinty-eyed glare he pushed himself to his feet and stomped away from the table. Blaine watched his departure in amusement. Standing, Rory was even more of a gremlin, with a wide hulking tor-so set precariously on spindly bowed legs, which gave him a scuttling walk as he moved between the tables and out the door.

But gremlins had their evil side, she remembered, her smile fading. Gruff spluttering men like Rory MacPherson should be nothing more than amusing oddities, harmless relics from another era. His barbed comments alone wouldn't have mattered. They hadn't hurt, really; certainly not the way Garrath's had. But Rory had also warned of trouble on Sithein One, and that was not so easily dismissed.

"I apologize for Rory,'' Miles said. "He takes some getting used to. He's got a mean tongue and old-fashioned ideas, but there's no man on this rig I—or anyone else—would rather team up with. He knows his job and does it well.''

Blaine nodded. "I understand. My father was a bit like Rory.'' Even more than a bit when it came to a woman's position, she thought. He had believed men should do their jobs and women should wait at home for their return, even if the waiting went on for weeks or months at a time, over and over again, until it eventually drained the women of all happiness.

"Well then, you realize men like Rory are all bluster. It doesn't mean a thing," Miles assured her. "Though I must admit to sharing a few of his reservations about your system. Sithein One was outfitted with the most modern equipment we could find to aid us in making decisions. We have ten different safety systems, some automatic, some manual. Our control room is a forest of dials registering the information from valves, gauges and sensors, and we've got computers to analyze that data and provide me with projections. None of that has given us any trouble."

Miles hesitated, rubbing two fingers over a bronzed cheek as if trying to massage away an ache. Blaine knew exactly what was coming.

"But your system goes one step further, doesn't it?" he continued. "It not only puts out the data, it makes the decisions, too. And I can't be entirely comfortable with a machine that can overrule me even when I know I'm right. Its installation was the only thing Garrath and I have ever argued about. Of course he's the boss, so we've got it and will have to make do. But so far its record hasn't been very reassuring."

Miles's complaint was a familiar one, one Computec had faced before. Many toolpushers relied heavily on a sixth sense, a "feel" for the oil, to tell them when and where to drill. Their prestige rested on that intuitive sense and the results of their decisions. For that reason they had no trouble accepting the most sophisticated equipment as long as it served them and provided information to aid in the making of those decisions. But a system that occasionally usurped some of their power by making decisions on its own, even in the name of safety, wasn't as enthusiastically welcomed. Usually the Computec system was able to quickly prove itself a help rather than a hindrance and so was just as quickly accepted. But so far on Sithein One the doubts were being borne out instead.

"I'm sorry," she apologized, feeling like the mother of an unruly child. "But I think that as soon as the system is repaired you'll find it a good friend."

"I'm sure I will," he agreed. But he didn't sound sure. In fact for a moment he sounded almost sarcastic.

When Blaine glanced at him, however, wondering if she'd heard correctly, his expression was hidden by his cup as he drained the last of his coffee. And when he faced her again, his gleaming smile was firmly in place.

"With a saleswoman as attractive as you to talk it up, I've no doubt I'll be kissing it cheerio every day quite soon," he said lightly. "So tell me more about my new mate."

Blaine did, finding that Miles was avidly interested in spite of his reservations. He asked about the system's inner workings, the kinds of failures that might occur, the scope of the computer's abilities, exactly how long she thought it might take to get the system running again. Only on the latter question did she hedge.

"Forever, unless I get to work pretty soon." She scraped the last bit of food off her plate.

"Well, in the interest of our mutual friend's speedy recovery, may I walk you to your office?" he offered. "Though I must warn you I'll try to persuade you to give me a personalized tour when we get there."

"Sure," Blaine agreed, but had to quell a momentary flash of irritation at receiving a second offer of an escort. The reaction was unfair, she knew. Miles was not Garrath; his invitation had nothing to do with thinking she needed a nanny. She shouldn't blame Miles for the faults of his boss.

"I'd love to," she added with more warmth. "And maybe later you could reciprocate in your territory. Until yesterday the only rigs I'd ever seen were on paper." She was rewarded by Miles's grateful look, that of a little boy just asked to show his spider collection.

They stopped in front of the rack of hard hats outside the galley, and Blaine looked at the assortment in dismay. The mosaic had shifted, with additions and subtractions. How would she ever find hers when so many of them were the same color?

Miles himself moved without hesitation, picking a silver one off the rack and setting it very carefully on his well-groomed hair.

"Tell me how you did that," she pleaded, and he laughed.

"It's easy. I'll bet I can find yours for you almost as easily." It took him a minute, scanning the line of hats, but the first one he pulled off was hers. "The stickers give the game away," he explained, handing it to her. "Everyone puts them on; usually the logos from rigs and companies you've worked with. Or whatever takes your fancy. Add to that the color, the familiar dents and scratches and the general area you left it, and it's not hard. Yours is brand new, the only one with nothing but the St. Clair logo.''

On the pristine yellow of her hat the logo stood out, distinctive and surprising. A white unicorn pranced on a field of blue, and around the mythical beast's neck hung a silver medallion on a gold ribbon. Written on the medallion was ''Sithein One.''

''An odd name for a rig,'' she mused.

Miles nodded. ''*Sithein* is Gaelic for fairy hill, the mythological home of the fairies. Legend has it that a man who entered a fairy hill would be trapped there, held by a magical enchantment forever. Garrath's always been a trifle fey about his Celtic heritage.''

''But isn't St. Clair a French name?''

''Yes, but the French and the Scots had close ties, closer than the ties between England and Scotland, throughout much of history. And a lot of those ties were knotted in the marriage bed, such as the one with the 'original' St. Clair. Depending on the version of the story he was either the dashing captain of a French ship sailing the seas on the business of the French crown or a dashing pirate interested in no business but his own. Either way he was dashing. At least we can assume the daughter of a fierce Highland chief found him sufficiently so, because she married him and thus brought the land where Glenclair Manor now stands to the St. Clairs.''

''You seem to know a lot about St. Clair history. Have you known Gar...Mr. St. Clair long?''

''Since he inherited St. Clair Corporation from his father. Almost fifteen years ago, I guess. But I've worked for St. Clair's most of my life. Oil work was the only thing I ever wanted to do. I was roughnecking for a small independent oil company when the old man, Stewart St. Clair, bought it. That was back when the possibility of there being big oil fields out here in the North Sea was still a pipe dream—forgive the pun. I worked my way up from roughneck to foreman the hard way, but the operation never did well. We sank a lot of dry holes, found a few small reserves but never anything to justify the enormous expenses. We'd just started work in a new area, one that I somehow knew was right, when the old man died. We all heard rumors that Garrath was being advised to sell out to one of the big oil companies, not to pour any more money into a losing proposition.''

Miles paused, and Blaine saw him slip deeply into the past. A faraway, almost wistful look dulled his eyes to a flat gray.

''I'll never forget the day I fought my way past a long line of prune-faced secretaries to Garrath. He was just a scared kid trying to fit into his father's huge chair then. And I was just a foreman on one of his rigs—not even a toolpusher—with no right to be barging into his office at all. But I did,'' he declared, and there was a whisper of pride in his voice that grew as he related the rest of the story. ''I told him the oil was there, that I would bring it up—soon—if he would put me in charge and give us the necessary funds. Garrath trusted me, took my advice against that of all his fancy advisers, made me headman on the rig right then and there. And I did what I'd promised. We paid back the original investment, and then some.''

Blaine hardly heard the last part of Miles's reminiscences. She was too caught up in trying to imagine the formidable Garrath St. Clair as a ''scared kid'' prematurely stepping into his father's large shoes.

But both she and Miles were abruptly recalled to the present by the sudden shouting of Miles's name.

"Miles Ramsey to the office. Miles Ramsey to the office immediately."

Grimacing, Miles pointed to a black box on the wall next to Blaine. "Intercom, although you might hear it referred to in less delicate terms since it can and does find a person anywhere on the rig. And whenever it does, it means there's a real...winner of a problem in the offing." As he explained he moved to the box and jabbed at a button.

"Ramsey here. Be right up," he said, before turning back to Blaine, his expression conspicuously regretful. "Sorry. Duty calls. We're going in opposite directions, so I guess I'll have to renege on my offer. Another time?"

"Of course," she replied too enthusiastically, ashamed of the direction of her thoughts. She'd noticed that Miles hadn't bothered to ask what the problem was that required his attention and guessed the omission was intentional. In spite of his well-displayed impatience and regret, she would bet he was pleased by this chance to appear important and indispensable and wasn't going to let her know that the urgent summons actually concerned something routine.

But her unflattering assessment hadn't shown, for Miles's smile was as wide and brilliant as ever as he said goodbye and strode briskly away.

Blaine still didn't escape having an escort. She had just arranged the hard hat securely on her head and was on her way to the exit when a familiar voice drawled her name.

"Miss Christensen, ma'am. Hold up, will ya?"

Blaine smiled. She was genuinely pleased to see Andy, even if the sight did cause a bittersweet lump to fill her throat as his resemblance to Len struck her anew. He was loping toward her from the other end of the corridor. A sky blue cowboy shirt was jammed into tight western jeans that tapered down into the same boots he'd worn at the airport, and his pile-lined jacket was hooked over his shoulder on one finger. Andy was clearly off duty.

He didn't show the slightest sign of having spent a long hard-working sleepless night. He looked fresh from a shower with dampness lingering in the reddish brown curls of his hair and a soap-and-water flush in his cheeks. His eyes sparkled a clear-morning blue and his smile was as irrepressible and infectious as ever.

They exchanged "good-mornings" and Andy asked if she was on her way to work.

"Yes," Blaine answered, nodding. "It seems our esteemed boss has had a change of heart."

"I'd say it was Mother Nature that had the change of heart," Andy contradicted, his mustache twitching over his grin.

"Mother Nature?"

"Well, sure. Y'know—the weather that came up during the night. Since the helicopters don't fly in winds like this unless there's an emergency, you couldn't leave if you wanted to. And Mother's working to keep you here awhile, it seems. The forecast is for a real gale heading our way."

"A gale heading this way," Blaine echoed. She was seeing the smile on Garrath's lips and hearing his voice as he told her he'd spoken with Richard and was willing to give her a try. Why hadn't she known immediately that Garrath St. Clair would never have changed his mind no matter how glowingly Richard presented her credentials?

Because you were too befuddled by his closeness, his light touch, his deep brown eyes, came the answer. He'd made a fool of her again, letting her think he was going to give her a chance to prove herself, when in reality he was doing the only thing he could do, short of locking her up somewhere. He was letting her work because he couldn't get rid of her—yet. He was probably just as certain as ever that she would fail and just as determined to send her home at the first opportunity.

"I have to get to work right now, Andy. Can you show me the way?" Blaine asked, her reluctance to being chaperoned around the rig suddenly forgotten. All that mattered was getting to the trailer as quickly as possible.

"Well, ah, sure thing, ma'am. But, ah, I think...." Andy's stuttering matched the rhythm of his hand slapping back and forth across his thigh.

"What is it?" she demanded. "You don't have to worry about Garrath objecting." Not as long as the wind keeps blowing, she added silently. "He said I could go to work."

Andy's eyes shifted over Blaine and then quickly away, and a wash of apple-red splashed from his throat to his hairline. "No, ma'am. It's not that. But it's really blowin' out there, y'know. And you are... well, you just might want to consider, ah, takin' a coat or something. In case."

Understanding dawned and the dimple bloomed in her cheek. "Don't worry," she assured him. "You can tell me straight out that I'm not dressed right, and I promise not to bite your head off this time. I've learned my lesson.''

Blaine smiled at Andy, but her thoughts were far away, on a lesson that had nothing to do with dressing correctly.

"Yes, I've learned my lesson,'' she repeated. "Now I think it's about time I had a turn as the teacher. And boy, am I going to teach him. . . .'' The smile and the dimple were gone.

CHAPTER SIX

BLAINE EXPECTED WORK TO DRIVE ALL THOUGHTS of Garrath and his deceit from her mind. She had always been able to lose herself in data printouts, equations and calculations, forgetting problems and worries while under the computer's spell. But shortly after Andy left her in the Computec trailer she knew that this time the magic wasn't going to happen. How could it, when every few minutes a gust of wind slammed against the trailer walls like the blow of a large and unfriendly hand, reminding her of the real reason she was still on Sithein One instead of on a helicopter halfway back to Aberdeen.

Perhaps the wind was trying to grant Rory Mac-Pherson's wish to be rid of "American machines and fancy American women," she thought crossly as another blast sent a shudder through the building—and through her. Certainly each gust seemed stronger, more belligerent and one step closer to blowing the whole unit right off the side of the rig. But even more disturbing was the whisper she heard in the sound of the wind, the whisper of a name: Garrath St. Clair.

Between gusts she worked, however, quickly discovering that her exhaustion the night before hadn't led her on a false trail. With a clear head the whole thing seemed even more improbable, peculiar and suspicious.

Hindsight showed the malfunction to have had a ridiculously simple cause, but Blaine wasn't surprised that Walter hadn't discovered it. He had been looking, understandably, in the wrong place.

The system had been shutting down drilling on occasion as if it had sensed extreme and dangerous pressure building on the lines, when in reality no such excess pressure existed. The computer and the monitoring program were functioning perfectly in every other respect, so the obvious assumption was that the computer was somehow receiving incorrect data. Therefore the logical places to begin searching for the malfunction were in the pressure sensors located on every drilling bit and oil line and in the analog-to-digital converters, the specialized circuits that translated sensor information into computer language. That search, Blaine knew from Walter's reports, had been thoroughly and efficiently conducted—several times.

Which left Blaine with a single conclusion—that the computer had lost its mind, or at least a part of it. A circumstance that was very very unlikely.

The computer's "mind," the program that told it exactly what to do, how and when to react, was what she had spent months designing. These instructions were then recorded—or burned in—on "nonerasable" memory circuits called ROMs. Long before a ROM found its way into a computer in a Computec trailer, it was tested for the integrity of its program. And once it was proved valid and installed, the only way it could be changed was by exposure to intense ultraviolet light like that of a ROM eraser. But there was no ROM eraser on Sithein One, no need or purpose in having one aboard.

So the possibility of something being wrong with the program itself was nearly impossible. Nearly.

Blaine repeated her actions of the previous night. Her fingers flew over the terminal keyboard, composing a simple computer command, "DISPLAY PROGRAM." The computer obeyed instantly, filling the screen with the pattern of numbers and symbols that represented its intelligence.

The pattern was perfect, faultless most of the way through. But then a few lines of meaningless gibberish printed across the screen, just as they had the night before. A few nonsensical lines that confirmed her earlier diagnosis. There was a defect in the ROM.

The defect was in the section of memory enabling the computer to handle the rare circumstance of its receiving messages from two drill strings at the same instant. But due to the alteration in the program, the computer now "glitched"—malfunctioned—whenever the situation occurred. Instead of queuing the messages in order of importance as it was supposed to do, the computer responded as if it sensed a pressure overload, by shutting down the drilling and instituting safety measures.

Correcting the problem was simple, as simple as pulling out the drawer below the terminal that housed the inner workings of the computer, locating the right circuit board and replacing the faulty circuit. Blaine did that and then automatically began running the series of tests that would prove the fault was corrected.

The testing was routine and occupied only a small portion of her mind. The rest of her attention lingered on the question of how such a malfunction could have occurred.

Two hours later she was no closer to the answer. There seemed to be only two possibilities—one she couldn't believe and one she didn't want to believe.

The problem might be due to natural causes, might have developed on its own from an undiscovered flaw in the circuitry. When dealing with sensitive and intricate electronic equipment such a circumstance couldn't be completely ruled out. But it could be considered highly unlikely.

Which left the other unthinkable possibility. That the malfunction had been caused intentionally.

Blaine hit the computer's "BREAK" key, interrupting the current program, and wished she could break the pattern of her thoughts as easily. But already the word was printing itself in her mind, already she was considering how it could have been done. Sabotage.

With all the intensity she had once given to developing the program she now concentrated on how to destroy it. The alteration had been subtle and slight, its results enormous. Each shutdown of the drilling cost valuable time; time to discover if the shutdown was necessary, time to disengage the automatically instituted safety systems, time to restart the drilling. And on an oil rig time was very, very expensive.

So although the change in the program had been a minor one, it had been enough to cause severe trouble. And its very subtlety had made it difficult to discover. Total destruction of the system would have in the long run been less troublesome and much less costly. Had someone been smart enough to realize that fact?

Blaine could think of only one way the alteration

of the program could have been accomplished—with a strong ultraviolet light source carefully applied to the ROM circuit. She was computing just how strong a source would be necessary and for what length of time it would need to be applied, when the door of the trailer opened.

She didn't need to look up to know it was Garrath, come to check up on her as he'd warned her he would. She felt his searing scrutiny even before she dared meet the challenge of his gaze.

He closed the door against the weather, hung his hard hat on the rack, ran a hand absently through tousled black hair and greeted Walter. But his eyes never left Blaine.

Too late she realized she'd been wasting precious time. For the moment it didn't really matter exactly how the sabotage could have been accomplished. What mattered, what she should have been asking herself, was whether or not she was going to tell Garrath St. Clair her suspicions.

She didn't want to. She had no proof, not the smallest shred of tangible evidence to offer him, only her instinct insisting that although the failure might have been a freak accident, it wasn't. And she could well imagine Garrath's reaction to her instincts.

No, she wouldn't tell him, at least not right now, she decided. He hadn't believed her capable of fixing the system, had only let her work when he had no other choice. He certainly wasn't going to take her unsubstantiated word that there was a saboteur on his rig.

Three slow easy strides brought him to her side. Blaine bolted to her feet, not wanting him towering over her, making her feel like a not-too-intelligent schoolgirl whose work was about to be scrutinized by a stern unsympathetic teacher. But in her hurry she tangled herself in the metal legs of the chair, however, and would have fallen in a humiliating heap if Garrath hadn't put a steadying hand beneath her arm, at the same time carefully pulling back the chair.

It took only a moment for her to regain her balance, but in those few seconds she was all too aware once again of being supported by Garrath's strength, of his warmth penetrating even through her layers of clothing and of the amusement striking gold flecks in his brown eyes. She could almost hear him thinking he'd been right the first time; she did need a nanny and she certainly didn't belong on Sithein One.

In that instant she reversed the decision she'd so recently made. She pulled free of his touch and attacked his complacency with the only weapon she had.

"I've pinpointed the problem, Mr. St. Clair, and there's something about it you have to know. I don't think it happened by accident."

"What do you mean?" His hand was instantly back on her arm, seconding his demand, and the glint in his eyes was now of steel, cold and sharp.

"I mean someone tampered with the computer..." she began, then stopped, horrified. So baldly stated it sounded absurd even to her own ears. She wouldn't have been surprised to see Garrath laugh.

He didn't though. He was studying her, his eyes boring into hers as if he could determine the truth of what she had said in the spring-green depths.

With every ounce of willpower she possessed

Blaine forced herself not to flinch or turn away. And
when he had found the answer he was searching for
his hand tightened almost painfully on her arm.

"Not here," he said.

She nodded, understanding that he didn't want an
audience for the discussion that had to come. He
released her just long enough for her to pull her coat
on quickly, then he was guiding her out of the
warmth and protection of the trailer and into the full
fury of the wind.

Blaine squeezed her eyes halfway shut against the
sudden onslaught on her senses, the ear-splitting
grinding and groaning of the rig machinery and the
stinging chill of the wind. She let Garrath guide her
across the platform, up three flights of narrow steps
and around two buildings to a glass-enclosed observation deck set high on one corner of the rig.

Reaching the deck was like stepping into another
world. Sheltered from the rig noises by the buildings
and from the harshness of the wind by the glass, the
deck was a sanctuary, safe and peaceful. No longer
feeling under assault, Blaine opened her eyes and
forgot computers, sabotage and even the man standing beside her in wonder at the one-hundred-eighty-
degree panorama spread before her.

The force of the wind was clearly visible here.
Huge clouds in every shade from gray to black
writhed across a dark sky. Below, the silver gray
ocean thrashed, sending waves crashing against the
steel legs of the rig like watery battering rams. And in
the distance, rising and falling with the tumult of the
waves, was a long black shape.

Blaine pointed. "Garrath, is that a boat?"

"The supply boat." He barely glanced at it. All his

attention was on her and suddenly the force of the
wind seemed insignificant.

"Tell me," he ordered. Blaine complied.

His expression didn't change as she spoke, and
when she had finished there was no hint of his reaction in his first response.

"You think the system was intentionally disa-
bled?" It was less a question than a summation of
what she had said. Still something warned her she
should grasp this last chance to back out. She should
deny her suspicions, phrase them less dramatically,
claim less certainty. She should, but she wouldn't.

"I do," she answered firmly.

"But you can't give me any proof, nothing concrete to support your suspicions? Can you at least tell
me why someone would have done it? And more importantly, who?"

"Why? I'm not sure. Resentment, perhaps," she
suggested, taking the easier of the two questions first.
"Too many people still believe computers take jobs
from men and women. And the safety system does
make some decisions automatically that used to be
part of certain jobs on the rig. So there can be feelings that authority and status are being lost. We've
run into resentment on other rigs, though never to
the extent of sabotage."

"And what makes you think there is that kind of
resentment here?"

"Well, I overheard...." Blaine turned away from
Garrath as she gave a brief account of her run-in with
Rory MacPherson. She stared at the wildly bobbing
shape of the supply boat inching closer to the rig, not
wanting to witness the outrage she knew would be
building in Garrath as he listened. He wouldn't take

threats from one of his workers lightly. She just hoped his anger wouldn't extend to the bearer of the bad news.

She finished by repeating Rory's ominous words of warning and waited, gnawing nervously on her bottom lip, for Garrath's reaction.

It came, a low rumble. A growl of fury barely restrained, she guessed. But directed at whom? Hesitantly she chanced a peek at him and couldn't believe what she was seeing.

Garrath's eyes sparkled a warm golden brown and the corners of his mouth twitched upward, forming a broad smile even as he struggled visibly to prevent it. The rumble came again, deep in his throat, and suddenly Blaine was feeling as murderous as she'd expected Garrath to be.

The sound wasn't a growl at all. Garrath St. Clair was trying but failing miserably to hide laughter. He was laughing—at her!

"I fail to see why this amuses you," she said through lips of cardboard.

His voice rippled with suppressed emotion. "It amuses me," he said, "because I'm imagining Rory in the role of master villain, engaging in the subtle and highly technical bit of sabotage you've been so carefully explaining to me. And that is a very, very funny picture."

Garrath was right. Rory MacPherson was far more likely to bash the machine with a sledgehammer than to tamper with its inner workings, a conclusion she would have reached on her own had she been thinking logically. But somehow Blaine kept failing to think logically or even to think much at all when Garrath was around.

"But he did threaten trouble," she protested.

"Of course. Rory does that on every tour he's on. It's just his way. If he didn't have your computers to complain about this time, it would be something else, some other piece of new equipment or the weather or a new inexperienced hand, anything. But Rory's like an old dog with a loud bark. Absolutely toothless, no bite. He's a crusty harmless old man, the best hand I've got and completely loyal to St. Clair's. And no matter how much he resents your system, he wouldn't know a computer circuit if it 'nipped him on the bum,' as my dear old nanny used to so graphically put it."

Blaine accepted Garrath's assessment of Rory MacPherson; she had to. But though she might have been wrong about the perpetrator, that didn't mean she was wrong about the sabotage.

"If it wasn't Rory, it must have been someone else, someone familiar enough with computers to manage it. Someone like...someone like Miles."

Guilt surged through her the moment she said the name, and at the same time she wondered why it had come to mind at all. Miles might be accused of being a bit vain and something of a phony. But his interest and willingness to learn about the system had been real enough. There was no reason to suspect him.

Yet it was too late to call back the name. And Garrath was no longer having any difficulty keeping a smile from his lips.

"That's the most ridiculous thing I've ever heard," he said, his scowl as dark as the backdrop of stormy sky behind him. "Miles Ramsey lives for this business. Without him St. Clair's wouldn't even have an oil exploration division. He brought in our first important well when everyone else said I should dump the whole operation. He helped design this rig, oversaw every step of its building personally and is as concerned about our success as I am, if not more. That's the man you're accusing of trying to wreck the safety system without a shred of evidence to show that anything was even done to it. Is it that important to you to divert the blame from your precious system, where it most likely belongs in the first place?''

Business, she told herself; *this is business, not something personal. And business doesn't hurt.*

But it did. A prickly sensation filled her throat and eyes, as if Garrath had thrown pepper instead of words. She wanted to tell him how wrong he was, that she wasn't like that, that he was judging her unfairly. But the words wouldn't come.

At the same time Blaine couldn't help admiring his loyalty to Miles Ramsey, a loyalty more than evident in the way he stood—feet planted firmly apart, hands set sternly on hips, every muscle from jaw to toes tensed with his anger. It was a stance more appropriate to an ancient battlefield than to the observation deck of a modern oil rig. He was more an untamed Highland warrior protecting the honor of a member of his clan than the head of a multinational multimillion-dollar corporation.

And it fitted. Of course he would be fierce in his loyalty. He had been fierce about every other emotion she'd seen him express so far.

What if the emotion were love, a little voice inside her whispered. Would Garrath St. Clair be as fiercely committed to loving? That is, if he ever fell in love with something—or someone—besides his oil rig and his business?

She felt her face blanch. Her brain needed a "DELETE" key like that on a computer, she decided. Ever since she'd fallen into the man's arms her thoughts had been "glitching" all over the place. The question was pointless anyway. Garrath St. Clair would never love anything or anyone more than his oil rig. He was an oil man like her father, like Len. And to oil men everything else was of secondary importance. Even love.

She forced herself back to the questions that made sense. "I wasn't accusing Miles. I just used him as an example. You're the best judge of who on board might have the necessary know-how."

"It seems to me your technician, Walter, is the most likely candidate in that division," Garrath said, his brown eyes nearly black with coldness.

Blaine could be defensive, too. "Walter has been with Computec for years, has worked on many different rigs with a perfect record. The computers are his life as well as his business. What would be the benefit to him in injuring the system?"

"None, it seems," Garrath shot back. "Just as there would be no benefit to Miles. So unless you can come up with something more concrete than these juvenile fantasies, I don't want to hear anything more about this."

"Juvenile fantasies!"

"And I don't want you talking to anyone else about it, either," he ordered, cutting her off. "Not anyone. Rumors spread on a rig quicker than an oil fire. And I don't need my men suddenly seeing saboteurs in every corner."

"But I have to discuss this with Walter so he can...."

"Not anyone, Miss Christensen," Garrath said slowly, a direct nonnegotiable order. "I will speak to Walter about some extra precautions, just to be on the safe side. You are to forget about it and just get on with your job, which is repairing the system, not cloak-and-daggering. Have I made that quite clear?"

Crystal clear. Blaine nodded, reluctantly. She might not like his overbearing orders, but she had accomplished what she'd intended. He would take precautions.

Garrath hadn't bothered to wait for her answer. His attention and his scowl had already shifted to somewhere over her shoulder.

Blaine followed his gaze to the supply boat, now drawn up under one edge of the rig. She had almost forgotten the turbulence of the weather outside the observation deck, but the sight of the boat rising and falling to the violent rhythm of the waves left no doubt that the wind was still building.

The boat looked like a large badly constructed toy. It was little more than a long narrow deck riding barely above the waterline, and the bigger waves threatened even that claim. The wheelhouse and two huge black smokestacks squatting on one end didn't seem balanced by the load of drill pipe, machinery and boxes of supplies lined up on the stretch of deck.

"It doesn't look very seaworthy," she said, anxious on behalf of the small figures scurrying about the heaving deck.

"It is, though. It may not look it from here, but that boat is about two hundred feet long and weighs two hundred tons, most of that weight being below the waterline in the storage tanks for drill mud and water. Supply boats are built to stand most of what the North Sea can dish out. Wind and seas like this are merely a nuisance.''

He sounded certain enough, but there was still concern in his scowl.

"Just a nuisance? Even for the men on board?" Blaine asked.

Garrath looked at her for a moment in surprise, as if he couldn't believe Blaine had understood, then turned back to the boat. "Usually just a nuisance. Though I must admit I'm always a little concerned when they have to use the personnel basket in strong winds.''

"Personnel basket?''

Garrath pointed to the long line being swung out from the rig by the crane. On the end of the line was a bell-shaped net with a round platform bottom. And clinging to the outside of this contraption were two men, their arms tucked through the mesh and the toes of their shoes on the rim of the wooden platform.

"It typifies all the dangers of oil work for me. I've ridden it many times and I still don't like it. Few people can be comfortable swinging around on the end of a line that's dangling seventy-five feet above the water, and that's what it means to be lowered from the rig to the boat or vice versa. But in weather like this the boat doesn't dare pull in close enough to the legs of the rig to tie up and unload.''

Blaine suddenly recalled Len's tales of rides on the personnel basket. He, too, had hated it, hated the slow rise or descent fraught with the risk of being dropped straight into the water or bashed against the side of the rig. And all the while having nothing to hold on to but the loose netting that sagged and stretched in the worst moments.

The two men were set without mishap on the supply boat's deck. A winch and various hoses were also lowered and the unloading began. But there wasn't time to feel relief. Almost immediately the basket began to rise again, a single passenger clinging to the net.

The halting of the basket's rise about one-third of the way up from the boat didn't mean anything to Blaine. But the tensing of Garrath's whole body did. Something was wrong. He strained against the glass, his hands balled into fists on the rail, and this time there was no mistaking the growl low in his throat for suppressed laughter.

His tension found its echo in Blaine, and she too leaned against the glass to watch the basket and its small rider.

The basket wasn't rising, but neither was it still. It was twisting and swaying in the cruel hands of the wind. She could almost feel the cold vicious shoves slamming against the basket, which was tipped at an angle with the uneven weight of a single rider. The figure on the basket would be feeling them in a much more immediate way.

And the figure looked so frail and small in its orange life jacket, the black ocean below so huge and hungry. Suddenly Blaine understood exactly what Garrath had meant about the basket. It did typify all the risks of oil work—the danger and the uncertainty of being constantly at the mercy of the capricious elements and uncaring machines. Human beings didn't stand much of a chance of survival against that kind of odds. No wonder her father and Len had died on a rig. And what on earth was she doing on one, risking her life where she wasn't even wanted?

All at once it was as if the nightmare had reached out in the daytime, touching her with all the old fears, trying to engulf her and drag her down to the place where the screaming began. She couldn't let that happen, so she did the only thing she could think of. She put out a hand and grasped Garrath's arm.

He didn't seem to notice and she didn't care, not as long as he let her hang on. She focused on the reality of the tensed muscles of his arm beneath her fingertips, clung to his warmth and strength just as she had during the night. And suddenly she wasn't going under. Nothing could threaten her, not while he stood there beside her. The only nightmare was the one they were watching and then that one, too, ended.

"It's all right," Garrath said, his voice husky with a relieved sigh. "They're moving."

Blaine took her hand from his arm under cover of his explanation.

"Must have been a snag in the line," he said. "Not serious except to the poor bloke left dangling in mid-air while they untangled the mess."

The figure became clearer as the basket rose, until it was possible to make out a blue parka beneath the orange life jacket and an electric-blue knit cap covering the figure's head. But at that point another problem came into view, and a sick feeling thudded like a rock dropped into Blaine's stomach.

The rider of the basket was holding the net with just one arm looped through the mesh. The other arm was waving wildly, presumably at someone on the loading deck above.

"What the hell!" Garrath exclaimed, seeing the foolhardy action at the same moment. His palms came up against the glass, pushing until Blaine thought it would pop out of its frame under the pressure. "The bloody little idiot!"

The basket was just a few feet below the loading deck now, though still several yards out over the water, and close enough for them to see exactly what was happening.

The waving figure looked up, anxiously gauging the distance left to go, and in doing so dislodged the blue cap. Blaine gasped in horror as the figure automatically grabbed for the cap, tilting the unbalanced basket even more. It still might have been all right if a particularly strong gust of wind hadn't struck the basket at the same moment. The combination tilted the basket even more and the figure's feet slipped off the platform.

A scream rose in Blaine's throat and she closed her eyes against what had to happen—the small body following the blue hat into the ice-cold water over seventy feet below. Instantly her eyes flew open again; she had to see it all.

Impossibly, the figure was still on the basket—barely. It hung there, clutching the net with one hand while its feet scrabbled frantically in midair and its other hand waved, not in greeting now but in a wild effort to grasp the net again. The basket rocked crazily, swinging in a wide arc.

What would happen to a person who fell from there to the water below, Blaine wanted to ask Garrath. But she could see the answer on his face, in the muscle twitching violently beside his mouth, in the cords standing out in his neck. She sensed that he wanted to run to the deck below, to shout orders and conduct the rescue, but at the same time he was afraid to be even momentarily out of sight of the swaying basket, as if his will alone could hold the figure there safely.

"Bring it up fast," he ordered, the command a grated whisper. "Bring it up, damn you."

"Hold on, please hold on," Blaine breathed the prayer, knowing neither her nor Garrath's invocations would make any difference. There was no way the rider could hold on long enough to be pulled to safety.

And then another movement caught Blaine's eye and the whole scene lapsed into slow motion. A second figure appeared at the edge of the loading deck, a figure carefully positioned, tensed and intently watching the sway of the basket. Judging and waiting for the right moment—to jump.

Garrath saw it, too. "No!" he roared, slamming his palm against the glass.

"Yes!" Blaine shouted almost at the same time, automatically crossing her fingers.

The figure jumped and for one moment seemed suspended over the cold impossibly wide span of ocean, arms outstretched. The next it had landed on the basket with a jolt that set the mesh bell swinging erratically. But before Blaine could even wonder what such a strain would do to the first figure's slight hold, the two figures were together, the second pulling the first up safely onto the wooden platform.

Garrath headed for the stairs. Blaine ran after him, not pausing even when she stepped wrongly on her sore ankle and pain shot through it. The trek took forever, but when they reached the loading deck the basket with its two entwined figures was just being pulled in.

Blaine felt another slap of shock as she recognized the larger of the two figures, the one who had jumped from the rig and was now supporting the smaller with an arm snugly around its shoulders. Andy Walker.

And the smaller was a young woman! A woman whose identity Blaine guessed even before Garrath thundered, "'Tis murder you'll be drivin' me to one day, Janet St. Clair!"

CHAPTER SEVEN

BLAINE'S GREEN EYES WIDENED with surprise. It was the first time she had heard Garrath sounding really Scottish. This wasn't his usual slight burr but the musical cadence, the broad vowels and the rocking lilt of a born and bred, tartan-wrapped Highlander. She felt as if she'd heard it with her whole tingling body. There was nothing cold or dispassionate about that accent; it sang with emotion. Which was undoubtedly why it took a very special circumstance to make Garrath lapse into it.

And that "special circumstance" was answering Garrath with a similar but mischievously exaggerated accent.

"Och, now, is that any way to greet your poor wee sister who's been missin' ye so much that she braved the stormy seas just to visit ye on your inhospitable island? Of course I see now that ye had no need of my company—you already have a guest." And Janet St. Clair looked pointedly at Blaine. "But how was I to be knowin' that?"

"Don't you dare try to sidetrack me, Janet. This is Blaine Christensen. She's out from Computec, working on a malfunctioning computer. Which explains why *she's* here. What I want to know is what *you're* doing here, coming out on the supply boat in weather like this. And I hope you can do better than nonsense about missing me," Garrath warned, glaring from the young woman to Andy and back again.

Janet just smiled sweetly in the face of her brother's anger, and Blaine was reminded of a kitten playing with a panther. A touch of daring, a bit of affectionate teasing, a few amusing antics, all to charm the ferocious beast and keep it from biting off the kitten's head.

In appearance they were like kitten and panther, too. Janet possessed all of Garrath's devastating attractiveness beautifully translated into a smaller and very female version. His thick black hair on her was a crown of soft black curls, just touched by copper highlights. They shared deep-set brown eyes, but on Janet the lashes were longer and thicker, the sparkle merrier. Garrath's prominent cheek and jawline were delicately sculpted cheeks and chin on his sister. His bewitching mouth on her became slightly fuller, softer and a deep rosy pink, the perfect means for wrapping any male in sight around her little finger. Especially when pursed in a tiny pout, as it was at the moment.

"Well now, I had some papers for you to sign...."

"Which you had no need to bring yourself. If they were so urgent—" Garrath's brows arched with his doubts and Janet's scarlet blush confirmed his suspicions "—the supply boat captain could have brought them."

"Oh aye, but didn't you teach me well that if you want something done right you must do it yourself? I was just taking your advice." Silky lashes fluttered over soft doe eyes.

Garrath didn't stand a chance and he knew it.

"'Twould be the first time, Janet St. Clair," he said, and his laughter rippled like a flag of surrender. Janet flew from the shelter of Andy's arm to the haven of Garrath's, and they hugged each other. Fiercely.

Blaine closed her eyes briefly against an unexpected surge of pain. It was missing Len, she supposed, that made her envy Janet the comfort of her brother's strong arms. What else could it be?

Garrath ended the hug by holding Janet a little away from him and shaking her with all the exasperation of a parent scolding a careless headstrong child. "Don't ever do a thing like that again," he said, a plea more than an order. "You could have been killed."

"Not with Andy around," Janet answered brightly. It was the first tactical mistake Blaine had seen her make.

"Yes, Andy," Garrath said, biting out the name, the laughter and lilting accent gone. He turned to the young man in question. "The only thing worse than Janet's absurd display was your dangerous Hollywood stunt. This is an oil rig, not some Wild West show. You could have killed Janet as well as yourself with your foolhardy dramatics. And you're not even on shift now, are you? What are you doing out on deck, anyway?"

Andy straightened to his full lanky height. There was a deep red flush in his cheeks but no hint of submission.

"Just checking out a few things," he said evenly. "As for my 'stunt,' I knew there was a risk. But from where I stood it looked like the greater risk was that she wouldn't be able to hold on long enough. I thought it was her only chance."

"And from where I stood it looked like you went against every rule in the book," Garrath stated. "You know how I feel about that."

"I know," Andy replied without hesitation.

Blaine knew, too, remembering Andy's description of Garrath's concern with safety. One infraction and the individual lost his job—no second chances. And obviously no exceptions granted for saving the life of the boss's sister. Andy was about to be fired.

But no one had counted on Janet. "I know 'tis hard for you to thank someone properly, Garrath, and I'm sure Andy will understand if I do it for you...later. Right now, I think I'm needing a wee rest, after this dreadful ordeal, you know."

"And what about these urgent important papers you brought out for me to see?" Garrath demanded.

Janet renewed her smile. "Oh, I think I'll be recovered around—" she paused to slide a glance at Andy "—seven o'clock, I'd say. All right, big brother?"

Janet knew better than to wait for Garrath's agreement. Linking arms with a reluctant Andy she dragged him away in the direction of the quarters building.

Blaine couldn't help it, she burst out laughing. Seven o'clock! When the shift changed and Andy would be back on duty.

Garrath turned a thunderous scowl on her. "I fail to see what you find so amusing about this situation. My sister is a willful foolish child who is going to end up—"

"Not a child, I don't think," Blaine interrupted, still smiling.

"Nineteen is hardly a mature adult." He paused, shaking his head. "Perhaps it's my fault. I don't have enough time. And she needs a stronger hand, someone who's always around to keep an eye on her.''

"Like a jailer?'' she asked softly.

"Don't be cute about things you don't understand, Miss Christensen,'' Garrath warned.

Blaine refused to accept the warning. ''I understand that you don't approve of the relationship between Andy and Janet. What I can't understand is why.''

"There is no relationship,'' he snapped.

"You can't be that blind. Whether you want to admit it or not, those two are in love.''

"Oh, so now you're an expert on love as well as computers, are you?''

"No, I'm...that is I....'' Blaine stopped, confused. This was just what he intended to happen, she knew. He wanted to make her feel stupid and embarrassed; it was his way of winning an argument. Well, this time it wasn't going to work.

"You don't have to be an expert to see how they feel about each other.'' She plunged ahead, hardly knowing what she was saying, only that she wasn't going to let his unfair tactics stop her. "Why, it almost crackles between them. Surely you've felt that kind of attraction at some time, one so strong it becomes a compulsion....''

The question dwindled away, unfinished, as Blaine heard her own words. At the same time she realized that the loading deck, which had been bustling with activity a few minutes before, was now empty of everyone save Garrath and herself. And Garrath was moving toward her.

"A compulsive love?'' he asked. His eyes burned

with flecks of gold, a sparkle that had nothing to do with anger. "An attraction that knows no logic or sense? Perhaps I have. But how about you, Blaine? Have you ever felt that kind of attraction?" His question was a whisper that screamed in her veins.

"No, I...well, not exactly," she stumbled, knowing suddenly why she'd always hated seeing insects pinned to display boards. "But I know that Janet and Andy—"

"Are children," Garrath cut her off. "It takes a man and a woman to feel the depth of emotion you're speaking of, the kind of attraction that sets pulses to pounding so hard that it can be felt... here."

His hand was at her throat, two fingers resting gently in the hollow there.

"No!" she cried, backing away. Her hand reached up to cover the spot his had touched. A pulse throbbed wildly against her fingers.

He smiled knowingly.

"Your hand was cold," she defended against the unspoken accusation.

"I see," he said.

What, what did he see? Blaine wanted to ask. She saw only the way he intimidated her, trying to bend her to his will by embarrassing her with his innuendos and allusions. If her pulses raced when he was near, it was only her anger at his brashness. Nothing more.

"You're wrong, completely wrong," she told him, and turned and headed back to the Computec trailer.

It wasn't until she was back at work that a question whispered in her mind. A low velvety whisper that bore an uncomfortable resemblance to Garrath's voice. Just what was it she had so adamantly denied?

BLAINE WORKED THROUGH THE AFTERNOON and into
the evening. She completed the system tests to her
satisfaction in a couple of hours, all except the final
one. She started that by putting the system back on-
line and then was out of things to do. It would take
twenty-four to forty-eight hours of actual operation
to verify that the malfunction was corrected, and
Walter could computer-sit during that time as well as
she could.

But she stayed in the trailer, going over operating
procedures, checking out the rest of the equipment,
studying the incoming data. Busywork designed
primarily to give her a chance to talk to Walter.

The possibility of sabotage still nagged at her. She
trusted that Garrath would take precautions as he
had said he would, and that was really all she could
ask considering the lack of proof. But Walter was a
Computec employee and a friend, and she was going
to make sure he had all the facts, even if she had to
stretch Garrath's gag order a bit.

She didn't mention her suspicions; she didn't need
to. She simply gave Walter a basic explanation of the
cause of the malfunction and waited for him to draw
his own conclusions. When she saw by the slow repeated blinking of his eyes that his thoughts were following the same uneasy paths hers had, she merely
helped him along a bit by asking who among the rig
crew had spent much time in the trailer—with or
without his being there.

Unfortunately the answers weren't of much use.
Andy, Miles and Garrath were in and out frequently,
as was to be expected. And of course nearly all the
crew members had been present at the general

demonstrations always held when a system was first installed, to acquaint them with its operation.

As to who might have come in at other times, well, anyone with a key, Walter told her solemnly. There were only three keys that he knew of, and they belonged to Andy, Miles and Garrath.

Which made the whole thing seem as impossible as Garrath had declared. If there were only four possible suspects—Walter, Andy, Miles and Garrath—and each of them appeared totally innocent, she might as well toss her one piece of evidence, the damaged circuit, overboard and forget the whole thing.

Blaine sighed, determining to do just that. Precautions would be taken; Walter was warned. She would forget it and get on with her work.

When hunger pains finally drove her from the trailer, however, the small sharp-pronged piece of plastic was in her coat pocket, and she fingered it absently as she made her way across the deck.

She was grateful for the anonymity of her hard hat and coveralls as she hurried toward the quarters building. There were no leering stares like those that had greeted her calamitous arrival. In fact, her passing went basically unnoticed by the workers, who were giving the required strict attention to their work.

Even so, she didn't linger. The coming of night had increased the fury and strength of the wind, and although the rig was well-lighted, the spotlights were cold and harsh and the hiss of the flare far above eerie and unfriendly. She hadn't expected it to be any different. How could a drilling rig ever seem anything but inhospitable?

She had purposefully waited until after the shift change to leave the trailer. Now she lingered awhile in her room, exchanging the serviceable clothes she'd been in all day for the softest plushest outfit she'd brought with her. The chocolate brown, brushed flannel slacks and cowl-necked cashmere sweater of leaf green were cozily comforting, and she was in definite need of some kind of pampering.

She pulled the pins from her hair and shook it free, massaging away the tightness of her scalp. Then, eyes closed, she brushed until her arm ached, caring much more about the relaxation the effort brought than about the golden sheen it added to the long strands. Finally she tied it into a loose ponytail with a ribbon the exact color of her eyes.

Even after using up all that extra time, when she took the precaution of peeking into the dining room before going in, she found the coast wasn't quite clear. Seated by herself in one corner of the room, hands cradling a coffee cup, was Janet St. Clair.

Blaine's desire for solitude evaporated. Her brief and unusual introduction to Janet hardly counted as a basis for friendship, but she had taken an instant liking to Garrath's spirited sister. Besides, they had something very important in common. Garrath St. Clair wanted them both off his rig.

Deciding that that was enough of a bond to impose upon, Blaine walked over to Janet's table.

"Would you mind some company?" she asked, and was immediately welcomed by Janet's kittenish smile.

"Mind! I'd sell my soul for a kind word after all the yammering I've had to endure over the past few hours from the two men in my life," Janet exclaimed, motioning Blaine into a chair. The thick Scottish twist to her words was gone now, leaving a lyrical inflection that was delightful but not nearly as colorful. It seemed Janet, like Garrath, saved the "stronger" stuff for her sibling. Blaine envied them their sharing.

"The *two* men?" she asked.

"Aye, Andy as well as Garrath. Trust men to side together, can't you? Just because my arrival was a wee bit unexpected." She shrugged.

"But not totally so, I would guess," Blaine interjected, grinning, and her guess was unrepentantly confirmed by Janet.

"Well, I did get a bit of a word to Andy—that's why he was waiting on deck. But then, that was all to the good, wasn't it? So why they both had to go on and on about my not telling Garrath, I don't know. Not that I meant to deceive him, mind you. But with my brother and certain subjects, it's better to tell him what you're planning after it's done. Otherwise he's too apt to say no. He takes the big brother role a wee bit too seriously."

That wasn't the only role he took too seriously, as far as Blaine was concerned. Lord of the oil rig was another. But she kept that thought to herself.

"And then, of course," Janet continued, "they had to scold me over and over about how foolish it was to wave from the basket. As if I hadn't realized that the moment my feet slipped off the platform!"

Blaine laughed, but Janet shook her crown of black curls. "You'd think those two would get along better, since they both agree so heartily on how I'm to be scolded all the time," she said with a sigh.

"They don't get along? Then how did Andy get to be a drilling foreman?"

"Oh, Garrath respects Andy's work, and likes him, too, hard as that may be to credit. They got along like brothers from the first time they met. For weeks after that 'Tex' was all I heard about. How enthusiastic, responsible, intelligent and fun—especially fun—the new lad was. Tex did his job so well that Garrath just had to promote him and give him more and more responsibility. Tex was so much fun; they just had to spend a good measure of their free time together. And then Garrath brought Tex—Andy—home to Glenclair."

Having witnessed the glowing attraction between Janet and Andy, Blaine could almost imagine the fireworks of their first meeting.

"Love at first sight?" she asked, not doubting the possibility at all.

Janet nodded, golden stars twinkling in her brown eyes. "Just about. But when Andy and I went out the first time, Garrath acted like I was dating Jack the Ripper. He blew his top."

"But why?" Andy was so nice. Blaine couldn't imagine the reason for Garrath's opposition.

"I don't know for sure, but I suspect it has something to do with all the fun they were having up until then, as bachelors on the town. Garrath has always been able to find willing women friends but has never needed or wanted to form any kind of serious commitment. I gather Andy was about the same—which was fine with Garrath until it came to his sister. And he just refuses to believe that Andy could be serious about me. But," she paused, and her mouth bowed in a self-assured smile, "I'll wear him down, never fear."

Blaine laughed, tickled to know that there was at least one person in the world that Garrath St. Clair couldn't bend to his will. It was too bad that Janet's tactics wouldn't work for her.

They chatted on, Blaine finding Janet's company as enjoyable as her brother's was trying. So there was no hesitation at all in her response when Janet asked whether she would object to having a roommate.

"I'd love it," she replied quickly. "I'm still not used to being on a rig."

"But I thought you worked for Computec. Aren't you on rigs all the time?" Janet asked.

She could have answered with something innocuous about usually working in design. But instead Blaine found herself telling the story of Len, her father and her nightmares for the second time in two days. And the most amazing thing about it was how easy it was this time, how much less painful. Why, her voice barely trembled!

"Well, dinna fash yourself," Janet said softly when Blaine had finished, and Blaine felt warmed by the lilting words that she intuitively understood meant not to worry. "There are no nightmares in rooms where I'm sleeping. My nanny worked a charm for me when I was a child, and I havena had one since."

Blaine believed her. No self-respecting nightmare would dare enter a room with sunny down-to-earth Janet St. Clair. She smiled, but the smile turned into an irrepressible yawn.

"Since I know my company couldn't be boring you," Janet teased, "I must assume my slave-driving brother is working you too hard. 'Tis typical of him, I assure you. Just because he's gone daft about this silly oil business, he expects everyone else to be as dementedly dedicated as he is.''

"Is he? Daft about the oil business, I mean?" Blaine didn't know why she bothered to ask. She already knew the answer.

"He is that. Completely bonkers over it. You'd think drilling was all St. Clair Corporation was involved in from the way he spends so much time with it. The owners of major international corporations don't usually end up spending most of their time as roughnecks on an oil rig. But Garrath can't leave it alone. In every other division of St. Clair's he's delegating authority. With the oil he's assuming more personal control all the time. I think it's addictive and Garrath is getting too wrapped up in it. I wouldn't want him to end up like Miles Ramsey.''

"Like Miles?" Remembering her last discussion of Miles, Blaine hesitated to ask the question. "How?"

Janet didn't answer right away. Her finger traced three slow circles around the rim of her coffee cup before she spoke. "You've met Miles, then?"

Blaine nodded noncommittally.

"Well, he's all right, mind you. But no matter how he fights it with his bleached hair, his daily sessions under his fancy sunlamp and his lines right out of an old movie, he's getting on in years, and he's got no life outside of the rig. No family, no friends except Garrath, no special girl, nothing except being a tool-pusher. So he's built his job, the rig, drilling, all this—" Janet waved her hand in the air "—into the most important thing—the *only* thing—in his world. He spends a lot of his off time at our home, Glenclair, but even there all he wants to talk about is oil, oil, oil, and he's getting more fanatical about it all the time. I don't want to see something like that happen to Garrath.''

Janet paused, and then went on more lightly. ''And then again, perhaps I'm just jealous because Garrath has found something to care for besides his sister.''

Blaine laughed, but it was laughter tinged with sadness. She understood what Janet feared, perhaps even better than Janet did. The oil business was addictive and it sounded like Garrath St. Clair was badly hooked. She knew from experience that if he were, there wasn't anything that Janet or anyone else would be able to do about it. It was a spell that went on forever. The only escape from enchanted worlds like Sithein One was the one that had claimed her father and brother.

No, oil men didn't change, Blaine thought, and a tightness filled her throat. It was so damned unfair—to Janet, of course. Only to Janet.

CHAPTER EIGHT

THE NIGHTMARE DIDN'T DISTURB BLAINE that night, but she couldn't credit Janet's nanny-woven charm for its absence. She didn't dream because she didn't sleep. And after several hours of lying wide-eyed and rigid in the small bed for fear of waking Janet, Blaine began to wonder if grappling with the dream wasn't preferable.

She had expected sleep to come so easily. She and Janet had talked until late, "coincidentally" meeting Andy when he came in for his coffee break. And maybe the problem had begun there. For though Andy and Janet had included her in their conversation, Blaine couldn't help feeling like a definite third wheel. Andy didn't put his arm around Janet, they didn't hold hands, their chairs weren't even pulled unusually close together. But it seemed to Blaine that she would have known they were in love even if she were seeing them for the first time.

What she'd told Garrath was true—there was something almost visible between them. Talking, laughing or just sitting in companionable silence, they were like two powerful magnets held a short distance apart. They weren't touching, but they wanted to be. And would be, Blaine guessed, regardless of Garrath's efforts to prevent it.

When she realized she was envying them the

strength of their feelings, she asked—demanded of herself—why? Surely she felt something equally strong for Richard, didn't she? Wouldn't other people watching the two of them together see a similar picture?

Blaine imagined herself with Richard—at work, discussing work over dinner, she listening to Richard's recitation of company problems, he listening to her description of snags in design. But those were pictures of companionable co-workers, not a man and woman in love. And though she knew there had been other times, times when Richard had taken her in his arms to kiss and caress her, she couldn't find them now in her memory.

Desperately she tried harder, and then she did see herself enclosed in a tight embrace. But the picture was wrong. The arms holding her were too strong, the chest too broad. The eyes in the face bending toward hers weren't the color of weak tea but a deep vibrant brown. The hair that should have been fine and dun-colored was thick and black. And the mouth so close to hers wasn't Richard's, it belonged to a prince.

Blaine blinked rapidly, wiping the startling picture from her mind, refusing to consider the implications. Soon afterward she left Janet and Andy and returned to her room—to go to sleep, she thought.

But though the picture was gone, the questions remained. They kept her tossing and turning at first, and then after Janet came in, lying stiffly in the dark as the hours crawled by. She tried not to think, but it was difficult when the only distractions were the sounds and feel of the rig at work.

Like Blaine, the rig wasn't asleep. It never slept.

Night and day were one to the crews who worked twelve-hour alternate shifts to keep the drilling going round-the-clock. But because the quarters building was so well-insulated, only a hint of the activity on deck reached Blaine. Distant mumbling, a slight trembling, restless stirrings, as if another sleepless person joined her in her lonely vigil.

But Blaine didn't want company, especially such a disquieting kind. She wanted oblivion. And she wasn't finding it in her bed.

Finally she gave up. Still not wanting to disturb Janet, she didn't bother with underthings but slipped into the slacks and cashmere sweater she had worn earlier, the first pieces of clothing she found in the darkness. Grabbing her jacket she crept out of the room.

She considered going to one of the rig's many entertainment rooms—library, closed-circuit movies, games. But she wasn't likely to be alone there; she would have to smile, fend off questions. She might even run into...someone. A breath of fresh air and solitude would better be able to clear the clutter from her mind.

She hadn't realized just how fresh the air was going to be. She was nearly knocked off her unsuspecting feet by a frigid blast of wind the moment she opened the quarters building door.

She didn't even consider going back inside, however, and the fact made her pause in wonder. Two days ago she had been terrified by the thought of even being on a rig. Now she was wandering around it in bad weather as if it were home.

It wasn't home, of course, and as she fought her way along the foreign territory of the iron catwalk, she thought of the place that seemed as far away as the moon. The soul-soothing view from her apartment window of San Francisco Bay, the mind-soothing logic of work, the emotion-soothing company of undemanding Richard. Nice, ordinary, familiar home. But there was no ache of homesickness in the thought and Blaine couldn't understand why.

The catwalk edged around the quarters building, away from the busy main deck. On the other side, facing the sea, was a gallery, a spot somewhat sheltered from the wind and noise, not as completely as was the observation deck but sufficiently so for Blaine's purposes.

The wind was raw but freshly invigorating as it brushed her cheeks and combed through her hair, reminding her of the hard hat she'd left in her room. She ignored the twinge of guilt she felt at her breach of the safety rules. She wouldn't be long. Breathing deeply of the chilled air, she stood against the rail and watched the night world of the rig.

It was a Jekyll and Hyde panorama, the instrument of metamorphosis being the wind-whipped clouds scudding across the face of a half-circle moon. One moment a sparkling fairy-tale world existed, where the clouds were tipped with milky moonlight and the black rippled surface of the ocean was burnished with silver. The next a thick cloud swallowed the moon and its light, turning the world to wasteland, bleak, forbidding and cold.

It was a beguiling world of startling contrasts, the soft alternating with the harsh, each more vivid and impressive because of its juxtaposition to the other, and the perfect setting for Garrath St. Clair for just that reason. He, too, had contrasting sides to his nature that fascinated all the more deeply by virtue of the contrast.

With a sigh Blaine leaned back against the wall of the building, feeling the metal's chill immediately penetrate the thick cloth of her jacket. Garrath had invaded her thoughts again, but now there was none of the frustration that had kept her tossing and turning in her bed earlier. Instead a feeling of inevitability filled her. How could she hope to keep him from her mind? How could she expect to escape from him anywhere as long as she remained where even nature mirrored the man? It was impossible.

Having reached that conclusion, it wasn't at all surprising to find him standing at her side when the world became a silver palace again. He was only a few feet away, casually leaning one shoulder against the wall, turned to watch her instead of the view.

She glanced at him and then back out at the sea. "Still baby-sitting?" she asked, but not with anger. He was no more of an intruder in person than he'd been in her thoughts.

"No, just wandering. I get restless when a storm is brewing." He stepped closer, removing his hat and looping it over a post. "And you? Is it the nightmare again?"

She shook her head, and her hair fanned around her face like a billowing lace curtain. "Just...restless, too, I guess."

The clouds gobbled the moon again, darkening the world, but Blaine didn't need the light. She could feel Garrath's hand moving toward her as if it were a well-fired branding iron. The tips of his fingers touched her temple, brushing back the curtain of hair and tucking it gently behind her ear, then followed the hollow there down her neck until they rested lightly at the base of her throat.

She felt her pulse beating against his touch, an admission of the feelings his nearness alone had stirred, and there was no denial this time, no backing away. Then his lips were following the path his fingers had traced. This too, she thought, was inevitable.

"With the moonlight caught in your hair you looked like a fairy princess, too beautiful to be real," he whispered gruffly.

Blaine smiled. She had compared him to a prince, now he was calling her a princess. But she knew he was wrong. She was no ethereal being without feelings, without emotion. The sensations licking through her belonged to a very real, very human woman.

His hand went to the back of her neck, caressing with increasing pressure until she was forced to turn from the sea to him, to the lips lowering toward hers.

Garrath's mouth touched hers, once lightly, then again more demandingly. Then it fixed against hers with a certainty that robbed Blaine of her strength. Her knees buckled, but there was no threat of her falling. Garrath's arms were around her, pulling her tightly against him. And she no longer needed any strength of her own.

She couldn't tell where her breathing ended and Garrath's began; their heartbeats had synchronized into one strong pulse that pounded within her. Garrath's hands slipped beneath her coat, molding the plush softness of her sweater against the skin of her shoulders, her back, the curve of her waist, the flatness of her stomach.

"Blaine, oh Blaine," he whispered, and his fingers

splayed wide, so that his thumbs rested just beneath her breasts. For a moment they were still, their heat searing through her sweater and into her skin. And then they began to move slowly, in small circles that drew the downy cashmere back and forth tantalizingly across her breasts.

Blaine moaned as an exquisite ache blossomed inside her, a feeling like nothing she had ever known before. Her arms went around Garrath's neck, her fingers twining in the soft thickness of the hair at the back of his head and her mouth opened to his, the deepening kiss a plea for more.

His hands slid from her waist to her hips, drawing her length against him, and the soft flannel of her slacks was like no barrier at all. She felt the warmth and urgency in his stroking hands, the hard demanding strength of his hips and thighs pressed against hers, the heat leaping between them like that of a fire out of control. She reveled in it, and yielded willingly to the embrace, urging the flames higher.

And then the fire was in the sky, splitting the dark night with a jagged knife of lightning, closely followed by a roar of thunder. They sprang apart, but the tension of their meeting hung between them like static electricity, holding them both in place, separated only by inches.

Blaine's chest heaved with the effort to breathe on her own. Garrath's hands were out in front of him, still open as if trying to hold onto something that had disappeared.

"Wait, Blaine..." he began, but a second round of lightning cracked the sky, and the deluge began.

Rain slashed at them from every direction at once, stinging wind-driven droplets that drenched and blinded in spite of the protection of the building. It seemed to wash away the spell that had drawn them together.

Garrath's hand closed around Blaine's, but there was only business in the touch as he guided her along the catwalk, back toward the door. Even that contact ended when he dropped her hand and ushered her inside the building. He remained outside and the rain came down like a screen between them.

"I'd better do some checking to make sure everything is secure," he said. His hard hat was in his other hand and he raised it to his head. "You'd better get some dry clothes on and get to bed. Don't worry. This rig is meant to stand solid through much worse than this."

"Of course," she answered numbly, staring at him as he settled the hat over his wet hair. Those hands, which had been so strong and warm on her body, now held an oil man's hard hat. In the bright light of the hall the logo stood out in vivid relief: Sithein One.

The name lashed out at her like a slap in the face, wiping away the last bit of the spell the night and the man had woven. Garrath was an oil man first and foremost, and the rig was claiming him, the rig that was named so well. Sithein, the fairy hill to which men could be lured and enchanted, never to be free again. As her father had been. And Len.

As was Garrath St. Clair.

A fact she had nearly forgotten, caught in the sweep of physical sensations that had no logic or reason. The one sure thing she'd learned in her life was that caring for oil men resulted in misery, a lesson well emphasized by the deaths of her father and brother. And having learned the lesson so painfully well, she had been confident she knew better than to move willingly into the cruel jaws of that trap. Until tonight.

"Good night," she said, and turned to walk away. But his voice reached out to catch her.

"Blaine!" he called, and her heart jumped into her throat. He was going to call her back to him! What should she, what would she do? Be smart, reasonable, logical? Or let knowing better be damned?

She looked back.

"Don't go out without your hard hat again," he said sternly. "This can be a dangerous place."

He nodded briskly and was gone. Off to the demands of his real love, Blaine told herself. But it didn't matter. Even if he had called her, she wouldn't have gone. She was too rational to fall into the same trap twice. She wouldn't have gone.

She made it to her room, peeled off her wet clothing and tumbled into bed. Her hair was wet and cold around her, and she knew its damp would transfer to her pillow. But it didn't matter. The pillow was wet anyway, with a dampness that tasted faintly of salt.

SHE WAS STILL DEEPLY SUBMERGED in sleep when her name blared out of the intercom in the room.

"Blaine Christensen, to the Computec unit immediately. Blaine Christensen...."

The sudden startling awakening hurt. Her nerves screamed, her adrenaline surged and her heart hammered in her chest. But she didn't hesitate. She knew immediately what had happened. The monitoring system had shut down the drilling again.

Hurriedly she threw on coveralls and her jacket

and twisted her hair into a long rope that she tucked up loosely under her hard hat as she dashed out the door. In spite of her haste Andy was waiting at the end of the corridor when she got there.

He confirmed her guess that the system had caused another problem. "Your computer claims we're losing pressure on Line Number Three. It's already shut down the pumping on that line. But Miles says it's wrong. His figures show no problem."

The question was implicit. Was the system malfunctioning again?

Andy was holding out a large yellow oilskin. "It seems I'm always tellin' you how to dress, ma'am, and I do apologize. But the gale's full force now and you'll be needing this."

They grinned at each other over the shared joke as Blaine slipped into the heavy oversize coat. Its hem brushed below her knees, the sleeves hung to her fingertips even after she had turned them up twice, and she supposed she looked like a truant from the schoolroom again. But she was ready.

As Andy pushed open the door she had a glimpse of slanting rain and a dark unpolished pewter sky that hinted at dawn beginning somewhere behind the thick clouds. Then they stepped outside, and she was forced to lower her head and cling to whatever was available—the railing as they descended the steep stairs, then Andy's arm as they crossed the deck, which ran with water. Andy did what he could to protect her, but there was no real protection from the storm, and keeping on her feet soon became Blaine's sole aim. Though she knew the deck was railed to prevent things and people from slipping over, it was still easy to picture herself being washed right off the edge. The rhythmic shuddering of the metal flooring beneath them wasn't helping at all.

At the bottom of the steps leading to the trailer Blaine glanced up and saw she was expected. The door was open, despite the rain, and a rectangle of yellow light reached down to her like a beacon, signaling the impatience of the man waiting there.

"What's the problem?" Blaine demanded brusquely as she climbed the stairs. No matter that Andy had already explained; she needed a defense against the tremors setting in merely at the sight of Garrath. And business was that defense.

She forced herself to face him squarely without a hint of emotion and was rewarded by his look of surprise. But though his brows arched and one corner of his mouth quirked questioningly, he replied in kind, reiterating Andy's description of the difficulty.

"I see," she said flatly, and turned to shrug out of the wet oilskin. But Garrath's hands were suddenly there, at the collar of the rubbery coat.

"Let me help you," he spoke softly, and his fingers brushed her neck and shoulders as he pulled the coat from her. Before she could stop him his hands moved to the hat on her head.

"No!" she exclaimed, but was too late. He had already lifted it, and the rope of her hair fell, untwisted and spilled over her shoulders like golden rain.

He was close enough that Blaine felt the stiffening of his body, then one hand reaching to the hair brushing the side of her face.

"Blaine!" The one word was barely more than an expulsion of breath, an echo of the feelings that had gripped them a few hours before, feelings Blaine did not want revived.

She moved away quickly, into the room, roughly tucking her hair back behind her ears. Immediately she was greeted by Miles.

"I'm certainly glad you're here, Blaine, my love," he said brightly. "Please explain to the boss that this is just another of your machine's little temper tantrums so I can get back to work. Okay?"

He was leaning casually against a table, arms folded tightly across his chest, a sheaf of papers clutched in one hand. Despite the hour and the weather that he, too, must have faced, every blondish hair on Miles's head was perfectly in place, as was his Cheshire cat smile. The perfection was irritating; the tinge of gloating in the smile unbearable. The combination made Blaine reckless.

"What makes you assume there's something wrong with the computer?" she tossed out, praying *Please don't let it be the computer.* At the same time she moved toward Walter, who was busily punching demands for information into the computer, and looked over his shoulder.

"But, Blaine...I..." Miles faltered, then quickly recovered his confidence. "I should think that would be obvious. This is the same thing that happened before, and you told me this morning you hadn't finished the repairs. In fact, I was surprised to find the system in operation again."

"So was I," Garrath put in smoothly, his voice suddenly unnervingly close behind her. "I wasn't aware the repairs had progressed so well."

Blaine started guiltily. She had looked forward to

being able to tell Garrath that a "mere" woman had fixed his system but not this way. It was possible she hadn't really accomplished the job. And what was worse, she had forgotten to notify him before resuming operations. From everything she knew about him so far, she would have expected his severe censure over such a mistake.

But his comment had sounded more amused than reproachful, and when she looked at him, his eyes echoed the sentiment. Confused, she turned away, trying to think of a logical explanation for her omission. She couldn't very well say, "I didn't tell you because I was too busy hiding from you all afternoon." Before she could come up with anything better, Miles had a comment of his own.

"Well, the repairs obviously haven't gone well enough," he declared. "Because I've checked all the measurements and weights, and there's nothing indicating a leak in that pipe. We should stop wasting time with this nonsense."

Stung by the gibe, Blaine spoke without thinking. "You're wrong, Miles," she said, then could have bitten her tongue for phrasing her comment so badly. Miles's smile shattered into sharp disbelieving pieces.

She knew from her earlier conversation with him how much he resented being overruled by the computer, and from her later talk with Janet how much importance he attached to his job. She should have known better than to directly contradict him and blatantly challenge his authority. Now she could only try to make amends.

"Perhaps you haven't seen this sharp drop in the pressure and rate of flow of the oil through the line," she said placatingly, pointing to the computer display. "Wouldn't you say that indicates a problem?"

Line Number Three was a working line, one already pumping oil from a recently drilled hole. There was no visual access to the line that rested on the seabed far below, but there were monitors feeding information into the computer, and this information had led to the shutdown.

"Of course not. It doesn't mean a thing!" Miles scoffed. "The pressure returned to normal limits almost immediately. A little fluctuation in the pressure is to be expected. Anyone who's *worked* with the oil can tell you that."

Blaine tried to ignore the dig, but couldn't help feeling a shade less conciliatory. "I may not have worked with the oil itself, but I have worked with the figures. We studied data from a large number of rigs over a long period of time before designing the parameters of the system and the situations that would result in shutdowns. If the computer says the shutdown is necessary, then I believe it has good reason. We should wait until that pipeline can be inspected before pumping is resumed."

"And I'm telling you there isn't a leak. Your precious computer is just pulling the same trick it did before. There was nothing really wrong the other times and there isn't now."

"Those other shutdowns were of the drilling, not of a pumping line. That problem was due to a faulty circuit. But it's been replaced. And besides, this is a totally different situation. It needs checking out."

"And checking it out takes time. Perhaps you don't realize, Blaine, how costly shutdowns like this can be on an oil rig." Miles had patched together his smile, but it wasn't reaching his voice, and he was agitatedly rubbing two fingers against his cheek.

"I do realize it. But I also realize that the cost of
not shutting down can be much greater in the long
run if there really is a problem. What if the computer
isn't wrong, Miles? What could happen to a small
leak in a storm like this?"

"I'm telling you, there isn't a leak," he answered,
leaving no more room for argument. He turned to
Garrath. "We should put that line back to work.
Now."

Garrath was scowling down at the floor, and when
he looked up it was at Blaine, not at Miles.

"Are you sure?" he asked her slowly. "Very, very
sure?"

Blaine couldn't answer at once. Not because she
was trying to decide on her answer—that was clear-
cut. It was just that she was having trouble forming
the words because she was too busy struggling to keep
everything except the matter at hand out of her expression. And how could she manage that when the brown
depths of Garrath's eyes were focused on her, burning
with bright golden sparks, and it was almost like being
touched again by his hands, his mouth and his body?

Blaine knew the others were watching and wondered just what they were seeing. But she held her
gaze and her voice firm and steady, and finally
forced out her reply.

"Yes, Garrath. I'm positive the computer isn't
malfunctioning. There's a good reason for the shutdown."

"Walter? Andy? Any comments?" Garrath turned
to each of them in turn, receiving a slow blink and an
affirmative nod from Walter and a firm, "I agree
with Blaine," from Andy.

Finally Garrath turned to Miles and his voice was roughened by regret. "I'm sorry, Miles. I hate to overrule you on this, but I'm inclined to agree with the majority, to lean toward the side of safety. I'll take Blaine down in the mini-sub and personally check out the line as soon as the weather clears. But until then I think we should wait."

Blaine's hands tingled with the childish urge to clap them together in glee. Garrath was agreeing with her! He was accepting her professional assessment of the situation over that of his toolpusher.

But with that thought she looked at Miles and her happiness dissolved. She still felt a sense of triumph, but there was no enjoyment in it. There couldn't be, not when he was so obviously hurting.

A whole range of emotions were playing across his face, none of them pleasant. Disbelief, confusion, humiliation, anger—all made more pathetic by his almost palpable effort to keep them from showing.

"You and Blaine will take the sub down?" he asked dully, and his blue gray eyes were bleached to silver as they moved from Garrath to Blaine and back again to Garrath.

"Yes, I thought she would enjoy seeing what—" Garrath began, but Miles cut him off by slapping the sheaf of papers containing his computations and figures onto the table.

"I understand," he said, shrugging elaborately. There was something in the emphasis he gave to the words that made Blaine want to object, even though she couldn't have said just what it was she objected to.

But Garrath didn't hesitate. "Miles, I don't think you do understand."

The toolpusher was already at the door, grabbing his hat and coat from the rack. "Oh, I do, perfectly. It's your rig. So I guess you can lean toward the side of whatever—" he paused and turned back to Garrath, and the silver of his eyes was hot, white hot, "—or whoever, you want."

Pushing open the door, he stepped out into the rain.

CHAPTER NINE

TWENTY-TWO HOURS LATER the shock of Miles's
scathing comment had faded. As Blaine stood on one
of the rig's lower decks, watching a small blue submarine being readied for its trip beneath the North
Sea, it was a different part of the scene in the trailer
that she was remembering, a part she had almost disregarded at the time.

"I'll take Blaine down in the mini-sub and personally check the line. . ." Garrath had said. Blaine had
been so concerned with Miles's reaction to being
overruled by the Computec system that she'd hardly
noticed. But now, faced with the actuality, the words
took on all the force of a dire warning.

The lozenge-shaped ship, a mini-submersible, had
already been moved from its hangar to the deck.
Through the plastic bubble in the sub's nose she
caught glimpses of two crewmen inside, meticulously
checking out the equipment. Outside, other workers
were attaching the main hawser and secondary lines
from the launching crane that would lift the sub over
the edge of the rig and lower it into the sea. And
overseeing the work personally, as he insisted on doing so many things, was Garrath St. Clair.

In his present position, with one foot hitched up on
the rigging of the sub and arms extended to check the
attachment of a line, the powerful contours of his

body were limned by the tautly stretched fabric of his white coveralls. Blaine could easily follow the brawny musculature down his arms, over his shoulders and broad back to his waist, his lean hips, his legs.

But she didn't want to follow it, didn't want a revival of dangerous feelings. She caught her lower lip between her teeth and forced her gaze out to the teal-blue ocean, its surface calm now as if it were resting from its hours of storm-driven turbulence.

After the episode on the gallery Blaine had decided to keep the maximum amount of space possible between herself and Garrath for the duration of her stay on Sithein One. The scene with Miles had only intensified that resolve. Ridiculous as his insinuations were, what Miles could assume, others could, too. And Blaine refused to let that happen. No fleeting physical attraction for an egotistical oil man was going to threaten her professionally or personally.

But keeping distance between them wouldn't be easy in the close confines of the miniature submarine. That was why her first reaction when reminded of the trip had been an attempt to back out.

Garrath had found her and Janet at breakfast early that morning. His first words had been for his sister.

"A helicopter leaves in forty-five minutes, Janet St. Clair. Since we've taken care of the crucially important paperwork you felt obligated to bring out to me, I would like to see you on it," he'd said. Lightly spoken, but there was no mistaking that it was an order. "I'll see you next week—at Glenclair."

Janet nodded, her picture of meek obedience only slightly marred by the self-satisfaction underlying her rosy-lipped smile. Garrath, wisely, had accepted the victory without close inspection and had turned to Blaine.

"Our transportation leaves just after that. The submersible should be ready about ten." It wasn't really an invitation, but Blaine tried to decline anyway.

"I don't really need to see the line itself," she said, squirming in her hard oak chair. "The information will be enough to work with."

Garrath's brows arched mockingly, and Blaine gave her complete attention to scooping two spoonfuls of sugar into her coffee.

He remained silent, however, and it was Janet who protested. "Oh, Blaine," she cried, "don't miss the chance of the ride. It isn't often someone can con my all-business brother into letting passengers into the sub. I've been down and it's really special. There's a fascinating world down there, and the sub is just like I always imagined a magic carpet would be, so cozy and fun."

Cozy! Blaine felt herself pale just before color flooded her cheeks. Cozy was the last thing she wanted.

She raised her cup to her lips while her mind raced in search of another more pressing excuse. Would she look like too much of an idiot if she claimed a phobia of some sort? But what? Claustrophobia? Hydrophobia? Garrathophobia?

She took a quick gulp of coffee and gagged as unexpected sweetness hit her taste buds. No wonder she'd always taken it black! She forced down the cloying brew but not before Garrath had noticed her discomfort.

"Something go down wrong?" he asked innocently, while his eyes glittered with amusement. "You're not worried about being in the sub, are you? It's perfectly safe."

Blaine shook her head. Of course she wasn't worried about the safety of the sub, and she was sure he knew it.

"Well then, could it be that you and I will be all alone four hundred feet beneath the waves in a craft that's just thirty-one feet long and three and a half feet wide? Is that what's bothering you?" His voice was low and huskily suggestive.

Bingo, Blaine thought, but snapped "Of course not! I just didn't want to waste time, that's all."

"Oh, it won't be wasted," he leered.

"Oh, Garrath! Don't try and give Blaine the jitters," Janet scolded, jabbing her brother's chest with a finger before turning to Blaine. "It's fun, really. And you certainly won't be 'alone with Garrath,' a prospect any right-thinking woman would fear. The sub crew will protect you." And she giggled.

It had all been a cute joke to Janet, her brother teasing and Blaine playing the nervous maiden. But short of admitting that Garrath's humiliating guess was correct, there was nothing she could do but clutch the thought of a sub crew—how many would that be, four, five—and smile coolly at Garrath.

"Fine. I'll be ready," she'd said.

And now, ready or not, it was just about time to go, Blaine surmised. The crewmen had completed their last-minute checks and were leaving the submersible.

Head held high, she marched toward Garrath, who was climbing down from the edge of the craft. She didn't want to go, but since there didn't seem to be a way to gracefully avoid it, she was going to make sure Garrath didn't have occasion to remark on her reluctance or the reason for it.

"All set?" she asked brightly.

Garrath smiled slowly and nodded. "Just give me a moment to get out of these coveralls. I know how you feel about the trappings of my greasy grimy work."

Blaine's cheeks burned at his reference to their first meeting, and the traitorous pulse in the hollow of her throat started pounding as she watched him yank open the snaps at the front of his coveralls and pull it off, revealing a chamois shirt and jeans beneath.

Finished, he tossed the almost perfectly clean uniform aside and held out a hand. "Up we go," he said, indicating a ladder on the outside of the sub.

Still holding her hand he leaped onto the rigging of the sub and pulled her effortlessly up to the first rung of the narrow ladder. She grasped the ladder's metal tubing and began the climb up the conning tower, far too conscious of Garrath just behind her.

A similar ladder edged down inside the hatch. As she made the twisting turn from outside to inside, she faced Garrath for a moment and flinched from his pleased grin, that of a cat watching a mouse heading straight for a trap.

Her first glimpse of the interior of the sub made her glad she didn't actually suffer the claustrophobia she'd considered claiming earlier. It was three and a half feet in width as Garrath had told her and not much more in height. Most of the available space was occupied by black boxes and electronic gear. She moved away from the hatchway in a half crouch and wondered how Garrath's towering form would ever fit inside.

He dropped down after her almost immediately, and quickly satisfied her curiosity. If her crouch was half, his was whole; for Garrath the sub was strictly a bent-knees situation. But somehow he didn't look the least bit awkward. She was reminded of a panther again as he moved toward her. The gracefulness of a wild animal was in his movements, a strong vitality that she would have been better able to appreciate if she hadn't felt so much like a panther's prey.

"I think you'll do best sitting there," he said, pointing to a molded plastic chair. "I have to drive and the controls are in the nose."

Blaine looked at the chair and back to Garrath, pursing her lips. It was obvious that he should have entered the sub first. Now he would have to squeeze by her to reach his station, the very type of situation she had been afraid of. And one she had no doubt he'd deliberately stage-managed.

She swiveled the chair sideways and sat down, pulling her folded legs as much to one side as she could. Sucking in her breath, she closed her eyes and hugged her knees, much as she had as a child when she wanted to hide. If she didn't breathe and didn't look and made herself as small as possible, maybe nothing would happen.

It worked, almost. The side of Garrath's leg brushed hers as he edged by, but the contact was brief and not prolonged beyond necessity. She couldn't really blame him for the goose bumps that raced along her skin.

When she opened her eyes, he was lodged cross-legged in the nose of the sub, briskly punching dials and checking gauges. She heard the hatch slap shut and seal with a hiss, and Garrath announced his

readiness into a radio microphone. She felt the slight
lurch as they were lifted from the deck. They were on
their way—she and Garrath alone.

"The crew!" she cried, her voice unnaturally
shrill.

Garrath was smiling as he turned and jerked his
head toward the back of the craft. "Behind that
panel, Blaine."

A solid panel closed off the rest of the sub, starting
just behind the conning tower. Picturing the outside
of the small craft, Blaine realized that probably half
of the interior was behind the panel. But why? She
glared her question at Garrath.

"The divers are all back there," he explained
smoothly. "They'll check out the line and make repairs if necessary. But deep-water divers are satur-
ated, meaning they stay in a special high-pressure
chamber aboard the rig for their entire month's tour
of duty. The same pressure is maintained in the aft
chamber of the sub, so that they can move from their
rig quarters to the sub to the high pressure on the
seabed below and back again without worrying about
decompression. Without that system a trip such as
this wouldn't be feasible. The divers were loaded on
before the sub was brought out on the deck.

"As for the rest of the crew," he shrugged, "often
there are extra crewmen up here to operate special
equipment. But one man can handle the ship's controls without any trouble at all." And handle anything else, the fiery glint in his brown eyes seemed to
say.

A crew to protect her indeed! She'd been tricked,
but it didn't really matter. If Garrath thought this intimate exotic setup was going to make her fall into his

arms again, he was in for a big surprise. For now there was nothing for her to do but settle back, collect herself and enjoy the ride.

They bobbed a little as they were deposited in the water and the connecting lines were detached. After a few more words into the microphone Garrath flipped the switches to flood the sub's tanks, and the descent began.

The last direction Blaine wanted to look was toward Garrath. But since he was sitting in the only "window," it couldn't be avoided. The sub was equipped with a videotape unit providing a wide-angle view of the area in front of the craft, but its picture was in black and white, which meant the small screen was currently a uniform gray. So she chose the window, doing her best to blot Garrath out of her field of vision while she watched the color of the sea change rapidly from sky-reflecting blue to turquoise to a dark hazy green lighted by the glare of the craft's quartz-iodine spotlights.

Janet's comparison of the sub to a magic carpet had been apt, Blaine decided. There was very little sense of motion, only a light floaty feeling, and nothing but the soft reassuring whir of electric motors to indicate the source of that motion. The descent was rapid but uneventful, and in just a few minutes the flat sandy bottom of the North Sea was visible through the plastic bubble.

"We're equipped with an automatic pipe-tracking system." Garrath tossed the information over his shoulder at her, busy with another set of switches and dials as the sub began to move horizontally, gliding along just above the seabed. "We're over Line Number Three already. Now it's just a matter of finding the leak."

Suddenly Blaine discovered a new source of tension. What if Miles had been right? What if they didn't find anything wrong with the pipe? She wrestled uncomfortably with doubts for a moment, then mentally shook herself. She trusted the Computec system and her own analysis of the data. Why was she manufacturing problems?

The search was short. "Got it!" Garrath exclaimed, bringing the sub to a hovering standstill. "Your computer was right, Blaine, bless its little plastic brain. It doesn't look like much of a leak, but it's there, all right."

Blaine heaved a huge sigh of relief. She'd known it was there, but still. . . .

A few moments later her "chaperons" were visible on the video screen as two divers left their special compartment and swam toward the pipeline. They looked right at home, like some large and unusual species of fish. Encased in black wet suits, face masks and fins, they slid easily through the water, with only their hands betraying their humanness. Long narrow lifelines supplying them with air, heat and communication connected them to the sub.

They were soon over the pipe, pulling tools from the belts at their waists. The radio crackled with their assessment of the problem.

"Fine," Garrath replied. "Doesn't sound like much of a problem at all. Keep me posted." Then he casually hooked the mike on the control board and twisted around to look at Blaine.

"Now we just have to wait," he said.

The muscles beneath his shirt rippled visibly as he turned, and Blaine's breath caught and fluttered in her throat like a trapped butterfly. *Stop it,* she ordered herself. *He's just an ordinary man; irri-*

*tating, egotistical, impossible and in love with just
one thing—oil drilling.*

But in the small, confined space of the miniature
submarine, Garrath St. Clair didn't seem at all ordinary. He filled every inch of the station in the
bubble-shaped nose of the craft, and his imposing
figure drew Blaine's eyes like a flame draws an un-
wary moth. She didn't want to look at him—doing so
made her pulse race and a strange trembling begin to
flow through her. But she couldn't help herself.

Suddenly she was aware not just of being alone
with him but of being alone in a place from which
there was no escape. No matter what he chose to
say—or do—she couldn't walk away. She would
have to face it, and him, and her own reactions. It
was the latter she was most worried about.

"How long?" she finally managed to ask.

He smiled lazily. "Half an hour or so. So you
might as well make yourself comfortable. Why don't
you come up here where the view's better?"

It seemed like a good idea. Trading places might be
tricky, but once that was done, she would have the
bottom of the North Sea to divert her, and he would
be out of her sight.

She edged forward in the necessary half crouch.
When she was as close as she could get, Garrath
swiveled in his chair and stretched his legs out to their
full length before refolding them into their cross-
legged position.

Her eyes followed his movement along the taut
length of his jeans, up to the hips and waist snugly
molded by the blue denim—so snugly molded that
the sinewy strength of the body beneath was emphasized. Blaine was horrified to find herself wondering

just what that strength would look like without its covering of material.

The heat of embarrassment rushing from her head to her toes, she shifted her gaze to the only other place there was to look. His face.

That was no better. The greenish glow from the sea beyond lent a saturnine cast to the arched brows, the prominent cheek and jawline, the taunting smile that claimed he had read her unbidden thought and enjoyed the reading.

Crouching there before him was suddenly very uncomfortable, but he still wasn't making any effort to move out of her way. Surely he didn't expect her to squeeze in beside him!

"I don't think there's seating for two," she said, holding her breath.

He raised an eyebrow, then slowly nodded. "I think you're right." And he pulled her down onto his lap.

Before she could object or regain her balance, he'd swiveled both of them forward, effectively eliminating her chance of retreat. She was trapped between the window and his unyielding body.

I won't scream and fight and play his silly games, she thought. *I won't give him the satisfaction.* Besides, she sensed that struggling would only make the situation worse. Instead she sat stiff and straight, pretending she didn't feel the tingling that had begun at every point where their bodies touched.

Garrath, too, remained still and finally Blaine relaxed enough to look out the window. There was little to see. The divers were dim faraway shapes in the glare of the sub's lights. The seabed was bare and flat. The occasional darting fish and the divers' dancing air bubbles were the only signs of life in the watery world outside.

Inside there was far too much life for Blaine's comfort. She felt that her usually well-behaved emotions were very close to short-circuiting, that every one of her nerve endings was tensed, ready and waiting.

Garrath shifted and Blaine jumped, a whimper escaping her lips.

"Don't panic, kitten," he said, his laugh deep and low. "I was just going to make it easier for you to see." He reached up and flipped a switch, plunging the interior of the submarine into darkness.

"No!" she cried. "Garrath, turn the lights back on!"

"Why should I? You can see out much better now. You're not afraid of...anything, are you?"

Her heart was pulsing rapidly somewhere in her throat instead of beating quietly where it belonged. Not that she was afraid; not really. It was just that the darkness made the space feel smaller, more isolated, like a special intimate world occupied by just the two of them. It created the same feeling of rightness and inevitability she had felt on the gallery, and she didn't want that now. Not at all.

"I'm not afraid," she declared. "But isn't this dangerous?"

"There's only one danger I can think of, and it has little to do with the submarine."

"I don't know what you mean."

"I rather think you do. I think it's the reason you've kept a good distance between us since the other night when the storm broke." His hands grasped her shoulders and forced her to face him. "I see it in your emerald-green eyes. I see it in your very inviting mouth.''

His eyes had followed his words and her lips grew hot beneath his stare.

Her tongue darted out, trying to quench the flame he'd begun there. It didn't work. Her lips were moist and flushed, and still burning, and too late Blaine saw how her slight movement must have looked to him. Inviting.

''No!'' she whispered, just as his mouth came down on hers.

She didn't say no again. From the first moment she was lost, floating in a world of sensations as colorful and varied as the patterns in a kaleidoscope.

His mouth was gentle, then tender, then demanding, exacting a response she was more than willing to give.

Her head tilted back to draw his kisses closer, deeper. And he guided her body, so that she was lying in his arms, vulnerable, ready.

His hands began to move, trailing fire down her spine, up to her neck beneath her tied-back hair. A small tug and her hair was loose, freely flowing as his fingers slid sensuously through it.

His lips left hers, murmuring, ''Even without the moonlight, you're enchanting. You're everything....''

Her arms flew around his neck, pulling his mouth down again. It wasn't words she wanted.

Then one of his hands was at her throat, testing the pulse there, before moving lower to the skin exposed by the open neck of her blouse. His fingers slipped down, excruciatingly slowly, and Blaine felt her breasts grow taut against the soft material. Her whole body was quivering, begging those fingers to move on...and on.

One button, then two, were undone, and his hand slid beneath the material, caressing, stroking, beckoning her on to a new and glittering turn of the kaleidoscope. She arched upward, molding her softness against him, wanting every inch of her to be touching a part of him.

Garrath's arms closed around her, drawing her yielding body closer and closer, as if he could meld them together by force. His mouth claimed hers over and over again, demanding yet more. And she willed him to take whatever he wanted. *Now. Please, now.*

"Mr. St. Clair," the diver's voice blared out of the radio, lightning from a clear sky. "Repairs are finished. We're ready to come in now."

It was like being ripped from a dream. They separated in a daze, their eyes locked hungrily together as if that could keep the moment, the feelings, alive a little longer. But it wasn't enough, not nearly enough.

"Blaine, I..." he began. She turned away from him, hands going hastily to the undone buttons, shaking her head.

Garrath reached up and switched on the light.

CHAPTER TEN

RICHARD HAD ONCE TOLD BLAINE he could recognize a bag she had packed with one glimpse of the contents. No one else brought such logic and precision to the task of filling a suitcase. Each article of clothing was carefully folded and meticulously layered into the bag in order of planned use. Not one unnecessary item was included; not one inch of space was wasted. The result looked computer generated, he had concluded admiringly.

He wouldn't have recognized the case Blaine was packing now.

She tossed her toilet articles haphazardly into a cosmetics bag, then bit her lower lip in frustration when the zipper wouldn't close over the jumbled mess.

"Come *on*," she pleaded with the contents, at the same time shaking the bag in hopes that rejumbling would result in a more amenable assemblage. "You came out of there, you've got to go back in."

What begging didn't accomplish, a vicious tug did. Blaine forced the zipper's stubborn teeth together and heaved a sigh of relief. She was one step closer to going home.

Her decision to leave Sithein One had been made in the submersible, as she'd scuttled away from Garrath and back to her station after the diver's untimely—or

should she say just-in-time—interruption. Now that
the Computec system had proved itself repaired, her
job was finished. She had shown Garrath, and herself, that she could do the job, that she couldn't be
driven away by either her own fears or his disap-
proval. The possibility that the malfunction was a
result of sabotage still bothered her, but she'd seen to
it that precautions were being taken. That was all she
could do. There was no longer any reason to stay and
every reason to go.

So she was packing, as rapidly as she could. Not
having ever really unpacked, it wouldn't take long.
The room was already almost Andy's again, the few
signs of her occupancy disappearing one by one into
her suitcase. In a very few minutes she would be
ready to leave, except for one thing. She hadn't told
Garrath she wanted to go.

Blaine threw a pair of shoes into the suitcase with
more force than was good for their soft suede finish.
It wasn't that she was afraid to tell him. After all, he
was the one who had wanted so desperately to be rid
of her in the first place. Her decision would only
please him. It was just that so far the time hadn't
been right.

She couldn't, for instance, have blurted it out in
the submarine. He had been too busy then bringing
the divers aboard, navigating the sub to the surface
and directing the swimmers to attach the towing and
winch lines. And afterward, when the hatch had
opened and she had scrambled hastily out, the deck
crew had been there, securing the submersible and offering her a hand down. She couldn't have spoken
then, so it was just as well she hadn't waited for Garrath, that she had left the deck, heading for her

quarters while he was still performing his last tasks inside the sub.

Her actions made perfect sense to her, but somehow she knew Garrath wouldn't see it that way. He was going to be angry and that was going to make him disagreeable. The fact made her reluctant to face him, even with news she was positive he would relish.

It would be easier when she was all packed, when she was physically committed to leaving, she assured herself. To that end she looked around for the next victim of her frenzy and found it in a small turquoise ball tucked into the back of a drawer. It wasn't until she drew it out that she realized it was her silk blouse, and then she couldn't seem to either pack it or consign it to the wastebasket where it belonged.

She held it out in front of her at arm's length, her hand shaking. The blue green color was as appealing as ever, the material as soft and smooth in her fingers. But she would never wear the blouse again, she knew; not even if the two conspicuous stains on the front weren't permanent. For her the smudges would always be there.

She was still holding the blouse when the door opened. Between two beats of her heart, Garrath crossed the room, glaring at her furiously.

"Why did you run away, Blaine Christensen?"

The sudden racing of her pulse at the sight of him was clear proof of the rightness of her decision to leave. She swallowed the tightness in her throat.

"I didn't run away. You were busy, and I wanted to—"

"You're damned right I was busy. Shutting down the sub and explaining to Miles what we'd found."

Miles! Somehow, wrapped in her own concerns, Blaine had forgotten Miles, and now she felt horribly guilty. "How did he take it, the computer being right, I mean?"

"All right, I guess. I explained about the leak. He claims it would have shown up in his measurements soon enough, long before the problem would have grown serious. And possibly he's right. He thinks your system is redundant when it works, a hindrance when it doesn't. I think it's going to save lives sometime; maybe not on this rig but somewhere. And that's what counts. Whether he likes it or not, he has to learn to live with it." He sliced a hand through the air dismissively.

Blaine felt a pang of sympathy for Miles and his probably injured pride, but that didn't stop her from smiling at Garrath. His words had echoed her feelings so precisely. Saving lives was what mattered, and she was inordinately glad to hear him express it.

But Garrath didn't see her smile. He was staring, first at her suitcase open on the bed, and then at the blouse in her hand. He grabbed one end of the silky material and shook it, giving emphasis to his next words.

"Enough about Miles. I want to know what you're doing."

Blaine jerked the silk from his hand. "I'm getting packed to leave," she said curtly.

"Leave? What are you talking about?"

"My work here is done. The weather is fine. I have to go home."

She stuffed the ruined blouse deep into a corner of her suitcase, but even turned away from him she could feel his sudden tensing. She stiffened in response, waiting for him to speak or move, to react. But silence stretched between them.

"Is it because of your nightmares?" he asked at last, very softly and gently and so close that his breath whispered against her neck.

"My nightmares?" For a moment she couldn't imagine what he was talking about, and when she did she gasped in surprise—at herself. The dream hadn't recurred since that first night; here, on an oil rig, she'd barely even thought of the fears that had once haunted her constantly. But there wasn't time to reason that fact out to its conclusion. Garrath was still waiting for an explanation.

"No, it's got nothing to do with that," she said hastily. "I've told you, my work is finished. And after what Miles said, I—"

"Surely you don't believe that garbage!" Garrath exploded. His hands bit into her shoulders, forcing her around to face him. "You can't be as much of a fool as he is."

"Of course I don't believe it!" Her lips trembled. "But others among your crew might, especially if anyone happened to see...and it won't help the system being accepted if people think...well, anyway, I'm sorry about what happened that night and on the submarine."

"Sorry!"

"Yes, of course. I don't think business and...and pleasure should be mixed on the job. It's not professional and it just leads to difficulties."

"I guess I should be grateful for the pleasure part of that nonsense," Garrath sneered. "But the rest is pure bunk."

"It isn't. You should be able to see that from what

happened with Miles. Involvements on the job just don't work out.''

''Then how about you and Richard?''

''Me and Richard?''

''I understood you two were very. . .close. Yet he's your boss. I would think that constituted involvement.''

''That's different. Our relationship began long before we were business colleagues and it's grown slowly over the years. It's not like this. This is just a. . .a physical. . . .''

''Attraction? Is that the word you're groping for? An attraction so strong it becomes a compulsion?''

Blaine recognized the words—her words—immediately, and remembered just as easily what she'd been referring to at the time: Janet and Andy and the real consuming love between them. But that couldn't be applied to her and Garrath, and he knew it. He was just twisting her words as he always did, using her own arguments against her.

She moved away from him, away from the intensely burning gaze focused on her. Picking up a sweater, she concentrated on smoothing out every possible wrinkle as she folded it for packing.

''Yes, that's all it is,'' she answered without looking at him. ''A physical attraction—and a complication I can certainly do without. That's why I insist on leaving Sithein One as soon as possible. My work here is finished. I'm going home.''

''To Richard?''

''That's none of your business,'' she snapped. ''I'm leaving. Please arrange it.'' She carefully placed the sweater in the suitcase where its folded precision made a mockery of the rest of her packing.

She reached for another item of clothing, but Garrath's next question stopped her hand in mid-air.

"What are you afraid of, Blaine?" His hand shot out and grasped hers. "If it's nothing but a physical attraction, then all you have to do is refuse my advances. I don't force women into anything they don't want. If I touch you," he paused and his thumb started tracing sensuous circles in her palm, "and you say no, I'll stop." He paused again, waiting, challenging her to say the word, to call him to a halt. Her mouth formed the word. *No,* she thought. But no sound came from her parted lips.

His hands moved to her arms, turning her and pulling her close to him, and then one hand was cupping the back of her head, tilting her face up to his, so that she could feel the warm traces of his whisper against her mouth.

"Or is it that you know you won't say no, won't want me to stop?"

He was right. She didn't want him to stop. She was melting again, sliding away from all her firm resolutions, her better judgment, reality even. She tried to think of San Francisco and Richard. But she had never felt anything like this in Richard's embrace. Thoughts of home faded away.

She wanted to be held in Garrath's arms, just as she was. She wanted the taste of his mouth on hers. She wanted the glittering sensations only he could rouse in her in spite of everything.

She sighed, and it was the signal Garrath had been waiting for. His lips moved to claim hers, and Blaine's green eyes fluttered closed. But beneath her lowered lashes, an image formed of a blue and silver

logo vivid against a·white hat. And the words on the
logo: Sithein One.

Her eyes flew open and she jerked free of Garrath's embrace. "No!" she cried. And then, more
softly, "No, Garrath. I want to leave the rig."

She took two steps backward, out of his reach,
before she dared turn away. Even as the distance between them grew, some treacherous part of her was
longing for him to call after her, to come after her, to
blot her "no" from her lips with the hard pressure of
his own. But true to his word, he didn't, and when
she started to continue her packing, he didn't stop
her.

The silence screamed between them while Blaine
folded two shirts and another sweater and placed
them in the suitcase as carefully as if they were spun
glass. And then there was nothing left within her
reach. She took a deep breath and pivoted on her heel
to face him, ready to defy his anger and scorn.

Neither of those emotions was molding his features. He was staring at her, and though she couldn't
read his expression, she was sure it wasn't what she
had expected. His lips were compressed as if with
fierce determination, but the corners tilted up just the
slightest bit. His eyes flashed sharply, but their
brown depths glowed with warmth.

"Garrath?" she began, not having the faintest idea
what she wanted to ask.

"I'll arrange it," he said flatly. "For tomorrow
morning." And then he grinned.

THE GRIN WORRIED HER all afternoon and through
the night. It stayed in the back of her mind, where
she stumbled over it at odd moments. Had it been

smug, she wondered, and if so, why? But even as she wondered, she hoped without much hope that she wouldn't find out.

She finished her packing and had some last words with Walter, cautioning him to let her or Richard know if anything at all unusual happened. She was pleased to run into Andy so she could say her good-byes and wish him luck.

"With a certain young lady," she added, and Andy's freckles drowned in a sea of red.

"Aw, don't fret none, ma'am," he drawled, looking at his boots. "I can be stubborn as a mule. I'll hang in there."

Blaine stood on tiptoe and brushed her lips against his blushing cheek.

She looked for Miles, too, hoping to make amends for the trouble she knew she'd caused him. But the only time she saw him, he was deep in conversation with Rory MacPherson, and she didn't have the courage to take on both of them at once.

She couldn't fall asleep that night, plagued as she was by the memory of Garrath's grin. She was bothered as well by contrary feelings of impatience to be gone and regret that she was leaving, though the latter made no sense to her at all. She longed to get up and wander out again to the gallery, to let the fresh sea breezes sweep the turmoil from her mind, but didn't dare. So she tossed and turned and dozed fitfully until morning.

Even though it was early when, exhausted, she dragged herself from bed, she was just twisting her hair into a bun at the nape of her neck when Garrath's knock sounded on her door.

"Ready to go, Miss Christensen?" he greeted her.

He was wearing tan wool slacks and a brown suede jacket, the suede looking as rich and soft as velvet, the color as deep and warm as his eyes. Thick snow-white shearling showed at the wide collar of the coat, and the effect would have been royal except for one thing. On the face above the collar the grin was still unnervingly in place.

Smug. It was very definitely smug, she decided, and an apprehensive shudder slid down her spine.

She glared at his broad back as he hefted her bags and led the way toward the helicopter pad. Probably he was just happy to be getting rid of her, she thought sourly, but he didn't have to show it so openly. She was glad to be going, but she wasn't grinning like someone on the way to a party.

The chopper's huge blades were already whipping the air when they reached the deck, its roar almost blotting out the now-familiar clangs and groans of the rig. While Garrath was loading her suitcases aboard, Blaine's attention was drawn to the derrick towering over them. Shading her eyes from the gusting air she followed the steel latticework up and up, until she came to a metal plate attached close to the derrick's top. The St. Clair logo gleamed in the bright morning sunlight.

She turned away and, ducking low, scurried to where Garrath waited.

She had racked her brain all night for something to say, some appropriate farewell, something very adult and sophisticated. Nothing had come. But now she discovered it didn't matter. Garrath didn't give her a chance to say a thing. One moment she was standing beside him, the next his hands had spanned her waist and in one quick movement he hoisted her up onto the helicopter's black float. Even more startling, he climbed up after her.

"Get in," he shouted over the roar of the machine, pointing to the seat beside the pilot. When she had, he reached over her to the seat belt. His fingers brushed the tops of her thighs as he drew the belt across her lap and fastened it, and Blaine shivered. His look told her he hadn't missed her involuntary reaction, but he slammed the door closed without a word.

A cry rose in her throat. They were going to part without even a goodbye. It wasn't right. She raised her hand and pressed her palm against the rounded window beside her.

But Garrath didn't see her gesture. He had already moved away—not from the helicopter as Blaine expected but to the back door. There was a sharp burst of noise as he opened it and climbed into the rear seat, quickly muffled again when the door slammed shut.

Blaine twisted around, ignoring the belt digging into her hips. "What are you doing?" she shouted, the raising of her voice only partly due to the noise of the helicopter's jet engine beginning its screaming whine. She had no idea whether the pilot, insulated by his earphones, could hear her or not and didn't really care. Nothing mattered except the man in the back seat.

"We're leaving the rig, just as you wanted," he replied, his mouth twisted in what Blaine supposed was an attempt to look innocent. It wasn't successful. Innocence didn't sit well on eyes so knowing or a mouth so smug.

"What do you mean, we? Are you planning on escorting me all the way to San Francisco?"

He shook his head, and a lock of black hair fell across his forehead. "Oh, no. Didn't I explain? You're not going to San Francisco, not yet. I've arranged with your Richard for you to do another job for me."

The helicopter lifted into the air, leaving Blaine's stomach on the platform below.

Another job, and Richard had agreed. But of course Richard would agree, just as he had agreed to send her to the rig in the first place. He would do almost anything to please Garrath St. Clair.

"What job?"

"Nothing complicated. Just a computer link from the rig to my office."

"But surely that's already been done," she protested, puzzled. Establishing the remote sea-to-shore link from the Computec unit to the oil company's headquarters was an automatic part of the installation of the unit on the rig. She said as much to Garrath.

He nodded. "That was taken care of. But I'd like an additional link in my private office. I can't always be out here, so I might as well have the next best thing."

"You don't need me for that," Blaine said, bitterness at this further evidence of his obsession with the rig coloring her voice a cold flat gray. "We have plenty of installers who are actually more qualified than I for that type of work. I'll see that one gets out to you as soon as possible when I get home."

"Oh, I'm sorry. I should have realized you couldn't handle this kind of job."

"Of course I can handle it!" she snapped, then realized what she'd said. "That is," she tried to amend, "I *could*, but...." Too late. Garrath closed the jaws of the trap precisely around her.

"Good, then that's settled," he grinned.

Blaine glared at him for a moment, then sighed. She'd let her temper get her into trouble again; now she would just have to live with the results.

"All right, I'll do it," she gave in. "But I'll have to go back to the rig. The computers have to be programmed to accept a new link, the proper equipment has to be delivered to your office, and—"

"That's all been taken care of," he interrupted. "Walter is doing the on-board work, and your Richard is arranging for shipment of the necessary equipment. It's all arranged."

Blaine turned forward and flopped back in her seat, fuming. All arranged! It certainly was, between Richard Perry and Garrath St. Clair, and she didn't know who to be the most angry with. How could they treat her like a slave whose fate could be "arranged" to suit the two of them without even bothering to consult her? How dare they!

But there wasn't any point in arguing now. Strapped inside a St. Clair helicopter several hundred feet above the ice-cold North Sea was definitely a weak position. Not the best one for the kind of response the situation deserved.

Blaine massaged a crick in her neck—another thing she owed to Garrath! But even as she grumbled to herself, she realized things weren't so bad, not if she disregarded this newest insult to her pride. She was getting what she'd wanted—off Sithein One. True, she wasn't quite free of Garrath yet. But even if she agreed to install the remote link, the job wouldn't take much time to complete, and she would be in Aberdeen, not in a world where Garrath ruled undisputed, where he possessed keys to all the doors. She didn't understand what kind of game he was playing now, but he would find she had a few rules of her own to add once she was back on dry land.

Comforted by that conclusion, she relaxed and leaned against the window for a last glimpse of Sithein One. The helicopter was making a low circle around the rig, probably just for that effect.

It was a very different sight from her first glimpse of it. Then it had been lost in a murky twilight, the flare the only sign of its existence. Now, in the clear crisp morning light, every detail was discernible and surprisingly familiar. She could almost hear the sounds associated with what she saw. The groan and screech of a giant crane as its long arm was swung around, reaching for a load. The grunts of the roughnecks at the grueling task of attaching drill string, the new lengths of pipe that would allow the drill to bite deeper and deeper into the seabed far below. The thumping of the mud pumps, pouring their viscous concoction of water and chemicals down hole with the drill, to cool and stabilize the pressure.

And then the helicopter was passing over the corner of the rig where the observation deck perched. A figure stood there, head turned upward, hand raised to shade its eyes against the sun.

At first the figure was unidentifiable, just another worker relaxing on a break, watching their departure. Blaine raised her hand to wave.

But when the pilot tilted the helicopter in a farewell

salute, Blaine had a clear view of the face of the immobile figure. It was Miles.

She dropped her hand and shrank back from the window, no longer inclined to a friendly wave. Miles was no accidental observer. He was there on purpose, watching her leaving Sithein One with Garrath St. Clair.

And he wasn't smiling.

CHAPTER ELEVEN

WITH A LURCH the helicopter veered sharply away from the rig and there was nothing but teal-blue sea and turquoise sky to be seen out the bubble-shaped windows. But the image of Miles lingered. Blaine twisted in her seat again, daring a peek at Garrath to see if he, too, had noticed the unsmiling face witnessing their departure.

He hadn't. His attention was already elsewhere, on the papers spilling out of a brown leather briefcase open on the seat beside him. Reflected sunlight glittered from the gold plating of the felt-tipped pen he moved unhesitatingly over one page after another, slashing through text, stabbing sharp notations into margins and branding an occasional sheet with the bold flare of his signature.

Her look lasted much longer than she'd intended, all thoughts of Miles fading away. There was something different now about Garrath, something she couldn't quite put her finger on, and the chance to study him while he was unaware was just too tempting. She supposed it was only the trappings of his gold pen and expensive briefcase, but he seemed to have lost some of his rough edges. The angles of his face were less sharp, there was less arrogance in the set of his jaw, less tension in his neck and shoulders.

The fierce Highland warrior had set aside his claymore, at least for the moment.

Or was her judgment being rose tinted by the minutes carrying them farther and farther from Sithein One? Would he really change when he was away from the responsibilities and strains of the rig? Not likely, not when he was merely trading one set of responsibilities for another larger set. Still, there was something different. . . .

Blaine turned forward, surreptitiously rubbing the twin sore spots left on her hipbones by her straining against the seat belt. She didn't know what the difference in Garrath St. Clair was, but it didn't really matter anyway. Soon she would be free of him and back home to safe steady Richard. It shouldn't take more than two days to install his office link, and then she would never have to see Garrath again. Two more days.

Or. . . maybe three?

She leaned back in her seat, sighed once and fell promptly and deeply asleep, a tiny tentative smile dusting her lips.

TRACES OF THE SLIGHT SMILE REMAINED hours later when a touch on her shoulder roused Blaine from her nap. She wriggled a bit but resisted coming fully awake. She still hadn't made up for her lack of sleep the night before, as the lead weights on her eyelids and the cotton stuffing her head testified.

A voice whispered close to her ear, "Better wake up, princess, or you'll miss one of the best views in the world."

Princess.

Blaine's eyes flew open and she jerked upright in her seat. She whipped her head around toward the source of the voice and was staring into warm brown eyes.

Garrath's, and he had called her "princess"... just as he had another time? She'd thought it was a dream, that memory from the first night on the rig: of being tucked under a warm blanket, of gentle hands running through her hair and a soft deep voice whispering, "Sleep, silly princess." Just a dream. But now....

"What did you say?" she asked hoarsely.

He was leaning over the back of her seat, smiling that infuriating I-know-what-you're-thinking smile. For an answer he moved his finger from the protective thickness of her coat to the bared skin of her neck, turning what would have been an impersonal nudge into an intimate caress. Before she could protest he had pressed against the point of her chin.

"Look," he insisted, and it was easier to yield than to resist. Blaine looked out her side window.

"Oh, Garrath," she breathed.

Spread out before her was a city spun from some ancient sorcerer's spell, surely designed just to offer this one spectacular view. Beneath a sky piled with silver clouds it rose in tiers of gray and green, enticing the eye ever upward. The foreground was carpeted by the identical roofs of row houses layered up the steep slopes of low hills. Shooting up at random through this carpet were soaring church spires, delicate heaven-aimed arrows. But towering over even these skyscraping steeples was a bold upthrust of black rock, the base for the formidable battlements of a majestic castle. And beyond, looming benignly over all the rest, was the huge but softly contoured mound of a richly verdant hill.

It was dramatic, enthralling and definitely not Aberdeen.

Admittedly, Blaine's view of the Houston-of-the-North had been confined mostly to the airport and hindered by both her exhaustion and her distress. She'd had only the briefest glimpse of the city before the helicopter had shot out over the ocean, just enough to see that it, too, was a montage of gray buildings and lofty church spires.

But brief as her view had been, she was sure that the lovely fairy-tale scene now before her was not Aberdeen.

"Where are we?" she asked, confused.

"Edinburgh," he replied, pronouncing it Ed-in-burra, with rumbling "R's." "Scotland's capital, and her most regal city."

"Edinburgh!" Blaine exclaimed. "Why aren't we in Aberdeen?"

"Because St. Clair Corporation headquarters are here," Garrath said blithely. "Only our oil division offices are in Aberdeen."

"Then this is where you want the computer link? But why didn't you tell me?"

"Umm, well...oh, we're coming into the airport now," he said, quickly easing back into his seat and refastening his belt for the landing.

How typical, Blaine grumbled to herself. *First he acts with his usual infuriating arbitrariness, then when he's caught at it, he simply dodges the question!* Not that their change of destination made any real difference to her. As long as she was off the rig, one city could do as well as another, and certainly

Edinburgh was appealing. It was not being told that was so galling.

Her annoyance ebbed away, though, once they were on the ground and heading back into the center of Edinburgh. The highly polished black body of the taxi and the unpolished driver both looked of a vintage perfectly in keeping with the aged mien of the city. The grandeur visible from the air was even more impressive on closer inspection, and she couldn't stay miffed at Garrath when he was playing the perfect and most charming guide.

"Most of Britain's ancient cities grew up along river valleys. Edinburgh was built along the volcanic ridge sloping down from the castle. Over there." Garrath pointed unnecessarily.

From the ground the castle that seemed born of the thrust of black rock was even more overpowering. A stout and sternly visaged nanny, it stood guard over its charge, the city, with an air at once threatening and comforting.

"One of the earliest settlements on the Rock was known as Dun Eideann, the Fortress on the Slope. That name may have been somewhat inaccurately adapted to Edwin's Burgh in the sixth century, when Edwin of Northumbria built his own fortress on the old site. From there it was only a matter of one letter to Edinburgh."

"I like the original," Blaine said thoughtfully. The ancient name was appropriately lyrical, while its translation was the perfect description. She could easily imagine a fierce band of early Scotsmen rolling boulders down on their enemies from their wind-swept stronghold, while their leader, a black-haired stern-jawed man with gentle but fearless brown eyes, urged them on.

"I do, too," Garrath agreed warmly, his gentle but fearless brown eyes searching hers.

Blaine leaned forward, partly to escape his scrutiny but more in an effort to see. "It's so...so...." Words failed her and she sighed. "I wish I had the time to see everything."

"Do you?" Garrath asked softly. Blaine nodded without turning around. She was precariously balanced on the very edge of the car seat, straining forward for the best possible view and totally unprepared for what came next.

"Driver, stop here!" Garrath ordered suddenly. He was obeyed instantly, with a screech of brakes and a yank on the steering wheel that wrenched the taxi curbward and tossed Blaine in the opposite direction. The next thing she knew she was sprawled across Garrath's lap.

Flustered, all too conscious of his muscles tensing against her stomach, her breasts and her palms, Blaine struggled to right herself. It shouldn't have been difficult; one good push would do it. The only trouble was she couldn't seem to find a safe place to put her hands.

Her first automatic contact was with his leg just above the knee. Bad enough, but when she tried to draw back, her hand slipped into even more dangerous territory—the tautness of his upper thigh.

"Why, Miss Christensen!" Garrath chuckled, and Blaine had the uncivilized urge to sink her teeth into the leg so conveniently close. Restraining herself with superhuman effort, she shifted again, very carefully.

The impersonal leather of the car seat had to be there somewhere!

But she couldn't find it, and from Garrath's continuing laughter she knew she needn't expect any help from him. He was enjoying himself too much—at her expense.

Well, she'd be damned if she'd continue to flop around like an embarrassed fish out of water just so he could be amused! The show was over! Blaine closed her eyes, moved her hands and pushed.

Garrath, perhaps sensing her intentions, chose that moment to offer the necessary assistance, so Blaine didn't discover whether her imprudent action would have caused him permanent injury or not. But when she was sitting up again, she found that his arm was tightly around her shoulders.

Holding herself stiffly, she glared pointedly from the hand cupping her upper arm to his face.

He grinned. "Mere self-preservation," he defended cheerfully. "I never realized before how very risky having girls fall into your lap can be. Best not to take chances."

Blaine held onto her anger and her glare as long as she could. But Garrath's grin was teasing, not taunting, and highly contagious. Suddenly the absurdity of the whole episode struck her, and the corners of her mouth turned up into a tiny smile. Once it had begun she couldn't stop it. The smile turned into laughter and she slumped against Garrath, laughing until tears filled her green eyes.

Garrath joined her, the vibrance of his humor feeding hers. He released his hold on her shoulder, taking her hand instead, and then reached to wipe the tears from her cheeks.

"Come on," he said, pulling her toward the door. "I've got something to show you."

They climbed out of the taxi and Garrath leaned over to speak to the driver. Blaine didn't pay any attention to what was being said; she was savoring her first unimpeded taste of the city.

Signs of an earlier rain lingered in the shiny puddles on the sidewalk and the fresh-washed smell in the air. Moistness tinted the crisp wind nipping her cheeks. A park stretched to either side of them as far as she could see. It was lush; the grass, trees and shrubs all intensely green after their shower. A tall Gothic spire bloomed amidst the greenery like some immense exotic flower, watched over by the guardian walls of the castle.

"Is this what you wanted me to see?" she asked when Garrath was again by her side.

"Partly," he answered, taking her hand again. "It's a good place to start, at least. These are the Princes Street Gardens, and the architectural delicacy before us is the monument to Sir Walter Scott—poet, novelist and romanticizer of Scotland. The spire is two hundred feet tall and it's only two hundred eighty-seven steps to the top. Shall we make the ascent or press on?"

"Press on? What are you talking about?"

"Edinburgh," he said with a mock bow. "You're about to receive the world-famous St. Clair condensed tour of the Scottish capital, including a stroll up the Royal Mile, a bite to eat in a cozy pub in one of the courts of Old Town, the castle certainly and other points of interest as time permits."

Blaine laughed. "Don't be silly," she began, but squealing tires drew her attention to the taxi, which was pulling away from the curb with their luggage.

"You mean it!" she cried.

"Of course I do. Haven't you learned yet that I always mean exactly what I say?"

"But you can't! I don't have time for this. I have to get to work."

"Why?"

"Why? Because I...because I have to get back to...because it's my job and I should...." Blaine floundered to a halt, her thoughts racing.

"Should what?" he asked. "Since you're working for me for the time being, and I have no objections to the delay, I don't see why you should."

He might not, but Blaine did. Tours around a fairy-tale city were not part of her plan to return to safety and sanity as soon as possible.

But even as she told herself to refuse, she was glancing wistfully up at the ramparts of the castle looming over the tops of the trees and thinking of cathedrals and courts. It would be a shame to return home without seeing some part of Scotland. Surely there couldn't be any harm in indulging in a little sight-seeing with Garrath? They weren't going to end up in any romantic embraces in the middle of the city. It would be fun, and perfectly safe.

"Neither do I," she said at last, smiling. "I'll take one ticket for the deluxe guided tour of Dun Eideann, please."

Returning her smile, Garrath saluted. "'Tis pleased I'd be to escort you, lass." And he suited action to the words, leading her off at a brisk pace before she could change her mind.

See, everything is going to be fine, she assured herself. Garrath was going to keep it light. There was nothing to worry about.

And then, in a move as smooth and practiced as an intricate dance step, Garrath turned the hand holding hers and twisted both their arms back and around her waist, drawing her provocatively close against his side. As she looked up at him to protest, he brushed a kiss against her forehead.

"I'll collect the fare later tonight," he whispered.

"What!" she shrieked, trying to pull free of his grip.

He let go of her waist but not her hand, and increased his pace. "Come on," he ordered, laughing again. "Your guide frowns on stragglers."

There was nothing to do but follow along, wondering just what she'd got herself into now.

Her uneasiness didn't last, chiefly because Garrath didn't let it. After that one unnerving comment, he had gone back to being light and relaxed. Blaine stopped fretting and started enjoying her tour of the city, without worrying about the "fare."

Not that their walk bore much resemblance to a formal tour. It was more like getting to know a new friend. They wandered along, Garrath relating an occasional historical detail, or, more frequently, his private observations. Blaine enjoyed the latter most of all.

In the gardens they watched the tourists rushing from site to site, clicking cameras.

"I doubt they even know where they've been until they get home and have their slides developed," was Garrath's scathing comment.

Blaine smiled, agreeing. She never took a camera

when she traveled, preferring to spend her time experiencing the places instead of calculating distance and light. Her memories and a few picture postcards were what she took home.

But she wouldn't have minded a picture of some of the babies they saw out for their "wee walks." Pudgy pink-cheeked faces peeked from buntings, blankets and hooded coats that were not the usual pale pink and blue of infants wear but dark earth tones—browns, grays, navy blue, even black.

"Scottish mums are too practical to put their babies in light colors," Garrath observed. "Too easily stained."

"And just what do you know about babies and stains?" Blaine teased.

"Enough. I was fifteen when Janet was born and my mother died not long after. I helped out."

I helped out. A simple statement, but it said so much about Garrath the boy, a lot of it contradictory to Blaine's assumptions about Garrath the man.

A steep street led out of the gardens and up to the high ridge that housed the Old Town. An archway was cut through what would have been the bottom floor of one of a line of tall gabled buildings. Garrath turned back to look out over the emerald green foliage to Princes Street and the New Town beyond.

"New Town was designed in the late eighteenth century to allow for Edinburgh's expansion," he explained. "But the people were at first afraid to venture into the new territory away from the protective walls of the old city. Finally a twenty-pound bribe was offered to the first person to build a house there."

He swept a hand across the wide view. "Imagine

this almost completely empty, uncivilized, unpro-
tected, Blaine. Would you have taken the bribe?
Been one of the first?''

Blaine looked from the crowded ridge behind them
to the spacious sprawl of the New Town. Would she
have left security for a promise?

''I don't know,'' she said at last. ''Would you?''

''Of course,'' Garrath answered without hesitation. ''Think of the chance they had, to build, create!
Think of the challenge!'' He paused and turned from
the view to her.

''I think you would have done it, too,'' he claimed,
smiling. ''It would have been the logical choice and
I'll show you why.'' He led her through the archway.

Like Alice-Through-the-Looking-Glass, she
stepped into a totally different world. On one side
of the archway was the spacious lushly green garden,
on the other a dark narrow street where the buildings
pressed in from either side so close they almost
seemed to touch at the top. Even the air felt heavy.
She shivered.

''You can see why they are called 'closes,' '' Garrath said, letting go of her hand to put an arm around
her shoulder. Blaine didn't object to the warmth.

''When Edinburgh was still trapped inside its
walls, they built up instead of out, resulting in
tenements that were as much as fourteen stories high,
unique for that time,'' he explained. ''What we're
seeing are some of those buildings restored and
preserved but minus the dirt, grime and pestilence
that would have been part of living in the overcrowd-
ed conditions then. Somehow I don't mind at all not
having to keep an ear open for the shout 'Gardyloo,'
so we can dodge the contents of a chamber pot being

emptied from one of the upper windows as they did
in the Old Town's heyday.''

Blaine wrinkled her nose as her imagination provided an all too vivid picture of the scene.

At that moment someone pushed open a small window above them. Both Blaine and Garrath looked
up, and when something fluttered in the opening they
moved as one, ducking and half jumping a few feet
ahead.

From a position of safety they glanced back—at a
white curtain flapping in the chill breeze. Their
laughter echoed along the corridor of the close.

Garrath seemed to know his way perfectly through
the mazelike wynds—the passages connecting the
warren of courts and closes. Blaine was lost after one
turning but didn't care a bit. She happily let him
guide her past the shops, businesses, galleries and
numerous small museums dedicated to different aspects of the city's history that now occupied the tenements.

In the spotless window of a Clothiers shop she saw
a long woolen skirt, a high-necked blouse of silk and
lace and a fur-trimmed floor-length cape—and had
the mad impulse to rush in and buy the whole outfit.
How much better than her pants and sweater it would
fit in with the wrought-iron railings, crow-stepped
gables, conically topped towers, mullioned windows
and cobblestone streets.

Garrath's promised "bite to eat" turned out to be
steaming bowls of Scotch broth, thick with barley
and vegetables, and crusty loaves of bread taken in
The Thistledown, a cozy pub occupying a restored
seventeenth-century inn.

A delicate tinkling of bells had announced their

opening of the front door, and immediately a huge bear of a man had lumbered toward them, the exact flaming-haired clansman Blaine had imagined when Richard first mentioned her coming to Scotland.

He was wearing a tartan kilt that swayed as he walked, and long hair and a flowing beard obscured all but his blue eyes. Garrath, far from small, nearly disappeared as the larger man threw trunklike arms around him in greeting.

"Aye, now, 'tis a sight for sore eyes ye are!" he bellowed. More words followed that were totally incomprehensible to Blaine. Gaelic, she wondered? And then the man saw her.

He was double her size in width and almost that in height, she decided, as he advanced on her. Massive hands reached out and clamped around her waist, and she was swept off her feet and lifted upward until green eyes met blue.

Strangely she wasn't afraid or even alarmed. She'd seen the twinkle in the blue eyes, heard the warmth in the voice. And somehow it seemed the most natural thing in the world to be held a foot off the floor and studied by a total stranger.

Finally the great head nodded, the red beard twitched and a smile appeared. "I see ye're finally after takin' my advice, Garrath, old friend," he thundered over his shoulder.

"And what advice is that, Alexander Duncan?" Garrath asked dryly.

"Why, that ye find yerself a lass with fire instead of ice in her soul, of course," he roared, and lowered Blaine gently before turning and slapping Garrath's back with a force that would have knocked a lesser man across the room.

They were shown to a table that was instantly set with a kettle of thick soup, bread, fresh butter and steaming mugs of tea. Their host readily agreed to join them.

"Alex's family lives near Glenclair and he and I went to school together," Garrath introduced them. "He's been bullying me ever since we were children."

"Aye. Had to," the big man agreed, folding his arms across his chest and shaking his bushy head. He turned to Blaine. "Ye see, it was the only way we crofters could keep the little lord of the manor in line."

Blaine tilted her head to one side, studying Garrath. Had he been a stuck-up little boy, impressed by his family's wealth? Somehow she found that hard to believe. He could be arrogant, certainly, but not in that way. His arrogance, his power and his authority came from his capabilities, not his family fortune.

Alex proved her deduction. "Aye, he just never would stay in his place. Always wanted to be just one of the lads. Why it was well nigh impossible to keep him from movin' in with me family. My job was cut out for me, that's for dear sure. Do ye mind the time, Garrath, when ye gave away all yer fancy bought clothes and insisted ye wouldna wear anything but me mum's homespun shirts?"

Alex continued his tales of Garrath's boyhood to Blaine's enjoyment and Garrath's discomfort until the kettle was empty and there was nothing left of the bread but a few crumbs. But over second cups of tea he changed the subject to one that caused Garrath more than a little discomfort.

"By-the-by, have Janet and Andy set the date yet?" Alex asked. "I'm expectin' an invitation to the weddin', ye know."

Garrath was suddenly sitting bolt upright in his chair. "Wedding? When did you see them? Were they really talking about getting married?"

Alex took time to pull at his red beard thoughtfully, and Blaine thought she detected an almost mischievous twinkle in his blue eyes. "Weel, no, not exactly," he answered at last. "They were in here a few weeks back for lunch, and we had a nice long chat. I liked the lad fine, and it was obvious Janet did, too, so I assumed. . . ."

"Wrong!" Garrath declared, sinking back in his chair. "There's no date to be set. Not between those two."

"An' why not? Anyone wi' two eyes can be seein' they're well-suited and verra much in love."

Garrath shook his head. "Janet is simply infatuated and Andy Walker is just a—" He broke off, scowling, and left the sentence unfinished, beginning again. "They are not getting married."

"Hmm," Alex tempered his disbelief with a good-natured smile.

But Blaine wasn't smiling, and she couldn't resist commenting. "I don't see how you can be so sure of that," she said. "Or why you think you have any right to try and tell Janet who to love."

"I'm sure, and I have the right because I'm her brother. She'll do as I say," Garrath snapped, glaring at Blaine.

She glared right back. This was the old autocratic Garrath St. Clair, the one who arranged other people's lives, who gave orders and expected others to jump. Who was arrogant, presumptuous and dictatorial; the one she disliked so intensely.

She was just gearing up to tell him so when Alex intervened. Ignoring the suddenly black moods of his two guests, he gently eased the conversation into new channels, talking of friends he and Garrath had in common and relating funny anecdotes about life as a pub owner. When their cups were empty there was another less caustic disagreement as Garrath asked for the check. The big man started shaking his head, but Garrath put a hand on his shoulder.

"Alex, I had your word last time," he reminded gruffly. "Now, no arguing. The check, please."

"But it dinna seem right, not when it's yer siller that got me started here. Why, I wouldna have the place if not for you."

"It wasn't my money," Garrath denied hurriedly. "Your deal was with the corporation, strictly business. And this is your business. Please, Alex."

Despite much head shaking Alex gave in and Garrath quickly changed the subject. Very quickly, Blaine thought curiously.

When they were ready to leave, Blaine found herself enveloped in one of Alex's great bear hugs. "Ye're a bonnie wee thing, aren't ye, lass?" he said, and heat scorched her cheeks.

Alex's grin split his beard. He turned to Garrath. "Mind now, dinna let this one get away, mon, do ye hear? Why, the sweet thing even blushes."

Blaine couldn't help giving even more vivid testimony to the truth of Alexander's statement as she tried desperately to think of some witty sophisticated response, something to show she didn't take the comment at all seriously. But it was Garrath who supplied it.

"I won't, Alex," he said easily, lightly, leading Blaine to the door.

It meant nothing, of course. It was just the right kind of reply to Alex's teasing. But Blaine had the sudden desperate urge to pull free of the hand on her arm and go running down Edinburgh's narrow streets in any direction that would take her away from Garrath. Because just for a moment, for one single insane moment, she'd wished that he meant the offhand remark. And that was all wrong. All very, very wrong.

CHAPTER TWELVE

BLAINE HAD LOST HER TASTE for the "tour," but Garrath insisted she see Edinburgh Castle. She relented for lack of a good excuse to refuse, but her mood didn't improve within the castle's dark walls.

Moving back through time had been pleasant in the gardens and Old Town. But there was almost too much history in the castle's blackened stones, and much of it tragic. The Witches' Well marked the spot where more than three hundred witches were burned to death between 1479 and 1722. The Crown Room displayed the beautiful Scottish regalia, including golden crown, scepter and sword, but even these spoke of Scotland's long unsuccessful struggle to remain independent from England. The Scottish National War Memorial, with every type of war service depicted in bronze and stained glass, was impressive and designed to inspire pride, but it was a pride tinged with the tragedy of war.

What affected Blaine most strongly was the incredibly tiny room where the ill-fated Mary, queen of Scots, gave birth to James VI. Poor misguided Mary, whose heart had often overruled her head. *And look what happened to her,* Blaine thought grimly.

From the castle ramparts they saw that the clouds had thickened darkly. A bitterly cold wind hurtled up the steep slope of the Royal Mile.

"I think we'd best go," Garrath said, his eyes on the sky. "We may be caught in the rain as it is. Shall I try to get a cab or are you willing to risk it?"

Blaine agreed to gamble, and Garrath guided her down from the Castle Rock and into a section of elegantly pedimented and pilastered buildings set along the spacious tree-lined streets of the New Town. The clean formal lines of the Georgian architecture were reflected in the surroundings. Dried fall leaves were the only litter on the sidewalks; brass knobs and door knockers gleamed; steps were immaculate and surely always had been. No one would ever have dared empty a chamber pot from a window dignified by marble garlands and classical columns.

The gamble didn't pay off, though Blaine didn't realize what was happening at first. It began as the finest of mists, barely noticeable except against warm cheeks and hands. But it didn't stay fine. It thickened until the mist became drops and the drops became rain. And finally the rain became a downpour just one minute before Garrath guided her up the wide steps of a building of honey-colored stone.

Nothing so pedestrian as a sign identified the occupants of the building. Exquisitely designed stained glass filling the fanlight over the large front door handled that job. The "spokes" of the fan encompassed all shades of blue from the deepest cobalt to cerulean. And boldly prancing on this field of blue was the white unicorn, the medallion around its neck this time inscribed simply, "St. Clair."

"Like it?" Garrath asked from beside her.

Blaine nodded, impressed. "Very much. But I didn't realize we would be coming directly here to work. I'm not really dressed for this and with the rain...." She pushed strands of damp hair back from her face.

"You're fine," Garrath assured her. "Besides, we're not going to work. I just need to check in with my secretary, see what kind and number of crises are waiting for me, then we'll go back to the house and get settled in."

As he spoke he led her under the watchful eye of the unicorn and into the building's foyer.

"Not going to work? But, Garrath, I want to. I would just like a chance to change first."

Garrath ran a hand through his wet hair, ruffling the black thickness, and his mouth twisted as if he were biting the inside of his cheek. "Well, Blaine, there's something I ought to explain about the job...."

But he didn't explain, for at that moment they were discovered. Or rather Garrath was, and suddenly it seemed that hundreds of people swarmed around, nodding, smiling, welcoming. Blaine watched the faces, young and old, male and female, and could find nothing but honest warmth and respect in them. Like Andy, these employees loved their boss.

A few glances came her way as well, subtly curious and appraising. Blaine smiled, but her chin came up defiantly as she assumed her most professional air, one that had never failed to put a business associate in his or her place—except once, with the man now standing beside her.

Garrath either didn't notice or didn't care about satisfying the curiosity of his employees by introducing her and explaining what she had come to do. He led her through the tide of greetings to the polished-wood door of an elevator without a word, his hand never leaving her elbow, almost as if he feared she might bolt if given half a chance.

Stepping into the interior of the elevator was like being closed into an antique cupboard. But this cupboard rose smoothly and silently, proving that its machinery was completely modern. In seconds they were at the top of the building. The door opened automatically.

"Good afternoon, Mr. St. Clair," purred a sultry voice, the perfect complement to the dark curvaceous beauty of the woman before them.

"Diana," Garrath said. Just her name and a smile. Blaine felt as if someone had just poked her sharply in the ribs.

Then, "This is Blaine Christensen from Computec. Diana Mills, my secretary."

"Pleased to meet you, Ms. Christensen," the woman said formally, and dipped her head in a slight nod that brought a wave of silky sable brown hair forward across one artistically rouged cheekbone. Casually she reached a long red-lacquered fingernail up to brush the shoulder-length strands back into place.

Blaine made the appropriate response while inwardly cursing Garrath St. Clair. She felt like the country bumpkin come to the big city.

When she had arrived in Aberdeen dressed for an office meeting, Garrath had sent her to an oil rig. Now, drenched and wearing travel-weary slacks, a simple wool sweater over an oxford cloth blouse, warm knee socks and rubber-soled shoes, he took her to an office that looked like a classical monument and introduced her to a creature right out of the pages of *Vogue* magazine. She wanted a brush, a towel, dry clothes and her high heels!

Diana Mills was model tall and slender, except where slenderness was not an asset. Her black silk blouse was unbuttoned far enough to let any interested party be well assured of that fact, and just in case the point hadn't been taken, two dainty gold chains at her neck guided the eye down to the plentiful cleavage.

And, Blaine thought with a sigh, it was entirely possible that some people might need that extra guidance. They might be caught by the full lips and eyes lushly lashed and effectively shadowed to highlight their unusual shade, a dark dusky gray, like smoke.

"Was there some problem, Mr. St. Clair?" Diana asked silkily. "We expected you several hours ago."

"No problem," Garrath answered quickly. "I just gave Blaine a little tour around the city."

"I see," the secretary stated properly, impersonally. But her eyes slid sideways to Blaine, to Garrath's hand still resting on Blaine's arm, and they were no longer the color of smoke. This gray held the glint of cold tempered steel.

Garrath dropped his hand. Because of Diana's look, Blaine wondered?

"What have we got lined up?" Garrath asked his secretary, starting briskly down the hall. Diana glided smoothly into place beside him, flipping open a stenographer's notebook and beginning to list names and messages. Blaine was left to follow along behind.

Garrath dealt swiftly with each item mentioned, Diana taking note of his instructions as they walked. "Let Thomas deal with that." "Janet can handle him." "Set up an appointment." "Say yes in an appropriate letter." "No."

The pace didn't slow, not even when Garrath flung open the door to his office and tossed his briefcase and jacket onto a tufted brown leather couch. He seemed to have forgotten Blaine completely as he moved behind his massive oak desk and settled into a high-backed chair, his attention already on the next item on Diana's list. Or, Blaine thought nastily as she stood unnoticed in the doorway, perhaps just on Diana.

Attracting his attention certainly seemed to be Diana's goal. She was leaning over Garrath, letting her breast brush against his arm as she pointed out something on a piece of paper he held. Her face was close to his and she was speaking in a low airy voice. Her hand rested proprietarily on his arm, her bright red fingernails garish against the muted rust of his three-button pullover sweater. And Garrath wasn't objecting to any of it.

Disgusted, Blaine plopped down on the couch, sinking into leather luxury beside the abandoned briefcase and jacket. *Excess baggage, anyone?* she muttered to herself, unaware that she was absently stroking the soft shearling collar of Garrath's jacket.

Garrath's office was a striking combination of old and new. His desk and chair had the rich golden glow and solidarity of genuine antiques. Across one wall stretched the quiet jeweled colors of a tapestry depicting rolling green hills, a small turquoise lake and slanting rays of sunshine breaking through a clouded sky. In the opposite wall were set twin wooden panels, the type that usually opened to reveal a bar unit alcove. These, too, looked like antiques, though they were appropriately carved with matching unicorns rampant on a field of flowers.

But blended perfectly in with these elegant touches of an earlier age, complementing them in fact, were modern comforts—the contemporary contours of the couch, the thick, deep plush of champagne-colored carpet and a wide sweep of glass that the building's original architect couldn't have dreamed possible.

Perhaps it was the view exposed by that very modern plate-glass window that tied the old and new together, for it was part of both ages, then and now. The castle on the Rock and the turrets, gables and towers of the Royal Mile looming against a backdrop of pewter sky were ageless, forever.

But even that awe-inspiring panorama couldn't keep Blaine's eyes from Garrath. She looked at him behind the old desk and tried to imagine him as Miles Ramsey had described him at their first meeting—a scared kid trying to fit into his father's chair.

Was it the same chair, she wondered? Most young men coming into such a difficult situation would probably have redecorated, tossing out all reminders of their predecessor. But not Garrath, she realized. He would have kept things the same, precisely to preserve the reminder of what he had to live up to—and surpass.

And he'd succeeded. He certainly filled the chair now.

She was still watching Garrath when a flash of red caught her eye. Diana had raised a hand to brush at a sweep of dark hair, and when Blaine followed the movement she found herself fixed by Diana's steely look, a glare that shifted derisively from Blaine's face to her hand on Garrath's jacket and back again.

Begin a long love affair with SUPERROMANCE.
Accept *Love beyond Desire,* free. Mail the card
below, today.

SUPERROMANCE
1440 South Priest Drive, Tempe, AZ 85281.

⌐—Mail this card today.

A compelling love story of mystery and intrigue... conflicts and jealousies... and a forbidden love that threatens to shatter the lives of all involved with the aristocratic Lopez family.

Mail this card today for your FREE book.

Postage will be paid by addressee

BUSINESS REPLY CARD

First Class   Permit No. 70   Tempe, AZ

SUPERROMANCE
1440 South Priest Drive
Tempe, Arizona 85281

Blaine snatched her fingers from the silky shearling, and decided she didn't like Garrath's secretary at all.

She couldn't care less if Garrath and his secretary had a relationship out of as well as in the office, and she certainly didn't need Diana's hard-eyed looks to warn her off. Garrath himself, however unintentionally, had accomplished that quite well. But Diana's deliberate flaunting of a private matter was so...so unbusinesslike! Garrath deserved better, she thought, then nearly choked. What was she thinking of? His willingness to mix business and pleasure—at his convenience, of course—had been amply demonstrated! He deserved exactly what he was getting. In fact, Diana and her boss seemed well suited to one another.

"Blaine." Garrath's voice snapped her out of her uncharitable wanderings and she turned to him.

"Yes?"

"It looks like I'm going to be stuck here for a bit. There are a couple of things that won't wait."

"That's fine. I'd like to get started on the preliminaries of the installation anyway. If you could just tell me where—"

"Not now, Blaine," Garrath interrupted quickly. "Diana can take you to the dining room for a cup of tea or something, and I'll meet you there a little later. Not long, I promise."

"But Garrath, I would rather—"

"Tea is traditional and inescapable in the British Isles," he insisted. "Go with Diana. I'll join you soon."

Tradition or not, Blaine would have protested further if she hadn't noticed the effect Garrath's instructions were having on Diana. There was a tinge of green beneath her carefully applied makeup, and her eyes had narrowed into sharp-edged arrows of outrage. Anything that outraged Miss Diana Mills couldn't be all bad.

Blaine smiled sweetly. "Fine. Shall we, Diana?"

BLAINE SPREAD ANOTHER FEATHER LIGHT SCONE with orange marmalade and her taste buds tingled with anticipation. At least some part of her was enjoying itself, she thought wryly.

Although she had been certain she couldn't eat a bite so soon after lunch, the array of scones, biscuits, cakes and pies in addition to the carefully brewed tea soon changed her mind. The food, and almost everything else in the St. Clair Corporation dining room, was heavenly. The tables were spaciously arranged, the decor eye-pleasing in blue and gold. And smiling waiters hovered attentively over their patrons like a cadre of punctilious Scottish butlers straight out of an old-fashioned murder mystery. Only one thing ruined what should have been an extremely pleasurable experience—the company.

She and Diana had been verbally sparring since they'd been seated at an elegant table near the window and Diana had begun what Blaine now thought of as the Inquisition. Diana wanted information, but the tone of her very first question raised hackles Blaine hadn't realized she possessed and made her determined not to give away a thing.

"You look so young and inexperienced," Diana had purred as the china teapot and an extra pot of boiling water were placed in front of them. "Have you worked for Computec long?"

"Long enough," Blaine shot back curtly, fiercely

repressing the urge to raise a hand to her damp drooping hair.

"Computer work has always struck me as so cold and clinical, and if you'll forgive me, unfeminine."

"Really?" Blaine gritted out a smile. "It isn't unfeminine at all, of course, not for a woman who has the intelligence to handle it. And as for cold—well, a job can't be cold when you meet fascinating people like Garrath." The battle lines were drawn.

It had continued throughout the tea, which Blaine decided was otherwise a very civilized tradition.

"I imagine you'll be glad when you can go home. I know it must be lonely, not knowing anyone in a foreign country, feeling so different, so...out of place," Diana said, a twist of her full lips indicating exactly how out of place she thought Blaine was.

"Oh, I'm in no hurry," Blaine lied. "Janet St. Clair asked me to visit Glenclair, and I may take her up on the invitation. Somehow she and Garrath have made me feel right at home." She paused, letting the knife sink in deeper. "You do know Garrath's sister, Janet, don't you?"

But though Blaine was holding her own against Diana's increasingly sharp barbs, it wasn't any fun, and the worst part was that she didn't understand why she was doing it. Why was she bothering to exchange digs with the woman? They sounded like two dogs growling over one bone, and Blaine certainly had no interest in the bone in this case. Why didn't she just mention Richard and set Diana's unfounded suspicions to rest?

"It must be nice to have a job where it doesn't matter what you wear," Diana said silkily, letting her eyes travel disdainfully over Blaine's decidedly worse-for-wear sweater.

That was why, Blaine sighed to herself. "Yes, Garrath doesn't seem at all interested in the outer trappings, does he?"

An angry flush spread across Diana's cheeks and Blaine guessed that the sparring was over. The war was about to begin.

"Let me give you a word of advice, Miss Christensen," Diana said sharply. "I couldn't help noticing the way you were mooning over Mr. St. Clair, and I think I should warn you that even if some casual... flirting went on out on Sithein One under the romantic star-filled sky and Garrath has convinced you to continue the...affair awhile longer on land, don't take it seriously. I've been with him several years now and have seen numerous women come and go, usually with broken hearts. Garrath is like most men, willing to take what's available, but he isn't ready to settle down yet. And when he is he'll choose someone who understands and shares his work, his tastes, his temperament."

"And I suppose you think that someone will be you?" Blaine queried coolly, telling herself how grateful she was that all this nonsense didn't mean a thing to her. What would she be feeling if she really cared for Garrath?

"I think so, yes," Diana replied.

The waiter chose that moment to bring a fresh pot of tea. But in spite of the tantalizing aroma of the steaming brew, Blaine only pushed her spoon around the circle of her cup.

"Congratulations, then, Ms. Mills," she said flatly. "You and Garrath St. Clair seem perfectly matched. But you're way off base with your assumptions about me. I'm here to do a job and that's all there is to it."

"What job?"

"Installing a Computec linking system in Garrath's office. The moment that's done I'll be on my way, completely heart-whole."

Diana's upper lip curled. "If you want to keep the real reason you're here a secret, my dear, you'd better come up with something better than that. Perhaps you don't care; I understand Americans are very loose about things like this. But if you do, you can't just—"

"What are you talking about?" Blaine demanded. This was really getting out of hand. "I don't need to come up with anything better. I've told you the reason I'm here."

"To set up a Computec link in Garrath's office?" Diana asked scornfully.

"Yes," Blaine nodded, the motion beginning firmly but ending a bit hesitantly in the face of Diana's mocking disbelief.

"Then what is Garrath planning on doing with the one already there?"

Blaine's spoon dropped onto the saucer with a plaintive little plink. "I...didn't see it."

"But you did see the unicorn panels on one wall?" Diana waited for Blaine's weak nod. "A complete computer system was installed in a small room behind the panels months ago, including your Computec link."

"But I...he told me...I don't understand..." Blaine faltered.

"Don't you, Miss Christensen?" Diana sneered.

"Then you must be even more of an innocent than you appear."

Blaine didn't have a chance to reply to that. Her mind was still blank with the shock of Diana's disclosure when Garrath appeared at their table.

"Are you two enjoying yourselves?" he asked cheerily.

"Certainly," Diana replied. Her eyes were on Blaine, daring her to challenge Garrath about the job now, in front of her. "It's been very...amusing."

The woman rose smoothly to her feet and listened intently, her head cocked flatteringly to one side as Garrath gave her a few more instructions.

"Call me at Rose Crescent if there's any problem with the latter," he said. "Otherwise I'll see you tomorrow morning at ten."

"Fine," Diana agreed briskly, efficiently. "It was nice talking to you, Miss Christensen," she added smugly. Turning on one spiky high heel she was gone, without waiting for a reply.

CHAPTER THIRTEEN

BLAINE WAS GRATEFUL FOR THE DISTRACTION of the taxi driver, who seemed intent on airing all his Scottish Nationalist Party views indiscriminately of whether or not his passengers were interested. "Dinna ye agree?" he would demand after each of his proclamations, never waiting for an answer. But when he declared, "Scotland's oil should be for Scotland, not England! Dinna ye agree?" Garrath's voice overrode the beginning of his next tirade.

"No, I don't. We're one country and claims like that are irresponsible and impractical. What Scotland deserves from her oil is support-industry development and the jobs that that creates. Jobs are what Scotland needs most, so that our people don't have to leave Scotland to find work, and oil is already bringing us that."

"But dinna ye care about preservin' Scotland's heritage?" the driver squawked.

"Certainly I do. But not to the point of squabbling like children over what belongs to whom and dividing our country. There's a lot to the old saying, 'Divide and conquer.'"

At some other time Blaine might have joined the discussion, firmly on Garrath's side. But she knew that if she opened her mouth now the words that came out would have nothing to do with politics.

"Rose Crescent," a somewhat more subdued driver mumbled a few moments later, and Garrath indicated a narrow two-story stone house that in no way resembled a hotel. By the time Garrath helped her out of the cab Blaine was ready to burst.

"Where are we now?" she demanded, yanking her arm from his grasp so violently she felt something pull in her shoulder.

For once she had caught him off guard. "My... well, this is the house I keep here in the city. Edinburgh hotels do a thriving business, so much so that it's often difficult to get a room on short notice. This is more convenient."

"I'll just bet it is!"

"And what do you mean by that?" Surprise grew into a scowl.

"I mean that I can just imagine what your house is so convenient for. And I don't want any part of it, not your house or your so-called job."

"I don't know what's got into you, Blaine. And I don't intend to stand out here on the curb and argue." He grabbed her arm again. "If you have something to say, let's say it inside."

Blaine had to run to keep up with Garrath's angry pace as he manhandled her through the front garden. Well, naive young things were supposed to be led down the garden path, weren't they, Blaine thought derisively. And she certainly seemed to qualify for that label now. She'd been a complete fool, accepting Garrath's commands with little protest and less thought.

He jabbed a key into the lock on the door and propelled her into a paneled hallway, where their suitcases stood side by side. Then they were in a high-ceilinged living room and she was being pushed into an overstuffed armchair. Furiously she bounced back up, but Garrath's hands were immediately on her shoulders, forcing her down again.

"Stay there while I get a fire started!" he warned as she tensed to do just the opposite.

"Don't bother on my account. I'm not staying," she snapped. He ignored her, striking a match and tossing it into the already-laid kindling in the fireplace. When the flames were licking hungrily at the wood, he turned back to her, his eyes blazing brighter than the fire.

"Now, start explaining just what you're havering about."

She didn't require a translation of "havering," and was more than happy to oblige. "I'm 'havering' about ending up in Edinburgh instead of Aberdeen. And the computer system you already have in your office and this cozy little arrangement and...and your whole attitude toward women!"

A question mark appeared between Garrath's scowling brows. "What the devil does my attitude toward women have to do with anything?"

"Everything! You assumed I couldn't fix the computer on Sithein One because I was a woman. You wouldn't have let me stay at all if the weather hadn't intervened. It's obvious you think there's only one thing a woman is good for, and so you also assumed I would eagerly accept your pretense of a job in order to come here to your house, where I suppose you imagine I'll be happy to fall into your bed!"

"*If* I wanted you in my bed, I wouldn't resort to

the use of pretenses, Blaine Christensen. And as for the rest of this nonsense, we'll have to take things one at a time." He put a hand on each arm of her chair and leaned ominously over her.

"First, my objections to your presence on Sithein One had nothing—or at least very little—to do with your sex or females in general. What I objected to was one female in particular. You."

"I see," she said, not seeing at all. The word *you* was bouncing around painfully inside her.

"No, you don't see, but you will!" he thundered. She shrank back into her chair, startled by his fury. Seeing her reaction, he shook his head and pushed himself away from her. He jammed his hands into his pockets, and when he spoke his voice was several decibels lower.

"Look, Blaine, on the rig didn't you notice there were several female support-staff crew members aboard? We also have two female roughnecks on the other rotation."

"I did see one girl serving coffee," she admitted. "But no women in higher positions, positions of authority."

"Because right now there aren't any women ready for those positions. This is a new field for women, one just opening its ranks, and contrary to what you seem to believe, it isn't one hordes of women are clamoring to join. Roughnecking is hard dirty dangerous work and very few women want to tackle it. Those who do and can cut it are more than welcome on my rigs, and when they're ready they'll be promoted equally with the men. Ability is what counts with me, not gender."

"But you didn't even give me a chance to prove or disprove my ability," she protested.

"I thought you disproved it the moment I saw you." He paused and lifted broad shoulders in a slight shrug. "The first time I set eyes on you, you looked about as competent as Lolita. I wanted you off Sithein One not because you were a woman, but because I was certain you would be a danger both to yourself and my rig and its workers. A snap judgment I admit, and one I subsequently was forced to revise when other evidence—a talk with your boss and the difference in your appearance the next morning—came to light. But I did revise it. Can you believe that?"

Reluctantly, Blaine nodded. Remembering her arrival on Garrath's rig, she couldn't really blame him for his "snap judgment."

"But what about this job? Diana told me you already have a linking unit in your office here."

"We do. This isn't the office I meant. My private office is in my home, Glenclair. This was just a short detour because I had urgent business to attend to, and the necessary equipment won't reach Glenclair for a few days anyway. But that's where you agreed to install the system."

"Glenclair! I agreed to do an installation, not to go to. . .to wherever in the world Glenclair is, which is just another of the small details you forgot to mention! Garrath, why didn't you tell me all this in the beginning?"

"Why didn't you ask?"

Flippant as his answer was, it pricked the balloon of her anger. Truthfully, she was just as mad at herself as she was at him. She'd made possible any lies of omission he'd committed by not bothering to demand answers to her questions earlier. Desperate to get off Sithein One, she'd accepted his "job offer" without insisting on more information. And so she had agreed to work in the St. Clair ancestral home! A wry smile brushed her lips, and she collapsed back into the soft cushions of the chair.

"I didn't ask because I made the logical assumption that you meant your Aberdeen office—at least until we arrived in Edinburgh," Blaine replied weakly, staring into the fire. "Because I assumed you would have informed me if we were headed somewhere completely different."

Silence rang between them for a moment. It was broken by Garrath yanking a chair around, so that it was facing her. When he sat down, their knees touched.

"I should have told you," he said quietly. "I started to at the office today, but we were interrupted and...I'm sorry."

Blaine stared, and her hands clenched together in her lap. "You're...?"

"Sorry," he filled in the word. "I apologize for the...oversight."

Suddenly she felt exceedingly warm. A lock of black hair had fallen across Garrath's forehead, and she had the crazy impulse to brush it to one side. She'd imagined many possible outcomes of her confronting Garrath with Diana's revelation but not him apologizing. This couldn't be the same arrogant, infuriating man that she'd crossed swords with time and again on Sithein One—and lost. He had explained away his earlier treatment of her; he was apologizing for this latest mix-up. She was losing all her reasons for disliking him. And that could be a very dangerous thing.

"Well, fine, then. I'll get someone else out to handle the installation at Glenclair as soon as possible."

"Someone else? Why not you?"

"Because. . . because I have my own work to do—back in San Francisco. I can't go running all over Scotland. If it was here in Edinburgh, just a matter of a day or so, that would be one thing. But this—I don't have the time."

"Richard said you could take the time," he reminded her.

"Richard was wrong!" she snapped.

Garrath arched an eyebrow. "Are you sure, Blaine? Or are you using work as an excuse, something to hide behind so you won't have to face the truth?"

"What. . . what truth?" she breathed.

"This." He leaned forward, closing the distance between them. He brushed a kiss across her lips.

Just that one light touch, a grazing by live wires. And then he drew back two inches and waited.

Blaine felt like she'd been cut in two and was warring with herself. Her mind was screaming warnings, urging flight. But her body was vibrating with a different message. *Yes, stay, give in, risk it.*

Of their own accord her hands reached up. But whether she intended to push him away or draw his face across the chasm of those two inches, she never discovered. Just before her fingertips would have touched him a shrill ringing shattered the spell.

"Damn!" Garrath muttered, bounding up out of his chair. His footsteps echoed in the hallway and she heard him pick up the phone.

"Yes," he barked.

Moments later he was back in front of her.

"I have to go into the office, Blaine," he said. "Some business I intended to deal with tomorrow can't wait. But it shouldn't take long and we can go to dinner when I get back. In the meantime make yourself at home, choose whichever of the guest rooms upstairs you like best. Okay?"

Blaine nodded.

When he had gone, she stretched suddenly freezing hands out toward the fire. What had she been about to do before the phone stopped her, she asked herself? Listen to logic and reason, or give in to the whirlwind again? And of the two, which would have been the right choice?

"RICHARD? RICHARD? ARE YOU THERE?" she cried into the phone.

"Yes, Blaine. How are you? Is something the matter?"

She took a deep breath and closed her eyes, trying to picture the familiar face and thatch of dun-colored hair that went with the even, almost bland, voice coming over the wire.

"No, I'm fine. I just wanted to talk to you about this job for...St. Clair's."

"I hope nothing's wrong. You know how important that account is."

"Yes, I know. But I was a little curious about why you wanted *me* to install the office linkup. Any technician could handle that."

"I know that and you know that, but St. Clair seemed to expect first-class treatment. He knows you're tops and that's what he wants."

Blaine's knuckles went white on the receiver.

"Anyway," Richard continued, "I'm just as happy to have you there, since he's being so touchy. I know you can take care of any problems, soothe him, set whatever doubts he has to rest.''

"I'd rather not, Richard. He wants the unit at his home somewhere out in the middle of nowhere, and I'd rather not waste my time with this. Can't you arrange for someone else to—''

"Someone else? Of course not. You're already there. I know it's a little below you, but you can certainly do it. And nothing that pleases St. Clair is going to be a waste of time. I thought you understood that.''

"But I . . . I don't really want . . . I have to. . . .''

"Just finish up quickly and get back here, Blaine,'' Richard went on as if he hadn't heard. "I need you.''

"You . . . you need me?'' Blaine clutched at the words.

"Sure. Things have been so hectic around here, you wouldn't believe. A storm in the Gulf nearly destroyed one of our trailers, though the computer kept functioning through the whole mess. We've just got a large order from Shell, who wants the units yesterday, of course, and the latest bunch of trainees seem like they've never seen a computer before in their lives.''

Biting her lip in frustration, Blaine only half heard Richard's rundown of company problems. He wasn't listening to her at all, just as he hadn't listened to her when she'd tried to refuse to come to Scotland in the first place. It was Computec, not Richard, that needed her.

"Richard,'' Blaine tried again, "I don't really think I'm the best one for the job here. Gar . . . Mr. St. Clair wasn't too happy about a woman appearing on his rig in the first place.''

"Yes, so he told me, rather explicitly," Richard said dryly. "But you're not on the rig now."

"Still, he's a very demanding man, and I...I'm just uncomfortable."

"Oh, Blaine, you never did have any confidence in yourself. You do fine with the customers, but you always want to hide away with your machines. Now listen, you just give Garrath St. Clair whatever he wants, finish up and get back here to work. Okay?"

Blaine couldn't say anything for a moment, stunned as she was by Richard's description of her. Is that how he really saw her—as lacking confidence, hiding away with her machines? But she didn't do that, not at all. It was just that she was good with the computers, skilled at what she did; just as he was skilled at public relations. She wasn't hiding!

"Did you hear me, Blaine? Just give St. Clair anything he wants."

Anything, Richard, she thought.

"All right," she said flatly. "Goodbye."

It wasn't until she had dropped the receiver back into its cradle that she realized Richard had said much the same thing Garrath had, though the context had been slightly different. They had both accused her of hiding!

She stared at the telephone as if it had betrayed her. Not only had Richard not given her the out she'd hoped for, he had used the one expression that would trap her yet more securely. She wasn't hiding from anything, of course. True, she had used work to block out the worst of the pain after the deaths of her father, brother and mother. But that was natural. She wasn't hiding from anything now.

But it seemed she was going to have to prove that

to both of them. And there was only one way to do that—by going to Glenclair.

HAVING MADE THE DECISION to see the job through, Blaine felt a relaxation of tension she hadn't known was there. Every muscle in her body seemed to ache, partly, she imagined, from the long walk around Edinburgh, but mostly from the stress of this latest encounter with Garrath.

She decided to take him at his word and make herself at home, starting with a long soak in a hot tub. Upstairs she discovered three bedrooms, as well as a bathroom that was almost large enough to qualify as a fourth. Two of the bedrooms were similar, each furnished with antiques—beds, dressers and wardrobes—and Oriental rugs with fringed edges stretching across wooden floors. The one at the front of the house had the extra touch of a small table and two thin-legged chairs tucked into the alcove of the bay window looking out on the garden.

The third boasted a bed almost twice the size of the others, wide, high and piled deep with quilts. Next to it stood a highboy and an enormous desk that bore the tools of an executive's trade—telephone, pads of paper, a good reading lamp and a comfortable chair. She had no doubt which room was Garrath's.

She put her suitcase in the room at the front of the house—and farthest from his—and unpacked her robe. Then she headed for the tub.

That appliance, like the rest of the bathroom, was oversize and old-fashioned. Big enough for two, she thought, then blushed, pushing the thought away. But everything worked smoothly and perfectly: the water was scaldingly hot, the wall heater took the chill off the room instantly and a large glass jar held bath beads that claimed to smell of heather.

Blaine wrinkled her nose—not at the scent, which was a little like warm honey and very pleasant, but at the unbidden question of for whom the bath beads were supplied. Certainly not Garrath. But in direct challenge to the twinge of annoyance she felt, she liberally sprinkled the beads into the water before sinking into the lavender depths.

She didn't climb out until the tips of her fingers and pads of her toes were pink raisins. The warm water had soaked away the last of her tension, and she was humming as she wrapped herself in her robe.

As she tried to decide what to wear to the dinner Garrath had mentioned, the limited contents of her suitcase made her long again for the outfit, complete with cape, that she had seen in the shop window that afternoon. It would have been perfect whether Garrath was planning something elegant, in one of the posh hotels on Princes Street perhaps, or something cozy and atmospheric, somewhere like Alex Duncan's Thistledown. Both suddenly appealed very strongly to her.

She was still rummaging in her suitcase when the phone jangled imperiously. She dashed into Garrath's room and caught it on the second ring. Her "hello" was breathless.

"Blaine?" It wasn't the voice she'd expected.

"Yes, Diana. Garrath's not here."

The woman's laugh was a fingernail scratching across the blackboard of Blaine's mind.

"Oh, I know that. He's here, with me. He asked me to call and let you know he won't be coming home for some time. We're still quite...involved.

He suggested you might want to call a cab to take you to one of the hotels for dinner, or you're welcome to raid the pantry. And don't bother to wait up for him.''

''Fine,'' she replied curtly, but there was no one on the other end to hear her. Disgusted, she hung up with a force that made the phone's bell ring once in protest.

Not that Diana's far from subtle insinuations bothered her. She didn't believe what Diana so wanted her to, that she and Garrath were together for reasons other than business. It was only natural for Garrath to have his secretary with him when he was working. If she *had* believed they were mixing business and pleasure, she wouldn't have cared. But she didn't believe it.

She didn't believe it as she flipped the lid of her suitcase closed. She suddenly had no appetite for dinner in one of Edinburgh's hotels. Her robe would be fine for raiding the pantry—alone.

She didn't believe it when she scouted out the pantry and refrigerator that someone had lavishly stocked, or while she fixed herself an omelet from fresh eggs, milk and scallions, spending an unusual length of time beating the mixture. She ate the very fluffy result with part of a loaf of dark brown bread spread with rich creamy butter.

She didn't really believe it when she took a pad and pen up to her room and curled beneath the quilts on the bed. She started a list of things to check with Garrath to make sure the installation at Glenclair would proceed smoothly—and quickly. Did he want a ''smart'' or ''dumb'' terminal there; one with an independent ''brain'' or one that would primarily receive information from other computers? Was the telephone system needed for the modem—a special type of phone that would allow Garrath's individual computer to "talk" to the main computers both in his offices and on the rigs—already installed?

The list took longer than she would have expected, since it was a job she could have done in her sleep. But for some reason her mind refused to concentrate on work and kept asking her what time it was now.

She didn't believe Diana's insinuations at ten o'clock, nor even at eleven.

But at one-thirty, when she turned out the light and burrowed under the quilts, she had to remind herself that even if she did believe Garrath and Diana were *together* instead of *working together*, she wouldn't care. Because believe it she did.

THE TAPPING OF FOOTSTEPS ON THE FLAGSTONE WALK brought Blaine instantly awake, as if she'd been programmed to respond to just that sound. Goose bumps rose on her skin as she sat up and the mountain of quilts slipped away. Shivering in the frigid air, she pulled the topmost quilt from the bed and wrapped it around herself before padding to the window.

She pushed aside the heavy velvet curtain and peered out through the lace sheer. It was barely morning. A light drizzle fell from leaden skies, silvering the plants in the garden, the street, the horse and cart that stood just in front of the gate.

The milkman walked back down the front path, his load of empty bottles clinking musically in a wire carrier. Exchanging empties for three full ones, he patted the horse on the neck and headed toward the next house in the crescent. The horse nodded its long narrow head up and down as if saying, "Yes, I understand," and clip-clopped along behind the man, stopping when he turned up the next walkway.

Blaine smiled, glad she had awakened in time to see this charming bit of old-worldliness, even if her toes were curling with the cold. But just as she was about to make a dash back to the warmth of her bed, she saw something else that was definitely not old-world or charming.

Turning into the crescent was a sleek blue sports car. It purred its way slowly up the street and into the drive, blinking its windshield-wiper eyes.

She let the drapery fall back into place and crawled back into bed. Not just her feet were cold now. She glanced at the clock that affirmed what the dawn sky had already told her. Five-fifty; early morning. And Garrath St. Clair was just coming home.

Diana's brittle laughter seemed to fill the room. Blaine pulled the quilts tight around her body and hugged a pillow to her chest.

CHAPTER FOURTEEN

"RISE AND SHINE, princess," whispered a voice that fitted perfectly into the very pleasant dream Blaine was having. But the warm breath against her ear was reality enough to yank her abruptly from sleep.

"Garrath!" she named the face bending so close above her own. He smiled.

"The same," he said. "Were you expecting someone else?" His eyes dropped pointedly to her bare shoulder showing above the quilts.

Blaine flushed and clutched a quilt to her in a grip that whitened her knuckles, thanking her guardian angel that at least it hadn't been one of those nights when she had tossed and turned and kicked off all the covers.

"Haven't you ever heard of knocking?" she rasped out.

Garrath held up three fingers, nodding.

"You did...three times?" Blaine asked, wondering how she could have slept through even one of his typical raps on a door and still have come instantly awake at his whispered words.

"Three times," he affirmed. "And breakfast was getting cold."

"Breakfast?" She wriggled to the far edge of the bed and sat up, using two hands to anchor her covering up under her chin. Garrath waved a hand toward the small table in the alcove of the front window, now set for two.

He had pulled back the draperies—another thing she hadn't heard—and golden sunlight spilled through the lace sheers in delicate patterns, touching on silver dishes, white china plates that glistened like pearls and slender stemmed goblets with rainbows in their glass. And in a cut crystal vase next to one of the places was a single rose of a blushing pink—the very color she felt suffusing her cheeks.

"Come on," he called, moving to the table. "Before it gets cold and my great efforts go for naught."

"Your efforts? You mean you fixed breakfast?"

He nodded, his back to her. "Certainly. Bachelors develop all sorts of unusual skills, of which cooking is one of my best."

She could just imagine what some of those other bachelor "skills" were, Blaine thought, biting her lip. The kind that kept a man out all night, for instance.

"What time is it?"

"Just gone seven. I would have let you sleep a little longer, but I'm a bit anxious to get started."

"Started?" Why was everything she said coming out as an inane echo?

"For Glenclair." He lifted the lid from one of the silver dishes and the siren scent of bacon filled the air. "All's ready, and the chef does not like to be kept waiting. Do you need help getting free of those quilts?"

"No!"

He still had his back to her, his head bent over his chefly tasks, but his amused chuckle was clearly audible. "Well, then. . . ." He let the threat hang.

With an exasperated snort Blaine gave up. He obviously wasn't going to be a gentleman and leave the room to give her a chance to dress. But then what kind of gentleman returned home at five-fifty from his "business" with one woman and brought breakfast into the bedroom of another? The same kind who would make good his "offer" to help her get up!

Clutching her quilt she edged to the foot of the bed and reached for her robe. Keeping one eye on Garrath's back, she awkwardly struggled into it while managing to hold onto the patchwork shield until it was no longer necessary.

Her floor-length robe was her one packing extravagance. Of thick white velour sewn in vertical strips to simulate ermine, with a luxuriously large collar and wide princess sleeves, the room it took in a suitcase would have held two more complete outfits. But Blaine had gladly sacrificed the outfits to have the sensuous comfort of the robe.

Covered from neck to toe she slid out of the bed. Garrath turned to look at her, and all she could think of was that there was nothing beneath the robe—and that he knew it.

But the smell of bacon had done its work, and she was soon taking the chair Garrath gallantly held for her, only her high color betraying her discomfort.

"This is by way of apology for reneging on my dinner invitation last night," he said when she was settled and he was sitting opposite her. "I'm truly sorry, Blaine. The problem with the new production company we've set up near Invergarry turned out to be more serious than I thought it would be, and it was necessary that I get the whole mess straightened out right away. But the bonus is that as of this morning, we're free. We can leave for Glenclair.'' He paused and stared intently into her eyes. ''That is, if you're still willing to go?''

Free, she repeated silently. He might be free, but she was not, she thought, not while both he and Richard would interpret her refusal to go to Glenclair as a sign of weakness. But she couldn't help being pleased that he had asked instead of ordering this time.

''I'll go,'' she said simply. ''When should I be ready?''

They settled on forty-five minutes after breakfast. ''Now dig in,'' he said.

Blaine didn't need any more encouragement, especially not after her first bite. Garrath hadn't exaggerated his culinary talents. The eggs scrambled with bits of tomato and herbs were cloud light. The bacon was crisped to perfection. There were even hot muffins to spread with rich butter and thick orange marmalade. And the champagne-spiked orange juice made everything else taste twice as marvelous.

She looked at him as she sipped from the glass. Cooking and serving an elegant breakfast was not a side of him she would have expected. Sometimes he reminded her of the Russian nesting dolls, where a different one appears every time the outer shell is removed. She was beginning to want very badly to know exactly what was at the core.

The other thing that surprised her was his appearance. He certainly didn't look like a man who had spent very little time in his own bed the night before. He was dressed in a green and gray Fair Isle sweater over a shirt of darker green, and suede slacks molded his hips and legs tightly. His brown eyes were bright and his smile was hearty and cheerful. She, on the other hand, felt like she'd spent the night at hard labor. It wasn't fair.

"You still haven't told me where Glenclair is," she said, her eyes lowered to concentrate on the buttering of another muffin.

"Over the sea to Skye," he intoned.

Blaine tried to dredge a map of Scotland out of memory, without success. She knew Skye was an island off the coast somewhere, and that it had figured romantically in Scottish history somehow. But that was all she knew.

"Will. . .will Janet be there?" she asked, and her voice betrayed her by wavering.

Garrath grinned. "Yes. As will Mr. and Mrs. MacGuigan, the couple that 'does' for us and has been doing so since I was a tot. Charlie is ground-keeper and general handyman. Mrs. M. started as my nanny, then Janet's, and then was mother to both of us when we needed one. Now she's housekeeper, cook and chaperon when necessary."

Blaine blushed. He let her suffer a bit and then changed the subject. "I'd also like to stop briefly at the company whose problems I was working on all night, if you don't mind a slight detour."

"I don't mind," she replied, but she was thinking of the first part of his comment. This was his second mention of how he'd spent his night. Could he actually have been working on business until early morning? Not that it made any difference, but could Diana's insinuations have been as groundless as she had at first thought?

"What kind of company is it?"

"Fledgling computer chip production," he answered, and Blaine looked her surprise. He nodded. "There's a lot of electronics-type development in Scotland, mostly around the already industrialized areas like Glasgow. What we're doing is starting small-scale businesses in outlying areas so the people can get jobs without having to leave their towns and villages."

"But is that profitable?" She hadn't been listening to Richard's business speeches for so long without picking up a few things, and one of his major precepts was that bigger was better.

"Not the way some other areas are. But profitable enough. For years and years Scotland has been without enough jobs to hold people here, especially the young ones. There's a sad saying that Scotland's primary export is her people. And a country's people are her most valuable natural resource. This is just one way of conserving that resource."

"And is that the reason you set Alex Duncan up in business?"

"St. Clair Corporation *invested* in Alex's business for the same reason, yes," Garrath said sharply. But Blaine could tell the sharpness came from a touch of the same embarrassment she had sensed in him when Alex had mentioned the situation in the restaurant. And just as he had done before, he quickly put an end to that line of conversation, this time by pushing back his chair with a suddenness that made the thin legs squeak.

"Well, I have a few things to do before we leave," he said, striding toward the door without looking at her again. "Let me know when you're ready."

Blaine agreed with a smile. It was highly enjoyable

to see Garrath St. Clair flustered for once. She smiled
all the way through a second glass of champagned
orange juice.

IT TOOK BLAINE ABOUT HALF AN HOUR to become
accustomed to having the driver—Garrath—on the
"wrong" side of the car, and the car on the "wrong"
side of the road. It took a little bit longer to stop worrying about how very close to him she was forced to
sit because of the miniature dimensions of his sports
car. By then the rat's-nest snarl of traffic in Edinburgh was behind them and she became too absorbed
by the constantly changing Scottish countryside to
think about anything else.

Garrath had given her a large-scale map to follow,
and she soon discovered that the scale was large indeed, especially when it came to the listing of cities.
A name in large bold-faced type might be a very
small city, something the size of a suburb of San
Francisco. Medium bold-face was a town, each with
its Gothic steeple and castle tower. Small was a
village, where mortarless stone walls lined narrower
roads. And regular print represented a few houses
and shops clustered together, usually with their name
proudly displayed on a sign attached to a post or tree.

As they moved northwestward, the land changed
from flat verdant farmland to forested passes
through rolling green hills, and finally to wild wind-
swept moors spiked by rows of jagged peaks. The
distances between even the tiny names on the map
grew. Time lost its rigid forward movement in a
world of manor houses and fortified castles, arched
bridges and the remains of a wall of turf and clay
built by the Romans in A.D. 140. It could be anytime;

anything was possible. Even lunch was in the seventeenth century.

That unusual meal, like breakfast, was courtesy of
Garrath St. Clair. Just before one o'clock a narrow
pass took them from the bleak gorse-and-bracken-
covered Moor of Rannoch to the ominous beauty of
Glen Coe. Blaine leaned forward and clutched the
dashboard.

The smooth green velvet of a flat grassy valley was
crimped at the edges into rolling hills. Over these
brooded ancient mountains, soaring slopes and
jagged rocky peaks split by deep ravines. Gray-lined
clouds shrouded the slate-blue tops of the mountains
in secrecy. It wasn't the kind of beauty to exclaim
over; this took your breath away violently, so there
was a moment of panic and pain before you were
able to gasp air again. And in that moment lay the
essence of Glen Coe.

But Blaine didn't immediately realize that. All she
knew at first was that Garrath had stopped the car
and announced "Lunchtime," and she couldn't see
the slightest sign of habitation that might indicate a
possibility of lunch. But Garrath climbed out of the
car and pulled a canvas rucksack from the back.
Hefting the bulging pack over his shoulders, he in-
structed her to follow him.

A half-mile walk through mist-wet grassland
brought them to an energetically burbling stream.
Blaine glanced back to where they'd left the car. Both
it and the road were gone. They were totally alone.

A large flat rock overhanging the stream provided
the perfect table, and Garrath provided rolls, boiled
ham, hunks of cheese, olives, carrots, pickles and a
bottle of wine. As Blaine took her first bites of

potato flour roll and cheddar cheese, she felt it could be any fall day since the beginning of time. But Garrath placed them in the seventeenth century by beginning the story of the massacre of the MacDonalds by the Campbells in that century, the event that had given Glen Coe its second name, the Glen of Weeping.

It was the cold snowy winter of 1692 that the vile deed happened, one not so much viler than many of the deeds done by the untamed Highland clans of that period, but remembered chiefly because of its special infamy. The Campbells had visited the MacDonalds, accepting their hospitality for nearly two weeks before rising in the cold predawn to slaughter their hosts.

"Picture the passes filled with snow, the bitterness of the cold, the shock of waking to the unexpected attack," Garrath suggested, and it seemed to Blaine that the day darkened, the wind grew chillier and heavy with a hundred cries. "But the passes were the MacDonalds' only hope. Some died of exposure, but over a hundred of them escaped over the mountains, leaving behind the forty or so who died here in the glen."

"But why did the Campbells do it?" Blaine asked, and Garrath explained the politics of the time.

"Many of the clans had not willingly accepted William III in the place of James VII as monarch of England and Scotland, and William had demanded oaths of allegiance. When the Chief of the MacDonalds was late in swearing, Sir John Dalrymple, Master of Stair, decided to make an example of this troublesome clan—by exterminating them. Their hereditary enemies, the Campbells, were glad to take on the actual task."

He paused, and his gaze swept the rough wild scenery. "It wasn't the only time an extermination of the Highlanders was tried, by any means. Scotland's history is one of resistance against invasion and conquest by England. We paid the price for that resistance over and over again, but we always survived."

There was pride in his voice, as if he were speaking for all those centuries of men and women who had lived and loved and fought and died on the hard harsh land. And Blaine, seeing him against the dramatic background of Glen Coe, thought she'd just moved quite a bit closer to Garrath's core.

"You should have been a teacher, Garrath," she said around a thick slice of cheese.

"Is that your subtle way of telling me I'm talking too much?"

"Oh, no!" she exclaimed. Her smile was impish. "I just hope the test isn't too hard."

Garrath laughed, refilling his cup. He raised the bottle questioningly in her direction.

Blaine shook her head, still picturing him as a teacher, a college professor perhaps. Her comment had devolved into a joke, but the thought had been a serious one. He would make an excellent teacher. His classes would be wall to wall with nubile young girls suffering from severe infatuation with "the devastatingly handsome Dr. St. Clair," of course. But she would bet he'd have more than a few of them switching to history majors by the end of one term, and not because of his looks, either.

He certainly made her fervently wish she'd studied more history in school. She'd taken the required classes and passed easily because she could memorize dates, names and places with no trouble and regurgitate them back as answers (a), (b) or (c). But when it came to really learning about the past she hadn't been interested, not when there were numbers to manipulate and puzzles to solve in math and science and computer classes.

Or maybe she'd just never had teachers who could spark her interest the way her new teacher was. Or should she say teachers? Garrath was one, with his way of speaking about past centuries as she would speak of last week. Another was Scotland herself, where history seemed to echo in every field, moor, mountain and loch they'd passed since leaving Edinburgh.

When lunch was finished Blaine started packing away the things, but Garrath stopped her.

"Wait, there's one last thing to do." He took some crumbs from the last roll and the remaining wine and put them in a depression in the rock, saying "For the spirits of the glen." And Blaine, who all her life had been practical, logical and disbelieving of anything she couldn't prove by hard cold facts, didn't find this unbelievable at all. She leaned close to Garrath and added a sliver of cheese.

The car and the present were waiting for them at the road. A short time after they left the austere beauty of Glen Coe, Garrath turned off onto a side road that led to an assortment of oddly shaped buildings clustered on the shores of a cascading burn. Several tall smokestacks rose above the peaked roofs of the buildings, but there was no smoke rising from their tops.

"This is Janclair, Inc.," Garrath told her, leading her toward a long line of rectangular buildings placed side by side, sharing their long walls.

"Did you name it for Janet?"

He laughed. "Janet named it for Janet. She came up with the original idea and handled all the preliminaries for getting it started. This is really her baby, so it was her job to christen it."

Blaine was impressed, both with Janet's abilities and with Garrath's allowing her to undertake a project like this. But the latter didn't fit very well with the way he was treating her about Andy. She felt a familiar twinge of annoyance. Why should he assume Janet had a brain for business, but not for love?

The first thing she noticed when Garrath ushered her inside was a strange, almost indescribable smell— earthy, musty, pungent, a little like sherry but stronger. Much stronger. She wrinkled her nose and looked at Garrath.

"Whiskey," he said. "These buildings once housed a distillery making fine Highland malt. There were a lot of small distilleries like this before World War I that were driven out of business when there wasn't any grain available. But the buildings were still standing, and by knocking out a few walls here and adding some there, it makes a perfectly good plant. The workers don't mind the smell at all."

Blaine could understand that. After just seconds inside she was no longer wrinkling her nose but breathing in deeply, the rich scent seeming to warm her veins.

"Don't you get a lot of hyperventilating?" she asked, grinning.

"Only by the new employees. The old-timers have learned to ration themselves."

The outside of the buildings might be old, but inside was the most modern technology money could buy. Janclair, Inc. was clean, efficient and safe, the qualities Garrath seemed to insist on for all his projects. And productive, she discovered when he told her their output and the numbers of orders pouring in.

"I think Janet's baby is going to grow up fine," she commented after they had completed the tour, and Garrath had handled the bit of business that had brought them there. He agreed.

"And best of all, the workers are all locals who won't be forced to Glasgow or south to England, looking for a job. I think it's working out well for them, too."

Blaine concurred. She had seen very happy proud faces during the tour and heard their greetings to Garrath. They liked their work—and him.

Back in the closeness of the car, Blaine glanced sideways at Garrath without turning her head. The chiseled lines of his profile were sharp and stern, the grip of his hands on the steering wheel strong and unwavering. She saw a hard unyielding man.

That was all Blaine had seen at first, that obvious hard and unyielding side. But that wasn't his only side, she was discovering. Others saw him differently. Andy admired him in spite of their one area of disagreement. Janet loved her brother so much she excused his treating her like a child. The workers on the rig, in the Edinburgh office, at Janclair, all seemed not just to respect the boss but to actually like him.

And what about her, she asked herself, her insides somersaulting. Was she, in spite of everything, beginning to like him, too?

She steadfastly refused to answer that question as

they headed back to the Road to the Isles. It took them through a blur of glorious reds, oranges, browns and golds, the multitextured canopy of a mixed forest, before climbing to a wild lonely country studded by small lochs. Then they were descending into the dark defile of Glen Shiel, a narrow cleft between two chains of savage barren mountains, whose serrated ridges slashed across the dark gray sky. And when they were in the shadow of the corrugated hills, it began to rain.

Blaine leaned forward in her seat, enthralled. In the time it took Garrath to switch on the car's windshield wipers, a hundred waterfalls had bloomed in the gullies gouged into the rocky hillsides by past storms. Falls as wide and fine as bridal veils and those as narrow and heavy as white silk streamers foamed against the blackness of the slopes. They drove on for a few minutes with the rain pounding on the roof and mocking the feeble attempts of the wipers to clear the front window, and then Garrath pulled off onto a turnout.

"I think we'll have to wait it out," he said, switching off the engine. The tempo of the rain seemed to increase in triumph.

Blaine shivered. "I'm glad we're in here," she said, staring out through the streaming glass.

"Are you cold?" Without waiting for an answer, Garrath twisted in his seat to reach into the back and pull out a blue and green mohair blanket. "This should help."

He reached across Blaine and tucked a length of the soft material around her far shoulder.

It didn't start out as a caress. Blaine knew that because she felt the precise moment when Garrath's touch stopped being practical. One moment he was simply putting the blanket around her, the next all thought of the blanket was forgotten and it was his hand on her shoulder that mattered—to both of them.

A special kind of silence filled the car. The drumming of the rain was so steady, so rhythmic and so *outside*, that it only served to make the already close space inside seem closer yet, isolated, a place out of time where no normal rules applied. Blaine could no more prevent herself from turning to Garrath than she could stop breathing.

His fingers tightened, his other hand grasped her other shoulder and drew her to him. Slowly he bent his head, his gold-flecked eyes boring into hers.

There was time to draw away, had she wanted to. But this was not Garrath St. Clair, the oil man. This was Garrath who had brought her breakfast, shared his wine with the spirits of Glen Coe, and smiled gently. She didn't want to draw away.

She leaned into his embrace and raised her mouth for his kiss.

His lips were feathery against hers, nibbling lightly as if he were sampling delicacies too rich and rare to be gulped hastily. His hands left her shoulders to cup her face, his thumbs tracing tingling patterns on the sensitive skin of her jawline and neck. A soft sigh escaped her, a whisper of longing against his mouth. And suddenly his kisses deepened, no longer a nibbling, but the desperation of a starving man who must have the sustenance he needs or die.

Blaine was perfectly willing to be that sustenance, to be anything that would merge her forever with the source of the feelings whirling her in their vortex. She leaned toward Garrath.

And was stabbed in the ribs by the stick shift of the car.

"Ouch!" she cried, jerking backward out of Garrath's arms.

He saw the problem at once. "Damned sports cars!" he muttered. "Why didn't I buy a Rolls?"

They stared at each other a moment, passion still lingering in their eyes and in the rasp of their breathing. But their lips were already twitching with the humor of the situation.

"Or at least something with an automatic shift!" Blaine teased, elaborately rubbing her side. They laughed, the laughter tinged with a little embarrassment at being caught necking in the front seat of a car like teenagers. But even as they laughed, a memory of the feelings of moments before remained. Feelings that hadn't belonged to teenagers.

CHAPTER FIFTEEN

THE RAIN TOOK PITY ON THEM and stopped as suddenly as it had begun, allowing Garrath to risk the road again. In a short time they were driving onto the car ferry at Kyle of Lochalsh to go "over the sea to Skye."

There wasn't much sea to go over. The ferry ride was a brief five minutes across the straits to Kyle Akin, barely enough time to leave the car and make their way to the bow of the ferry to watch the approach to Eilean a Cheo, as Garrath called it. The Isle of Mist.

Skye was living up to its romantic nomenclature. A fine mist curtain stretched between the large island and the mainland. Like some magical Bali Ha'i, Skye rose hazily out of the water, a gathering of lofty peaks whose height could only be guessed at because clouds crouched protectively over the tops and stretched long misty fingers down the hillsides.

The ferry bumped against the Kyleakin dock, and, with the other cars, they rolled off onto the narrow streets of Skye. For a short distance they had the company of the other ferry passengers, but at Broadford most of these continued north. Garrath took a turn to the left onto a one-lane track that seemed to be aimed at a tall line of jagged and forbidding peaks.

THE FOREVER SPELL   217

Once on this road, Garrath leaned slightly forward, his eyes set anxiously on the hills ahead, as if he would go faster were it possible. It wasn't, of course. Meeting another car on the twisting narrow track would mean one vehicle's having to back up until it reached one of the infrequent turnouts to allow the other car to pass. But Blaine soon discovered that the real hazard of the road was not traffic, it was sheep.

The shaggy black-faced creatures were lying on the asphalt like dingy tea cozies, their legs tucked up out of sight under their matted wool. And there was no question of who was the trespasser. As the car drew near, the sheep would reluctantly and awkwardly stand on spindly black legs and shift just enough to let the car edge through, dolefully glaring their disgust at being disturbed. An occasional beast even roused himself enough to bleat a nasty "ma-aaa," before settling back onto the road after they had passed.

"The tarmac is comparatively warm and dry," Garrath explained. "And Highland sheep are notoriously unflappable. They seem to know they are a valuable commodity and not likely to be bumped off the road."

The sun was slipping toward the horizon. As they rounded the V-shaped head of Loch Slapin, it peeked beneath the clouds, shooting gold bars across the smooth surface of the water and the whitewashed walls of the few farmhouses nearby. They turned onto an even smaller road that climbed heather-clad slopes at the foot of a bluish gray mountain.

Blaine's attention was diverted from the scenery by Garrath's grip on the steering wheel. It seemed to be growing tighter with every turn of the road, and there were many turns. His jaw was set at a sharp tense angle, too. It was almost as if he were worrying about their arrival at Glenclair, but that didn't make any sense. Why should he be worried?

Blaine had tried to imagine what Garrath's home would be like. A castle? A stately manor house? Knowing the extent of the St. Clair fortunes, she hadn't ruled out a palace. But now that she saw Skye, the wild barrenness, the simplicity of the land and the scattered buildings, none of her earlier fantasies seemed likely.

When the road curved between low hills and opened suddenly into a narrow glen almost filled by a finger loch, she discovered this latter feeling was correct. At the head of the pencil of dark blue water, backed by the stark heights of the mountain, stood a house. Glenclair.

It was love at first sight.

Blaine had never been the kind of woman to become attached to places. Perhaps it was her early years, when her mother had followed her father from oil field to oil field, making a home as close to him as possible, that had made her cling more to certain belongings than to any four walls. By the time her mother had given up the nomadic life to settle down, with or without her husband as his business allowed, Blaine's ways were set. Even the selling of the family house after her mother's death hadn't really bothered her, not as long as she had certain pieces of furniture and pictures to take with her.

One look at Glenclair and all that changed. She wanted to belong there, to have the right to stay there forever, to have it be her home.

It was more manor than castle, but even manor was perhaps too grand a term. Glenclair was a house, large, unpretentious, perfect. Its golden brown stone was as rough as if it had just been dug from the moors, but its lines were sturdy enough to stand forever. A purplish gray slate roof peaked above the walls, an imitation of the mountainous peaks behind it. There was no symmetry to it, no unifying design. Glenclair had sprouted limbs as needed, a long wing here, an upper story there. It could have been a product of the seventeenth century or the twentieth, so timeless was it, and it blended in with the moors and mountains as if it had grown there naturally.

Blaine loved it with a longing she had never felt for anything before in her life. A longing that brought tears to her eyes.

Garrath had stopped the car and now Blaine felt his stare. She knew intuitively he was waiting for her comment on the house.

"It is the most wonderful place I've ever seen in my life," she managed. All that she was feeling rang in her voice, even though she had hoped to disguise the unusual intensity of it. Garrath heaved a sigh, flexing his hands on the steering wheel.

"I'm glad you think so, Blaine," he said gruffly.

She turned to him, amazed, realizing suddenly the reason for his earlier tension. He had been worried about her first reaction to his home. But why, she asked herself. What difference should her opinion make to him? Why should he care whether she liked Glenclair or not?

The sports car's wheels crunched over the graveled front drive, and the thick oak door in the deep recess of the entranceway arch flew open at the sound.

"Garrath!" squealed a voice, and Janet was dashing toward the car, flinging herself into her brother's arms the moment he levered himself from the low-slung seat.

Blaine opened her door, envying them once again. Their love was so uncomplicated, so freely given, so simply accepted. But her melancholy didn't last long, for Janet soon turned to her, and Blaine was enveloped in a hug just as exuberant and hearty.

"Ah, Blaine, 'tis glad I am to be seeing ye again," Janet cried as if they had been separated by years instead of days. "Thank goodness me daft brother didna let ye get away."

Even making allowances for Janet's teasingly exaggerated accent, it was a strange turn of phrase, Blaine thought. Thankfully she wasn't required to think of a reply, because Janet was pulling her up the front steps. Garrath was left to follow with the suitcases.

It wasn't until they were in the shadow of the archway that Blaine realized someone stood just inside the door, watching them. It was a sparrowish woman, all bird's-nest gray hair, beaky nose, thin prim lips and close-set dark eyes that narrowed as they fixed piercingly on Blaine. Unconsciously, Blaine's steps faltered and Janet had to tug on her hand to get her moving again.

"Mrs. M., I want you to meet Blaine Christensen," Janet said to the dour-faced woman. "Blaine is working for Garrath. Though I think there's more to it than that."

"Janet!" Blaine gasped, and glanced behind them to see if Garrath had heard. Fortunately he was several steps away and didn't seem to be listening. "What are you talking about? That's ridi—"

"Blaine, Mrs. MacGuigan. Glenclair's house-mum."

Blaine couldn't ignore the introduction, which had brought a wan smile to the woman's narrow lips.

"Nice to meet you," Blaine mumbled, and would have held out a hand if Janet hadn't already been using it to steer her inside the house.

Mrs. MacGuigan answered formally, "Welcome to Glenclair," but her continued sharp stare was an efficient negation of the formality.

There wasn't time to ponder the woman's strange manner because they were inside, and Blaine was falling as quickly in love with the interior of the house as she had with the exterior.

The entryway, and every room she saw thereafter, was oversize, with solid masonry and woodwork, the perfect setting for larger-than-life men—like Garrath. Yet there was nothing stark or cold about any of it. Like Garrath's Edinburgh office, a combination of old and new had been used to decorate Glenclair, the result being so comfortable that Blaine felt immediately at home.

The entryway floor was dark tile, but from there stretched polished hardwood overlaid with brilliantly colored Persian rugs. In the living room, what would have been the great hall at one time, an exposed granite fireplace took up most of one wall, its opening large enough to easily roast a side of beef. Thick oak beams supported the ceiling, contrasting with the rough white walls. High-backed sofas were clustered around the fire roaring in the hearth, and Janet led Blaine toward the welcoming warmth.

By the time Garrath had returned from carting the luggage upstairs, Janet had poured richly golden liquid into three small glasses. As Blaine took hers, she smelled the same pungent odor she remembered from the old distillery buildings at Janclair.

"Whiskey?" she questioned. Her infrequent drinking was usually confined to wine.

"A wee dram," Janet replied.

"*Uisge beatha*—the water of life," Garrath said, taking his glass. He raised it in Blaine's direction, then toward Janet. "*Slàinte!*"

Janet echoed him with a smile. "*Slàinte!*"

And then they were both looking expectantly at Blaine. Nervous, and uncertain of the etiquette of this Highland ritual, she repeated the unfamiliar toast, lifted the glass to her lips and took a huge gulp.

She felt it first in the back of her throat, acid burning its way right through her. The fire spread to her tongue, along the path down her throat to her stomach, even to her lips. Tears sprang to her eyes, and through a haze she knew she was going to start coughing and choking like a twelve-year-old sneaking her first drink. She wanted to die—until the fire hit her veins, and there it didn't hurt at all.

After a breathless blissful moment, Blaine smiled. "Lovely," she said hoarsely.

Garrath grinned. "Are you sure there's not a wee bit of Highland blood in your veins?" he asked, looking her up and down, the touch of his eyes as warming as the whiskey.

"There is now!" Blaine shot back, and the three of them were laughing.

Perhaps it was due to her first glass of pure Highland malt whiskey, or maybe her second, which Garrath insisted she savor properly. In any case the late afternoon slipped into evening pleasantly for Blaine. Janet and Garrath made her feel at home, not as a guest but more as if she had always been there. They discussed St. Clair Corporation business, surprising Blaine with how much power Garrath invested in Janet. When Janet led her up the wide sweep of the polished oak staircase to her room to change before dinner, she couldn't help commenting on the fact.

Janet nodded. "He's had me slaving away in the company since shortly after he took over. He inherited control of St. Clair's, though we share equally the financial aspects. But early on he told me that since it was my future, too, I should share the work and the decision making, as well. I love him very much for that."

"But if he's willing to let you make decisions affecting an international company like St. Clair's, why is he so...so Victorian when it comes to your personal life?"

Janet tossed her cap of black curls. "The business side of Garrath doesn't mind that I'm growing up. The big brother side does. And he's been a big brother for a lot longer than he's been heading up St. Clair's."

Blaine didn't reply. Janet might be willing to excuse Garrath so easily, but she wasn't.

The door squeaked as it opened onto the room that would be Blaine's. It was in a corner of the house, and a sloping ceiling, long rectangular windows in the two outside walls and a large fireplace straddling the corner gave it a towerlike impression. The major piece of furniture was the bed, an Elizabethan four-poster with huge intricately carved posts holding up a canopy, the whole draped with thick blue velvet that matched the draperies at the windows. A tapestry covered the wall opposite the bed.

"Is that Glen Coe?" she asked, moving closer to the stitched picture. It didn't seem possible, but she thought the scene on the tapestry was the very one she had been looking at over lunch with Garrath in the brooding glen.

Janet affirmed her guess. "It was specially commissioned by our father for our mother as a wedding present. He proposed to her in Glen Coe, and that is supposedly the view you would see if you were sitting in the very spot they were when the romantic moment occurred." She paused and looked at Blaine, her eyes sparkling mischievously. "It's a very unusual view, not the one you generally see in travel books, or even when driving through the Glen. I'm surprised you would recognize it."

"Oh...uhm...." Blaine mumbled weakly.

"Unless perhaps you've been there sometime. Maybe today, with Garrath."

Blaine's cheeks flamed. "Well, we did have lunch somewhere in Glen Coe. I suppose it might have been near that spot." She tried to make it sound inconsequential.

"I knew it!" Janet cried.

"Knew what?" Blaine demanded, trying to sound stern instead of embarrassed.

"Oh, nothing special," Janet grinned impishly. "The bathroom is two doors down the hall. Just come down whenever you want. We're having some of Mrs. M's stovies and cold roast beef that will be ready whenever we are, so there's no hurry." And she danced out the door like a child harboring a brand-new secret.

Maybe Garrath was right about her immaturity, Blaine grumbled irritably to herself. But her irritation was directed more at the way her heart was fluttering than at Janet's silliness. There was nothing to be made of Garrath's taking her to a place that had special meaning to his family. It was probably just the spot he knew best, the most convenient. He had probably thought of it on the spur of the moment.

But even as she argued with herself, another voice was reminding her of the elaborate lunch he'd packed and saying that kind of preparations didn't indicate convenience or spur of the moment. He'd planned that stop. Which didn't mean anything, of course. . . .

Her thoughts were still riding that merry-go-round when she saw her suitcases. The largest one was on a rack near a wardrobe carved as a companion piece to the bed; the smaller case on the floor. But it was what was on top of the large case that caused Blaine's sharply indrawn breath. Three boxes were stacked there, tied together with a blue and gold ribbon. Her hand shook as she reached for them.

The first and smallest box contained a handwritten note.

> To replace the one I ruined.
>
>   Garrath
>
> P.S. It was worth it.

Beneath the small square of linen notepaper was the lacy blouse from the shop window in Edinburgh. Lips parted in excitement, Blaine tore the lids from the other two boxes to disclose the long woolen skirt and the fur-trimmed cape.

How could he have known, she asked herself, lifting the charcoal-gray cape from its cradle of tissue paper. She had barely hesitated when she gazed in the window. Yet somehow he'd been watching her carefully enough to see her longing. When had he bought it, and why? One ruined blouse was not an excuse for the skirt and cape.

She looked at the note again, especially the postscript. "It was worth it." How like him that sounded! She could see him smiling his infuriating smile as he wrote that, knowing the comment would bring a flush to her cheeks and the memory of his hands on her body to her mind. Was that why?

She started to refold the cape. She couldn't wear the things, of course. The etiquette of accepting such an expensive personal gift aside, if she wore the clothes she would constantly be thinking of the touch that had ruined her other blouse.

Then another thought struck her. If she didn't wear them, wouldn't he assume she didn't dare face the reminder? Wouldn't his look brand her a coward again, afraid of her feelings?

Thirty-five minutes later Blaine was at the top of the staircase, no longer caring why she'd decided to wear the skirt and blouse, only glad that she had. She liked what she saw in the full-length oval mirror hanging there.

It had been worth every one of the fifteen minutes of struggle and contortions it had taken her to do up the tiny pearl buttons closing the back of the blouse. The antique white silk and lace that felt so lovely against her skin also brought a rich warm glow to her complexion. The soft lavender wool swirling elegantly from the wide waistband to her ankles highlighted the narrowness of her waist and the curve of her hips. She had plaited her hair over one shoulder and tied it with a thin black velvet ribbon, a style that seemed to fit in with the aura of the outfit. She felt even more at home in Glenclair now than she had before.

She was tucking in a stray wisp of hair when another face appeared in the mirror, a small dark face with eyes that peered sharply at Blaine's reflection. She gasped and whirled around.

"Oh, Mrs. MacGuigan! I didn't hear you coming. You startled me!"

"I was just after bringin' some fresh towels in to ye, miss."

Blaine's eyes fell to the stack of fluffy pale blue towels the woman clutched in one arm, her other hand tightly grasping the banister.

"Thank you," she mumbled. "I'll. . .I can take them." Blaine put out a hand.

"Well, if you dinna mind," the old woman said curtly, with another look that seemed to cut right through Blaine. She thrust the stack out in front of her, and when Blaine had taken it, she turned away. Still holding the banister tightly, she made her soundless way back down the stairs.

Blaine returned to her room just long enough to drop off the towels before heading back to the stairs. This time she didn't stop to look at herself in the mirror. A little of the charm of resembling the heroine of a Gothic novel had faded with her encounter with another character from the book—the mysterious dour housekeeper who dislikes the heroine on sight. Blaine couldn't think of a reason for Mrs. MacGuigan's animosity, but she felt it every time the woman stared at her so intently and with such seeming displeasure.

Garrath came out of a room at the back of the hall just as Blaine reached the bottom of the stairs, and his look more than made up for any lack in Mrs. MacGuigan's. Even in the dim light she could see his sudden stiffening, the flare of gold lights in his eyes, the parting of his lips over an indrawn breath. She stood very still as he crossed the hall to her.

"I didn't think you would wear it," he said, and took her hand. "I'm honored that you did. You're beautiful."

After that, dinner was a pleasurable haze for Blaine. Janet explained that Mrs. MacGuigan usually prepared the meal and then retired to her own quarters with her husband—or Charlie. Garrath and Janet served themselves and cleared the dishes. And it was that way with all the household chores. Two local girls came in once a week to do the heavy cleaning, but mostly they fended for themselves.

"Stovies" turned out to be onions and potatoes browned in thick beef drippings and then simmered. With the lean roast beef redolent of basil and thyme, with hot rolls and salad and several glasses of wine, it made a wonderful meal. When they were finished, Blaine followed them into the kitchen, dishes in hand.

That room was bright with gleaming copper and polished steel. Shiny pots hung from an overhead rack and a huge old-fashioned range squatted against one wall. A center island was of dark aged wood. No microwave ovens and food processors here, Blaine thought, but when she voiced the thought, Garrath contradicted her by pulling open several cupboard doors. The latest in time-saving devices were hidden inside. Even the dishwasher was hidden behind a door.

"Mrs. MacGuigan calls them my 'abominations' and insists they be out of the way. She only grudgingly let me have the range reoutfitted with new wiring and such. It came to Glenclair in the early eighteenth century, imported from Hampshire at great expense, and you'd think she was here at the time from the way she cherishes the old relic."

Blaine received another shock when Garrath pushed up his sleeves, ran water into a pot that was too large to fit into the dishwasher, and started scrubbing. Garrath St. Clair—doing dishes! She didn't know what to think.

After the kitchen was spotless once again—"We daren't leave it otherwise! Mrs. M's wrath is best not unleashed," Janet said, rolling her long-lashed eyes; and Blaine could well believe that—they returned to the living room, which was dark now except for the golden glow of the fire.

Feeling the effects of the whiskey earlier, as well as the wine at dinner, Blaine sank gratefully into the luxury of the high-backed sofa. Slipping off her shoes, she tucked her legs up onto the cushion and her feet beneath the warmth of her skirt. She was perfectly relaxed and mellow as she watched Garrath hefting another huge log into the fireplace and stirring the coals. But then Janet announced she was going to her room.

"I have those papers from Janclair to go over. See

you in the morning." And she scooted out the door, with a sly look over her shoulder that told Blaine this was her not-too-subtle way of leaving her and Garrath alone.

Blaine's first inclination was for flight. The inclination wasn't strong enough to overcome the lethargy induced by the warmth she felt, however. She was comfortable; she belonged where she was.

"You look like a kitten who's been at the cream," Garrath said, easing onto the sofa beside her. Close beside her.

"That's precisely how I feel," she said, smiling up at him. "I've enjoyed today very much, Garrath. Seeing the countryside, our picnic lunch, but especially Glenclair. I'm glad you. . . talked me into coming here."

"I'm glad, too," he echoed and bent his head to kiss her, lightly, tentatively, questioningly.

Every logical reason for answering no ran through Blaine's mind without affecting her actions in the least. Even while logic was reasonably arguing that nothing good could come of this moment, her mouth was saying a definite yes in a language far more vivid than words.

Their lips met, parted, melded together, and the rest of the room, the house, the city, the world, faded away into oblivion. The only real thing was the safe haven of Garrath's arms and the sensations he was awakening in her body.

She was a flat empty canvas, he the painter creating a masterpiece there. A bold sweep of fiery red—their mouths moving in a passionate dance. Scorching yellow—the stroking of his hands on her neck, shoulder, back. A flash of orange—the hardness of his body pressing against hers. Electric blue—the molten heat growing at the center of her being, which threatened to consume them both.

She felt Garrath's hand at the pearl buttons of her blouse and wondered how he could undo so quickly what had taken her so long to do. As each tiny button slipped from its loop his fingers brushed her backbone tantalizingly, his mouth echoing the motion on hers until, when every one was undone and he leaned away from her to slip the silk off her shoulders, she nearly cried out with the sense of loss. But then his sweater followed her blouse to the floor and she was leaning into him, a mewling starting deep in her throat at the heat of his skin against her bared breasts.

He eased her backward until she was arched over the soft arm of the sofa, and then he bent his head. His mouth took warm moist possession of first one breast and then the other, and now she did cry out with wild pleasure.

Her fingers combed and then clenched in the thick black waves of his hair. This was torment, and she wanted it to end, and to go on forever. Her hands slid down over the muscles of his back and she felt the taut trembling of rising desire. But was the trembling his or hers?

Then his hand was at her ankle, pushing the soft wool of her skirt out of the way. Stroking, massaging there a moment before sliding slowly up her calf to the sensitive skin at the back of her knee. Then farther up, over thigh, hip, all the way to her waist before traveling the same fiery path back down again.

He stood and pulled her to her feet, tightly against him. He claimed her mouth again, his hands caress-

ing her bare back and her waist, then moving down
over the curve of her hips where the covering of
material suddenly seemed an unneeded and unwanted barrier.

His fingers were on the waistband of the skirt when
the voice poured over them like a sudden dousing of
turpentine.

"Garrath? Miss Mills has rung up, askin' for you.
She insists it's urgent," Mrs. MacGuigan said tonelessly, and washed away all the color and the
warmth.

CHAPTER SIXTEEN

GARRATH'S ARMS TIGHTENED, holding Blaine immobile against the length of him.

"Would you tell them I'll be there in just a moment, Mrs. M.," he said calmly, as if nothing had happened, as if they weren't standing there half naked in front of the cold dark eyes of his housekeeper. "And then, if you wouldn't mind, we'd appreciate a pot of something warm to drink."

"And am I ever mindin' such things?" she huffed. But her eyes never left Blaine's bare back.

The moment they were alone Blaine pulled free of Garrath's arms. She turned away, pressing her fists against her mouth and her arms against her chest, too embarrassed to even dive for her clothing.

She heard him pulling on his sweater, and then he was reaching around her with her blouse. She grabbed it with one hand and quickly slipped her arms into the sleeves.

"Do you want some help?" he asked softly, and she shook her head violently. "All right, I'd better take that phone call. I'll be back in just a second, okay?"

She nodded. But when the sound of his footsteps told her he was gone, she ran out of the room and upstairs.

In her bedroom she threw off the blouse and skirt

and wrapped herself in her robe. Shivering, she climbed into the canopied bed and pulled the covers up around her. She would never come out, she decided. Never.

But she'd been alone only a short time when the squeaking of the door announced that someone was coming in. Blaine looked up through tear-dotted lashes to see Garrath striding into the room, carrying a mug in each hand.

"Are you up here dying of mortification?" he teased, amusement twinkling in his eyes, and Blaine could happily have murdered him. "Some of Mrs. M.'s cocoa should cheer you up."

"I don't think cocoa will help," she snapped. "And I'd rather be alone."

"Hey, aren't you overreacting?"

"Overreacting! When right this minute your Mrs. M. is probably using terms like wanton and shameless, and a few others not so nice, to describe me to Mr. MacGuigan? She disliked me from the first moment she saw me, and now she's undoubtedly congratulating herself on how very right her intuition was."

"She disliked you? Why on earth do you think that?"

"Because of the way she's been looking at me, or rather through me, the whole time. I've never felt so...so small!"

"Oh, Blaine, that's not true."

"It...is...so...." she stammered, and tears spilled over her lashes and rolled down her cheeks. Garrath set the mugs on the small table near the bed and sat down beside her. His amused grin became a sympathetic smile.

"It isn't. And there's no reason to be so bothered by this. . .situation, either."

She started to protest, but he put a finger across her lips. "Wait. I'll explain. But before I do, I want you to know I don't see anything shameful in what was happening between us. Imprudent, perhaps, in our choice of location, but we can chalk that up to. . .to our compulsive attraction or something like that. But not shameful. And since I don't see anything wrong in our behavior, I don't really care what anyone, including Mrs. M., chooses to think. If she had been scandalized and wanted to condemn me, I would consider that her problem, not mine."

"Oh, I don't imagine it would be you she condemned. It's the woman who always gets the scarlet letter, you know."

"Perhaps. But not from Mrs. M."

"And why are you so sure? I know how she's been looking at me and—"

"And you jumped six feet to a very wrong conclusion," Garrath interrupted her sternly.

Blaine's chin came up. "How do you know it's wrong?"

"Because I know Mrs. MacGuigan. She's gruff, she grumbles incessantly and smiles seldom. But I've known her for most of my life, and in all that time I've never known her to judge anyone unfairly or unkindly. She knows the facts of life and love and human nature. If she had seen us, she would perhaps have scolded us for not throwing another log on the fire, so we wouldn't catch a chill, but she wouldn't have done any condemning."

"*If* she saw us! Garrath, she couldn't have missed us!"

He put his fist beneath her tilted chin and rubbed softly, shaking his head. "She might have seen that we were standing rather close together, but that's all. She wasn't wearing her glasses, Blaine, and without them she's very nearly blind."

"Nearly blind?" Blaine's mind refused to accept it. "She can't be. She hasn't worn glasses at all since I've been here. She served the dinner and walked around the house without any hesitation, and she...."

"Looked right through you?"

Slowly, reluctantly, Blaine nodded.

"She never wears them, not when anyone's around," Garrath said, smiling again. "She vehemently denies she needs them at all. So she's developed tricks to handle everyday tasks. She shoos everyone out of her kitchen if she needs to read a recipe and squints and stares when she's trying to make out what a stranger looks like."

"But that's incredible!"

"That's Mrs. M. So now you can stop worrying. And the next time, we'll choose a more private time and place. In fact, if I didn't have to make a few calls right now to handle the problem Diana called about...." He raised a finger to stroke Blaine's cheek and his eyes smoldered with desire.

With a small cry she slapped his hand away. "There isn't going to be any next time," she said through clenched teeth. "This whole thing was due to a combination of whiskey and wine. It won't happen again."

Garrath stiffened and the fire in his eyes died. "Are you sure about that, Blaine? Your words say one thing, but your body keeps telling me something quite different. Why are you trying so hard to re-sist?''

''I'm not trying—I am resisting. I won't have you ordering my life and my emotions to suit yourself the way you do Janet's. Now please, leave me alone.''

With one hard, cold look, he did.

BLAINE WOKE EARLY for no reason she could think of and pulled back the velvet draperies on a morning sharp with frost. The long bluish shadow still stretching across the small loch was evidence that the sun had not yet crested the mountains behind Glenclair, but the clear sky was tinged with the pinkish promise of its coming.

She decided to head for the kitchen in search of a cup of coffee. She knew she was going to have to face Garrath and Mrs. M. some time today, and wasn't looking forward to either encounter. But delaying wasn't going to make the prospect any more appealing. If she hurried, there was a chance no one else would be up and about yet, and she could get a shot of fortifying caffeine to bolster her courage.

But would there even be any coffee in a Scottish house, she wondered as she tiptoed down the long staircase. Would Mrs. M. allow it?

The moment she pushed open the swinging door to the copper and steel kitchen, she knew there was indeed coffee at Glenclair, and freshly brewed if her nose was any judge. The brewer turned out to be Mr. MacGuigan.

He was the antithesis of his wife in every way but height. He was no taller than she, but roly-poly was the only description for his figure. His face was round, jowly and ruddy, his eyes actually twinkled and his mouth spread into a jack-o'-lantern grin when he saw her.

"Charlie," he corrected her firmly as, assuming his identity, she said a shy good-morning. "And ye must be the lass my Mary was chattering about 'til the wee hours."

"Mrs. MacGuigan was...talking...about me?" Blaine stammered, the heat of a blush rushing up from her toes to the top of her head.

"Aye. All aboot how very nice ye sounded, yer voice like spring breezes, yer step gentle and ladylike. Since her sight dimmed, Mary's ears have become very good at tellin' her things. And they certainly were right this time."

Blaine smiled her thanks for the compliment, the smile lighted by an extra brightness that was due to relief. Charlie offered her some coffee and Blaine accepted gratefully. It was rich, very strong and delicious, and had all the fortifying power she could want.

"I was afraid coffee might be against the law in the Highlands," she said, and Charlie grinned.

"Aye, almost. My Mary considers my liking for coffee my one major failing, a sort of blasphemy. So I fix it meself and she never *says* a word."

Blaine discovered the explanation for Charlie's emphasis on the word "says" when his wife came into the kitchen. She said a gruff good-morning to both of them, went to various cupboards to take out pans and supplies to start breakfast, and all the while was sniffing the air quite audibly and shaking her gray head.

Blaine also quickly discovered the truth of what Garrath had told her, now that she was looking for the signs. The woman's movements were swift and sure but also careful. She used her hands more than most people did, feeling the shapes of canisters and bottles. She laid one hand against the tea kettle's metal body as she filled it, too, to judge the level of the water from the cold penetrating through. Blaine felt enormously guilty for misjudging her, and also for the relief she couldn't help feeling.

A bit hesitantly she offered to help with the breakfast preparations. Mrs. M. accepted.

"Though I doubt ye know how to make decent porridge," the woman muttered. "I'll have to be showin' ye, which will take longer than doin' it meself." A great sigh shook her thin body. From behind his wife's back, Charlie's grin showed the years he'd lived with Mary MacGuigan's sharp-tongued ways, and Blaine smiled knowingly back at him.

She soon discovered that the grumbling hadn't been entirely without foundation. She didn't know how to make proper porridge, at least not according to Mrs. M.'s definition. The quick-cooking oatmeal Blaine was familiar with wasn't allowed in Mrs. M.'s kitchen, of course, so it wasn't a matter of just throwing everything together in a pot. To make Scots porridge meant adding steel-cut oats to spring water just at the boiling point, while stirring briskly with a spurtle—a small wooden stick. After ten minutes it was time to add the salt.

"And would ye be rushin' and thus hardening your oats?" Mrs. M. demanded archly when Blaine mentioned she always put the salt in first. Blaine didn't make any further suggestions.

It seemed a lot of fuss and bother for a bowl of

oatmeal, Blaine thought, until Mrs. M. thrust a spoonful of the result into her mouth. It had a rich nutty flavor and texture that was as far from instant oatmeal as one could get.

A large trolley was loaded with the breakfast things and wheeled to a room at the back of the house, one that immediately became Blaine's favorite. The solarium, Mrs. M. called it. Back home the decorating magazines were calling them sunrooms, Blaine thought, stepping into the space roofed and walled in glass. It was Garrath's own design, she was informed pridefully, this newest of Glenclair's limbs. It worked beautifully. A large rug woven in shades of green covered the floor, ferns and philodendrons spread their lush foliage all around, and a small glass-topped table with cane chairs had the place of honor in the center of the room.

But what made it so special was the view the clear walls exposed. The green carpeting seemed to flow beyond the glass into grassy turf and then up to rolling hills. There the green gave way to brown, lavender and orangey rust ground cover and then to darker shades as the hills became peaks stacked one behind the other, climbing steeper and higher like a skyward thrust of stairs. As she watched, the rim of the sun rose above the far mountain, and magic wands of sunshine made a crystal palace of the room.

Mrs. M. headed back to the kitchen for a kettle of hot water, and moments later Janet bounced in as if she were riding one of those rays of sunshine. The red highlights in her black hair gleamed copper in the sparkle of light, and the devilish gleam in her eyes was equally bright.

"Did you and Garrath have a nice evening?" she asked, not at all casually.

"Fine," Blaine lied.

Janet pouted. "Blaine Christensen, fine is not an answer at all. Come on, how did it go?"

"How did what go? We just...talked and then went to bed." She hoped her nose wasn't growing, Pinocchio fashion.

"Bed! Terrific! Things are moving—"

"Janet! We went to bed separately, of course," Blaine remonstrated sternly, and Janet's gleeful grin faded. "I think you've been watching too many X-rated movies or something. Your comment to Mrs. M. yesterday, and now this! I don't know what makes you think there's anything between Garrath and me."

Janet tossed her head. "I see the way he looks at you. And you look at him the same way, even if you don't want to admit it. I saw it on Sithein One that first day. I was just afraid there wouldn't be time enough for things to develop. But now it seems there is. He brought you here and that's proof in itself. He's never brought a woman to Glenclair before. Not ever."

"I came here to do a job," Blaine countered. "That's all there is to it."

Janet didn't look convinced.

"Maybe, but that doesn't explain the rest. I'm sure I'm right and nothing would suit me better. If he falls in love, he'll understand about Andy and me. Garrath has always been the ultimate bachelor, never allowing himself to get serious about anyone. He needs someone like you, someone he could settle down with."

"Oil men don't settle down," Blaine said grimly. "My father was perfect evidence of that, always putting work before everything else. And my brother would have been just like him if. . . . Well, anyway, I know better than to really care for a man whose first love is oil.''

"But Garrath wouldn't be that way if he was in love. He just needs to marry the right woman. He needs—''

"What do I need, little sister?" a voice drawled from the doorway.

Blaine looked up, already knowing who would be standing there. But for how long had he been, she wondered. How much had he heard? Enough to know they were discussing his love life—and marriage, if the sardonic twist of his full lips was any indication. And he would undoubtedly assume that Blaine had instigated the conversation. Her stomach sank to her heels.

Janet didn't bat an eye. "You need to spend more time enjoying yourself. You work too much and too hard. You're going to get old before your time.''

Garrath saluted. "Thank you for the sage advice," he said curtly, taking a seat at the table. "I'll take it under consideration. . . sometime when my work schedule permits.''

Janet looked unperturbed by his sarcasm. "Well, just make sure your schedule permits time for Eileen's spree tonight.'' She turned to Blaine. "You're invited, too.''

"What's a spree?"

"It's the most lovely sort of party, given for an engaged couple—a dance, a *ceilidh*, a celebration of love all rolled into one,'' Janet enthused.

Before Blaine could ask about the unfamiliar word, "kay-lie," as Janet pronounced it, Garrath broke in.

"It's something like an American wedding shower, a chance for everyone to gossip about what a good or bad catch the girl has made."

Blaine winced.

"Oh, go on with ye, Garrath St. Clair, ye old sourpuss," Janet admonished. "You enjoy them as much as I do. And this one's special, since the engaged girl is a good friend of mine, and I'm to be best maid."

"Bridesmaid," Garrath translated dryly, with a challenging look at Blaine, as if this conversation about wedding showers was all part of her plan.

"Which reminds me," Janet rushed on, turning her sweetest look on her brother. "Could you go over to Armadale to pick up the tea set that's coming in on the ferry? It was supposed to be here last week, but you know how that goes. I've promised to help Eileen with the preparations today."

"Are you sure you aren't just trying to get me away from the evils of work?"

Janet's lower lip protruded prettily. "Now, isn't the china tea set the traditional gift from best maid to the bride? Of course, I could tell Eileen I canna be helping her, but . . . ."

"I'll go, Janet," Garrath succumbed grumpily, and immediately Janet's elfin face brightened.

"Ooh, thanks, luv!" She leaned forward and gave him a quick kiss. But her smile was coy. "And you might as well take Blaine with you. It's such a lovely ride and she could see some more of Skye."

The object of this untimely matchmaking would cheerfully have throttled Janet at that moment. Now Garrath would be certain they had cooked up this convenient trip for two together as the first step toward roping him into marriage. And that her ardent denials of the previous night were just her way of playing hard to get.

"No, I . . . I would like to get to work this morning," she said hastily. "Right after breakfast."

"Of course," Garrath agreed, and it was almost a sneer. "Unfortunately your computer equipment hasn't arrived yet, though I can show you the office. I suppose there's some preliminary work you might want to do."

"Yes," Blaine replied firmly. But her firmness wilted quickly under the scorching intensity of Garrath's gaze. Fortunately before she collapsed completely, Mrs. M. brought in the pot of freshly boiled water.

"Are ye no goin' to eat afore everythin's cold?" she demanded. Obediently they loaded their plates from the scrumptious array of dishes Mrs. M. had prepared while overseeing Blaine's cooking lesson. There were mild sausages, eggs, kippers and baps— big soft floury rolls that melted in the mouth—with honey-sweetened Darjeeling to wash it all down.

The conversation was minimal, even Janet's normal garrulousness subdued by Garrath's continued glowering. But the food more than made up for the lack.

"I won't need to eat for the rest of the day," Blaine sighed when she was finished.

"Wait 'til you see lunch," Janet warned, laughing, and Blaine groaned.

"Are you ready, then?" Garrath cut in, but he didn't wait for an answer. Blaine jumped immediately to her feet, but he was already striding from the room.

Janet shook her head. "I think he got up on the

wrong side of the wrong bed this morning,'' she said innocently, and then ruined the effort with a wicked wink.

Blaine made a face at the younger girl and hurried after Garrath.

His office turned out to be a huge library. Floor-to-ceiling shelves packed with books lined the walls. Comfortable leather chairs were grouped in one corner, served by a brass swivel-arm lamp. An antique globe with raised-relief mountains balanced on a wooden stand, and the desk was the largest rolltop Blaine had ever seen. The corner closest to the desk had already been cleared and was obviously waiting for Blaine's computer.

"Will that be sufficient space?" he asked coldly, leaning against the desk. When she replied that she thought it would, he said, "Good. Then I'll leave you to whatever it is you need to do."

But he didn't leave her, not physically. Mentally, Blaine wasn't sure about. He sat at his desk, going over papers, making phone calls and dictating into a pocket recorder with what looked like intense concentration. He didn't seem to be at all aware of anyone else being in the room. Unlike Blaine.

She worked, measuring, checking availability of outlets and wiring, arranging the system in her mind to fit the space and still provide optimum convenience of usage. But at no time did she forget she wasn't alone. She could feel the tension radiating from him, tension she didn't understand.

But what was even worse was the way her eyes kept straying to the tilt of his head over the paper he was reading, the curl of dark hair lying silkily against his neck, the line of his shoulder and arm and hand. And each time her eyes strayed, it was the tilt of his head as his mouth bent to hers, the feel of her fingers twined in his dark hair and the warmth of his shoulders and arms and hands she was remembering. It didn't make for efficient working.

As Garrath had promised, he'd arranged most of the preliminary details, so there wasn't really much for her to do. She stretched out the job as long as she could, hoping he would finish and take his sulky mood elsewhere. But finally even the busywork ran out.

Somehow he seemed to sense that precise moment. He tossed down his pen.

"Done? Let's go then."

"Go?"

"To Armadale for the tea set. I know you'd rather be slaving away over a hot computer, but since that isn't possible, perhaps your conscience can be salved by looking at this as a job. I need someone to hold the china so it has a chance of surviving the roads in one piece. You'll do."

The invitation was as unexpected as it was ungracious. Why should he want to take her? But one look at Garrath's dark expression told her it wasn't really an invitation at all. For whatever reason, he was ordering her to accompany him.

Blaine conducted a small brief war with herself. Her principles versus the possibility of victory and the importance of the skirmish. She decided her weapons were better saved for another battle.

"I'll get my coat," she said.

HALF AN HOUR LATER Garrath's small blue sports car was creeping along a road in the southern part of the island, the Sleat peninsula. This time their slow pace wasn't due to sheep, but to cattle—a herd of huge rust red cows being driven along by a man with a big stick.

The sloping embankments on either side of the road would have created a natural barrier for the herdsman to run his animals between, if only the slopes hadn't been covered with lush green grass that the cows found irresistible. One after another of the beasts veered off the road to snatch a few tearing bites of grass before the herdsman came after them, whacking them soundly with the long thick stick he carried.

Blaine cried out the first time she saw and heard the force of the blows across a cow's back. But she quickly realized how little fazed the sturdy animals were by even the loudest and hardest crack from the stick. Getting their attention was the hard thing.

When the ground leveled out again, the herdsman shifted his charges off the road onto the grassy bank to allow Garrath to pass, much to the cows' delight. Garrath called out his thanks and sympathy as they drove by.

Sleat was a series of picturesque bays, where tiny islands were sprinkled across the teal blue water. Less stark, not dominated by the jagged faces of the mountains backdropping the area around Glenclair, it had grassy slopes and trees, neat fields and trim farms. Tall yellow haystacks with pointed tops stood like straw sentries near many of the crofts, ready for winter. Far across the Sound were the mountains of the mainland, their sharp edges gentled by mist.

The tea set had already arrived, they discovered, and was being kept at a cottage near the ferry quay. Blaine waited in the car while Garrath fetched it. She couldn't help hearing the enthusiasm with which the

pretty red-haired young woman who answered Garrath's knock greeted him. She refused to let him go
until he promised her a dance at the spree that night.
When he had complied she threw her arms around his
neck and pressed a fervent kiss against his lips.

Acid burned in Blaine's stomach and her hands
clenched into fists. She turned to look out at the bay
without seeing it; then Garrath was back in the car,
handing her the sizable box. As they drove off she
held her head as carefully as she held the box on her
lap, keeping her eyes away from the doorway of the
cottage, where she knew a smiling figure watched and
waved.

This was why he'd decided to bring her along, she
thought. He wanted her to know that his lovemaking
had no serious feeling behind it, so her rejection
wouldn't bother him. He wanted her to see that there
were other women not so unwilling, who would do
just as well.

Well, she did see. She most certainly did.

CHAPTER SEVENTEEN

BLAINE WASN'T LOOKING FORWARD to the spree. The ride back from Armadale had been uncomfortably strained and silent. At Glenclair she found herself alone and at loose ends. Garrath had shut himself in his office as soon as they arrived and stayed there, a grouchy bear in his cave, for the rest of the afternoon. Janet was at her friend's and Charlie had gone to a neighboring farm to help repair a roof. Mrs. M. was in the kitchen baking her special marzipan fruitcake for the party, but when Blaine peeked in with an offer to help, she was brusquely refused.

"Out wi' ye! I dinna want pesterin' now!" Mrs. M. snapped, and Blaine quickly closed the door. But not before she caught a glimpse of the thick-lensed glasses perched on Mrs. M.'s nose.

Amusing as the episode was, it still left her with nothing to do but simmer in a stew of inactivity that left far too much time for thinking.

She chose to wear the outfit Garrath had given her, despite the trembling in her fingers as she worked on the numerous pearl buttons. It was more appropriate for the party than anything else she'd brought with her, and she decided there was no reason she shouldn't wear it. She fashioned her long hair into a complementary Victorian topknot that pleased her with its cool sophisticated air.

When she had finished dressing she draped the soft gray cape around her shoulders and went downstairs. Charlie and Mrs. M., who were going to drive over to the party with them, were already waiting. As was Garrath.

His dark magnetism struck her with an almost physical force. He was wearing a black vested suit that was tailored precisely to the lean musculature of his body, the black heightening the intensity of his coloring. His hair shone like a thick sable that her fingers itched to touch. His lips, curved now in a smile, radiated a heat that set her mouth to burning. And that smile, sensual and appraising as it traveled slowly over the length of her, made her regret her defiant choice of clothing.

One look from him and she was again feeling his hands undoing the buttons down her back, was again tasting his kisses and longing for it to happen again. She squashed the feeling mercilessly, assuming her coldest haughtiest expression as camouflage, but her mood was not improved.

It was Mrs. M. and Janet who made bearable the drive from Glenclair to the farmhouse hosting the spree. Janet was bubbling over with news and local gossip garnered from her day spent helping Eileen, and Mrs. M.'s caustic grumbling about frivolous doings and wasted time provided a special kind of amusement of its own.

The farmhouse was large and filled with more people than Blaine had thought lived on the whole Isle of Skye. They were crowded into several rooms, drinking wee drams that were not so very "wee"; talking in Gaelic or such heavily accented English that it was nearly as incomprehensible; laughing, dancing, helping themselves to the buffet supper. It was lively, fun and as "lovely" as Janet had described it, and Blaine would have enjoyed it immensely, she thought, if only she hadn't been so constantly infuriatingly aware of Garrath St. Clair.

The red-haired young woman from the Armadale cottage claimed her dance from Garrath shortly after their arrival, and she wasn't the only one asking for—and getting—his attention. He seemed to know and be quite friendly with a good number of the local young women. Blaine missed many of the introductions Janet was making as she watched Garrath dance.

His pantherish grace served him well on the improvised dance floor. His movements were sure and smooth in the waltzes, Scottish reels and flings, and Blaine's stomach was burning again just as it had been that afternoon.

I must be catching something, she thought. *The flu, perhaps.* Surreptitiously she put a hand to her forehead. There didn't seem to be any fever, but still. . . .

The pain doubled when Garrath suddenly appeared in front of her, asking rather formally for a dance.

"I. . .I can't dance Scottish dances," she stammered, her ears roaring with panic. If he held her, her body would betray her, she knew; would make a fool of her with illogical messages and yearnings that he would easily read.

"This is a waltz, Blaine," he said tauntingly. "Surely that isn't too Scottish for you?" And he held out his hand. What else could she do but take it? She went into his dancer's embrace.

Funny, she hadn't noticed him holding his other partners especially close, Blaine thought. But he had drawn her tightly to him, tight enough for her to feel the brush of their bodies as they moved, to feel the whisper of his breath on her hair. And her reaction was immediate. Every part of her cried out that this was where she belonged, here and nowhere else.

His hand at her back moved caressingly, its heat in direct contrast to the coolness of the silk of her blouse. "I like having you in my arms," he whispered, drawing her yet closer until she was all too aware of the strength, the power of him. "The way I did last night, especially. But this is nice, too."

"Yes, I noticed you liked dancing," she shot back bitingly.

He chuckled. "You sound jealous, kitten."

"Jealous!" She leaned back enough to glare up at him. "Why would I be jealous?"

"Why, indeed?" was his cryptic reply, and then he pulled her yet closer, precluding further conversation.

Blaine seethed for the rest of the dance. How dare he accuse her of being jealous! What an inflated ego the man had! Did he really think every woman in sight was head over heels in love with him? Well, he certainly was wrong about her!

The moment the dance ended she whirled as far away from him as the room permitted.

She was still seething over his ridiculous insinuations when glasses of whiskey were passed around to toast the engaged couple. Even so, she might not have acted so foolishly if her eyes hadn't met Garrath's just as she raised her glass to her lips. He was across the room, next to the curvaceous redhead again. When his dark eyes met Blaine's, he leaned close to the woman and whispered something. She looked across at Blaine, then up at Garrath. And she smiled.

Anger turned Blaine's veins to gunpowder. The golden liquid she tossed back with complete abandon lighted the fuse. Scottish hospitality saw to it that her glass stayed well filled after that, and she saw to it that she didn't miss a toast. Soon the numbing fire in her throat had spread throughout the rest of her body.

Fortunately, just about the time the farmhouse began to spin the party wound down into a *ceilidh*, the Scottish version of a hootenanny. It began when one young boy, a cousin of Eileen's, began singing what Janet told Blaine was the "Bride's Song," a traditional well-wishing tune. It was sung in Gaelic, but understanding the words wasn't necessary to sense the meaning, which ran richly through the melody. The boy's voice had the haunting quality of one as yet unbroken, and there were many damp eyes when the song came to an end, including, Blaine was tickled to note, Mrs. M.'s.

Despite her earlier grumbling the housekeeper seemed to be enjoying herself now. With Charlie's arm snug around her slight shoulders and bright nostalgic tears in her eyes, she actually looked happy. Was she remembering when she had been the bride being sung to, Blaine wondered absently.

The song acted like a signal. The guests settled into chairs or onto the floor around the boy and his cousin, an area that then became an improvised stage as one person after another gave an impromptu performance. Most of the songs were in the ancient

language of the Highlanders, the Gaelic. But like the
first, there was no need for a translation to experience their rich mood. There were the songs of
work—reaping, sowing, fishing, weaving—and more
of love in all its guises, happy and sad, sweet and
melancholy. There were pantomimes, including a
bawdy one depicting the wedding night. And then
there were the Lowland songs: "My Love Is like a
Red, Red Rose," "Comin' thro' the Rye," where
everyone joined in.

Blaine never knew how Garrath managed to be beside her when the music began, or how they ended up
sitting together on the floor, his arm firmly around
her. But she, floating on the "water of life," didn't
really care. She knew she'd been furious with him a
little while ago, but that didn't seem to matter now.
Not with the age-old songs wending their way into
her soul and her heavy head drooping to his shoulder.

Then, from outside the house, came the mournful
call of bagpipes, and as one, the guests stood up and
moved silently out to the front porch, answering the
call. Blaine stood, too, but everything tilted at a wild
angle that would have swept her off her feet if Garrath hadn't been there. He lifted her easily and his
smile was like another shot of Scotch whiskey. She
grinned crazily.

"Oh, my poor wee princess," he said with a soft
chuckle. "Are you going to have a head in the morning!"

But she didn't take in the words. All she knew was
that the cradle of his arms was the most warm, safe
and comfortable place she could have found to listen
to the song of the pipes.

The piper was a tiny old man, his face as wrinkled as that of an apple doll. Kilt swaying gracefully over thin legs, he marched forward and back before the porch, squeezing his tune from the instrument that was as much a part of Scotland as the hills and moors and lochs. When the last skirl faded into the night, the party was over.

The ride home was a fuzzy-edged blur to Blaine. She heard Mrs. M. suggest that Charlie drive and mumbled her thanks to the woman because it meant she didn't have to lift her head from the haven of Garrath's shoulder. Then they were back at Glenclair and she was being carried upstairs to her room.

"Are you sure you can manage?" she heard Garrath asking.

"We'll manage!" Mrs. M. answered sternly. "When ye want to be undressin' the lass, it'll be asking her first ye are, Garrath St. Clair. And she's in no condition to be sayin' yea or nae now. So if that fire's well started, be off with ye!"

Janet was giggling.

Mrs. M.'s hands were gentle, though a bit uncertain dealing with the unfamiliar clothing. Even so, Blaine was soon undressed.

"I can't find her nightie," Janet said.

"Well, I suppose she'll survive the night without," came the nannyish comment. The pins were pulled from Blaine's hair and she was finally allowed to lie down. The warm weight of quilts settled over her and she sighed.

"You should have worn your glasses tonight, Mrs. M., just to see her and Garrath dancing." Janet's voice barely reached through the fog filling Blaine's mind. "They looked perfect together."

"I dinna need glasses to be seein', miss. And who are ye to be judgin' perfect couples, I'm wonderin'? Now get off to your own bed and stop all this havering."

Janet's laughter faded as she obeyed. There were a few more rustlings in the room as Mrs. M. hung up Blaine's clothing.

"A perfect couple," the woman muttered, tucking the quilts up around Blaine's shoulder. "Aye, well, perhaps so. Havena I been hearin' something special in his speakin' of the lass's name? So... perhaps."

But Blaine had already slipped into a deep, deep sleep.

SHE HAD A VERY DEFINITE "HEAD" in the morning. Before she even opened her eyes she knew that burying herself as deeply as possible beneath the quilts for the next twenty-four hours was the wisest course of action. Getting up, dressing, eating, facing the world, those actions were for other people. People not suffering from the first hangover of their lives.

But Garrath had other ideas.

Somehow when she heard the scraping and thumping of a fire being laid in the grate, she knew without even taking the two down-filled pillows from her head that he was the perpetrator of this torture. Who else could be so cruel?

"Go 'way," she moaned as he snatched away her pillows. Now only her tightly squeezed eyelids were between her and agony.

"Come on, princess. I know it hurts now, but I'll have you feeling better in no time."

"Tomorrow."

"Today. This morning, what's left of it. I've arranged everything."

"Arranged...everything?" Her eyes snapped open, painfully. It was Garrath's arranging of a few other things that had landed her here at Glenclair. What did he have in mind for her now?

He was nodding. "As soon as we get you up and dressed we're going out for a walk."

"A walk! You're mad. I'll consider myself successful if I can manage crawling at this point."

"That's why a walk is just what you need. I've had Mrs. M. prepare a portable brunch...."

"No food," Blaine groaned as the room zigzagged. "I'm never going to eat again."

"...which you'll be ready for by the time we're halfway up the first hill. The fresh air is just what you need."

"What I need is...."

Garrath cupped her face with his hands and stared deep into her eyes. "Fresh air. I promise it will make you feel much better. Trust me, Blaine."

Calling herself all kinds of a fool, she did.

IT WORKED. The fresh air fulfilled Garrath's promise very soon after they started the climb into the hills behind Glenclair, magically sweeping the ache from Blaine's head with a broom of heather-sweetened breezes. He had also been right about the return of her appetite, though she did manage to wait until they were at the *top* of the first hill before asking him what Mrs. M. had sent along.

"I thought you weren't eating ever again?" he teased, ushering her to a slab of black granite poking through the tangle of ground cover. He pulled sausage rolls, hard-boiled eggs, fat dill pickles, dried apricots and a thermos of hot tea from his rucksack.

"Well, maybe just a bite," she admitted, the dimple deeply etched in her cheek. She felt as wonderful now as she had felt horrible earlier. It was a marvelous morning. Looking back toward Glenclair, she saw a scene that could have been created specially for travel brochures. The sky was a deep azure blue, with only a few whipped-cream clouds hovering on the horizon. The roof of the house and the still surface of the loch sparkled golden in the bright sunlight, two precious jewels nestled in the green velvet-lined box of the little valley.

But then she noticed something that didn't quite fit the idyllic image. On the far side of the house a circle of turf had been cleared away, and crouching on the smooth brown patch was a helicopter.

"For emergencies," Garrath told her. "I'm a licensed pilot, as is Janet."

"Janet can handle one of those things?"

"Sure. She's a very capable girl."

Blaine popped a sausage roll into her mouth, grimacing. "Garrath, I don't understand. You see how capable Janet is, you let her deal with the business of a major international corporation, you even teach her to fly helicopters, and yet you won't let her take responsibility for choosing someone to love. That doesn't make any sense at all."

"You don't mean someone, you mean Andy Walker," he said, suddenly curt.

"Well, suppose I do mean Andy? You seem to think he's a good worker, good enough to be promoted quickly on the rigs. He's sweet and good-natured, and really cares for Janet, so I don't see why—"

"Because I know what's best for my sister," he snapped, and then seemed to hear the unreasonableness of what he'd just said. He paused, took a deep breath and leaned back against a protruding rock to stare up at the sky for a thoughtful moment before continuing.

"Look, Blaine," he began finally. "Janet is a very wealthy and, through St. Clair's, a powerful young lady. I've learned from painful personal experience that wealth and power can attract the wrong kind of caring."

What personal experiences he was referring to didn't bear thinking of. Blaine focused on the other part of his explanation. "But surely you don't think Andy is some kind of fortune hunter!"

"I wouldn't have thought so, not at first. But...." He cut himself off, shaking his head. "Let's just say that I do know that Andy was very much a ladies' man when he first came to work for me, always looking for the good time only. And he found it quite often. His little-boy-lost looks charm a fair number of women."

He was very much like you, wasn't he, she felt like saying. But prudently she held her tongue.

"And I just find it difficult to believe that he's given all that up for true love's sake. But for a share of St. Clair's? That I might believe."

"Garrath! That's...that's disgusting!" She thumped a hard-boiled egg against the rock, splintering its shell. "I'm sure Andy isn't like that at all. But even if you were right, I would still say Janet should be allowed to make her own decisions and mistakes, just as you were. You can tell her your feelings and doubts, but if you keep on with the overbearing big brother act, she's liable to end up hating you.''

"Janet won't hate me. She'll understand that what I'm doing, I'm doing for her own good.''

"People who do things for our own good are the ones we usually hate the most!'' Blaine pronounced, biting into the shelled egg.

The rest of their conversation was less controversial. After Blaine had stuffed herself completely, they continued walking, following a deer path worn through knee-high heather to a gorge cut through the hills by a quick-running stream. From the bottom of the narrow valley the presence of the mountains seemed even more overpowering.

The bluish one looking down on them was named for its color, Garrath said. Blaven, the blue mountain. And beyond Blaven loomed the serrated ridges of the Black Cuillins, the most savage mountain range in the British Isles. Each year rescue squads had to go out to save climbers caught by sudden weather changes or by a lack of the necessary skill on the precipitous and dangerous peaks.

"Occasionally the rescue comes too late," Garrath said solemnly, staring up at the dark masses. "There's some evidence that ancient tribes may have made sacrifices of one sort or another to the spirits of the Cuillins. Though that practice has fallen into disfavor in our enlightened age, the mountains seem to demand a sacrifice of their own now and again.''

Blaine shivered. The Cuillins did indeed look both demanding and unforgiving.

A little farther on the stream widened into a small

dark pool at the foot of a small but forceful water-fall. The cascade gushed over sharp rocks, dropping about six feet into the pool. Trying desperately to leap from the pool to the stream above the waterfall were salmon.

The silvery brown fish wriggled forward in the pool, fighting the current. Inch by hard-won inch they struggled, until they were as close as they could get to the falls. Then they would leap wildly, right at the rock face—and fall short. The frothing torrent would catch them and fling them viciously back into the pool.

But immediately they would begin the fight to get into position for another try. And they tried and tried and tried. The only thing stronger than the force of the rushing water was the instinct driving them on.

"The poor things," Blaine said. She sympathized totally with their irrational illogical struggles but refused to think of why she should be in such sympathy.

"They aren't the only inhabitants of pools like this," Garrath said. "There are kelpies, too."

"Kelpies?" Blaine, kneeling on the bank next to the pool, leaned over to peer deeper into the water. "Is that a kind of fish?"

Garrath sat beside her. "No, though they do live in places of flowing water like this. They appear, espe-cially to young beautiful women, in the guise of a sleek handsome stallion. But if the young woman is foolish enough to climb onto the horse's back, he dashes with her into the depths of the pool, and . . . ." He paused ominously.

Blaine waited, not looking at him. She had caught on about halfway through Garrath's calm recital of his outrageous tale and had dropped her fingers into the pool. She was ready.

"...she is never heard of again!"

He had barely spoken the last word when Blaine dashed him with a handful of the icy cold water.

"Why, you little devil!" he accused, smiling dangerously.

"You were teasing me!" she defended.

"Now I've a good mind to put you over my knee for a good skelping," he threatened, his look leaving her in no doubt as to the meaning of the word.

"You wouldn't dare!"

"Wouldn't I?" he asked, but he was laughing. And when he grabbed her shoulders and pulled her to him it was a totally different part of her anatomy that received his attention.

He kissed her, a kiss tasting of the cold stream water and their mutual amusement. It was sweet and exhilarating and tantalizing, and it deepened so quickly that there wasn't time for Blaine to wonder if she should or shouldn't. She was.

An instinct as elemental as that driving the salmon upstream occupied them for some time. And then the fog came down.

Not a little-cat-feet fog but a great lion's paw dropped suddenly over them. The sun became a flat white circle and then was swallowed completely by a cold damp shadow rolling across the sky.

"Damn!" Garrath muttered as the change in temperature broke through the spell of their kisses. He stood abruptly and pulled Blaine to her feet. "I'm sorry, I should have seen this coming sooner. But you distracted me, you know."

She blushed, but this was one time when she didn't

have to worry about his seeing the signs of her embarrassment. He was looking elsewhere.

She looked, too, and saw almost nothing but swirling and rapidly thickening gray around them. The sun had disappeared, leaving a cold gloomy twilight behind. Blaven, the Cuillins, even the nearby hills were vague dark shapes. But when she looked in the direction in which she expected to see Glenclair, there was nothing, not even the slightest hint of a landmark. They were all at once marooned on a small island lost in a sea of mist.

Blaine shivered now for real. Garrath was pulling the extra sweaters he had brought along from his pack. "Put this on, quickly," he said, and she obeyed without argument. "We'll have to head for the cottage."

Panic touched her. How could they head for anything in this fog? How could he possibly know which way to go? She thought of the mountains, unseen now, but still there, and the sacrifices they sometimes demanded. Was this going to be one of those times? She didn't think she could move, she was so frightened.

And then Garrath took her hand. "Don't let go," he said, and started walking. The fear left her.

It wasn't logical; the danger was very present. The fog thickened with every passing minute until she was blindly following Garrath, barely able to see her own feet much less the terrain they were traveling. And some of it was very rough, scree that shifted and slipped beneath her feet, bracken-covered slopes where there wasn't a path, boulder-strewn places where Garrath practically carried her. But throughout it all she was never really afraid, except for one brief moment—when her hand slipped out of Garrath's as he jumped down from a ledge. She cried out then, unable to see him. But his hand grasped hers instantly and she was fine again.

It wasn't logical or rational or sensible, Blaine thought, stumbling along behind him. It didn't take into account all their differences or the fact that he was an overbearing brother, an ultimate bachelor and an oil man. But suddenly she saw how little those things mattered in a situation like this. She believed Garrath would keep her safe, not because she'd arranged some data into an equation and the answer came out right. She just trusted him, without proof, without reason. She just did.

And she loved him the same way.

CHAPTER EIGHTEEN

THE WHITEWASHED WALLS OF THE COTTAGE LOOMED suddenly out of the fog, just feet in front of them. In moments Garrath was shoving open the door and pulling Blaine inside. He closed the door behind him, thwarting the fog trailing in at their heels like a lost puppy. There was the rasp of a match and the flare of the wick on a brass oil lamp. Light blossomed in its tall glass chimney.

"Make yourself at home, Blaine," Garrath said. "I'll get a fire going."

Wood, kindling and squares of peat were neatly stacked next to the wide open-hearth fireplace. Garrath bent to the task of laying the fire.

The cottage was basically one large room, though there was a small alcove that housed a propane stove and some cupboards in one corner; next to it an open door gave a glimpse of a bathroom sink. Rough exposed beams held up a peaked ceiling, and the small high windows cut through the thick walls were curtainless. The wood floor was smooth with age and bare, except for an occasional throw rug and a huge snow-white sheepskin sprawling in front of the fireplace. A couch and two chairs were grouped there, while tucked into the opposite corner of the room was a wide wood-framed bed.

"My father renovated this old shieling, or cottage.

It was once used by shepherds when they took their flocks to the high pastures in the spring,'' Garrath explained, his voice echoing hollowly as he leaned over the hearth. ''It was his hideaway whenever business or life in general got to be too much. No phones, no television, no radio. But he never managed to stay up here for more than a day before he would come rushing down to find out if St. Clair's had collapsed in his absence.''

''And how about you?'' Blaine asked, her voice just as hollow as his had been. ''Do you use it for the same purpose? And how long do you manage to stay away?''

Garrath laughed, touching a match to the kindling. ''Yes, I've kept it as a refuge. I added more modern plumbing but not electricity or other amenities that would bring in the outside world. And I've been known to hole up in here for...oh, three or four days at a time!''

Confident that the fire was catching, he stood and turned to Blaine, his laughter still molding his features. But his smile faded as he saw her standing exactly where he had left her.

''Good grief, woman, why are you still standing there, and in those damp things! Come over here near the fire immediately.''

Blaine didn't feel cold or damp, just numb. And that feeling, she knew, had nothing to do with the weather. It was a result of being struck by lightning, the bolt out of the blue that had told her she loved Garrath St. Clair.

She'd been caught off guard, the realization sneaking up on her in a moment of weakness, or she might have warded off the knowledge as she had been doing for so long by simply refusing to think it. But once thought, it couldn't be unthought or avoided anymore. The longing, the panic, the sick feeling when she saw him with other women, all were symptoms a schoolgirl could have recognized. Not of physical attraction alone but of love.

She hadn't recognized it because she hadn't wanted to, hadn't wanted the complications and possible hurt that loving him could bring. But now she couldn't hide any longer.

Hide! That was just what Garrath had accused her of, hiding from her feelings, and she had vehemently denied doing so. She saw now that she had indeed been hiding, but could he have seen that before? Could he have known all along that she loved him? Did he know even now?

She looked at him, unable to move. And then he was at her side, concern darkening his eyes.

"Blaine, are you all right?" He put his arm around her and drew her in the direction of the fire. "I'm sorry, I should have realized how this whole thing might have affected you. The fog can be pretty frightening even when you're used to it. I can imagine how you must have felt."

"No...it's not that...I wasn't afraid...not with you..." she tried to explain, but her teeth were chattering so badly the words came out all garbled.

"You're cold! Come on, let's get you out of those wet things."

He pulled off the extra sweater, which was almost white with the mist caught in its wool, then pushed her down onto the couch so he could unlace her shoes and slip them from her feet.

"You don't have to worry, we're safe here. We'll

probably have to stay till morning, but we keep food stored up here, so we won't starve.'' From the rucksack he took the thermos, pouring what was left of the tea into a cup and folding her hands around its warmth.

"Try to drink this,'' he said. He pulled off his own sweater and then went into the bathroom, returning with a large white towel.

In her befuddled state that morning she had just twisted an elastic band around her hair, leaving the long ponytail streaming loosely down her back. Now with one knee on the couch Garrath leaned over her, gently easing the band from her hair and tossing the towel over her head. He began rubbing the long strands with the terry cloth.

"Mrs. M. will have my head if I let you catch a cold, you know. I already received one lecture last night after she tucked you in bed, for not taking better care of you at the spree. I think she likes you.''

"I like her, too,'' Blaine replied, the words muffled by the towel.

"What?'' Garrath asked.

"I like her, too,'' Blaine repeated, but Garrath's ministrations were still causing interference. When he again asked what she'd said, she twisted around, pushed the towel back from her face and looked up at him.

"I said I . . . .''

She never finished the sentence. One glimpse of his deep brown eyes soft with caring, the sensuous line of his mouth, the curl of damp hair lying temptingly across his forehead, and all thoughts of Mrs. M. and everything else fled her mind. Her breath seemed to be coming twice as fast as normal, spurred on by the wild thumping of her heart, and each breath drew in the male muskiness of him, which mixed tantalizingly with the woody smell of the fire clinging to his shirt. Of its own accord her hand reached up to brush that lock of hair back off his forehead and then stayed in the damp curls, sliding around to the back of his neck.

He drew in his breath sharply, and she felt the muscles in his neck cord at her touch. A frown appeared between his black brows.

"Blaine?" Just the one word, coming huskily from deep in his throat.

She knew what he was asking. There was no stick shift here to jab at an inopportune moment, no telephones or Mrs. MacGuigan to interrupt. An isolated cottage, a blazing fire, a man and a woman alone—there would be no stopping if she went into his arms this time.

She put down the cup of tea, then shifted position so that she was kneeling on the couch, more on a level with him. She let her eyes meet his unwaveringly, knowing he would be able to read her answer in their green depths. Then she put her other arm around his neck and leaned forward to press her lips against his.

It was not a gentle kiss. Her movement was soft, tentative; his response was not. His arms went fiercely around her, pulling her up against him and crushing his lips down on hers. The whole world became their mouths moving hungrily together, exploring, tasting, arousing.

It was different, Blaine realized, without the restraint that had made her fight against her feelings before. Then, even as she was swept away by the sensations Garrath could awaken in her, some part of her energy had been diverted to her internal fight against those very sensations. Now there was no struggle, nothing holding her back. She could respond fully to the passion he kindled in her.

And then she didn't think anymore.

The towel fell to the floor as he ran his hands through the long fall of her hair.

"Burnished gold," he whispered, his mouth moving along her jawline to her neck. "I want to see you dressed in only that gold and the firelight."

Slowly he eased them both to their feet, never pausing in the rain of kisses he was loosing on her mouth, her cheeks, neck, the tender lobe of her ear, the pulse at the base of her throat. When they were standing, he began to undress her, his hands moving surely over the buttons of her blouse, the zipper of her jeans, the transparent nylon and lace of her underthings. In moments she was standing before him, the hair falling to her waist her only covering.

He pulled back then, his eyes devouring her, and the warmth of the fire was suddenly eclipsed by the heat on her skin wherever his eyes touched and lingered. He reached up to push the hair back over her shoulders, exposing her breasts to his sight, and their tips hardened in anticipation even before his fingertips moved beguilingly over them.

His hands slid across the silk of her skin, his caressing fingers electrifying at her breasts, her waist, the curve of her hip, weaving a magic spell of desire that made her weak. She swayed against him.

He lifted her in his arms, his mouth capturing hers again. Then he was lowering her to the sheepskin rug spread before the fireplace.

Its downy softness brushed the skin of her back and legs like another pleasuring hand. Garrath kneeled over her and his mouth slowly traveled the path his fingers had blazed. She arched against that moist warmth, caught by a longing so intense it bordered on pain.

"Garrath, please..." she moaned.

"Yes," he breathed. He stood just long enough to throw off his clothing and then he was bending over her again, easing the hard weight of his body onto her softness. His lips covered hers, plundering, enticing her to a feverish yearning, his hands continued to brand her with their fiery touch. His body demanded, hers yielded willingly.

It was a mystical dance, as old as the earth, yet new every time. Choreographed by their passion, orchestrated by desire, they melded together in perfect step, each giving, each taking, each urging the other on until the dance became a dizzying whirl of exquisite pleasure that flashed and flamed and finally crescendoed in a shower of glory and fulfillment.

BLAINE WOKE SUDDENLY. Her eyes flew open and she sat up, clutching the mound of wool blankets to her upper body. There had been a dream, though not *the* dream. But something about this dream had been nearly as disturbing. She had been at home in her apartment and the bell had rung. She was about to open the door when suddenly she knew something horrible waited on the other side of the panel, something that could destroy her.

She shivered, and then the dream lost all importance as she realized she was staring wide-eyed into the room and not seeing a thing.

She knew where she was, in the cottage, and that her eyes were open and she was awake. The soft warmth of the bed beneath her contrasted with the biting chill of the unheated room around her. She remembered the details of the croft, the door to her left, the fireplace in the wall directly ahead, the small unadorned windows. But she couldn't see any of it.

The fire might have gone out, taking away its red gold glow, she reasoned. But still there should be some light, somewhere; not this dark so total that there weren't even slight gradations in the blackness. Never in her life had she seen—felt—darkness so complete, and it terrified her. This was the black night of childhood with its unnamed fears and unknown things lurking in dark corners, only this whole room was dark.

She trembled, and there was a movement in the bed beside her.

"Blaine, are you all right?" Garrath sat up and his arm slipped around her shoulders without hesitation, as if he were attuned to some special homing signal she was giving off. "Is it your nightmare again?"

She shook her head, not realizing that he couldn't see her response. "It's so. . .so dark."

"Oh, my poor city girl," he sympathized. "No neon and fluorescent up here. This is just a mountain night when the fog blots out the stars. But I should have thought about your nightmares and made sure the fire would burn till morning."

"No, it's all right, I didn't—"

"Ssh," he cut off her protests, pulling her back down into the bed with him. "It doesn't matter. Now I can chase away your bad dreams the way I wanted to that first night, on the rig. Holding you then without touching you like this...and this...was the worst torture I've ever endured.''

The darkness suddenly didn't matter. It was just a black velvet cloak wrapping them in its snug intimacy. Garrath's breath was hot against her ear, while his hands were lighting wildfires over the rest of her.

''I'll drive out those dreams, Blaine. There won't be room in your nights for them, only for me and the passion we share. I'll burn them out of your soul. I will,'' he said fiercely.

And he proceeded to show her how.

PALE LEMON GLIMMERED AT THE WINDOWS, but the room was still shadowy when Blaine woke in the morning. Garrath's eyes remained closed, and she lay motionless for a few moments, savoring the feeling of waking up beside him. How had she ever endured twenty-five years of sleeping alone, she wondered. She'd heard of some tribal societies where whole families slept together all the time and thought she understood their reasoning now. Company was so utterly wonderful and comforting, especially when the company in your bed was the man you loved.

Loved. Smiling, she hugged the word to her. *I love you, Garrath St. Clair,* she spelled out secretly in her mind.

They hadn't verbalized their love yet. Their passion hadn't needed or allowed time for words. But they would, she knew. And until then it was nice to hold the words within her like a cache of precious jewels.

She knew now why she'd sympathized so strongly with the salmon in their instinctual battle. She, too, had been fighting, but in her case she'd been fighting *against* her instinct, against the force she couldn't escape. There were still obstacles to leap, problems she and Garrath would have to face and deal with, but at least now she was swimming in the right direction.

"You look very pleased with yourself this morning." The teasing voice snapped her out of her reverie. Garrath's eyes were open and focused intently on her.

"And why shouldn't I be? I've discovered the answer to a question that's been nagging at me since before I met you."

"And what is this mysterious question?"

"Which of your names fit you better. The strong bold Garrath or the gentle tender St. Clair."

"And what did you decide, dear analyst?"

A smile cut her dimple deep into her cheek. "My findings are—both. You are strong, bold, gentle and tender."

"And on what are your findings based, Dr. Christensen?"

"Personal experimentation." Blaine paused and twined her arms around Garrath's neck. "Very, very personal."

He laughed, richly and unrestrained, happiness easing the hard lines of his cheek and jaw. Then he reached down and delivered a light slap to her bottom.

"Well, doctor, unless you're planning a few more similar experiments right now, you'd better get up and out of this bed," he warned.

"Is that a threat. . .or a promise?" Blaine delivered the old line with a perfectly straight face and a wriggling that got her an immediate nonverbal response.

"Blaine. . ." he groaned. "I'm trying to obey my

conscience that says we should head back to Glenclair as soon as possible, so Janet and Mrs. M.
won't send out the rescue squad. But when you do
that...."

Blaine changed tactics instantly, easing away from
his hands, which were definitely not listening to his
conscience.

"Oh, Garrath, I didn't even think about them!"
she exclaimed remorsefully. "Will they have been
worrying all night while we—" She broke off, red
staining her cheeks.

"They'll have expected that we would head for the
cottage if we were caught in the fog," he reassured
her, grinning over her discomfort. "But," he added
reluctantly, "I'm sure they'll feel a lot better when
they get concrete proof that we're safe and sound."

With all good intentions she sat up quickly and
swung her legs over the edge of the bed. But when the
icy morning air hit her bare legs and shoulders, and
she realized the rest of her was equally as vulnerable
to the cold and Garrath's very interested eyes, she
slid back beneath the blankets, pulling them up to her
chin.

"Could I talk you into starting the fire first?" she
begged.

His expression was decidedly devilish as he leaned
over her possessively. "For a price," he intoned.

"Garrath! Your sister and dear old nanny are waiting!"

It was a close thing, but eventually conscience won
out. Garrath threw back his side of the covers and
bounded up out of the bed. Blaine savored the sight
of his lithe virile body as he moved to the fireplace,
remembering the feel of that body against hers, the

pleasure it had given, and taken of her. It was all she could do not to call him back into the bed.

Breakfast was filling, if not gourmet, assembled from the selection of freeze-dried and canned foods kept at the cottage. But Blaine didn't think she would have noticed if coddled newsprint had been served up, not with Garrath sitting across from her, occasionally reaching out to rub a finger along the curve of her cheek.

They were two lovesick teenagers on the walk back, stopping often to kiss and hug, holding hands, laughing over nothing whenever their eyes met. They rested again by the salmon leap, and Blaine cheered wildly when one of the persevering fish succeeded and swam off in the upper stream with a triumphant swish of his silverish tail.

She hadn't realized how far they had walked the day before, but it took them a good two hours to reach the hill above Glenclair. They raced like children down that last slope. When Blaine reached the back door first, Garrath pinned her there with caressing hands and demanded a consolation prize. "For coming in second," he said.

"Last," she rubbed it in.

"Then I need even more consolation," he returned. She obliged willingly. The consolation might have continued for some time if her stomach hadn't decided to growl.

Garrath pulled back, grinning. "Hungry again? Or is this just your sneaky way of getting out of a compromising situation?"

"Well, breakfast was rather meager," she temporized.

Laughing, he released her and pulled open the

door. "I concede. Why don't you go fetch up Janet while I beard Mrs. M. in her kitchen and beg some sustenance. Of course I will first have to endure a scolding for missing last night's dinner, so it may take a while."

Blaine was humming as she headed toward the main part of the house. She felt perfect, whole again, as if a piece of her had been missing for years and she'd finally found it. Would Janet be able to tell all that had happened at the cottage, she wondered. Probably so; and if it wasn't completely obvious, Janet wouldn't hesitate to ask. She imagined they were going to have a very lively, interesting conversation.

Blaine danced joyfully into the entryway hall—and then stopped, frozen suddenly in her tracks. Standing there, looking at her with a thin smile, was the last person on earth she would have expected to see.

"Richard! What are you doing here?"

His smile faltered just slightly. "Surprising you. Pleasantly, I'd hoped."

With a guilty start she realized how unwelcoming her comment had sounded. This was Richard Perry, she told herself, and her first reaction to seeing him couldn't be resentment. Not of Richard.

"Of course pleasantly," she said, hoping her monumental effort was producing the smile she intended. She forced her feet to carry her toward him, where he stood next to a bewildered-looking Janet. "You just. . . startled me."

"I guess that's the risk of surprising someone," he said blandly, and Blaine managed a light almost-natural-sounding laugh.

"Did you meet Janet?" she asked inanely. Of

course they had met! They hadn't been standing there talking without introducing themselves. But she was floundering, trying to regain her balance in a world turned suddenly upside down.

For the truth was she hadn't thought of Richard since the night she'd spoken to him on the phone in Garrath's house in Edinburgh. He'd totally ignored her plea for help then, or so it had seemed. She had felt that he'd betrayed her by thinking more of business and of pleasing Garrath than of her. Then she and Garrath had left Edinburgh and begun the journey that was to take her all the way to last night's discovery—of a whole new universe of emotions she hadn't known existed. San Francisco and Richard and her life with him had faded into nonexistence. Except perhaps in her dream early this morning.

But now he was here. Steady familiar Richard with his weed-brown hair attractively styled in what Blaine always thought of as entrepreneur wave and his pale calculating brown eyes. Richard, who had been there for her through the difficult times, even if recently he had let business come between them. Richard, whom she wouldn't hurt for anything, not if she could help it. But was she going to be able to help it?

"We met," Janet said. Richard nodded in turn.

"Yes, she was just telling me that you and Garrath were hill walking yesterday when the fog came down, that you hadn't come back last night, but she assumed you'd made it to their cottage. Are you all right, Blaine? You don't look any the worse for wear after your night in the wilds."

"No...I...the cottage is very nice, with all the necessities. And Garrath is a good...guide." *Don't blush, please don't blush.* "There wasn't really any danger."

"Good," he said. "I was worried." And staid, undemonstrative Richard reached out, pulled Blaine to him, and pressed his cool lips to hers.

She would have been less shocked had he bitten her. Never in all the years they had known each other had he shown more than polite formality toward her in public. Hand holding, arms around shoulders in a movie, a spontaneous kiss on the cheek—these were foreign to Richard. So a proprietary display in front of a virtual stranger was unbelievable. So unbelievable that Blaine was too stunned to ward it off or even shorten its duration. A coldly sardonic voice took care of that.

"You must be Richard Perry," Garrath said.

CHAPTER NINETEEN

LATE THAT NIGHT, as Blaine soaked in a tub so hot that the room was misting over, she tried to decide which of the two men in her life she was angriest with—without success. Both of them had acted like children. They'd played a vicious game of tug-of-war with Blaine as the rope, and it had left her more than a little frayed around the edges. She still couldn't believe it had all happened.

Admittedly, the episode in the entryway hall had not got things off to a perfect start. She could imagine how she would have felt were the positions reversed, and she had walked into a room to find Garrath holding another woman. But even so, it seemed he overreacted.

When Blaine had turned around, she'd found herself facing a stranger. All the happiness and love that had lightened Garrath's features just minutes before as they'd run down the hill to Glenclair was gone, replaced by a closed dark look and a twisted accusing smile, neither of which improved with Richard's cheerful response.

"And you must be St. Clair. Glad to meet you," he said, thrusting out a hand. "I've brought the equipment you ordered."

After a painfully protracted hesitation, Garrath shook the offered hand—one abrupt shake. But his eyes were on Richard's other arm, the one still firmly around Blaine's shoulders.

"Such personal service," he drawled. "I'm honored."

"Well, it wasn't in the original plan, I must admit. It's not typical procedure." Richard smiled deprecatingly. "But Blaine's call from Edinburgh persuaded me to make an exception in this case."

Garrath's glance was corrosive. "Oh, Blaine called you, did she? And persuaded you to come over. I see."

He didn't see, of course. She wanted to tell him not to be so stupid, that yes, she'd called Richard, and yes, she'd even wanted to get out of the job and away from him then. But that was before, long before, when she was still resisting her feelings. It had nothing to do with last night in the cottage or what she felt now. It certainly wasn't the betrayal his eyes were accusing her of.

But she couldn't say any of that in front of Janet and Richard. As the afternoon wore painfully on, she kept trying to get a moment alone with Garrath, but she never managed it, and she wasn't sure just why. Had he purposely avoided her? Or was it because Richard had clung like a burr to her side?

That was the second unbelievable thing: Richard's behavior.

They had always kept the business and personal aspects of their relationship strictly separate. It had been easy enough to do since Richard had never been particularly demonstrative in public or in private. Blaine hadn't minded and it wasn't until now that she realized why. With the new awareness loving Garrath had brought, she saw that she hadn't minded Richard's restraint because there hadn't been any fire between the two of them to make her care. The love they shared was not at all the kind she felt for Garrath, with whom such a hands-off policy would be unthinkable.

Richard had come into her life saying he would take the place of Len, and he'd succeeded much better, possibly, than he'd planned. With much the same suddenness that she'd realized she loved Garrath, Blaine now saw that she loved Richard, not as a woman loves a man but as a sister loves a brother.

The old restrained Richard seemed to have disappeared with his arrival at Glenclair, however. That first kiss in the hall was just the beginning. From that point on he was never far away, slipping an arm around her waist as they walked to the dining room for lunch, hovering over her as they unpacked the computer equipment in the office—under Garrath's malevolent eye—and appropriating the space beside her on the couch after dinner as they sat around the fire having a drink. His usual easy-going charm was well displayed as he told stories about his trip over, inquired about Sithein One, drew Janet out about Janclair. But too many of his comments included, "Blaine and I," "we often," and "we always," until Blaine was ready to scream. He seemed to be purposely flaunting their personal relationship and she couldn't understand why.

And then she did understand, after the worst moment of the whole miserable day.

It was while they were having their after-dinner drinks, brandy for Janet and herself, whiskey for Garrath and Richard. Blaine, her "head" of the previous morning still too fresh in her mind, was sipping slowly. Richard had already consumed two Highland drams and Blaine was beginning to wonder if she should, using her experience as an example, urge caution, when he set down his glass and took her hand. Standing up, he pulled her to her feet.

"I think Janet and Garrath will excuse us now, don't you, darling?" he said, compounding her puzzled look. "After the long trip I'm ready for an early...sleep."

Blaine gaped at him, unable to believe her ears. The Richard Perry she knew could not possibly have delivered that line complete with deliberately suggestive pause! But it seemed he had. Garrath's thunderous scowl and undisguisedly sarcastic comment confirmed it.

"Of course we'll excuse you," he sneered. "I understand perfectly why you might want an early night. And Blaine is probably just as in need of one as you are, Richard. We didn't get much sleep last night." His pause matched Richard's. "Strange surroundings, you know."

And then she knew. If they had been knights in the Middle Ages, they would have been jousting in some tournament for "my lady's favors." They'd been tilting at each other all afternoon and evening, Richard with sharp subtle thrusts, Garrath in a full charge. And the lady in this case was her.

There were some women, Blaine knew, who would be thrilled by the sight of two grown men acting like fools over them. She wasn't one of them, being too aware that there was going to be a lot of hurt resulting from the situation. But for the moment, the emotion gripping her most strongly was anger. Whatever their reasons, they were both acting unpardonably. It was time to put an end to this nonsense.

"I'm going to stay up awhile longer," she told Richard, deliberately disengaging her hand from his. Just as deliberately she added, "I'll see you in the morning."

A choleric purple pink suffused his pale skin. "Oh, well, I can wait if you want. . . ." he backpedaled, but Blaine cut him off firmly.

"You're tired. Please, go ahead. We'll have plenty of time to visit more tomorrow."

There was nothing Richard could do but go. With a brusque good-night to the others and a last imploring look at Blaine, he walked out and up the stairs.

Blaine stared after him for a moment, thinking sadly of what their "visit" tomorrow would have to include, and then turned, eyes flashing with emerald fury, to Garrath.

Beside him, Janet popped out of her chair. "I'm for bed, too," she announced, and Blaine flashed her a grateful look. Janet had been doing her fair share all day, trying to steer an even course through choppy waters she accurately sensed but couldn't fathom. Blaine had lost count of the number of times she had filled in the gaping silences after some of Garrath's most biting contributions to the conversation. And now she had correctly assumed that Blaine wanted to be alone with Garrath.

"See you two in the mornin', luvs," she called, heading rapidly for the door. But Garrath forestalled the plan.

"I'll go up with you." He moved beside his sister. "Good-night, Blaine." Ignoring Janet's despairing look and the beginning of Blaine's protest, he had left.

Which was how Blaine had ended up in a steaming tub, trying to soak away her tension and her fury.

Well, she told herself in the immortal words of that model for womanhood everywhere, Scarlett O'Hara, tomorrow is another day. She would see to it that she got a chance to tell Garrath precisely what she thought of his unreasonable and unfair jealousy, even if she had to do it in front of an audience.

But first would come the confrontation she thought of with less pleasurable anticipation—the one with Richard.

It wasn't going to be easy to tell him what she had discovered about her feelings, but she knew it had to be done, and the sooner the better. With a sigh she slipped her toe into the silver ring on the bathtub plug and pulled. Between one thing and another she didn't think she was going to get much sleep tonight, but she might as well try.

She dried herself and unclipped her hair from the top of her head. She started brushing out the loosened length but stopped when she caught sight of her reflection in the mirror. The long strands hanging over her shoulders were too vivid a reminder of last night, of Garrath pushing her hair back from her naked body to let his eyes, and then his mouth and hands, caress her. That kind of reminder she could do without, especially since she was going to be spending this night far differently than she had expected. Miserably alone instead of ecstatically in Garrath's arms again.

She slipped into her fleecy white robe and pulled the tie belt tight before opening the door and hurrying down the hall to her room. Whether it was the hot bath or simply the exhaustion brought on by a trying day, she was beginning to feel a bit woolly-headed. Not sleepy, exactly; but taken advantage of at the right moment, it just might be sufficient to win her some oblivion.

The door to her bedroom shut behind her with its usual protesting squeak, and Blaine moved toward the luxury of the fireplace. The fire she'd lighted before going for her bath had poured wall-to-wall warmth into the room, making it toasty and welcoming. She smiled. And then a movement made her turn toward the bed and her smile disappeared.

"What are you doing in here, Richard?" she demanded icily of the man sitting on the edge of her bed.

"I wanted to talk to you," he said softly. "To apologize first of all. I was a boor tonight."

His thin lips were curved in a sheepish smile that gave him a slightly vague, highly vulnerable and entirely innocent look. She had seen him sit through business meetings with that same look on his face, lulling others into a false sense of superiority—until he went in for the kill. But knowing that the look was at least part facade didn't make her immune. The ice was melting.

"Yes, you were." It didn't come out particularly chastising.

"I honestly don't know what got into me. I've never acted that way in my life, especially not with a client as important and influential as St. Clair. I'm sorry."

Blaine smiled then, faintly but fondly. Richard was apologizing to her, but she strongly suspected he was sorriest for the damage he might have done to his relationship with Garrath. Which sounded very much like the Richard Perry she knew.

"All right, Richard. I understand."

"Then won't you come over here and let me talk to you?"

"Talk?" Dread cut through her like a North Sea breeze. "What do we have to talk about that can't wait till morning? I'm not angry with you anymore, but I am awfully tired."

"It might be just as difficult to get you alone to-morrow as it was today," he said ruefully. "And it's important. Please."

She wasn't ready for this, she knew. She'd assumed she had at least until morning to decide on the best way to explain things to Richard. But something in his voice told her that what he was about to say would force her to tell him, somehow, right now.

Her feet felt weighted with lead as she crossed to where he sat on the edge of the bed. Gingerly she eased down beside him, racking her brain, trying to decide whether or not it would be best to forestall him by delivering her news first. But how? How could she tell him she loved someone else?

He took the decision out of her hands. "I want us to get married, Blaine. Right away. As soon as we can finish up this job and get back home."

"Married?" This was the last thing she had expected. Oh, Richard had proposed several times in the past, but always in a very casual way. He had never pressed her for an answer or seemed bothered by her hesitation.

"But you know I...we decided to wait awhile, to not rush into anything."

"I've changed my mind. I don't want to wait, don't see any reason to. We love each other, and no one could really accuse us of rushing into it after all this time. I want you to be my wife now."

"Oh, Richard!" she cried miserably. This was not a casual proposal; he wasn't going to be put off by some temporizing remark. She was going to have to refuse him and tell him why. But how could she? She did love him; not in the way he was talking about, of course, but she still didn't want to hurt him. What was she going to do?

His arm slid around her waist. "We can get rid of your apartment. Mine's larger. I think our furniture will consolidate nicely. And the operating expenses of one household will be a lot cheaper than for two."

"You make it sound like a business merger." No dimple appeared with her wan smile.

"Were you expecting flowers and candy and a ring and me down on my knees?" he asked, a faint bitterness in his voice.

She shook her head. "No, Richard, it isn't that. But I...I can't marry you."

"I don't see any point in waiting."

"I'm not talking about waiting. I can't marry you, ever."

There, she had said it. Now he would ask why and the whole hurtful thing would come out. She felt like crying already, but at least it would soon be over.

He didn't ask why, though, didn't say anything. He just looked at her steadily for a moment, in the same coolly calculating way he looked over contracts or profit-and-loss sheets. Then the arm that had been loosely circling her waist tightened, and his other hand was suddenly on the material of her robe where it covered her knee. He leaned forward and pressed his dry lips to hers.

"Richard..." she admonished gently, pulling back from his kiss, which tasted faintly of whiskey.

The hand on her waist moved to the back of her neck, holding her head so that he could find her lips again, while the other one pressed upward to her thigh. His mouth was moving insistently on hers as he tried to part her lips to his more intimate invasion.

She wasn't worried, except about finding the right words to tell him about her love for Garrath, words that would end this situation as quickly and painlessly as possible. After all, this was Richard, ordinary reasonable Richard. She reached up, pushing lightly at his shoulders.

His response was the opposite of what she expected. He leaned roughly against her, shoving her backward onto the bed. One of his legs came down across hers, trapping her. She felt the first stirrings of fear.

She wrested her mouth from his. "Richard, stop this right now! Let me up! We need to talk."

"I don't want to talk. We've had enough talk between us. I love you, Blaine, I want you. And I'm tired of waiting."

Hysterical laughter bubbled in her throat. "You can't mean this. Don't be silly." But even as she said the words, she knew the situation was not at all funny. His fingers were digging painfully into the back of her neck, while his mouth was at her throat. When his other hand went to the belt of her robe, panic welled up in her.

She didn't know what to do. She had never felt so vulnerable, so confused. Pushing against his chest with all her might didn't seem to be having any effect on him; the weight of his body and his leg across hers prevented her wriggling free. She couldn't scream, not when doing so would probably bring Garrath in to witness the scene. Could she hit Richard Perry?

The traitorous belt gave way easily and he pushed apart the edges of her robe. His hand went to her breast, pressing roughly.

"Blaine, Blaine, I need you. We belong together. I'll prove it to you."

She grabbed his wrist, sinking her nails into the skin, but he didn't seem to notice. *Hit him,* she thought. *You're going to have to hit him.* But she didn't know if she could do it.

"No," she moaned, tears filling her eyes. "Richard, please, no."

But he wasn't listening; he didn't see her tears. His breath was hot against her neck and then his lips were closing over hers again. His hand moved lower and his knee pressed between her legs.

Bile rose in Blaine's throat. This couldn't be happening. Not with Richard, who had always taken care of her, protected her, loved her. It wasn't possible.

And then a wail filled the room. Not the scream building deep inside Blaine but the high-pitched squeak of the unoiled hinge on the door.

"Blaine, are you asleep? An hour alone in my bed made me realize what an idiot...."

Garrath had taken three long steps into the firelit room before he saw Blaine—and Richard. For an eternity the three of them were frozen, a tableau from some ridiculous French farce. Until Garrath spoke again, his voice venomous.

"But I see you aren't alone. Which makes me doubly an idiot." There was another squeak, but this time it ended with the crash of the door slamming shut.

"Garrath!" she cried. But he was gone.

She would have fought Richard then, hitting, biting, kicking, scratching. But none of that was necessary. He'd frozen at the sound of Garrath's voice, and with the slamming of the door he went limp. Blaine pushed him away easily.

She sat up, clutching the edges of her robe together. Her first instinct, to race after Garrath and explain, was already fading. How could she explain what she didn't understand?

Next to her, Richard sat up, slowly, like an old, old man. His face looked gray even in the golden light of the fire.

"Blaine, oh Blaine," he moaned, not looking at her.

"Get out of here," she said flatly, and her nails dug deep into her palms. "Right now."

"But I have to—"

"Now, Richard."

He looked at her then, with bleary old-man eyes, and whatever he saw convinced him she meant what she said. At the door he turned back. But he didn't say anything, and the door creaked very plaintively as he closed it behind himself.

Blaine was alone. She buried her face in her pillow and let the tears come. And come.

SHE WOKE WITH A FRESH OUTLOOK in spite of the previous night's horrible muddle. It was a new day, after all. She would straighten out everything—and everyone—this morning. Somehow.

The morning itself wasn't as optimistic. A light drizzle was dripping from skies piled high with dirty laundry. The surface of the small loch was gray and dull, its sheen tarnished by wind and rain. Though it was after eight o'clock, it didn't look as if the sun had even bothered to rise.

Blaine had just pulled a sweater on over her blouse and jeans when a light tapping at her door made her breath catch in her throat. Garrath or Richard, she wondered. Who was she going to have to face first?

It turned out to be neither. The head that poked around the door in answer to her "Come in," was Janet's.

"Is the coast clear?" she asked, grinning at Blaine. "No poisoned darts flying, no grenades being lobbed?"

Blaine laughed, relieved. "All's quiet on the front for the moment," she said.

Janet crossed the room to perch on the end of Blaine's bed, leaning against the thick velvet draping the canopy post. "The front wasn't so quiet late last night, though, was it? With all the traffic in the upper hall, it sounded a lot like an Edwardian house party."

"Edwardian... house party? What's that?"

"Tsk, tsk. I can see your education has been sadly neglected, my dear." Janet's impersonation of a snobbish society matron was perfect, including the exaggerated roll of the eyes. "At the turn of the century in merry old England, during the reign of King Edward VIII, the upper class was known for its weekend house parties. Apparently, after the formal retiring, the halls were often filled with the patter of not-so-little feet as the guests regrouped for the after hours entertainment—if you take my meaning. They say that truly understanding hostesses attached name cards to the bedroom doors, to make sure a gentleman had no trouble finding his way to the right lady's chamber."

She tilted her curl-capped head coyly. "But even without such courtesies, none of last night's traffic found its way to my door, so I have to assume it was all in your direction." She looked expectantly at Blaine.

"Janet St. Clair, you are a terror!" Blaine laughed, then sobered. "But your romantic imagination is working overtime again. The traffic, as you put it, was not at all entertaining. It was awful."

"After the sparks flying all of yesterday, I'm not surprised. Was it Garrath or Richard?"

Blaine had to pick up her brush and start drawing it through her hair as an excuse to turn away from Janet before she could answer. "Both."

"Both! Good grief! I would have thought you'd got enough of their thrust and parry without carrying on through the night."

"Janet! I was not carrying on and it wasn't my idea anyway. And I certainly did have enough of their nonsense, and...oh...oh, damn!" To her shame, tears sprang to her eyes and rippled in her voice.

Immediately Janet's teasing grin disappeared. She bounded off the bed and was instantly at Blaine's side.

"Oh, dearie, I'm sorry. Forgive my runaway mouth. Was it really that bad?"

Blaine nodded, looking around desperately for a tissue. "Worse. For all of us." She gave a brief, highly expurgated account of the previous evening's events. "And now I have to think of some way to explain things to Garrath, and something to say to Richard when I would rather never set eyes on him again. So far I haven't been too successful," she con-

cluded, giving up the search for a hankie and wiping
her eyes with the back of her hand.

"Well, if it's any consolation, you'll have a day or
two before you have to do any explaining to my dear
dim-witted brother," Janet said sympathetically.

"What . . . what do you mean?"

"I mean Garrath left Glenclair a couple of hours
ago."

"Left! But why? Where did he go?"

"The where I can answer: Edinburgh. The why
I'm a little vague on. I only got the message second-
hand from Mrs. M. But it seems Diana Mills called
about some trouble, and Garrath went rushing off to
the rescue. He wasn't sure when he would be back."

"Diana. . ." Blaine breathed around the knife
stuck in her heart, its blade honed by the memory of
Diana Mills's high-fashion beauty, her smoke gray
eyes and sultry voice, her bright red nails lying possessively on Garrath's arm.

Garrath, furious, believing the worst of Blaine,
hadn't stayed to work things out. He'd taken his injured male pride to Edinburgh, to the beautiful
Diana. Would they be together at the house on Rose
Crescent this time? Would Diana bathe in the huge
tub, scenting her bath with the heather bath beads?
Would Garrath join her in the honey-sweet water?

"Oh, Blaine, don't look like that," Janet said.
"Garrath doesn't care anything for that woman except as an efficient machine. She's a good secretary,
if you disregard her snootiness. I'm sure it's business
and nothing else."

Blaine didn't believe it, though she tried to put on
a good face for Janet's benefit. She agreed to the
younger girl's suggestion that they get some break-

fast, willing to put off facing Richard until she'd had time to absorb this new shock. But as they sat in the solarium, which was minus its cheering sunshine, it wasn't easy to keep her thoughts from Garrath and Diana and his wide bed at Rose Crescent.

Her spirits took another plunge when they finished eating and took their dishes into the kitchen. Mrs. M. was just lifting two golden-crusted berry pies from the oven of the antique stove, and the room was thick with their sweet fruity smell.

"Ah, Blaine," she said as they greeted her. "I have a note for you from Garrath."

"For...me?"

"Aye, so he told me. 'Make sure she gets it first thing this mornin', Mrs. M.,' didn't he say? And in a right snit, he was, too, his voice dark as a cloud over the Cuillins," she said gruffly, pulling off her oven mitts and taking a folded piece of paper from her apron pocket. "So here 'tis."

Blaine's hand trembled as she took the single sheet of cream-colored stationery from the woman, whose small head was now cocked, birdlike, to one side as if she were listening to, or for, something. Blaine was hesitating, trying to decide if she dared open the note in front of an audience, when Mrs. M. turned to Janet.

"And as for you, miss, I've the supply list to be goin' over with ye, and now's as good a time as any." She had Janet by the arm and was dragging her away toward the pantry, ignoring Janet's protests that she thought they had finished that task just a few days ago. "Dinna be puttin' off things, lass. It willna take long."

Blaine smiled to herself. It probably *wouldn't* take

long, she guessed. Just long enough to give Blaine some privacy, bless the woman. As Charlie had said, Mrs. M.'s ears were indeed good at telling her things, even when there wasn't anything to hear except strained silence.

She leaned against the range, taking comfort from the residual warmth left from the morning's baking. Biting her lower lip nervously, she unfolded the note.

It was brief, unsigned and to the point.

Blaine—
Please work on the computer installation while I'm gone. I want it completed as soon as possible.

The last three words were boldly underlined—twice.

She could picture him sitting at his massive rolltop desk, callously dashing off the message, could see the gleaming gold of the felt-tipped pen in his hand, the vicious slashing motion as he underlined his orders once, and then, not satisfied, again.

A sad smile touched her lips. It seemed they had come full circle. Once again he wanted her out of his life as quickly as possible, having decided she wasn't exactly what he had expected. Only this wasn't Sithein One, and it wasn't his job he didn't think she was worthy of; it was his love.

It wasn't fair this time any more than it had been the last time. He'd condemned her without hesitation, hadn't given her a chance to explain. Granted, the evidence had been pretty damning, especially after the impression of their relationship Richard had worked so hard to give Garrath. But if he had truly loved her, wouldn't he have wanted to give her that chance in spite of everything?

He hadn't said he loved her, of course, not in words. But she hadn't voiced her love for him either and had assumed that the feeling was there for him anyway just as it was for her. Now she knew she'd been wrong. The physical attraction was all he'd ever felt, and once his male vanity was injured by the thought that his "conquest" was not unique, that attraction had ended.

Blaine looked once again at the cruel note with its harsh underlining, then crumpled the paper. Opening cupboards until she found the trash basket, she hurled it inside.

She wouldn't need the note to remember her instructions, she thought coldly. They were engraved on her mind and she would follow them. She would complete the installation as rapidly as she knew how and head back to San Francisco. She couldn't really say "back home" anymore, because some time in the past few days San Francisco had stopped being home. But homey or not, it was where she belonged, and it was time for her to do as she'd intended before the magic of moors and glens had sidetracked her into believing in fairy tales and handsome princes, before she'd forgotten that she knew better than to love a hard unfeeling oil man. But she remembered now. There wouldn't be any reason to forget again.

CHAPTER TWENTY

SHE HATED HIM, she thought as she trudged up the stairs. She had often heard that love and hate were the closest of emotions; now she knew it was true. She hated Garrath St. Clair now as fervently as she'd loved him before. Unfortunately she also still loved him—and that was what hurt.

Love and hate, misery and anger were raging inside her like some exotic tropical disease. Her heart felt cracked down the middle, breathing seemed too much of an effort and her head ached with a spate of unshed tears. But though the symptoms were painful, she knew the disease wasn't terminal.

She would survive loving, and losing, Garrath. She might never feel completely well again, but she would survive. A good cry in the seclusion of her room and then she would get to work, finish her job, and leave Glenclair. With any luck she could be done and gone before he returned from Edinburgh.

But thinking of that castle-dominated city was a mistake. Edinburgh meant Diana and the thought of her in Garrath's arms was too much. Tears flooded Blaine's eyes. Her vision blurred, and she didn't notice the open door of the room next to hers until a voice called to her.

"Blaine, may I talk to you?"

Talking to Richard was the last thing she wanted to

do at the moment. Too much of what had happened was his fault.

"I don't really think we have anything to say," she said without looking at him.

"We do. Or at least I do. I need to try to explain. Blaine, won't you please give me that chance?"

A chance! She'd condemned Garrath for not giving her a chance to explain. Could she really refuse Richard the same thing?

Hurriedly she brushed at the wetness on her cheeks. "All right. But I don't have long. I have to get to work." She walked past him into the room, her eyes lowered to avoid his. She didn't want to look at him, at the face she knew almost as well as her own.

But when she was inside she saw something else that was disturbing in a different way. Open on the bed was his suitcase. Richard was packing.

"Are. . .are you leaving?"

"Yes, soon," he said, crossing the room to the bed. He continued haphazardly adding things to the jumble in the case as he spoke.

"But before I go, I want you to know I'm sorry, so very sorry. I never wanted to hurt you—you have to believe that. I'd like to explain what happened, but I'm not sure that I can." He shook his head miserably.

This apology sounded very much like the one last night, but Blaine sensed a difference. There was nothing contrived in his expression this time; he wasn't trying to manipulate her. He was suffering.

"Try, Richard, please!" The cry tore from her involuntarily, and she realized she really did want to understand, to have a reason to forgive him.

He looked at her then, a quick glance of surprise—

and hope, before he turned back to stare at the gaping suitcase.

"Well, I guess it started when I realized you were in love with St. Clair."

"You knew that?" Her words came out in a strangled gasp.

"I began to suspect back in San Francisco, after your phone call from Edinburgh. I couldn't get some of the things you'd said and the way you'd said them, out of my mind. The next thing I knew I was on a plane. But when you came waltzing so happily into the hall downstairs yesterday, fresh from your night in the hills, I knew."

"But then why.... Last night you still asked me to marry you."

"Last night I was insane." He turned to her then, his smile as pale as the watery brown of his eyes. "We've been together a long time, Blaine. Our relationship might not have been the swept-off-your-feet variety, but it suited me. We share so much, work and Len and all. I didn't want to lose that."

A protest formed on Blaine's lips. Work and the memory of another man were not the right basis for two people staying together. But there was no point in saying that now.

"And despite my suspicions, I didn't really believe I could lose it," Richard continued. "After all, I don't often blow a deal, do I? I figured it was just a matter of reestablishing my territory, so to speak. Which I tried to do yesterday, until you put me firmly in my place. Even then, I still thought I could hold you by pressuring you into marrying me. But when that didn't work something snapped, I guess. I went crazy. I know that's not much of an explanation, but it's all I have. I just hope someday you can understand a little, and perhaps forgive me."

Blaine didn't think she would have understood an hour before. But she did now; now when she was hurting so badly from Garrath's rejection. Now she could understand easily how rejection could drive someone insane.

She wanted to tell him so, but the memory of the previous night kept closing off her throat. Silence stretched awkwardly between them.

"Well, that's really all I wanted to say," he sighed at last. "And now I'd better get on with this. I have to catch a plane to London." He picked up another shirt and tossed it on top of the rest of his belongings.

Blaine looked at the pathetic mess in the suitcase, then at the defeated droop of his shoulders. These were the shoulders she had leaned on and cried on so often through the years.... Suddenly she knew she couldn't let him go this way, regardless of what had happened. They had shared too much for too long to throw it all away because of one mistake.

"You...you don't have to go," she said.

He looked at her for a long moment. "Thank you, Blaine," he said huskily. "But I still think it would be best if I do."

"I thought you were going to help me with the installation."

He shook his head. "You don't need any help and we both know it. That wasn't the reason I came and there's really no point in my staying now." He paused deliberately. "Is there?"

For a brief moment she contemplated telling him yes, yes he should stay, that she had changed her mind. Now that she knew nothing could ever come of her love for Garrath, it was tempting to go back to Richard's safe undemanding untumultuous love. True, she didn't love him in return, not the way she loved Garrath. But as he had said, they shared many things—affection, business, memories of Len, their years together. Surely that was more than many married people had. Why shouldn't she take this chance to blot out all thoughts of what might have been?

But the temptation didn't last, chiefly because of how much she really did care for Richard. She couldn't give him only a part of herself and that was all that was left. Garrath had the rest, whether he wanted it or not.

The tears welled in her eyes again as she looked at him, wishing the answer could be different. "No," she said softly at last.

"Hey, now, none of that." He pulled out a starched white handkerchief and dabbed at the wetness on her cheeks. "Don't worry, I'll survive, as long as you promise not to leave me in the lurch at the company. Now that would be a tragedy."

He was joking, trying to ease a painful situation. But Blaine heard more truth in what he said than he perhaps realized. He probably would miss her more in the office than he did outside work if she disappeared from both. But at the moment she had no intention of leaving her job. It was about all she had left.

"Of course I won't," she said.

"Good. Then are you also willing to help me with this mess?" He pointed to the suitcase. "You've always been so good at packing, and at the rate I'm going, I'll never make my connections."

As she restored his suitcase to order, Richard

enthusiastically followed her lead in switching the conversation to the safe impersonal ground of Computec. Almost too enthusiastically, she thought wryly. She knew Richard was hurt by the way things had turned out, but she guessed that his recovery was not going to take very long. Not while there was still business to be done.

If she'd needed any confirmation of her guess, she got it when Richard snapped the latches on the case closed with two very final-sounding clicks.

"Thanks, Blaine. I wouldn't want to miss this plane. It gives me time to drop into the Department of Energy before my flight home. I can give them some of our newest literature and my personal spiel. Never know, I might be able to drum up a few new contracts."

He took the suitcase in one hand and his bulging briefcase in the other, and the glint in his lukewarm brown eyes told Blaine that his thoughts were already in London on his meetings, not on heartbreak.

"Oh, Richard," she said, reaching up to give him a quick platonic kiss. "I love you."

They both understood exactly what she meant—and didn't mean.

AFTER RICHARD WAS GONE Blaine set to work with a fervor. Her first task was the installation of the computer hardware in Garrath's office—arranging the components of the system, interconnecting cables, loading circuit boards—all the time-consuming basics she could have done in her sleep. And in a way she did. She used work as homemade novocaine, to numb her feelings and blank out her thoughts. It was the only way she knew to get through the two days or so it was going to take her to finish the job.

And she definitely was going to finish before she left. She didn't want Garrath to accuse her of running away, even if she wouldn't be around to hear him say it or see the accusation in his eyes.

As she worked she fended off Janet's several attempts to lure her out of the office. She knew the other girl was curious about the note Garrath had left for her and about Richard's sudden departure. But she had no wish to exchange confidences now. Janet's inquisitive probing might counteract the numbness, and she still needed its protection.

She skipped lunch and declined to share Janet's afternoon tea, even though her stomach growled angrily and her head pounded its protest. But at dinner time it was Mrs. MacGuigan who came to fetch her, and Blaine quickly discovered that a former nanny didn't accept work or any other excuse for refusing a meal.

"I'd like to be knowin' how ye think ye can keep workin' without keepin' up yer strength," she snapped, and didn't wait for a reply. "It canna be done. I'll expect ye washed and at the table in five minutes. Not a second more!"

Blaine smiled fondly, and sadly, at the old woman bustling from the room. Mrs. M.'s gruff but loving dictates would be one of the many things she would miss severely once she left Glenclair. But she quickly closed off that line of thought and ran up the stairs to her bedroom. Five minutes wasn't long and she didn't even consider being late.

When she hurried back downstairs and into the dining room she found an unexpected and very welcome guest at the table.

"Andy!" she exclaimed as he scrambled awkwardly up from his chair. "I didn't know you were here."

His blush was every bit as brilliant as she remembered. "I . . . ah, just got in, ma'am. I wanted to . . . ah, visit a bit with Janet . . . and you, of course."

She grinned at his confusion. "Of course."

Janet's eyes were twinkling with her happiness, and Blaine felt a new surge of annoyance at the absent Garrath. Just because he didn't want love, couldn't feel anything deeper than a momentary physical desire, didn't mean he should keep these two apart when they so obviously did feel it. It wasn't right.

But she was in no position now to interfere in that war. Janet and Andy were on their own.

"How long are you staying?" she asked, sitting down.

"Until Mr. St . . . ah, that is, a few days, I guess."

Blaine began to suspect that there was a bit more to Andy's visit than just wanting to see Janet. Could he be planning on confronting Garrath about their relationship? She couldn't tell from the two flushed faces at the table with her. Regardless of the reason for it, however, Blaine was pleased by Andy's presence. He would distract Janet from uncomfortable questions Blaine didn't want to answer, and that suited her very well. Finishing her job and leaving without having to explain anything to Janet would be a lot easier—on both of them.

His powers of distraction were amply demonstrated after the meal. When Blaine declined an after-dinner drink with them, their objections were mild, to say the least. The last she saw of them they were walking, arms around each other, toward the living room, where a fire was already burning brightly.

Blaine resolutely turned her back on the romantic picture they made and headed for the office again. Love was a wondrous thing to see—but not at the moment.

THE NEXT DAY OFFERED MORE of the same. She worked feverishly and tried not to envy the love between Janet and Andy, which was so touchingly obvious. Mrs. M. insisted Blaine stop for meals and a "wee walk to refresh yerself" in the afternoon, but otherwise she stayed steadily at her job.

With the basic hookup completed, Blaine turned her attention to configuring the system. She had to customize the standard hardware to Garrath's specific needs, a process that included entering information about the systems that the computer would be connected with, setting up separate files for the categories of information that would be coming in, designating values for various parameters, establishing access restrictions, passwords and sign-on procedures.

Then it was time to make the connections with the units on Sithein One and the St. Clair offices. She had one especially bad moment when she plugged into the Edinburgh office. As well as data, the computer was programmed to receive and relay messages much like an answering service. As she started testing this program she was suddenly afraid that some further scathing message from Garrath would appear on her screen. But there was no message at all. When disappointment tied a knot in her stomach, she realized that even though she had been dreading an angry message, she'd been hoping for a conciliatory one.

The work was detailed and complicated, and it was

late evening before she pushed herself away from the
unit, stood up and stretched her cramped muscles. A
miniature gold-faced clock on one of the shelves had
recently chimed midnight. Janet and Andy had come
in to say good-night over an hour ago. Mrs. M. had
been in a bit later, clucking about overdoing and
leaving a pot of tea covered by a quilted tea cozy on
the desk with the admonition "make sure ye drink it
afore it cools."

Guiltily Blaine poured herself a cup and took it
over to the leather chairs in the corner. Sitting in one,
with her feet up on another, she sipped at the lukewarm tea, trying to decide whether another hour or
two of work might enable her to finish tonight. She
still didn't have any idea when Garrath would tire of
his interlude with Diana, but the sooner she could
leave, the less chance there would be of meeting him.
In the past day and a half keeping their paths from
crossing had become even more important to Blaine
than it had seemed at first.

As she'd read his note, leaving before his return
had seemed the best way to spare herself more heartbreak and embarrassment. But in the intervening
hours, getting away had become crucial. As the sharp
edge of her anger and hate dulled, she found herself
in unguarded moments longing to see him again, to
touch him and feel his touch in return. She had even
caught herself wondering if things might not be
worked out in spite of everything.

Which was ridiculous. He would never admit he
had been wrong in his harsh judgment of her. Any
apologizing between them would have to be on her
side; it would always be that way with him. Which
was why she definitely had to get away without seeing

him. If she saw him, she was afraid she would want
him—on any terms. She didn't trust herself to resist.

She put her empty cup on a nearby table and undid
the hammered copper clip holding back her hair.
Yes, she thought, letting her head slump back against
the chair cushion, *I will go back to work. I can finish
tonight and be on a plane tomorrow, away from
Glenclair and Scotland and Garrath.*

A prickly sensation began in her eyes, and she
squeezed them shut against the start of tears.

She would get busy, she told herself, in just a moment.

THE NIGHTMARE CAME in all its horrible glory. She
was running even more desperately than usual, and
the name she called over and over again this time was
Garrath's. When the explosion came and the flames
began, it was some bizarre composite of Sithein One
and Glenclair that was burning.

"Garrath! Garrath!" she screamed, knowing that
if she didn't find him soon, she never would, and that
if she lost him she wouldn't be able to go on living.
But the flames only rose higher, surrounding her,
cutting off any chance she had of reaching him.

And then another voice was calling her, a voice not
part of the dream. It was outside, where security and
safety lay. Struggling, she followed the sound up and
out of the nightmare world.

To Garrath.

Impossibly, he was there, his hands warm on her
shoulders as he shook her from the dream. For one
brief instant Blaine's heart leaped with joy—and then
she remembered. Remembered all that had happened
and that she couldn't, wouldn't love him. In the cot-

tage he had promised to drive out her nightmares, to burn them from her soul. But he hadn't protected her from them at all. Instead, he'd become the cause.

"I'm awake. Let go of me," she said coldly.

"Are you sure you're all right? Was it the nightmare again?"

Viciously she pushed at his hands, telling herself it wasn't concern she saw in his eyes. "Of course, it was the dream, if it's any business of yours," she hissed. "And it will keep coming and coming until this job is over, and I get away from you and your stupid oil business. Which, thankfully, will be very, very soon. Now let go of me."

He did, and she no longer had to tell herself that there was no softness in his eyes. They were two hard coals set in a stiff closed face. It was also a tired face—almost haggard, she realized, really looking at him for the first time. Fatigue showed in his reddened eyes and in the rigid set of his neck and shoulders. But in the thin line of his mouth there was more, a weariness not so much of the body but of the mind. Something was wrong, she realized, suddenly regretting her harshness.

"Garrath, are you—" she began, but it was too late. He had already pivoted on his heel and was heading out the door without another word.

His heavy footsteps as he climbed the stairs spoke volumes, however—angry hate-filled volumes.

Blaine didn't work anymore that night. The little gold clock cheerfully chimed three as the echo of Garrath's footsteps died away. She dragged herself upstairs to her room and crawled into bed, clothes and all.

IN SPITE OF GETTING TO BED SO LATE, she was up early
the next morning and back at work, her determination to finish the job and leave Glenclair only
strengthened by the scene of the night before. Any
hopes she might have secretly and foolishly har-
bored—that Garrath would return to throw himself
at her feet, apologizing profusely and begging her
forgiveness—had been decisively dashed to pieces.
She was sure now that he had no regrets about putting her firmly out of his life. And, she told herself
over and over again, as if repetition was the key to
believing, she had no regrets about going.

She was running some program tests when a prickly sensation slithered coldly from the back of her
neck down her spine. Although her back was to the
door and not a sound betrayed his arrival, she knew
Garrath was behind her. Slowly she swiveled the secretary chair around.

Her first glimpse of his tall form lounging casually
against the doorjamb, arms tightly crossed over his
chest, quickened her pulse painfully. He was dressed
in a smoke gray sweater over a navy shirt and wide-
wale cords, and every muscle in his body was tautly
outlined. Her physical response couldn't have been
stronger had he reached out for her.

But his greeting quickly squashed those feelings.

"Hard at work so early! What industry!" he said.
But there was no praise in his dry tone or in his dark
scowl. "Ah, but then I forgot, you're anxious to get
away from—let's see, how was it you phrased it—me
and my rotten oil business, wasn't it? Or was it my
stupid oil business? Oh, well, I got the general idea."

"Yes, I am rather busy," Blaine slapped back. "Is
there something you want?"

"Breakfast," he said shortly. "Mrs. M. said I should fetch you to breakfast, and not take any excuses for your not coming. So. . . ." He waved a hand toward the door. "Shall we?"

She would have rebuffed any such invitation from him, but she knew better than to try to refuse Mrs. M. She certainly didn't need to have him as an escort, however.

"I'll be along soon," she said and swung back to the computer.

"I'll wait," he replied.

Although she started to work, her head held studiously aloof, she was still very aware of his movements as he strode across the room and pulled the chair from his desk over to the computer. While her nerve endings screamed in agony, he sat down, positioning himself just behind her, his chin nearly on her shoulder as he peered at what she was doing.

Her hands trembled on the keys, and she made several mistakes in a row before she gave up in disgust. She set the computer to print out some information and stood up, glaring at Garrath.

But he had jumped to his feet, too, lithe as a cat, and they were face to face. Blaine couldn't move, and Garrath didn't, so for a moment their eyes were locked together, fireworks flaring at the meeting of golden brown and green. Then Blaine shoved her chair backward, so she could move away. Tearing her eyes from his, she walked around him and out of the room, head held high. She deliberately ignored the fact that he followed close on her heels.

Mrs. M. was in the solarium, setting dishes on the glass table that, Blaine noticed with alarm, was already set for two. No serving oneself from the trolley this morning. The thin white china plates had a delicate blue border, the silver flatware sported a monogram composed of an "S" and a "C" intricately entwined. Purple heather and fronds of green fern were arranged in a similarly engraved silver vase. All very elegant and intimate, and totally wrong for her and Garrath.

Blaine's alarm stemmed from two sources. She couldn't imagine sitting down to this cozily arranged meal with Garrath; she wouldn't be able to force a forkful of food down her throat. But secondly, and more disturbing, she realized there should have been two other people at breakfast this morning—and one of them was Andy.

Did Garrath know about Janet's guest yet? Blaine seriously doubted he did. And did Janet and Andy realize that Garrath had returned? Was that why they weren't there? But she had got the distinct impression Andy planned on confronting Garrath over Janet....

She didn't have time to reason out the answers to her questions. Garrath was also surveying the breakfast arrangements, and with as little pleasure as she was.

"Isn't Janet joining us?" he asked. Mrs. M.'s reply was so immediate that Blaine couldn't have got in a word had she wanted to.

"No, Garrath. Out she went at the crack of dawn this mornin'—for a hill walk up to the cottage, and I was not to expect her back until late this afternoon. Now sit and eat!" Mrs. M. delivered this last order over her shoulder as she bustled from the room.

Blaine stared after her in amazement. The old woman hadn't even mentioned Andy, an omission that had to be deliberate. Blaine herself wouldn't have expected such subterfuge from her, but she was more than willing to follow her lead. If Mrs. M. thought it better for Garrath to be kept in the dark about Andy's presence, she would be happy to go along. She certainly wasn't going to be the one to tell him!

"And what about your...friend? Richard?" Garrath cut into her thoughts, holding out her chair. "Is he a late riser?"

Before she could decide how to answer his mocking question, he had taken the opposite seat. His knees brushed hers and the magnetism of the man struck her again. Suddenly she wanted to explain how Richard had happened to be in her room that night, how his advances had been totally unwelcome and had led to nothing. She wanted to apologize, to do whatever was necessary to make things right between them again. She wanted to make him love her.

The words were already forming on her lips when she furiously bit them back. She'd be damned if she'd try to explain to him when he hadn't bothered to ask for an explanation. He would never believe her anyway.

"Richard is gone," she replied simply. "He had an urgent meeting in London."

Garrath's head snapped up and his mouth quirked as he stared at her. In what? Surprise? Derision?

"I'll be meeting him there," she added quickly.

Whatever emotion had been in his expression disappeared with her words. He savagely tore a floury bap in half. "As soon as you're finished here? No wonder you're so anxious to be away."

The taste of the lie still chalky in her mouth, Blaine didn't respond to his provocation. She served herself sparingly from the breakfast dishes, the idea of eating becoming more and more repugnant. Her first bite had to be washed down with scalding tea.

"And how much work do you have left to do on the computer?" Garrath asked.

"An hour, perhaps. That's all. I suppose I should arrange for a taxi for this afternoon, and a plane reservation."

"There isn't any taxi service out here. When it's time for you to leave, I'll take you. But I can't see how you expect to be finished with everything by this afternoon."

"What do you mean? There are just a few more tests I'd like to run, and then—"

"And then you need to teach me how to operate the equipment, don't you?"

"Teach you! Surely you already know how!"

He shook his head.

"But you have a duplicate system in Edinburgh," she protested. "You must know how to—"

"I let Diana handle most of that. But here I'll be on my own, so I need lessons. Which I understood came with the equipment where necessary." He smiled nastily, a cat toying with a mouse in a trap. "And unfortunately for your romantic plans, I'm a very slow learner."

"You know instruction was not part of our deal," Blaine said. She didn't understand what game he was playing now, but she wanted no part of it. "If you really aren't able to operate the equipment—which I doubt—then I'll arrange for some lessons for you. But I am leaving this afternoon."

Garrath sat forward in his chair, leaning over the table to fix her with his stare. "And if you do, Miss

Christensen, I will cancel all my contracts with your precious Richard Perry and Computec, and I'll make sure that no other company in Great Britain will have anything to do with him, either. A word here and there, it won't be hard to do. I have plenty of influence in the business community and I won't hesitate to use it."

"Why, Garrath?" she asked hoarsely, feeling every bit of blood draining from her face. "Why would you threaten such a thing? And why do you want me to stay here?"

He stood up, flinging his napkin onto the table. "Because I don't like being made a fool of. And keeping you here when you would rather be off with Richard is the only revenge I can think of at the moment. That's why."

"It wasn't the way you think!" she cried, but she was speaking to herself. Garrath had gone.

CHAPTER TWENTY-ONE

BLAINE'S PLATE WAS ONLY HALF-EMPTY, but what little appetite she'd had was gone. With shaking hands she loaded the trolley with the breakfast things and wheeled it slowly back to the kitchen.

Mrs. MacGuigan was standing at the hardwood island in the center of the large room, kneading bread dough. She looked up as Blaine entered the room, squinting until Blaine greeted her. Then she smiled—a rarity, Blaine thought fondly.

"And did the two of ye enjoy yer meal?" she asked.

"Delicious," Blaine answered, surreptitiously scraping the remains on her plate into the disposal and hoping Mrs. M. was too absorbed in her baking to notice.

"Hmm. And did ye get on with settlin' yer differences, then?"

"Differences?" Blaine's voice was a faint echo.

Mrs. M. raised her head to stare accusingly in Blaine's general direction for a moment before returning her attention to her kneading. Her small hands pounded, flattened, folded and turned, releasing the rich sweet smell of yeast into the kitchen.

"Yes, differences, miss. Whatever was naggin' at the two of ye. Do ye think I dinna ken when somethin' is wrong with the lad? After all these years?" She snorted.

"When he races off in the wee hours of a morn without a kind word for me or my Charlie and nary even a goodbye to his sister, I ken well that somethin' is amiss. And when ye give up eatin' and sleepin' and tears are in every word ye speak, I'm well able to figure out that the somethin' wrong is between the two of you, now aren't I? What I want to know is if ye've made it up."

Blaine felt she'd just endured a bit of kneading at Mrs. M.'s busy hands.

"Well, it's true there was a little disagreement between Garrath and me, but it's just to do with the work I'm doing. Nothing important."

"'Tis my experience, lass, that the kind of things I've been hearin' in yer two voices are not the things of work. They're of love."

"Love!" Blaine exclaimed, and then smiled bitterly. She concentrated on not letting her trembling hands drop one of the china plates she was loading into the dishwasher. "Love has nothing to do with this."

The other woman clucked disbelievingly. "Well, I hope ye are better at foolin' yerself than ye are at foolin' me with yer pretense."

"It's not pretense. I'm not in love with Garrath and he certainly isn't in love with me. Quite the contrary, actually."

"Oh, the contrary, is it now? Are ye sure 'tisn't injured pride that's speakin' for ye, Blaine Christensen?"

"No!" she denied, and when Mrs. M.'s silence became a challenge, she said it again. "No. There's an attraction, I'll admit, but it's not love. Love is different—gentle, rational, based on trust and respect and understanding. Whatever is between Garrath and me isn't that.''

Mrs. M. shook her head. ''I fear ye've got a braw lot to learn about love, lass. Gentle, rational—pah! I know love; it's wild as the wind, stormy as the seas in winter and beautiful as the heather in bloom. But ye'll never find that out if ye let a stubborn head get in the way of yer heart. Remember that, lassie. Remember that.''

Stubborn! Blaine bristled. She wasn't being stubborn, just rational. Garrath didn't love her, wouldn't ever love her, so why should she hand him any more ways to hurt her by admitting she loved him? No, she was just protecting herself, wisely.

But she wasn't going to argue the point further; she doubted it was possible to win an argument with Mrs. M. She decided to ask a question of her own instead. ''Why didn't you tell Garrath that Andy's here?''

Mrs. MacGuigan's thin shoulders twitched in a shrug. ''Because there's no use letting him have any extra time to work himself into a proper dither. There'll be the devil to pay when he finds out anyway; no need to rise the price.''

Blaine smiled. The answer made perfect sense to her. But Garrath's attitude still didn't. ''I don't understand why Garrath should be so against Andy. He's so nice.''

''Aye, and verra much in love with our bonnie Janet.'' She was separating the dough into sections now, and using her hands to roll each section into a long ''snake.'' ''But Garrath was hurt a time or two in his younger days by women more attracted to the St. Clair name and fortune than to himself. He's always been afraid Janet would get hurt the same way, and so he's blinded himself to the possibility that she might find the right man the first time out.'' She twisted the ''snakes'' into braids and laid the loaves on large cookie sheets, covered them with a towel and set them on top of the antique range.

"The best place for risin' bread," she said, wiping her hands on her muslin apron. Then she looked at Blaine with her piercing stare. "Now I've no more time for this tongue waggin'. I've other work to be doin', as I imagine ye have, too.''

Color rouging her cheeks, Blaine agreed that she did indeed have work to do, and she headed out of the kitchen.

"Good," she heard Mrs. M. mumble as the door swung shut behind her.

She grimaced. Obviously the woman's idea of Blaine's work was slightly different than her own. Mrs. M. was undoubtedly expecting her to march off to make up her ''differences'' with Garrath, while Blaine knew no such thing was possible. All she was hoping to do was somehow survive the next few hours—surely it couldn't be longer—while Garrath exacted his revenge, whatever that was to be.

Though her first instinct had been to refuse his ultimatum, she'd quickly realized she couldn't do it. Garrath meant what he had said about ruining Computec's chances for British contracts, and she suspected he had the power to accomplish it if he wanted. She also knew how much Richard wanted this expansion. So she was going to stay. But it wouldn't be easy, and it certainly wasn't going to be done for the sake of love.

It wasn't easy. Garrath was waiting for her in the

office. He was working at the desk but looked up expectantly as she walked in. He didn't say anything,
just sat there, waiting for her agreement to his
demands.

She had no intention of capitulating any sooner
than she had to. She ignored him, therefore, settling
in front of the computer terminal to complete her
testing.

She didn't know whether to cheer or cry when the
system tested out perfectly. Finishing the installation
meant she was closer to leaving Glenclair. But if there
had been a few bugs to deal with she could have de-
layed the moment when she had to turn to Garrath
and admit she was submitting to his blackmail. As it
was. . . . She went over to stand before the desk.

"The system's ready. We can begin your lessons
now," she said stonily. "If you're ready."

"Oh, I'm more than ready," he said, his grin already filled with gloating.

He pulled the second chair over to the computer
again and sat in it. Blaine shook her head, pointing to
the chair directly in front of the machine.

"The pupil sits there," she ordered.

"I like this seat. I'd rather. . . watch you."

And lean intimidatingly over her shoulder, breathing on her neck the way he had this morning, she
thought. That she could do without.

"This is a learn-by-doing class, Mr. St. Clair. Now
take the other chair."

Scowling, he did. And then the battle began. For
as determined as Blaine was to keep her distance,
Garrath seemed equally determined to keep her from
doing so. They each had their weapons.

Blaine started the lesson with the most elementary

aspects of computer operation. She spoke to Garrath as if he were still in grammar school, and was a not very intelligent student, at that, hoping to bore him into canceling the whole thing.

"First we turn on the machine," she intoned. "The button is here. Although you'll be leaving it on the majority of the time, so it can receive and file information for your later study, you should know how to start up in case of power outages or such. Now let's see you do it. Good. And again, just to make sure you've got it right. What is the first step?"

"I know how to turn the bloody thing on!" he growled. "Get on with it!"

"I can't teach you if you won't cooperate," she said as sweetly as she could manage. "But if you're not satisfied with my methods, I could arrange for another teacher."

The white-hot heat of his glare could have melted the polar ice caps—at both poles simultaneously. But, disappointingly, he did as she asked. And a bit later he brought his own weaponry into the fray.

"How can you tell if the disk is properly loaded into the disk drive?" he asked with mock innocence. "I don't think I understand."

"It's simple. You aren't trying."

He shrugged. "I warned you I was a slow learner."

So she was forced to lean over him to illustrate the click as the disk slipped into place. He, of course, just happened to move as she did, so that his arm brushed her breast.

It didn't take many such engineered encounters to set the pulse at the base of Blaine's throat to pounding violently. But at least, she thought, his irritation at her condescending instructions also seemed to be increasing. All she had to do was hold on awhile longer and she was sure he would break.

But holding on became ever more difficult. Even stopping for lunch didn't help because, though they ate mostly in silence, his eyes never seemed to leave her. They roved, from the hair she'd pinned into a rather careless bun atop her head to her face and down to her body, to linger intimately until redness flooded her cheeks. And then he stared derisively at her blush. "See what I can do to you with just a look," was written in the glance.

The afternoon session was exactly like the morning's, only the barbs became sharper as both their tempers grew shorter. It was when Blaine was showing Garrath the computer's message function that matters came to a definite head.

"You can transmit messages to the other computers this one is linked to," she told him. "For instance instructions to Diana in Edinburgh—such as appointments to make or cancel; letters to write; calls to make; what time she should be at Rose Crescent, running the bathwater."

"Bathwater!" Garrath glared at her. "What the hell are you talking about?"

"Never mind," she said quickly. "You can ask the computer to list any messages for you, and if there's something urgent it will flash a signal at the bottom of the screen. Composing the messages, or letters and documents, is easy. Word processing functions are built in."

She pointed to several different keys, shuddering as he leaned toward her so that their shoulders touched. Defiantly, she didn't pull away. She wasn't going to admit to the reaction.

"You can insert or delete words, lines or whole paragraphs of text with these keys. Why don't you type something and I'll show you how easy it is."

She made the suggestion so he would be the one to break their contact. But when the words he typed printed across the computer screen, she heartily regretted the idea.

SOME WOMEN HAVE SHALLOW FEELINGS, he wrote, and then turned to her with a smile that was a dare.

She accepted the challenge, reaching past him to delete and insert, and came up with, SOME MEN HAVE NO FEELINGS AT ALL.

SOME WOMEN PREFER SAFE DULL MEN, he entered.

SOME MEN PREFER OBVIOUS OVERSEXED DOORMATS, she countered. And it continued, with both of them intent on the screen and the keys as they sparred back and forth.

SOME WOMEN WANT THEIR CAKE AND ICING, TOO.

SOME MEN TAKE THE ICING AND TOSS OUT THE CAKE.

SOME WOMEN ARE FICKLE.

SOME MEN THINK A WOMAN'S FICKLE IF SHE DOES WHAT HE'S BEEN DOING ALL ALONG.

SOME WOMEN HAVE A COMPUTER FOR A HEART.

SOME MEN TAKE PLEASURE FROM BREAKING COMPUTERS.

Garrath's hands had replaced Blaine's on the keys the moment she finished typing her latest response. But no new words obliterated hers, not even after she was certain he'd had sufficient time to read it—twice. She looked up at him.

The mocking derision in his eyes and on his mouth was gone. He looked confused and worried, and the tiniest bit hopeful.

"What did you mean by that?" he asked, saying

each word sharply, as if they were torn from some
place deep inside of him.

Suddenly she realized the mistake she'd made.
"I...well, I guess I...oh, Garrath, I don't know,"
she lied, though she knew very well. Garrath had
broken her heart, computerized or not, and the admission had slipped out in their free-association
clash. She turned her head away from him.

His hands grasped her shoulders, forcing her back
around to face the burning intensity of his eyes.
"Blaine, tell me what you meant. I have to know. I
need to know."

His need, his touch, the tension and longing that
had been building the whole day broke over Blaine.
She knew that to tell him she loved him and admit
how his rejection had hurt her was to risk further and
deeper pain. But she was going to do it anyway.

And then, before she could find the words to
begin, there were footsteps and the sound of two
happy voices, one female, one male, in the hall. In
the split second that it took Blaine to realize whose
voices they were, the owners reached the door of the
office.

"Blaine, we're back!" Janet trilled.

And the other voice chimed in with, "What a great
day!" The second voice, naturally, was Andy's.

At first sight of the young man, Garrath jack-
knifed out of his chair, his face the pasty gray of
alarm.

"Tex! What's wrong with the rig?" he demanded.

Both Janet and Andy froze in the doorway at the
sight of Garrath, their relaxed cheery expressions
changing to ones of dismay.

"Ah...nothin', sir. At least nothin' that I know

of," Andy stammered. "But I've been off shift for a bit, so I—"

"Then what are you doing here?" Garrath cut Andy off coldly, as he looked from Andy to Janet and his gaze caught on their hands twined together.

It was Janet who answered, with none of her usual sunniness. "I invited him."

Garrath's brows arched tauntingly. "While the cat's away, so to speak, hmm? How inconvenient for your little love tryst that I came back so soon."

"Garrath! Don't be silly! We didn't plan it that way."

"We certainly didn't," Andy spoke up. "In fact, I came out here hopin' to talk to you about Janet and me. But you'd left, so...."

"So you just made yourself at home," Garrath said, and Andy's face suffused with an angry red. Blaine wanted to cry out to Garrath to stop before something irrevocable was said or done.

"But we don't really have anything to talk about, do we, Tex?" Garrath went on. "I think I've already made my feelings about any relationship between you and my sister quite clear."

"I reckon you have. But Janet and I, we kept hopin' you'd come to your senses."

"My senses! I have come to my senses, just now. I see that I should have thrown you out of my house and out of a job the first time I brought you here and saw how you fawned over Janet. But I thought she would be smart enough to see through you, to realize that you aren't the type that gets serious about any one girl, at least not without a very...tangible reason."

"You're right about that," Andy drawled lazily,

though Blaine could see he was holding onto his temper with very thin reins. "And the tangible reason I'm serious about Janet is that I love her, and she loves me, and all we'd like is your permission to be married."

"All you'd like...!" Garrath laughed, a cruel nasty laugh. He looked down at the carpeting for a moment, and when he raised his head again he was glaring with near hatred at Andy.

"I'm sure that's all you'd like," he said. "After all, you said you'd only get married to a woman who could support you, didn't you? And Janet certainly qualifies as that."

"I said what?" Andy dropped Janet's hand and crossed the room to stand squarely in front of Garrath.

"Oh, you've forgotten your life's plan so soon?" Garrath sneered. "Don't you remember an evening a couple of months ago in Aberdeen, after we dropped off two lovely lassies with promises to call them again sometime, and I asked you if you really would? And you said you doubted it, there were plenty of pretty fishes in the sea, why should you use fresh bait on one already hooked? No, you intended to play the field as long as you had breath to do so, unless a rich lady came along, one so rich she could support you for the rest of your days. For a really rich lady you might be willing to give up your wandering days, you said, at least until the ring was on her finger and your name was on the bank account. Can you have forgotten that conversation so soon?"

Andy's face paled until there were just two red spots high on his cheeks. "Garrath, you can't believe I ever meant a thing like that. Why, we were both pretty high that night, if I recall. It was just big talk. That's all.''

"Exactly what I thought, at the time. In fact, I forgot all about it until a few days later, when I brought you here to Glenclair and saw you with my eligible, gullible and very wealthy sister. And then I did think about it, a lot. I didn't want to believe it of you, not after how well you and I had got along, after how much I'd come to like you. I guess that's why I didn't put a stop to this nonsense before. I didn't believe you'd dare go on with it, even go so far as to ask her to marry you. But you have and now the game is over. You won't get my permission to ruin Janet's life. Not now or ever!''

Andy turned and started back toward Janet, but she was already hurrying to his side. He never even had a chance to speak the denials written all over his face.

"I don't believe him,'' Janet said softly, looking up into sad blue eyes. "I know you love me.''

Blaine was watching Garrath as Janet spoke and saw his stricken look. She ached for him because he was pushing Janet's love for him away with both hands, but she didn't know of any way to stop him.

Andy smiled gratefully at Janet, but he wasn't smiling as he looked back toward Garrath. He slapped his hand back and forth nervously across his thigh, but there wasn't a hint of timidity in his voice.

"Are you sure you won't reconsider, sir?'' he said. "Because since Janet is of age, asking your permission is just...well, a politeness, I guess you could say. We don't really need it, y'know.''

Garrath's arm was already drawn back for the punch when Blaine grabbed him.

"No!" she cried, and heard an echoing scream from Janet. The other girl put a restraining hand on Andy's arm, too, though if Blaine read the younger man's body language correctly, he didn't need the extra restraint. Andy looked braced to block the attack if it came and ready to deliver a blow or two of his own if it was necessary to defend himself. But he wasn't intending to strike first.

"No, Garrath. You can't," Blaine repeated, tugging. After an eternity he lowered his arm. But the scene wasn't over.

"I want you out of Glenclair," he hissed at Andy. "Now."

"I'm not going until we straighten this—" Andy began.

But Janet interrupted him. Still clutching his sleeve, she stared up at him, her long-lashed brown eyes pleading. "Please, go for now. Go to Eileen's; they've got an extra room. Let me talk to Garrath by myself, it'll be better that way. Please, Andy."

Andy's emotional struggle was obvious. He didn't want to leave Janet alone to deal with Garrath's wrath, but at the same time he realized the wisdom of what she said. His love and concern shone like the flare atop Sithein One.

Garrath didn't seem to see it. He was still glaring, his body rigidly tensed.

"Are you sure you'll be all right?" Andy asked Janet, and she nodded.

"I'll call you soon," she promised, and with one last loving look Andy turned and went out of the room. No one else moved until they heard the front door slam.

The sound brought Blaine to her senses. This

scene, this argument, wasn't hers. She felt dreadfully sorry for Janet, and even for Garrath, but there was nothing she could do to help. She started for the door.

"Blaine, stay, please!" Janet cried. "You know Garrath is wrong about Andy. You have to help me convince him."

"No, I can't. This is between the two of you. You don't need outsiders...."

"Oh, that's all right, Blaine," Garrath interrupted. "You might as well stay, though don't expect to do any convincing. But since you were willing to encourage them in sneaking around behind my back, you might as well see the end result."

Blaine's mind went numb with shock at the unfairness of his attack. It was Janet who protested.

"We weren't sneaking around. Why do you insist on misconstruing everything? Why are you doing this?"

Garrath rubbed a hand across his forehead as if he were suddenly overwhelmingly tired. "Because I love you," he said. "And I refuse to let some childish infatuation ruin your life. I don't want you to be hurt. That's why."

"But you're the one who's hurting me. How can I make you understand?"

"You can't. I won't let you marry him and that's all there is to it."

"No, Garrath," Janet contradicted him, her voice heavy. "That isn't all there is to it. Because I'm going to marry Andy whether you approve or not. I...I want you to, because I love you. But if you won't, I'll do it without your approval."

He really hadn't considered that Janet might defy

him, that she might put her love for Andy above her love for her brother, Blaine realized, seeing the disbelief and hurt, and then the anger, on Garrath's face. And it was anger—unreasoning unthinking anger—that formed his next words, Blaine was sure.

"You won't see Tex—Andy Walker—again," he said flatly. "Not if you care for him as much as you claim. Because if you do he will no longer be an employee of St. Clair Corporation. And after I put out a quiet word here and there about him no other oil company will be willing to hire him either. His career in the oil business will be at an end."

"Oh, Garrath, no!" Blaine exclaimed. "You can't mean that."

"Oh, but I do," Garrath said, his eyes fixed on his sister as fiercely as hers were leveled on him. "Don't I, Janet?"

Their eyes, so very much alike, remained locked together in an emotional duel for a full minute before Janet answered him bitterly.

"I suppose you do. But you're wrong. And I will never, ever forgive you for this, Garrath St. Clair." She whirled and ran from the room, one small fist pressed tightly against her pale lips.

CHAPTER TWENTY-TWO

IN THE DEAD SILENCE that followed Janet's departure, Garrath carefully avoided looking at Blaine. He turned instead back to the computer, slumping into the chair in front of the terminal.

"Shall we get on with the lesson?" he asked tonelessly.

"No, Garrath," Blaine answered with as little expression. "The lesson is finished. I'm leaving."

"But you—"

"If you're about to try your blackmail methods on me again, forget it. Cancel whatever you like. Computec will survive better than I would if I stayed here much longer."

She walked quickly from the room. But before she was midway up the long staircase he was behind her, grabbing her arm and whirling her around to face him.

"And just what do you think I should have done?" he demanded fiercely. "Smiled sweetly over Andy and Janet spending the day alone together at the cottage doing God knows what?"

Blaine's eyes widened with contempt. "Oh, that's part of it, is it?" she queried. "You're worried about what they might have been doing at the cottage."

"Of course I am!"

"Funny, you didn't seem the least bit concerned

about what you and I were doing when we were
there.''

"That was different," he snapped.

"Different how? The only difference I can see is
that we had a whole night and they had only an afternoon. So what happened to 'I don't see anything
shameful in it, Blaine?' ''

Abruptly he dropped her arm, turning slightly
away and gripping the banister as if he were suddenly
in need of its support. "That was between you and
me and not the same situation at all. We were...."
He shook his head. "It just wasn't the same."

"Why wasn't it?" she insisted, picking at the first
chink in his armor she'd seen. "How could it have
been right for us and wrong for them? What makes
us—you—so different? What, Garrath? Tell me
what!''

Savagely he pushed himself away from the banister
and whipped around toward her. "Because I loved
you, dammit, and I thought you loved me! That's
what made the difference!''

"You...loved me?" It was so hard to form words
when her heart had stopped beating.

"Yes, I loved you," he growled, and there was
pain swimming deep in his brown eyes. "And, heav-
en help me, I still do." He pulled her roughly against
him, his mouth coming down on hers even as she
gasped in surprise.

It was a kiss like none of their others. He was
angry, desperate, demanding a response he didn't expect to get. And Blaine, not believing what she'd
heard but wanting to with every part of her being,
was too disoriented to think, to weigh the action for
right or wrong. She just let the feelings carry her—
and Garrath—away.

When their kisses deepened and his hands began to move passionately over her body, a last flicker of rationality made her whisper, "Not here. Please."

He swept her up into his arms easily, and she nuzzled against his neck, flicking her tongue along his skin till she reached the lobe of his ear.

"If you don't stop that, I'm going to drop you smack on your pretty little bottom, Miss Christensen," he warned. But they made it to his bedroom without mishap, due more to his determination than her forbearance.

She noticed very little of the room. He kicked the door shut behind them, cutting off the light from the hall. The only other illumination was the golden firelight that danced with the shadows across walls and furniture. It was to the fire that Garrath carried her.

A large sheepskin rug, much like the one at the cottage, lay before the fireplace, and at one end was a hill of fur-covered floor pillows. The private bower of a lusty Highland prince, she thought, a place of softness and warmth, enticing and sensual. Made for love. Made for them.

He set her on her feet, and they pulled apart just long enough to shed their clothing, and then she was in his arms again. The heat of the fire was like a caressing hand against her bare skin, each flicker of flame brushing warmly over her from head to toe, while Garrath's hands and mouth generated a glow of another kind.

"I love you, Blaine," he said again, and the fire became a conflagration.

Together they sank to the fleecy rug. The firelight bronzed Garrath's virile body as he kneeled over her, making an ancient god of him. And then he lowered his body to hers, and the flame was inside her, a bright and glorious blaze that went on forever.

LATER, THE HEAT OF THEIR PASSION SPENT, they sat propped against the pillows, the soft dark fur of the spread from his bed tucked about them. Blaine snuggled against Garrath and his arm went around her.

"Your feet are cold," she accused, giggling.

"Then do your duty and warm them," was his unrepentant reply. She covered his toes with hers and did her best.

"I thought you hated me," she murmured hazily as he lightly kissed her bare shoulder.

"Hated you! I thought you scientist types were supposed to be so smart."

"We are. I weighed all the evidence and came to the logical conclusion."

"What evidence?"

"The way you went straight off to Diana, and your note that said you wanted me out of your life."

He held her away from him just far enough to look deeply into her eyes. "What note?"

"The one you left with Mrs. M. when you went to...Edinburgh," Blaine mumbled, wishing she'd never mentioned it. She didn't really care about the note, not now. Now she didn't want anything to intrude on this moment. She tried to turn away again, but Garrath held her fast.

"My note said I wanted you out of my life? Blaine, it couldn't have. I don't remember just what I wrote; I was pretty upset at the time and dashed it off without much thought. But I couldn't have said that."

"Well, not in so many words," Blaine admitted under his intent gaze. "But the idea was clear enough.'' She recited the exact words. "So I knew you wanted me to finish the job and get out. As soon as possible.''

He laughed, shaking his head. "Oh, Blaine, you little idiot! I didn't mean I wanted you to finish and get out. I wanted you and *Richard* to finish, so that when I got back I could justify throwing *him* out. You, I never intended to let go. Not from the night on the rig when you were weak as a kitten from your nightmare and still spit fire when I said I was sending you home. In fact, I've been going crazy trying to think up ways to keep you with me long enough for you to fall in love with me—including insisting on this latest job, which I knew perfectly well could be done anytime, by anyone.''

He kissed her then, a long stirring kiss that was indisputable evidence of what he said.

"But if you felt that way," Blaine said breathlessly when she could speak again, "why did you leave here to go to Diana? Why didn't you stay and rant and rave and shout and demand to know how I could possibly have been with Richard after what you and I shared at the cottage? Garrath, why didn't you ask me what happened?''

He slumped down against the pillows, supporting his head with his hand. "I didn't go to Diana, Blaine. Why would I—she means nothing to me. I didn't even go to Edinburgh.''

"But Mrs. M. said Diana called and—''

"And gave me a message from Walter.''

"My Walter?'' Blaine twisted around onto her knees, staring at Garrath. He nodded.

"Before you and I left the rig I told Walter to contact me if there was any further trouble. I wasn't quite as undisturbed by the possibility of sabotage as I tried to make you believe. And that night, or rather early morning, Walter called."

"There was another attempt?"

"No, not exactly." Garrath turned to stare into the fire, and some of the weariness Blaine had seen the night before was back in the taut lines of his face. "It seems that Miles ordered Walter to shut down the Computec system, and Walter, knowing that order should come only from me, refused and called Edinburgh." He paused and smiled weakly. "Your Walter is one feisty little man. Anyway, he spoke to Diana, who relayed the message to me. I went straight out to Sithein One, Blaine, to give Miles an ultimatum. It was the hardest thing I think I've ever had to do."

Blaine lay down again and put a hand against Garrath's cheek, smoothing out the grim lines. "What happened?"

"I would have fired anyone but him on the spot for countermanding my direct orders that way. But I couldn't do that to Miles, not after all these years and all he's done for me. Even if he has been getting more and more difficult to work with since we started on Sithein One."

He turned his head to kiss Blaine's palm, then continued. "Miles is a brilliant man but too closed into his job. It's become everything to him and I guess he feels threatened. Part of that is my fault, I see now. I've been spending more and more time on Sithein One because I enjoyed it, but I realize how he could construe that as my usurping his authority. And when your system was installed and overruled him...."

"He was the one who sabotaged the system, wasn't he?" Blaine asked gently.

"I honestly don't know. I don't want to believe it now any more than I wanted to when you first suggested it. But I guess I probably have to." He took a deep sighing breath. "Anyway, I made it plain this time that I won't tolerate any more interference with the system—of any kind. I told him that if it came down to a choice between the computers and him, he would have to go. I felt like the worst kind of traitor in the world, but I'm sure things will be okay now."

It explained so much: why Garrath had left that morning, why he had returned so haggard and so on edge that he had flown wildly off the handle about Andy and Janet. It also explained one other thing—why he had at first jumped to the conclusion that Andy was bringing bad news from the rig. Despite his assurances Blaine didn't believe he was so very certain everything was going to be okay with Miles. He was more worried than he was willing to let on.

But Garrath interrupted her musings. "Enough of that. Miles has caused too much trouble between us already," he said seriously. "Now I'll ask what I should have the other night instead of letting my pride and my temper get in the way. What did happen, Blaine? Why were you and Richard...together?"

Blaine smiled, the dimple sinking deep into her cheek. He was finally asking. Late, but better late than never, as the worn old saying went. Things would be all right now.

"Richard and I weren't..." she began, and proceeded to tell him exactly what had happened, including Richard's apologies and her acceptance.

"I lied when I said I was supposed to meet him in London," she admitted. "I was hurt because I thought you'd been with Diana, and I wanted to hurt back. The worst possible motive. I'm sorry, Garrath. Can you forgive me?"

His hands found the curve of her hips and drew her unresisting body closer to his. "I think I can force myself," he whispered huskily. And he didn't have any difficulty at all.

THE NEXT TIME THEY RETURNED to the everyday world the windows with their undrawn curtains were pitch-black rectangles and the fire had burned down to glowing embers. Blaine sat up and nudged a drowsing Garrath.

"Wake up, lazy! It's very late. I wonder why no one's called us for dinner?"

"Always thinking of your stomach, aren't you?" he grumbled good-naturedly. "But I'd say it was rather a good thing that no one did come looking for us, wouldn't you?" To illustrate his point he reached a caressing hand to Blaine's breast, which was exposed by the slipping away of the spread.

Blushing hotly, she pushed his hand away. "Come on, you insatiable man! We have to get moving!"

"Why this sudden rush?" he asked, smiling.

"We have to—or rather, you have to—talk to Janet."

Garrath sobered immediately, rolling over onto his stomach and putting fists beneath a set chin. "Blaine, let's not get into this."

"We have to. Oh, Garrath, think of what's happened between us over the past couple of days," she pleaded. "All the wrong conclusions we've jumped to, the misunderstandings and misinterpretations. Couldn't your desire to protect Janet be leading you to make similar mistakes about her and Andy?''

He was silent so long, his face so hard and inscrutable that Blaine began to think she hadn't reached him at all. She was trying to think of something else to say when he turned to her, pulling her against him and kissing her soundly.

"You're right, Blaine. I've been mother and father to Janet for too long, and like all parents, I'm finding it hard to admit I can't protect her forever. I guess I was looking for excuses to keep from having to let her go.''

Blaine smiled at the faint mistiness she detected in his brown eyes and held him tightly. "I know, darling,'' she whispered. "I know.''

When they were dressed she gave him one final encouraging kiss before heading downstairs.

"Don't worry. Janet loves you very much,'' she said. "She'll understand.''

"I hope so,'' was Garrath's worried reply. Her last glimpse of him was standing before Janet's bedroom door, head bowed as if he were gathering his courage before knocking. Blaine made no attempt to descend the staircase quietly; he might as well be confident of his privacy for the reconciliation.

And reconciliation she was sure it would be. She knew enough of Janet St. Clair by now to know she wouldn't stay angry with her brother when the cause was gone. Garrath would find an eager reception for his apologies.

Blaine was not so certain of the kind of reception she would get downstairs. It was somewhat after the usual Glenclair dinner hour. Was Mrs. M. just behind schedule in her preparations? Or had she come upstairs looking for her charges and guessed what was going on behind at least one of the closed doors?

Well, at least they hadn't caught a chill, Blaine thought with a smile, remembering Garrath's comment about what would most likely disturb Mrs. M. should she witness a "compromising" situation between them. She pushed open the kitchen door.

Both Charlie and Mrs. M. were there, the housekeeper brushing fresh-cooked salmon with melted butter and sprinkling fennel over the butter, while her husband stole a parsleyed new potato from the covered dish on a warmer tray whenever Mrs. M.'s back was turned.

"Ah, I was just aboot to send Charlie up after ye and t'others. I left supper for late, thinkin' ye all might be busy," Mrs. M. said vaguely, and Blaine blushed. "But 'tis ready now."

"And it smells heavenly," Blaine enthused, her taste buds perking up at the aroma and sight of the succulent pink flesh of the fish. "I'm suddenly starved."

"Weel, then, let's..." Mrs. M. began, but broke off at the sound of heavy rapid footsteps approaching. A second later Garrath burst through the door.

He looked wildly around the room and then said, "Oh, God, Blaine, Janet is gone!"

The next few minutes were a flurry of questions and replies. Neither Mrs. M. nor Charlie had seen Janet since she'd come home from her walk with Andy. No, her car wasn't gone. Yes, Garrath had searched the rest of the house after he'd found her room empty. No one had any idea where else she could be.

"Niver would she go out without lettin' one of us know," Charlie said soothingly. But Mrs. M. was not so certain.

"No, not unless somethin' was a-naggin' at her," she said, looking fiercely at Garrath.

"Yes, Mrs. M., you're right, as always. We had a horrible row, and I was on my way to apologize when I found she was gone." He ran a hand through his dark hair. "But where would she go?"

He looked desperately at Blaine, and the thought occurred to both of them at once. To Andy. They didn't even have to form the words.

"But how?" Blaine asked. "If she didn't take her car...."

"Maybe he picked her up."

"Wouldn't someone have heard his car?" But even as she asked the question, she knew she and Garrath wouldn't have heard it, probably wouldn't have heard the house falling down around them. Mrs. M. and Charlie, though, had been less absorbed, and they were almost certain no other car had arrived at Glenclair that afternoon.

"We heard Janet's young man leavin'," Charlie said, "but nothin' after that."

It was still the only answer any of them could think of. Janet had to be with Andy, in defiance of Garrath's threats. But would they still be with Eileen's family or would they have left together?

"Let's go," Garrath said grimly.

"Shouldn't we call to see if—" Blaine suggested, but Garrath cut her off.

"I don't want to waste the time. Charlie, will you call and tell Janet I'm on my way, to wait for me?" He paused, then added, "Tell her I said...please." And taking Blaine's hand, he pulled her toward the door.

"Dinna be killin' yerself and the lassie in yer haste, Garrath St. Clair," Mrs. M. called after them. "If Janet is there, she'll bide a bit longer, and if she isn't, a few minutes willna make any difference. Mind now?"

Seeing the driven look on Garrath's face as he raced to the front hall, Blaine wasn't at all sure he had "minded." She debated asking him to let her drive but decided even a frantic driver who was familiar with the Highland roads was preferable to one who favored public transportation whenever it was available.

But there was no need to test her theory. Just before they reached Garrath's car, a pair of headlights crested the last hill before the road dipped into the glen that cradled Glenclair.

"They're coming back!" Blaine exclaimed, praying it was true.

She and Garrath waited impatiently, watching the approach of the lights, which seemed to be moving at little better than a crawl. Finally the car crunched its way across the graveled front drive and came to a stop near them, and Andy stepped out from behind the wheel. The other door stayed frustratingly closed.

"Where's Janet?" The strident demand came from the two male throats at the same time.

"What are you talking about?" Andy asked, puzzlement marking his forehead with a frown. "She's here, of course. But she hasn't called me as she promised, so I came out to see what was going on."

Garrath was stunned into silence by disappointment and Blaine was the one who answered.

"She's disappeared, Andy. We don't know where.

We assumed she was with you and we were just on our way to Eileen's.''

This time it was Andy's hands that bunched into fists. ''This is your fault, Garrath. If anything's happened to Janet I swear I'll—''

''Stop it, Andy!'' Blaine interjected sternly. ''The important thing now is to find her. So where would she go? Think!''

Once Andy had subdued his rage he came up with the answer almost immediately.

''To the cottage,'' he said.

''Of course!'' Garrath exclaimed. ''We've always used it as a refuge when something was bothering us, when we wanted to escape our problems for a while. She must be there!''

They ran as one into the house and to Janet's room, where a search of her things quickly confirmed the guess. She had taken her rucksack and torch, Garrath said, and her hiking boots were gone as well.

But their elation at knowing Janet's destination was soon tempered by the less happy thought that seemed to occur to all of them at the same time. It had been late afternoon when the argument occurred. Even if she had left not long after that, it still would have been dark before she could have reached the cottage. And the hills of Skye could be treacherous to one alone in the dark.

''Let's go,'' Andy said grimly. But Garrath shook his head.

''I'm going alone.''

''No way!'' Andy was equally adamant.

''Janet knows these hills well, just as I do,'' Garrath argued. ''It's a clear moonlit night, no fog, and she had her torch, so there's really no danger that she didn't reach the cottage. I'll be able to make better time alone."

Andy looked stubbornly unconvinced, so Garrath tried again. "Look, I realize I've acted like an idiot over the two of you, and I'm sorry. You were right when you said it was my fault that Janet ran away. Now I need time to mend things between her and me, and that can best be done if we're alone. Please, Andy, I need this chance." And this time it was a request, not a demand.

A "V" appeared between Andy's reddish brows and his mustache twitched. "But what if something happened to you? Even knowing the trails, there's still the risk of falls, broken legs and such. We could end up with both of you lying out there hurt, and we wouldn't know."

"You're right," Garrath agreed readily. "There's a flare pistol in the helicopter; I'll take it with me. I should be able to reach the cottage in at least two and a half hours, so at ten o'clock, let's say, I'll shoot off two flares—if Janet's there. I'll use one if she isn't or in case I'm injured. If you see just the one, or nothing at all, you can call for the search parties. All right?"

Reluctantly Andy agreed, and the next fifteen tense minutes were used in preparing Garrath for the hike. Andy got the pistol from the helicopter while Garrath changed clothes. Blaine helped a grumbling Mrs. M. prepare food for Garrath's pack.

"Whisht!" the woman snorted. "Such carryin' on! I wouldna have believed the whole house could've gone daft like this."

But when Garrath was packed and ready to leave, she gave him a quick fierce hug and there were tears in her dark eyes. ''Bring her back safely, lad. An God gae wi' ye.''

Blaine, too, offered him a hug and added a kiss that she noticed brought a knowing smile to Mrs. M.'s thin lips. It was decided that if—when, Garrath corrected—he found Janet at the cottage, the two of them would spend the night there and return in the morning, the most reasonable course of action. Blaine felt she was missing him even before he was out the door and striding briskly away from the house.

From the solarium Blaine and Andy watched him crossing the back lawn, where light from the house spilled across the green turf. Just as he reached the edge of that circle of light, he turned and waved, then stepped into the darkness. For a while the bobbing circle of his flashlight could be seen, and then that, too, disappeared, and the waiting began.

Blaine and Andy took turns trying to cheer each other up, with equally dismal success. Although logic told them that Garrath was right, that Janet had to be safe at the cottage, their less logical parts continued to worry. Mrs. M. served rolls, salad, and her now cold salmon garnished with cucumbers and lemon. When most of it was left over for another meal, she didn't even scold them for their lack of appetite, a true sign of her concern.

Later, as they sat in front of the living-room fire, fortifying glasses of pure Highland malt in hand, Andy asked Blaine about Garrath's change of heart.

''Did he really mean it? About realizing he was wrong? Do you think he won't be against Janet and me bein' together now?''

Blaine smiled. ''I don't think he'll be against it,

though he may want you to have a lengthy engagement since Janet is still a bit young."

"Oh, that wouldn't bother us none, ma'am. Not
as long as we could be seein' each other in the meantime."

"Well, I don't think Garrath will object to that
from now on. And knowing Janet, she'll see to it that
you see each other quite often enough."

They tried a round of chess, which drifted to an in-
sipid draw, then switched to poker. But when Andy
drew successfully to an inside straight and yet folded
absentmindedly, they gave that game up, too.

"Old maid?" Blaine suggested, the only game she
could think of that required almost no concentration.
Andy nodded with an apologetic grin.

They were waiting outside at nine-thirty, bundled
thickly against the cold but still freezing. They could
have remained in the warmth of the house, watching
from an upstairs window as Mrs. M. and Charlie
were doing, but they wanted to be able to see every
inch of the sky. They weren't taking any chances on
missing the signal.

The minutes ticked by on the green luminous dial
of Andy's watch. At five minutes before ten, Andy
took Blaine's mittened hand. She squeezed back her
appreciation for the comfort but didn't look at him.
Except for checking the time nearly once a minute,
neither of them dared look anywhere but the star-
dusted sky.

It was ten o'clock; two minutes after, then three.
Blaine was ready to start running for the hill path
leading to the cottage. Where was the flare? Where,
oh, where was Garrath?

And then at last it came, a comet brilliant against

the darkness, arcing high into the sky. At its zenith it seemed to pause a moment suspended, as if trying to decide whether or not to succumb to the laws of gravity. Then it gave in and became a falling star, burning out its life as it cascaded down to the earth.

One flare.

Neither of them breathed or blinked. There had to be a twin to that first flare; there had to be. Blaine's jaw hurt from the way her teeth were clamped tensely together, and the increasing pressure of Andy's hand on hers was beginning to crush her fingers. But she didn't move.

Finally it came, that second light that told them everything was all right.

Andy let out a whoop and began whirling Blaine around in a wild gleeful dance. Like two bewitched souls they cavorted around the damp lawn, laughing, hugging, even singing crazy songs. Until Mrs. M. appeared at the back door and ordered them into the house.

"Did you see it?" Andy demanded when he saw her. "Janet's safe!"

"Aye, I saw it. And of course she's safe; I niver doobted it. Now get ye inside here afore ye both catch yer deaths."

But in spite of Mrs. M.'s seeming calm, Blaine saw evidence that the woman was not quite as blasé about the situation as she was trying to pretend. Settled firmly on her beaky nose were her thick black-framed glasses. Vanity had succumbed to her need to watch for the flares.

Blaine and Andy stayed up awhile longer, buoyed by cups of Mrs. M.'s hot cocoa and by relief. Andy talked of his future plans, and Blaine was pleased to hear that though he enjoyed oil work and intended to make it a career, it hadn't become an obsession with him and never would. He wanted the work, but he wanted a home life, too.

As she listened, she realized she had never thought of Andy as an "oil man," had never thought of warning Janet of the dangers of loving one of that ilk. Even from the first she had sensed the difference in him, almost without knowing it. This conversation was only affirmation. She believed he and Janet would make it, very happily.

She was exhausted when they climbed the stairs to bed. This had been one of the worst and best days of her life, and the emotional seesawing had left her completely drained.

"Are you sure Garrath won't blow a gasket if I stay the night?" Andy asked hesitantly.

Blaine grinned. "Why should he?" she teased. "Janet isn't here."

But once she was in her bed, she found she couldn't sleep. Too much had happened; too much was still left to happen. Garrath loved her, and she loved him with a totality that she wouldn't have believed possible. But there were still hurdles to be overcome before any kind of lasting relationship could form between them—the main one being Garrath's fascination with the oil business, an enchantment that might well last forever.

What did that mean for her? She couldn't ask him to change; that would be wrong, as well as useless, most likely. Could she do the changing? Could she put aside her memories and live with the uncertainty, the separations, the danger? Could she keep it from destroying her?

Still without an answer, and unable to sleep without one, she gave up trying. Instead she slipped into her robe and padded downstairs. She would search for some nice boring book on the shelves in Garrath's office, something she could take to bed with her, that could guarantee oblivion.

But when she reached the office, even before she found a switch to turn on the light, something caught her eye. The message light on the computer was blinking.

A dreadful sense of foreboding made her fingers tremble on the keys as she ordered the computer to display the message, foreboding that was immediately borne out as words printed across the screen. It was from the Computec unit on Sithein One.

EMERGENCY. MILES LOCKED US IN TRAILER. THREATENING DESTRUCTION. NEEDS TALKING DOWN. WALTER.

Blaine was screaming Andy's name as she ran up the stairs.

CHAPTER TWENTY-THREE

IT WAS SO MUCH like that first trip, Blaine thought. The dreadful pounding beat of the helicopter's huge blade; the whine of its engine; the cold that numbed her hands and feet; the exhaustion that was due much more to unbearable tension than to the late hour. Only this time, instead of dreading her arrival at Sithein One, she would have given anything had they been able to fly faster through the dark night.

As if sensing her impatience, Andy turned to her, shouting above the helicopter's roar. "Not long now. Maybe fifteen minutes."

Blaine nodded with a faint smile, but inside she was trembling. Fifteen minutes—not long. But it had been almost two hours since her cries had brought a white-faced Andy, catapulting down the stairs at Glenclair, to view the message on the computer screen.

"Can this be for real?" he asked incredulously.

"I'm afraid so," Blaine replied grimly. She had proceeded to fill him in on the probability that Miles had sabotaged the system once already, had tried to shut it down a second time in Garrath's absence, had been warned by Garrath against any further interference.

"I've wondered a time or two if Miles was having some kind of personal problem but never guessed it could be anything like this." He shook his head. "I'd better call the rig."

Mrs. M. and Charlie rushed in while Andy was placing the call, and Blaine hastily assured them that there was nothing wrong with Janet, Garrath, Andy or herself; that this was a serious problem involving the rig. Once she had that assurance, Mrs. M. was off to her kitchen to deal with the crisis in the way she knew best—by preparing a "wee somethin' to keep yer strength up."

Andy's fingers tapped a nervous rhythm against his thigh as he spoke to the foreman on the other shift. No, he was told, so far there hadn't been any sign of trouble. Yes, Miles was on board, but that wasn't unusual; he often stayed on even when he was off shift.

Andy explained the situation and asked the man to cautiously check out the Computec unit. Minutes later he was back, reporting that from the outside there didn't seem to be anything wrong, but that that was all he'd been able to ascertain. His key hadn't opened the door and there had been no response to his knock. Did they think he should break in?

Did they? Blaine and Andy looked at one another. There was so little on which to base such a crucial decision—just Walter's message and a lot of supposition.

"Do you think Miles will really do anything?" Andy asked her.

"I just don't know."

"He's ignored Garrath's warning; that isn't a good sign," Andy judged.

"True, but Walter would have chosen the words for his message carefully. If he thinks there's a chance Miles can be talked down, I would assume things aren't too bad,'' she argued. "But then the question becomes, 'who might have a chance of reaching Miles?'''

"Garrath is the only one I can think of. Miles didn't make friends with the crew; I can't imagine him listening to any of them."

"But it would take hours to reach Garrath!"

Andy turned to Charlie. "Is there anywhere near the cottage where I could land the helicopter?"

Charlie wagged his head. "I dinna think so. Even the rescue parties have to go into these hills on foot."

"Andy!" Blaine exclaimed. "Can you pilot the chopper?"

"Sure thing. But if we can't land it up there, I don't see what—"

"We'll go to Sithein One."

"Us?"

"Yes, us. I think I might be able to get into the trailer to talk to Miles. I could tell him that he was right, that there is something wrong with the system and that I've come to shut it down."

"It might work," he agreed reluctantly, "but I don't think you should be the one to try it. Miles can't be operating with a full deck to pull a trick like this. And if you're right and he's blaming your system for all his troubles, it could be dangerous. He might not make the distinction between your machines and you if things get really bad."

"I know there's a risk. But it's Computec equipment and a Computec employee—and a friend—involved, and that makes the risk worth it."

"It'll take two hours or so to get to the rig from here," Andy advised her. "A lot could happen in that time."

"And a lot could happen if they try to force the door in. If Miles is on the edge of some emotional breakdown, there's no telling what he might do if he's pushed. Walter might be hurt."

Up to that point Blaine had been discussing it, had been knocking the idea around with Andy to see if it worked. With the latter thought she was decided. She didn't wait for Andy to comment.

"I'm sure it's the right thing to do," she insisted. "There's no use trying to talk me out of it."

He tilted his head to one side and grinned. "I've known there was no use tryin' to talk you out of anything you wanted to do from our first meetin', ma'am. Let's go."

Now, nearly two hours later, they were almost there, and Blaine was no longer so certain her decision had been the right one. They'd asked the rig foreman to set a watch on the trailer but to take no action unless it seemed absolutely necessary. Charlie had already been heading for the cottage and Garrath when they took off, the helicopter laden with the thermos of hot tea and sack of sandwiches Mrs. M. had prepared as if she had known they would be leaving even before they had. And by now the second helicopter they'd radioed for was probably at Glenclair, waiting for Garrath. They had done everything they could, but still. . . . Blaine bit her lower lip and stared out the bubble-shaped window, searching for a sign of Sithein One.

But there was only the darkness, which added to her apprehension. At least during her first twilight flight she had been able to see something of ocean and sky, no matter how misty and vague. Now there was total blackness, made more eerie by the knowledge that beneath them was the cold deep ocean, rising and falling in its endless rhythm. Just how far beneath them she couldn't tell.

Nervously she jammed her hands deep into the pockets of her jacket and felt a sudden stinging on one finger. Knowing what she would find, she slowly drew out a sharp-pronged bit of plastic—the computer circuit whose malfunction had originally brought her to Sithein One. She remembered putting it in her pocket, still wondering about it even after Garrath had assured her that precautions would be taken. Why hadn't she done something then? Why, she asked herself. Now she might be too late.

And then suddenly the darkness was broken. A candle flame appeared in the distance, small but growing bigger with every passing second. The flare atop Sithein One.

Blaine glanced at Andy. There was nothing boyish about him now, in pilot's headphones, with his hands busy on the helicopter's controls. It wasn't just the outer trappings that made the difference, however. There was a grim set to his face, a determination that worried her because she was pretty sure she could guess its source.

He had changed his mind about letting her carry out her plan, she thought. Or perhaps he'd never intended to let her do so at all. She'd had plenty of time during the long flight to go over their conversation at Glenclair. She'd realized that although he'd agreed to fly her out to the rig and had even agreed with her plan to get someone into the trailer to talk to Miles, he had never exactly said he'd let her be the one to try it.

He was probably planning on sending her to some safe spot and taking the risk himself. And once they were on the rig he would have the authority to order things that way if he wanted to. Her only option was to keep him from using his authority in the first place.

So she was ready. The instant the helicopter touched down on the pad, she unlatched her seat belt and jumped out. Andy called after her, but she ignored him, knowing he would be involved with the craft's shutdown for at least a few minutes. Long enough for her to get to the trailer.

She ducked under the still-whirling blades and ran for the stairs. The rig noises, the smells and the strange motion assaulted her at once, seeming more pronounced than ever. The vibration and the almost imperceptible sway of the rig added to the unsteadiness of her legs.

No one stopped her, though she guessed she was breaking more than a few of Garrath's stringent safety regulations as she ran across the deck without hard hat or coveralls. In relief she noticed that work seemed to be progressing normally. There was no sign that anything unusual was going on until she reached the trailer. Several men stood just outside it; the watch they'd asked for, she presumed.

There was no time to waste; Andy wouldn't be far behind her. Assuming her most authoritative air, she ordered them back from the trailer, saying that she was from Computec and was going in, that they should stay well away. While they were still dazed by surprise she ran up the steps and pounded on the door.

"Miles!" she screamed his name. "Miles, it's Blaine Christensen. I'd like to talk to you."

She thought she heard the sound of movement on

the other side of the door, though it was hard to tell with the rig noises ringing in her ears. She pounded and called again.

"Miles, can you hear me? There's something wrong with the system, just as you thought all along. I've been ordered to shut it down."

The door opened the slightest crack. A blue gray eye peered out at her.

"Hi, Miles," she said brightly. "Can I come in? It's awfully cold out here."

"You're going to shut down the system?" he asked.

She nodded vigorously. "You were right. It's not working correctly."

The crack inched a bit wider. "I was right?"

"Yes. So if you'll let me in, I'll get right to work."

Still Miles hesitated, rubbing two fingers against the faded bronze of his cheek. "I...I'm not sure. I didn't want...."

Just then Blaine heard a shout behind her—Andy. "Miles, please," she begged, and grasping the edge of the door, tugged.

He didn't resist and she squeezed inside. But he immediately pulled the door closed after her. He locked it, and then picked up a long piece of rope, one end of which was already knotted around the handle of the door. He swiftly tied the other end to the metal coat rack screwed into the wall of the trailer.

"Can't...can't be interrupted," he muttered as he pulled the elaborate series of knots tighter. "Not 'til I decide...what to do." Then Miles turned to her.

She smiled at him. She knew she was smiling because she could feel the pain of forcing her rigid facial muscles into that arrangement. But there was no hint of a smile inside of her, only stark numbing fear.

What had she been thinking as she'd planned this situation, she wondered as a chill slid down her spine. That Miles was just a little upset with the system and that a word or two from her would make everything all right? Had she really been so naive?

For Miles was not just a little upset. There was something dreadfully wrong with him. His speech was slurred, and the vain pretentious man of a week ago, whose age had been so hard to guess, now had the pinched drawn look of an old, old man—one not entirely in possession of all his faculties. She didn't have the faintest idea what to say to him.

"Where's Walter?" she asked tremulously, turning to look for her ally.

"Walter? Walter was upset with me for...something. I can't remember," Miles was saying. "We talked for a while about...shutting off the system. And then...." He paused. "But you're here to do that now, aren't you? So it will be okay."

Blaine had never felt such panic as when she heard Miles's rambling words. She rushed forward into the trailer, looking around desperately.

It seemed she viewed the room through the eye of a motion-picture camera, a series of freeze frames flashing at her in a rapid succession that moved from ordinary to nightmarish in seconds. Frame #1: the monitors blinking their various views of the rig; frame #2: a printer rat-a-tat-tatting out its information; frame #3: the circuit board drawer below the computer terminal hanging open, with a portable sunlamp fixed to its edge, shining its ultraviolet light down onto the vulnerable circuitry; frame #4:

Walter, crumpled in a pathetically small heap on the floor, blood smeared across the back of his head.

"Oh, Walter," she breathed, rushing over to kneel beside him. His wire-framed glasses had fallen off and the owlish eyes were closed, the rounded face a cold dead white. But there was a pulse, she found, and tears of relief flooded her eyes.

"He...ah...he's been like that for a while," Miles said, sounding childishly annoyed, as if Walter was at fault. "I didn't mean to hurt him, you know. But he told me I couldn't shut off the system without knowing the proper sequence, or else I would be shutting down power all over the rig, too. I didn't want that, of course. But then...then he wouldn't tell me how to do it right. He was trying to...talk me out of it, I think. And something happened. I...I don't quite remember...and he's been lying there ever since."

Oh, Walter, Blaine thought, dear foolish man, trying to protect the equipment by putting himself in danger. But there wasn't time to think of that. Miles suddenly reached out and grasped her arm, pulling her to her feet. There was a strange cast to the blue gray eyes staring at her.

"But he doesn't matter now, because you're here. You can do it right. You will, won't you?" His grip on her arm tightened, until even through her coat his fingers were digging painfully into her soft flesh.

"Sure I will," she said quickly. "It won't be difficult at all. But why don't we go and get a cup of coffee in the galley first? I promise not to spill yours this time like I did the morning we met."

She wasn't able to infuse the joke with much humor, but Miles didn't notice—either the failed humor or the reference. He just looked at her blankly and raised two fingers to rub absently at his cheek again.

"No, I have to finish here," he said.

"We can. But there's no hurry, is there? We can do it after some coffee. Please, Miles," Blaine pleaded. Walter was so still, so very still. She had to get help to him soon.

"No...no, I have to finish what I started. There's a reason, you know. I...I can't seem to remember just what it is, but there is a reason."

A sudden pounding made them both jump and whip around toward the door.

"They can't get in," Miles said. His too-brilliant smile flashed, but a bit crookedly, as if in a parody of what it had once been. "Not until I let them." But then a voice followed another round of knocking and Miles's smile twisted into a grimace.

"Miles, open this door! It's me, Garrath!"

It couldn't be, Blaine thought. He couldn't be here, not for hours yet. But that voice, the command, the authority, was unmistakable, and hope surged through her. If anyone could reach Miles, it would be Garrath.

Miles had already recognized the voice, but his reaction was not what Blaine had hoped for. The tool-pusher cringed, his face going a chalky gray.

"It's Garrath, Miles. He wants to talk to you. I'll let him in, okay?" She took two steps toward the door.

"No!" Miles's voice, ragged with anger and bitterness, stopped her. "He doesn't want to talk; he wants to get rid of me. He used to talk, used to listen to me, too. He took my advice, respected me, looked up to me. Until you and your machines came. I can't let him get rid of me. That's why I have to destroy your machines. Then he'll see, then he'll need me again.''

Before Blaine could say another word he turned and grabbed the sunlamp from the edge of the circuit board drawer. Swinging wildly, he smashed the still-burning lamp into the nearest computer terminal screen.

There was a flash and the screen exploded in a shower of sparks and glass, but Blaine was never sure exactly how the fire started. One moment there was nothing but the hissing and spitting of the innards of the broken screen and the shattered lamp, the next the acrid smell of burning electrical wiring filled the room and a pile of computer printouts stacked nearby burst into flames. And lying almost directly beneath the burning mass was Walter.

''Miles, help me!'' she cried as bits of flaming paper fluttered down onto Walter's unconscious form. But Miles stood frozen in place, seemingly mesmerized by the vivid results of his destruction. Smoke began to cloud the small room even as Blaine reached for Walter.

He was a small man, but Blaine was slight herself, and his dead weight was almost more than she could manage. Every muscle in her body screamed with the effort of dragging him out of danger.

She became aware of the continued pounding at the door and opened her mouth to yell a warning in reply. But the breath she drew was full of smoke, which singed her throat and brought tears to her eyes. Her cry for help was a strangled cough.

As soon as Walter as out of immediate danger, she turned to search for the fire extinguisher every trailer had as standard equipment. But the hungry flames had moved faster than she had, and in the worst possible direction. They blazed between her and the wall where the red canister hung, and in the far corner of the room where the small emergency generator stood. The gas generator.

"Miles!" she screamed. "We have to get out of here."

But he still didn't move, except to raise his palms to the sides of his head, pressing as if he were in pain. Even as she called again, she knew it couldn't make any difference, for the flames were already licking at the small gas tank. She grabbed Walter's body and tugged as hard as she could, dragging him closer to the door. Then the world exploded, and she was knocked against the wall, hitting her head with a force that stunned her.

There was a moment's blankness and then her nightmare suddenly became reality. Smoke and heat threatened to suck the breath from her. She knew it was hopeless, but she reached up anyway to tug on the rope, ripping her nails on the rough sisal. She couldn't even loosen the first loop.

But it wasn't quite like her dream, she thought, sinking down beside Walter. This time the flames were coming and there was nowhere to run. She would never see Glenclair or Garrath again.

There was a crash against the door, a crash that shook the whole building. Then a second and a third. Unbelievably, the door buckled. And even more unbelievably, Garrath was there, reaching for her, pulling her out of the nightmare and into the safety of his arms. Just as he had promised he would.

"Garrath. . ." she sighed, and slipped gratefully into unconsciousness.

CHAPTER TWENTY-FOUR

THE MISTS CLEARED a little, not enough for full consciousness, but just enough for her to feel the small aches and pains that were everywhere and the one not-so-small ache in her head. Enough for her to start to remember. She moaned.

"She's hurting, Doc," a voice said. Garrath's voice, raw with worry. His hand softly brushed the hair back from her temple. "Can't you give her something?"

"Not until we get some X rays. That bump on her head doesn't look serious, but she has been out quite awhile, and there's always a risk with head injuries. We'll be at the hospital soon."

No! The protest formed somewhere deep inside Blaine's mind. Not a hospital! She didn't need cold sterile rooms and doctors and medicine. She needed Garrath. Even now she felt better, just hearing his voice, feeling his hand against her skin. He was what she needed; she couldn't be separated from him.

"Garrath, I want to go home," she murmured weakly. "Please. Home."

There was a long, long silence, so long that she began to wonder if she had said the words aloud or only in her head. She tried again.

"Home, I want to go home," she begged. "Please, Garrath. I have to."

He answered then. "All right, *mo mhuirnín*, my darling," he said gently. "You'll go home. Soon. I promise."

And Blaine, clinging tightly to his promise, was content to let the mists come down again. It was only in the last moment before she slipped away that she wondered why Garrath had sounded so sad as he promised. Why wouldn't he want to take her home?

WHEN THE MISTS FINALLY LIFTED completely, Blaine woke to find that the standard cliché was wrong. Her first question wasn't where am I, it was where is Garrath. Only her voice was rusty with disuse and it came out as a whispered, one-word croak.

"Garrath?"

The bright-faced nurse holding her wrist and solemnly counting pulse beats jumped.

"Ah...ye're with us again then, are ye, Miss Christensen? A right turn ye gave me!" And tucking Blaine's wrist back beneath the crisp sheets, she marched out of the room, returning in a few moments with Doc. He bustled over to Blaine's bedside and stared down at her, at the alertness of her green eyes, the rosy glow in her cheeks, the crease between her brows.

"You'll do, I'd guess," he said, smiling. "But let's just make sure before you start bombarding me with the questions I see written in your pretty frown."

So Blaine waited, the number of her questions multiplying while he flashed a light into her eyes, put a stethoscope to her heart, felt the spot on the side of her head that was still tender enough to make her wince and checked various reflexes. Then, putting away the tools of his trade, he pulled a chair close to the bed and leaned back, folding his hands over his Ben Franklin paunch.

"Ready," he said solemnly. Before she could get in a word, however, he started on the basics. "You're in the hospital in Aberdeen. You received some kind of blow to the side of your head that left you with a concussion but, fortunately, no more serious damage. You've been here about thirty-six hours and I'll want to keep you here at least one more day as a precaution before I let you go home, no matter how you fight me."

Blaine felt newborn-kitten weak and couldn't imagine fighting Doc or anyone, about anything. She told him so.

"Well, that'll be a change," he chuckled. "You've been begging to go home every time you were the least bit awake right from the first, when Garrath and I were bringing you here on the chopper."

"Have I? Yes, I guess I do remember. . . ." She had wanted to make sure Garrath stayed with her then. Had wanted his comforting, the only thing that could ease the pain of that other memory—of what had happened on the rig. She wanted him for the same reason now.

"Where is Garrath?" she asked.

It was Doc's turn to frown. "On Sithein One, probably. And working too hard, I'd wager, though I haven't actually seen him since we brought you in. But I hear he's—" He broke off, and cleared his throat noisily. "He's as well as can be expected."

"Then the rig was badly damaged?" she asked fearfully, knowing the catastrophe that fire could mean on an oil platform.

Doc was shaking his head. "No, not at all. The explosion and fire were contained in the trailer, a compliment to Computec's construction job. A new unit is already being installed.''

Blaine stared at him, not quite wanting to believe what he had said. Garrath was back on the rig, not here with her, and the rig hadn't even been damaged. He could have stayed with her, but he hadn't! Why?

She pushed the thought away. There was a new aching starting somewhere inside her, one she sensed was going to be worse than any of the others. But she couldn't think about it now, not while there were so many other vital questions she had to have answered.

Doc told her all he knew, straight, without embellishment, but also without holding anything back. Walter was fine; his head was harder than Blaine's and he was being released that morning. No one else had been hurt. The only casualty was Miles.

"He's dead, Blaine," Doc said.

A wave of nausea surged through her, and she pressed her eyes closed against the start of tears. She'd known Miles couldn't have survived, not when he wasn't even trying to escape, but still it hurt. She remembered now her last glimpse of him just standing there, his hands pressed to his head. She should have done something.

As if reading her thoughts, Doc shook his head. "There was nothing you could have done. It wasn't the fire that killed Miles. He died of a stroke."

"A stroke?" Blaine opened her eyes, wide.

Doc nodded. "He'd probably been having small ones for some time, which would account for the personality changes and even the delusions that led to what happened at the end. One big one killed him. Garrath pulled him out after you and Walter, but he was already gone. No one could have saved him."

"Poor Miles," she whispered, thinking of him as she had first seen him, his smile so impossibly bright, his flirtatious manner so absurdly contrived. Saddened as she was by his death, she was glad to know about the strokes. There had been a reason for it all; it was nothing evil or malicious in Miles himself.

"But how did Garrath get out to the rig so soon? He was up at the cottage...."

Doc held up a pudgy hand. "You'll have to wait with the rest of your questions. I don't know any more. Get some rest now; there are people anxious to see you, and I think you could manage a few visitors this afternoon. Okay?"

"Okay," Blaine said, willing to wait to fill in the remaining blanks.

But after Doc had left, rest didn't come easily. Disappointment was a growing ache in her heart that made every beat ask, why, why. There were visitors anxious to see her, but Garrath wasn't one of them. He was on Sithein One, not here with her, and she didn't understand why. Not at all.

THE REST OF THE STORY CAME to Blaine in bits and pieces, brought by her visitors along with hothouse flowers and beribboned boxes of sweets.

Walter was the first, sneaking in before visiting hours officially began, with a violet plant potted in a silver bowl.

"I thought you'd like violets," he mumbled, blinking slowly. "They're dainty—like you." Red faced, he perched on the edge of the chair by her bed, looking more owlish than ever, and related his part of the events of that night.

He'd returned to the trailer in the middle of the night to check on a temperamental printer and found Miles there, his sunlamp hooked to the circuitry drawer.

"He was trying the same thing he must have done before," Walter said, blinking several times. "And I was the one who told him how."

"You?"

"He was always coming in, asking lots of questions. I remember telling him once about how programs were erased with ultraviolet light. But I never thought he was trying to find ways to hurt the system."

"He asked me questions, too, and I never thought a thing about it, either," Blaine commiserated. "But what happened after you caught him?"

"Well, I was going to go directly to the foreman, but Miles threatened to smash everything in sight if I did. So I went in and tried to talk to him. It worked for a while." He wriggled on his chair like an owl shifting on its tree branch. "But then his talk got crazier and he rigged that rope on the door. That was when I sent the message. I kept trying to talk him out of doing anything, and he got mad and hit me. I'm really sorry. I nearly got you killed."

"No, Walter. I nearly got us both killed. I suspected there was something wrong with Miles when I was on the rig the first time, but I didn't press it. It's my fault. The only thing you did wrong was to try to protect the equipment by putting yourself in danger. No set of computers is worth that."

Walter looked disbelieving, both at her assessment of the computers' value and at her placing of the blame. He wasn't going to let himself off that easily.

He was on his way back to work, in the new unit on Sithein One, and Blaine knew his guilt would drive him to longer hours and harder efforts. And he would love every minute of it.

Janet came in a bit later, bearing a box of Mrs. M.'s butter-rich shortbread. Large diamonds of happiness sparkled in her eyes, mirroring the smallish engagement diamond on her finger. She assured Blaine that everything between her and Andy was fine.

"Exceptin' that the daft laddie thinks we should be waitin' a bit before we get married. Says I'm so young!" she grumbled, pouting. "But I'll wear him down." Blaine smiled, knowing Andy didn't stand a chance.

But Janet's bubbliness went a little flat when Blaine couldn't restrain herself any longer and asked about Garrath.

"Oh, he's very busy, I'm sure, but fine. I guess. He's...he's...." Her glib response faltered to a complete standstill, and she started over again with a question. "He hasn't been to see you, has he?" When Blaine admitted he hadn't, Janet shook her black curls miserably.

"I honestly don't know what's wrong with him, Blaine," she said. "That night, when he came up to the cottage, we made up right quick. Then he said he knew it made more sense to stay the night, but he wanted to get back to Glenclair, to you. I didn't object to seeing Andy again, either, so we hiked back down, only to find you two were gone. We were about half an hour behind you. Garrath nearly went out of his mind right there. I would have sworn he would never let you out of his sight again once he found you."

"But then what happened?" Blaine cried.

Janet looked as heartsick as Blaine felt. "I just don't know," she said worriedly. "He's taken Miles's death hard, but that doesn't explain why he's avoiding you. I asked him about it, and all he said was that Doc was keeping him posted on your recovery. That he would try to see you sometime before you left for home, but he was awfully busy. Just that way. I'm sorry, Blaine."

Blaine suddenly regretted Janet's propensity for mimicry. She had done too good a job in conveying Garrath's cold unforgiving tone. Her faint hope that there was really nothing seriously wrong faded away.

It wasn't just that he was putting off seeing her because he considered the rig more important. He didn't *want* to see her. But why?

He was taking Miles's death hard, Janet had said. Could his change of attitude have something to do with that, she wondered. Miles's delusions had focused on her machines, and she had been the one with him just before he died. Though Garrath must know about Miles's strokes, could he still somehow blame her for the part she had played in the whole thing? Was that the reason he didn't want to see her?

The why of Garrath's attitude became unimportant late that afternoon when Richard called her from San Francisco.

"I've spoken to St. Clair," he said, after receiving her assurances that she was fine. "He says he's made arrangements for you to come home as soon as you're released from the hospital."

There was a pause, and Blaine could almost hear Richard wondering what had happened between her and Garrath. But she couldn't answer the unspoken question, and suddenly the answer didn't matter much anyway. All that mattered was that something had and Garrath was sending her away. He hadn't loved her enough.

"Let me know which plane and I'll be there," Richard said. There was just the fraction of a moment's hesitation before he added, "If you'd like me to be."

"Yes, I would," Blaine agreed, grateful for his tact and his concern. She wondered if she was going to be able to cry this one out on Richard's shoulder without giving him the wrong idea but didn't struggle to find an answer. She'd have the whole trip back in which to debate the issue.

"It will be soon," she added, then hung up quickly, before he could hear the start of her tears.

It was soon. The following morning, after checking her over once more, Doc said she could leave that afternoon. Half an hour later a messenger from St. Clair's Aberdeen office delivered a first-class ticket for a flight to San Francisco leaving London that evening. She would be picked up and taken to the Aberdeen airport in plenty of time to make a connecting flight; her belongings would be on the plane.

Blaine's hand shook as she took the airline folder. Not even a note this time, she thought, misery warring with anger. No matter what he thought of her now, how could he do this? How could he send her away without even a goodbye?

By the afternoon, when a nurse came in to tell her a car and driver were waiting, Blaine had convinced herself she was ready to go. She had known from the start that caring for Garrath St. Clair could only lead to this kind of heartbreak. It was time to accept it and find a way to go on, her rational logical self insisted.

Doc walked her from her room. He was leaving the hospital, too, he explained. He had only stayed on to oversee her care. He would be going back to Sithein One at the next shift change.

Blaine was glad of his hand beneath her arm when they reached the reception area. For leaning against the reception desk was a familiar figure in boots, jeans, cowhide jacket and cowboy hat. Andy.

"You've gotten the 'special' job again?" she asked wryly, her emotions mixed. It was nice to see Andy again, to have a chance to wish him well. But the feeling of coming full circle made the whole thing seem much more final, much more crushing.

"Asked for it this time, ma'am," he drawled. "We've got a couple of new men, Texas boys, comin' in later today, so I had a good excuse to do double duty."

"Thank you, Andy," she said softly, and her eyes filled with tears.

"Sure thing, ma'am," he said, tactfully looking away as he led her outside.

For a short while the only sound inside the car was the drumming of Andy's fingers on the steering wheel. Then he started speaking abruptly, as if he'd finally decided what to say.

"Did you hear I've been promoted—to toolpusher? Miles's job."

Blaine was surprised, not by Andy's promotion, but by his mentioning it at all. He had been so painfully modest before. She congratulated him heartily.

"Yeah, well, I'm not sure how it's goin' to work, though. What with the new owners and all."

He suddenly had Blaine's complete attention. "New owners? What do you mean?"

"Didn't Janet mention it? She's real upset about it."

Blaine shook her head vigorously.

"Well, Garrath is selling Sithein One and the rest of the St. Clair oil division to one of the big conglomerates—at a mighty huge loss, too. He's dumping it."

"He wouldn't," she denied it. "He'd never give up the rigs."

"He is, ma'am. And though he's put in the contracts that all personnel will keep their jobs, I'm not sure I'm goin' to like workin' for anyone else but him."

"But why would he sell it all?"

"Rumor says it's because of Miles, y'know. But I'm inclined to think Garrath is too levelheaded not to put the blame about that right where it belongs, on Miles's illness. I think there's something else eatin' at him. I sure wish I knew what it was." He shrugged his thin shoulders. "But then, I reckon it's too late to worry about that now, anyway. They're his rigs and he's sellin'."

"But he can't do that!" she exclaimed, wondering at her attitude even as she said the words. Once she'd wanted nothing more than to pry Garrath away from the spell cast by the oil business. But this wasn't the way. "Someone should stop him."

"We tried," Andy said, his fingers drumming faster. "His advisers all were full tilt against it. Janet fought like a little bobcat to bring him round. I even risked my neck to try and make him mad enough to see sense. He wouldn't listen. And now he's out at

Glenclair just waitin' for the papers to be ready to sign.''

"Glenclair? I thought he was on the rig.''

"Oh, he was, working like a wild man until this morning. But then—right after he got the call from Doc sayin' you were fine and could be goin' home, in fact—he took off for Glenclair, saying he wouldn't be back.''

Blaine stared at Andy, who was looking very carefully straight ahead.

"Right after...?''

"...he heard you were goin' home.''

The last word rang in Blaine's head. Home. Home, where she had begged Garrath to take her as they'd flown from the rig to the hospital after the explosion. And everyone thought she was going home now. Everyone—including Garrath?

"Oh, Andy,'' she murmured, hope stirring in her. Was it possible that this whole thing was the result of one misunderstood word?

Andy had parked the car, and they were already heading into the terminal when Blaine made her decision.

"Andy, is there a helicopter waiting to take you and the new men out to the rig?''

He nodded quickly.

"How long is it before you have to meet them?'' she asked, praying quietly.

"Oh, just about as long as it would take us to get from here to Glenclair and back, I reckon,'' he said, with just the barest twitch of his mustache. "And I did happen to mention to them about a pub right close to the airport that they might wait in if I was a bit late. Just in case, y'know.''

Blaine grinned at him, not knowing if what Andy was maneuvering her into was right, only certain that she had to give it a try.

"Let's go!" she said, the dimple deep in her cheek.

He grabbed her hand and turned her in the direction of the helicopter pad, his grin as broad as hers. "Somehow I figured that's what you'd say, ma'am. Somehow I just figured it."

ANDY SET THE CHOPPER DOWN on Glenclair's landing area just long enough for Blaine to jump out.

"My men are waitin', y'know," he excused his haste, rather transparently. "I ought to get hold of 'em while they can still stand up."

The moment the helicopter disappeared over the nearby hills, Blaine turned, and knew immediately that Andy's strategy had been right. Garrath was advancing on her, his scowl black with rage. His greeting made it obvious that he would have stuffed her right back into the craft if it were still there.

"What the hell are you doing here!" he ranted. "You're supposed to be on a plane right now!"

"I couldn't go," she said, starting resolutely for the back of the house and leaving Garrath with no choice but to follow.

"And why not?" he demanded.

"There's something I forgot to do when I was working on your computer system here. I couldn't leave without finishing the job."

"The system's working fine!"

"Oh, but we never did complete your lessons, did we? You probably just don't know enough about it yet to tell there's a problem."

She didn't dare look at him, but she could feel his

rage coming at her in waves. Good, she thought. What she was going to try would be impossible if he just coldly ignored her. Anger was better. Of course her plan might not work anyway, and what she would do then she didn't know. It didn't bear thinking of.

Mrs. M. was at the back door. Her glasses were slightly askew but definitely on her nose, and her smile was almost as wide as Charlie's.

"Welcome home, Blaine," she said.

"She's not staying," Garrath growled.

"Thank you, Mrs. M.," Blaine said.

Still ignoring Garrath, she headed directly for his office, and once there settled herself in front of the terminal. As she began typing in various bits of information, he was right behind her, but there was no hanging over the back of her chair today, no breathing on her neck. He went to his desk, sat down heavily with his back to her and started noisily moving papers about.

"I hear you're selling Sithein One," she said, continuing to type.

"Yes." Nothing more.

"Doesn't seem like a very wise move."

"I don't recall asking for your advice on my business affairs."

"Rumor has it St. Clair Corporation is liquidating assets because it's in trouble."

"Rumor is wrong, as usual."

"Then why are you selling?"

"That's my concern, not yours!" he burst out, and Blaine heard his chair swiveling violently. She didn't turn.

"No, I don't suppose it is," she said evenly. "Not

unless your decision has something to do with me and Miles and what happened on Sithein One. And with your sending me away—without even a goodbye.''

Blaine felt battered by the silence that followed her words. When Garrath's answer came it was so softly said, she almost missed it.

"You wanted to go," he said, a low broken whisper.

Her fingers had finished their job on the computer, all but the punching of the last key. Everything within her wanted to turn and fly into Garrath's arms, but she sensed he wasn't ready. She forced herself to stay still.

"I didn't," she said.

"You did," he insisted, his voice louder this time but so heavy with resignation that she almost didn't recognize it. "Look, Blaine, I knew from the start how you felt about oil work. You told me straight enough when I held you after your nightmare. And all along you insisted that what was between us was only a physical attraction.''

He paused and Blaine thought of all the times she had said those very words, to him and to herself. Had it ever been true?

"I even heard you telling Janet one morning at breakfast that you would never love an oil man,'' Garrath continued. "I just didn't want to believe you. I thought I could change your mind—I even thought maybe I had, that night in my room, though you didn't say you loved me even then.''

Hadn't she said the words, Blaine asked herself. She remembered his declaration, vividly. Had she only answered with her body?

Garrath went on, "But after the explosion, when I

held you in my arms on the way to Aberdeen and all you wanted was to go home, I knew.''

"You knew what?" she asked gently, her heart aching for the pain they had so unintentionally caused one another.

"That you could never love me, no matter how strong our physical relationship was. And knowing what Sithein One had cost me, I didn't want to see it ever again.''

"And what about me? Didn't you want to see me again? If you thought it was your oil work keeping us apart, why didn't you come and tell me you were selling it?"

"Because I wouldn't bargain for your love, Blaine," he said gruffly. "I wouldn't and I won't. So I'd like you to finish whatever you're doing there and get out. Now.''

Blaine took a deep painful breath. They had come to the point she'd been waiting for. Everything depended on the next few moments.

"I am finished," she said. "If you'll just come over here, I can show you what I've done.''

She heard his footsteps behind her, reluctantly bringing him closer. Then she could feel his presence behind her.

"All right. What is it?''

Blaine reached out and hit a key. The printer came to life and three words printed across a blank sheet of paper. She looked up at Garrath.

She watched him read the words, a second's task. But his eyes stayed much longer on the page, as if he were trying to see more or perhaps trying to be sure the words were really there.

"Garrath, I've loved you for so long, I'm not sure

now when it began. I fought it, yes, because of your work; I admit that. I was afraid, afraid you were like my father and my brother, caught forever in the spell of the oil business, and that there would never be room in your life for anything or anyone else. So I fought my feelings.''

Blaine stopped. He was still staring at the paper, but there was disbelief in the set of his shoulders and in the deep lines etched around his mouth. She put a hand on his arm and he flinched, but she held onto the contact as she continued.

''When we were lost in the fog in the hills, though, I wasn't afraid. And when I asked myself why, I knew it was because I loved you. I didn't care about your work or anything else. I just loved you. And I didn't fight it any more after that.'' She moved her hand up to his shoulder. ''Garrath, in the helicopter, when I begged to be taken home, this was where I wanted to be. Glenclair. Or anywhere, with you. That's what home has become for me. I love you, and that's the only spell that matters to me, now and forever.''

He looked at her then, his brown eyes velvety with wanting to believe her, with longing.

''Are you telling me you could love and live with and marry an oil man?''

''Yes, Garrath, as long as I knew he loved me, really loved me. But I wouldn't let him sink himself so far into his work that he forgot about us.'' She grinned. ''I'd insist on at least equal time.''

He laughed then, that rich wonderful laugh, and reached out to draw her close to him. His hands cupped her face and he stared deep into her eyes.

''I can't believe it,'' he said huskily. ''Are you sure?''

Blaine leaned against him, against the warmth and strength of his body. "There must be a way I can convince you," she said coyly. "Let me see. . . ."

But when his hands moved to draw her into an embrace, she pulled back just a little.

"Would a hundred times do it?" she asked. "A thousand? Five thousand?"

"Five thousand what?" he demanded, his brows darting together. "What are you talking about?"

"Convincing you that I love you," she said, reaching back to press quickly several keys on the computer. "I think we'd better be safe and make it five thousand."

As she turned back to Garrath the printer rattled to life again, obeying the instructions Blaine had typed. Its staccato beat started printing out her message, over and over and over.

    I LOVE YOU.
    I LOVE YOU.
    I LOVE YOU.

The first sheet of paper was only half-filled when Garrath took her into his arms.

"That wasn't the kind of convincing I had in mind," he whispered against Blaine's lips.

"Good," she answered. And neither of them needed, or noticed, the next 4,970 times the message repeated. They had learned it already. By heart.

What readers say about SUPERROMANCE

Harlequin Salutes... ANNE MATHER

The author whose romances have sold more than 90 million copies!

Harlequin is proud to salute Anne Mather with 6 of her bestselling Presents novels—

1 **Master of Falcon's Head** (#69)
2 **The Japanese Screen** (#77)
3 **Rachel Trevellyan** (#86)
4 **Mask of Scars** (#92)
5 **Dark Moonless Night** (#100)
6 **Witchstone** (#110)

Wherever paperback books are sold, or complete and mail the coupon below.✷
